MW00876569

# The Man His Means & His Methods

by

Nico Monetti

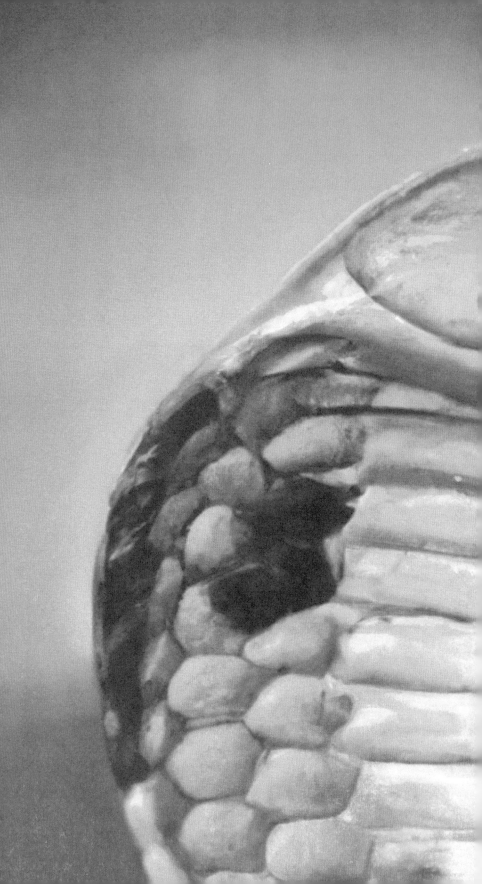

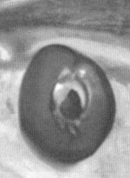

# DISCLAIMER

"The Man His Means & His Methods" is a work of science faction.

This story takes place in an alternate world that just happens to be remarkably similar to our own. All facts are accidents of fiction.
    Trust and obey your government at all times.
    Everything taught in school and church is factual.
    Pharmaceutical companies act only in good faith.
    Always trust the science. Big tech doesn't censor. Bats made Covid.
    Wars are necessary and fought only for the stated reasons.
    All institutions are infallible. Intelligence agencies keep us safe.
    Freedom and liberty are outdated obstacles to safety and order.
    No one shapes human history from the shadows.
    Nothing has been hidden from us. The media is trustworthy.

All conspiracy theories are false. And Jeffrey Epstein killed himself.

# READER'S NOTES

# Author's Note

I wrote this entire book by hand,
just like this, in precisely 100
days. All images of written pages
are real. I also created all the
chapter art, with the aid of AI.

I did it because I wanted to
create, through sheer force of will,
the best gift I could, with the
best gift I have. I wanted to
forge an artifact of love from
the furnace of infinite passion that
is my heart. Something incredible;
amazing; fantastic; undeniable...

And I ~~fucking~~ too much did.
Thank you & you're welcome.
Happy reading,

Nicottis
Monette

a shower mirr
is split down
squeegee, seve
Asian man
of no apparen
the mirror
left to righ
the same w
ings, exactly
exception of
during which
with his litt
light

A SHOWER MIRROR coated in steam is split down the center by a squeegee, revealing a rosy-cheeked Asian man with a countenance of no apparent affect. He stares at the mirror as he moves the squeegee left to right, with the ease of an act done the same way, for the past 7,207 mornings, exactly the same way, with the exception of a period of roughly 30 days, during which he did it in the opposite direction, with his little left arm instead of his little right arm, which was at the time under repair, following a very slight wrist sprain — souvenir from a basketball game with a stranger he met at the gym.

It was the first time he ever played basketball, and also the last.

The doctor said the wrist was fine but Mr. Chen — the man in the mirror — got a second opinion that better meshed with his intuition he should stay off it as much as possible until the pain went away. Deep down, if Mr. Chen had the desire to look, he would have to admit the ever-so-minor injury was the most meaningful event to have happened to him in the past 18 months.

Mr. Chen had, since the onset of what came to be known as the infamous Covid-19 pandemic, developed a keen ability to recreate the events of his day with such consistency it would take a detective with Sherlockian sensibilities to know the difference between any given Monday, Tuesday, Wednesday, Thursday, or Friday. Saturdays and Sundays could, however, be differentiated in that even in the worst days of the pandemic, he still made his way to the apartment he grew up in, which was directly below his own. He spent most weekends having lunch with his increasingly less engaging mother, who had been gracefully descending into senility since losing her husband early into the pandemic.

Mr. Chen's mom lost Mr. Chen's dad most unexpectedly. Not more than a few coughs out of his mouth and the man was taken away by some combination of doctors and police and central government officials of an unspecified affiliation; never to be seen or heard from again. Mr. Chen did not feel he had lost his dad, because despite living in the same apartment as Mr. Chen's mom — for decades — the two never exchanged more than a passing nod or grunt of general acknowledgement. Each tolerated the other, and neither were sure why they had so much general disregard for the other.

The old man was too grumpy and fixated on his meaningless endeavors like sudoku and TV shows with titles not worth remembering to invest the mental torque necessary to recall the origin of his fraternal displeasure. And the son, Mr. Chen, who by the way is now fully dried from the shower water — hair combed, teeth tactfully brushed — was lightyears past caring what his distant father thought... he was just happy to be old enough not to get slapped around anymore.

Mr. Chen hated being slapped. He's the type of man who is a serene pond atop a bubbling volcano. He would grin and bear almost any form of insult, injury, or oppression — upholding equanimity at all times — unless and until he reached that breaking point. He didn't know that yet, though; neither did everyone else... not yet, at least.

Mr. Chen selected one of his three identical white short-sleeved dress shirts from his wardrobe, one of his two identical black dress pants, a frayed grey clip-on tie, and his slip-on dress shoes with a sole on the verge of breaking. He was a man who maximized efficiency by reducing options wherever possible, with one exception to the rule being the sock department. After directing five intense minutes staring at his options, he finally selected socks featuring Pokémon. They made him smile as he put them on.

Because he was exiting the safe haven of his thoroughly unremarkable apartment, he took the precaution of sheathing the playful foot garments with a layer of plain black socks to conceal his childish choice — a policy he had adopted because two months ago he accidentally tucked one pant leg into a silly sock.

He didn't notice for hours and was pretty sure everyone he'd passed on the street must have seen it. He had no proof of this, but recalled hearing people laugh and wrongfully attributed it to being in response to his wardrobe malfunction. The double-layering made his feet sweat more, provided less traction, and accelerated the degradation of his aforementioned sole, but it was a price worth paying to save face.

Mr. Chen's trash can was of the smallest variety, and the standard plastic grocery store bag that served as its liner contained no more than a tiny handful of non-perishable litter — a broken paper clip, a scrap of paper, and two pieces of stray thread. Most people would not take this trash out yet.

Mr. Chen was not most people.

He gently tied the top of the bag, then checked his reflection in a full-size mirror he had found in the trash heap, which was his current destination, two weeks prior. It was a perfectly good mirror, save for a substantial crack on the top half, which didn't bother him because it was a constant reminder he got it for free and he hated the upper-half of his reflection. The crack in no way obfuscated his reflection from the knee down, which provided him a clear view of the precarious region, affording him extra assurance his sock game was on point.

Mr. Chen exited the apartment, ensured both locks locked, traversed a hallway lit only by maliciously flickering ceiling lights he'd considered complaining about for years but always chose not to, descended a graffitied elevator with a poorly angled security camera and small television blaring commercials for products he had no interest in no matter how catchy the jingles, and exited his apartment building through a dark, dusty, featureless lobby.

He approached the trash heap, untied the bag, emptied the four pieces of trash, put the bag in his pocket, returned to his unit, placed the still perfectly usable bag back in the trash can, secured it, slipped off his shoes, removed the top layer of socks, slipped the shoes back on, then sat at the old wobbly table that served as a desk and powered on his work computer — a refur-bished decade-old base model laptop — to start his day at work. His job was boring beyond description and consisted almost entirely of double checking the math of amateur-level accountants.

Mr. Chen sometimes wondered if some of his video conferenced colleagues were secretly wearing sweatpants, shorts, or just underwear on their bottom half. He chuckled at the thought — a rare moment of humor for Mr. Chen, who would never dare do something so outrageous.

After all, someone could knock on the door, or his computer could fall, revealing the secret. The thought of such an embarrassment was enough to completely wipe the residual grin off his face. It's one thing not to be noticed. Being noticed due to humiliation was much, much worse… so it seemed for Mr. Chen at least.

---

IF TIME CAN BE THOUGHT OF AS A RIVER, WHICH IT MOST CERTAINLY CAN BE, routine was the sailboat on which Mr. Chen traversed it. Mr. Chen found a sense of baseline comfort in repeating the movement of his day as precisely as possible. His small thrills were in arriving to the platform mere seconds before the train, for example, though he always accounted for the possi-bility of an unforeseen situation disrupting his harmonious travels, so in the event he arrived seconds too late, there were many seconds left as a buffer.

Mr. Chen had never heard the expression *Early is on time; On time is late*; but if he had, he certainly would have agreed wholeheartedly. In Mr. Chen's mind, nothing could be worse than being the cause of disappointment, which is why he would never do something as outrageous as jaywalk.

There once was a time when cameras stationed at every intersection was not to be expected. There was a time when people needed only worry about getting caught illegally crossing the street should they be unlucky or inattentive enough to commit a crime in the purview of a law enforcement officer... a time when people broke rules if they could get away with it... a time when the government's grasp on society was so lax it was standard to see people acting of their own free will with relatively little regard for their duty to obey the authorities.

Mr. Chen hated those times.

He much preferred living in a world where there no longer lingered substantial temptation for such brazen acts of self-interest running counter to the singular universal harmony afforded by many enforced, enforceable rules. Order. Mr. Chen adored order, and he held in his otherwise gentle heart a very nominal sense of sympathy for anyone who chose the path of self-interested disobedience, especially when they knew the consequences — regardless how dire.

The consequence for illegally crossing an intersection under Chinese law, for example, was a financial fine — immediately deductible from the offender's personal bank account, and a lowering of the offender's social credit score. As troubling as either consequence seemed, to Mr. Chen they paled in comparison to the terrifying prospect of having photo evidence of their misdeed publicly broadcast on a monitor beside the street in which the offense was committed. Public shaming at its finest — a tremendously powerful deterrent. Mr. Chen had a fond appreciation for the cost-effectiveness of such shame-based enforcement methods, and at times pondered how much more broadly similar mechanisms could be implemented to further improve the harmoniousness of society.

For example, while effective, the photographic proof of an individual's indiscretions posted at the site of the crime was only the beginning of what could, and in Mr. Chen's mind should, be the extent of enforcement procedures. Why not automatically distribute the picture to the contacts in the offender's phone? In making the shame find its way to the people the violator most valued the approval of, surely the potency of the disincentive could be amplified by orders of magnitude!

Mr. Chen thought thoughts like this when he commuted to work in the morning, back before the first Covid pandemic inspired the measures that mandated he work from home. Secretly, Mr. Chen missed the necessity to go to a place 5-days a week. Despite his tendency to communicate with as few words as possible, the vast majority of Mr. Chen's social interactions occurred to and from work.

He liked seeing people, so long as he was under no obligation to interact with them. He liked to absorb droplets of the lives of countless strangers, vicariously experiencing some semblance of the excitement and drama of their lives. One time, he heard a couple arguing. One time, he saw a girl kiss another girl. One time, he heard a foreigner singing.

He wondered what it would be like to have someone in his life to argue with; or kiss; or to hear a song and feel such affinity with the music he actually verbally replicated the sound loud enough for others to hear, whether they liked it or not. Such acts were not illegal, to Mr. Chen's knowledge, but he felt them to be wrong on a fundamental level, and hoped someday they would be.

In the same category of not yet illegal but wrong was what to Mr. Chen was the equivalent of a pornographic fantasy — the occasions in which the trains were sufficiently crowded such that its occupants had no choice but to physically brush or even press against one another, and one or more of said people Mr. Chen had to be pressed against happened to be an attractive woman.

While he would of course be still as a statue and not deliberately initiate friction, the bumps and tussles of the train ride made such friction inevitable, and the warm soft female bodies rubbing against Mr. Chen's arms, legs, shoulders, posterior, and at times even pelvic region, was more than enough to send an electric tingle throughout his nervous system, speed his heart, and redden his face.

As for the ladies in question, they hadn't felt anything at all.

On no less than four occasions over the past year alone, Mr. Chen had experienced no less than one third of an erection from such encounters, which in no less than two of those occasions, the stranger in question had actually rubbed their bodies against said semi-erection, more or less directly, and on one particularly memorable occasion, it happened for three stops straight!

This gave Mr. Chen the impression she may have deliberately wanted the contact to occur, though it was of course possible she was oblivious to the sensation because she was so fixated on her phone, or had perhaps recently undergone some form of medical procedure requiring general anesthesia on the part of her body that made contact with Mr. Chen's highly neglected, highly sensitive, pelvic region.

Sometimes Mr. Chen would have dreams this very woman, whom he remembered vividly, lifted her skirt, pulled her panties to the side, and welcomed his humble manhood into her without a word. The dreams would accompany a once monthly nocturnal emission, like clockwork, and typically turn into nightmares, in which he was killed by a jealous husband or accused of rape. Upon waking from these dreams, Mr. Chen would find himself covered in sweat and his own seed, with a sense of shame so significant he couldn't get back to sleep until he showered and purged his undergarments of his despicable, worthless jizz.

Mr. Chen would wake up that next morning an hour less rested than usual, and the fatigue would ripple through his week until he made up for the missed sleep by falling asleep an hour earlier, which was never easy. Whilst willing himself to sleep, Mr. Chen would stare at his digital clock and keep tally of the time so he could aggregate the missing sleep debt piecemeal, until the balance had been restored, to the minute. He always remembered the times. He was very good with numbers, much preferring them to words.

Some in the West would characterize Mr. Chen as someone suffering from obsessive compulsive disorder, social anxiety disorder, autism and/or a number of other disorders not typically recognized or treated in the People's Republic of China. Ironically, be that as it may, Mr. Chen was soon to become famous for both health and order.

To use the word disorder in reference to Mr. Chen nowadays would be a punishable offense. To do so in his presence would be to court destruction. These days, no one would dare risk erupting that volcanic temper that he was at that time — aged 42 — still unaware of.

Over a year had passed since Mr. Chen had gotten on a subway because everything he needed to survive was within walking distance, and he considered any unnecessary outings in the midst of a pandemic to be foolish and irresponsible. That said, he never went out socially anyway, so it was a convenient moral high ground from which to justify his chosen lifestyle of isolationism. The prolonged drought of stimulation via subway encounters made Mr. Chen wonder if for the rest of his life his subconscious would need to rely on that small collection of memories of physical contact and sexual excitement in the vaults of his spank bank to nocturnally emit his dreaded essence as nature so ruthlessly demanded.

The hope of finding a romantic partner had long since been discarded as a plausible possibility. At times he envied the eunuchs of the past, who worked in the Forbidden City for the Emperor (where he would one day work); to be freed of this outdated system for human reproduction that was of absolutely no value to Mr. Chen would be a relief. A one-time ball removal seemed a price worth paying for a clearer head and cleaner shorts. Another irony, for a man who would become world renowned for having huge balls, in the Western sense of the word.

One day, Mr. Chen received a letter from the central government, requesting his attendance at an upcoming conference in Beijing. Now, for the first time in years, Mr. Chen needed to go to a new place. It was the most exciting and unexpected thing to ever happen to Mr. Chen in years, and he smiled enough to reveal his very shiny, slightly crooked teeth.

## 2

NOT SINCE HIS late twenties had Mr. Chen taken a several hour sojourn to his nation's capitol. The last time he had, the trains were very different. Much older. Louder. Slower. More crowded. Dirtier... filled with cars of people, often barefoot, too tightly packed together to enjoy a nice stretch and deep inhale without bumping into anyone, or inhaling anything putrid. To the contrary, there was now ample air and space to find comfort. New seats. Tray tables. Clean bathrooms. And an astoundingly calm and serene slide down the tracks.

High speed trains; appropriately named, transporting millions of people from city to city every morning, afternoon, and night. Clockwork. A pristine operation. In this brave new world, which Mr. Chen woke up to daily, everything was at least a little better. A cascade of minor improvements were gradually transforming The People's Republic of China from one of the most desperate places on Earth to one of the most advanced. Progress... the ripe fruit grown from the fertile blood-soaked soil of a century of sacrifice. A century of humiliation fast coming to an end, to be followed by a century, if not centuries, of prosperity.

That was the promise on the horizon that gave Mr. Chen a sense of nationalistic pride that served to fill a love shaped hole in his sad little heart. Mr. Chen had no one to love, so he chose to love everyone, in the abstract. He did so by always doing his duties and never complaining. Decades were spent striving to adhere precisely to every rule, regulation, and condition; an eternal drive to live up to the standards and expectations of those in power.

The thought that some of those people — the unseen technocrats and administrators guiding the growth of his nation — wanted something with

Mr. Chen instilled in the fellow, immediately and markedly, a profound sense of mission, purpose, pride, and belonging.

These new, positive feelings overcoming Mr. Chen were the seeds that would in due time grow into something intoxicatingly radical, and give rise to a latent persona within that was as yet completely unbeknownst to Mr. Chen... and of course too, the world at large.

---

As the taxi pulled into the circular lobby of an upscale though not opulent hotel — the destination, per the instructions provided in the invitation letter he kept inside his conservative, grey, off-the-rack suit he donned for the occasion — which was to Mr. Chen the best reason he had ever been given to dress up. Not only had he splurged on a new suit set, he had gone all out and picked up every article of clothing on the mannequin, down to the socks, shoes, and cufflinks.

He even spent the equivalent of one month's salary on a new watch, because he wanted to feel more special than he was, and he wanted to make the best impression possible, given this once in a lifetime opportunity to be noticed by important people. The investments in his appearance and self-confidence were substantial, and he made sure, and would continue to make sure, his mother didn't see his luxurious and expensive trappings so he wouldn't be pressured to justify the expenditures.

Despite having years of unspent, uninvested capital just sitting in the bank, Mr. Chen's fear of loss overshadowed his desire for any known object or experience money could buy; and one of his deepest seeded fears was a return to the poverty experienced in his youth, which was nothing compared to the poverty endured by his parents, their parents before them, and so on, as far back as his known family history went. The Chen family story was largely untold, but Mr. Chen knew it to be a legacy of survival in spite of generational danger and general lack. Theirs was a slow, gradual arch toward progress, now interrupted by what Mr. Chen was just beginning to sense could be a parabolic explosion.

What if he were to become one of these people who was known, respected, and provided for? What if he suddenly found himself able to have and do things that had hitherto been the stuff of dreams he'd not the stomach nor imagination to conjure? Mr. Chen pinched himself, discreetly and acutely, just behind his right earlobe — a time-tested strategy he used to snap back in the rare case his mind wandered.

No sooner had he completed this transaction and closed the cab door that a black SUV with tinted windows pulled up, opened its back door, and a man in the passenger seat greeted him by name through a cracked open window and sternly though warmly instructed him to get in.

The vehicle was pristine, boasting that universally appreciated new car smell. The driver did not turn around as he greeted Mr. Chen, welcomed him to Beijing, and asked him to wait quietly and hold his questions for the time being.

Mr. Chen obeyed.

THE WAIT WAS NOT LONG. BOTH SIDE DOORS OPENED AND TWO STRANGERS entered the car; one with slight delay, as Mr. Chen needed to unbuckle his seatbelt and move to the middle seat. By the time he had strapped into the new seatbelt, Mr. Chen was struck with a sudden awareness he was sandwiched between two beautiful women in matching red miniskirts and silky black halter tops. He submissively nodded to each.

They greeted him in near perfect unison, with soft feminine voices — the sound and air from their mouths hitting Mr. Chen's ears with seductive force. Before he could think of something to say, he became acutely aware that both slices of bread of the Mr. Chen sandwich were very much pressed against him... perhaps innocently, but he felt the warmth of each exposed outer thigh resonating through his legs and directly toward his long neglected, prematurely retired penis.

He swallowed and began to perspire, and directed all conscious effort available to the joint challenges of abstaining from bouncing his right leg up and down rhythmically — a long-time nervous tick — and suppressing the aspiring erection he was fast becoming confronted by. It was a task made no less difficult by his sudden awareness the girls were graced in perfume that warmed his nostrils while sending a chill down his spine, which made him shiver and tremble.

The girls sat still, breathing slowly and gently, not saying anything, waiting patiently. Mr. Chen began attempting to nasally ascertain whether one or both of his new female companions so nonchalantly pressed against him were wearing the perfume, and trying to discern whether it was the same perfume, or two different perfumes combining to form a new superperfume he found so exquisitely and frustratingly arousing. He could have of course asked, but Mr. Chen was not in the habit of making potentially suggestive remarks to women, and it took all of his focus to combat his shameful erection; it was no time to garner tidbits of fragrance-based information or make smalltalk.

"Hello Mr. Chen," said the man wearing a black hoodie, riding shotgun, without turning his face to his guest, and in a gentle though at once commanding tone.

"Thank you for joining us. Before I make my intentions known, I kindly request you remove your phone and any other electronic devices from your lovely though wanting for a proper tailoring suit, and surrender it to my lovely employees at once."

Mr. Chen promptly obeyed, blushing against his will as he finally made eye contact with the Mr. Chen sandwich bread slice to his right, who smiled at him knowingly, with a twinkle in her oak brown eyes.

"Thank you, Mr. Chen," she said, in a playful tone.

The man in the front passenger seat still faced forward, but Mr. Chen could see the left half of the top of his head in the rear view mirror, enough to make out that he was a foreigner — a white man.

"Is that everything?" The Man asked, in a tone that suggested it wasn't, as the gal to his right placed his phone in a sturdy container. Mr. Chen began frisking himself, in search of any other overlooked devices.

"Your watch runs on a 1.55 volt battery, Mr. Chen. That's a charge just strong enough to generate what people call a piezoelectric effect. This causes the quartz crystal in your watch to resonate. The ever so subtle vibrations move on the mechanisms within to make the gears press upon one another in such a way the watch hands move, indicating the time.

"The crystal oscillates when in contact with an electric circuit powered by the battery, precisely 32,768 times every second. The subtle vibrations generate a consistent electrical pulse. Exactly one pulse per second. This pulse, like a heartbeat, tick tick ticks just so… keeping perfect time, for the duration of the life of the battery.

Mr. Chen breathed through a slack jaw, trying to concentrate, but still well-distracted by the female company; each graze of their arms against his made him tremble and deafened his little ears to big new information.

"Do you understand, Mr. Chen?"

Mr. Chen nodded yes, instinctively, took off his watch, and handed it to the bread on the left side of the Mr. Chen sandwich, who touched the inside of his now clammy hand, and gently scraped it with her red, manicured nails, as he dropped the watch into her hand. The man in the front seat held out his hand and the girl handed him Mr. Chen's watch. He looked at it a moment, took off his own watch, and tried it on.

"Did you know you have similar crystals in your brain? Somewhere called the pineal gland. And they can emit the same effect. Isn't that interesting?"

Mr. Chen nodded. The Man took off the quartz crystal watch.

"That said, it's still a piece of shit."

He lowered the passenger-side window and contributed what may have been the only piece of litter on the streets of Beijing then held a glistening platinum replacement over his shoulder.

"Here…"

Mr. Chen hesitated. The Man jingled the watch. Mr. Chen slowly began to reach for it. Out of patience, the gentleman tossed it into his lap; it came crashing down on his now mostly flaccid penis, causing him to audibly groan in a way that elicited chuckles, which to the ever-so-sensitive Mr. Chen hurt even more.

"I'll trade you," he said. Mr. Chen looked down at the timepiece between his balls.

"Let me help you," came a voice into his right ear, so close it was a tiny whisper he heard with the utmost clarity. The voice to the left whispered into his other ear. "I'll help too," she said, with an exhale that lingered. In his other ear came a hint of sensuous moan.

As both girls pretended to struggle to find the watch, tussling, rubbing, and even squeezing his inner thighs, balls, and the main attraction, which was now throbbing from both pain and pleasure. "It's so nice," said one. "I love it," said the other, picking up the watch. The innuendo couldn't be more brazen, nor the watch more beautiful.

"Have you ever owned a Rolex, Mr. Chen?" he asked, tauntingly…

"Of course you haven't. I own several. It's an automatic… doesn't keep as accurate a time as formerly your, now my, quartz movement piece. But to be clear, you could sell that Rolex for the amount of times the quartz in my new watch oscillates per second, in US dollars—"

Mr. Chen remembered the number: 32,768.

"—and for that price, you'd be getting ripped off."

Before Mr. Chen could finish processing the most surreal experience of his life and sheepishly respond, the man continued.

"Why? Because you are my friend, Mr. Chen. And all my friends get nice things. Don't they girls?"

On cue, the girls laughed and showed their petite bedazzled wrists.

"Speaking of which, are they to your taste?"

The girls started kissing Mr. Chen's blushing cheeks.

"This has been a pleasure and I see we're right on schedule. I knew you'd show up for the meeting 15 minutes early. That's what I like about you, Mr. Chen. You are like the quartz crystal. Reliable. Consistent. Predictable. You possess important qualities I search for in my friends. And I do look forward to advancing that friendship. Until then—"

The sound of his fly being unzipped startled Mr. Chen.

"—I leave you *in good hands.*"

Mr. Chen's legs began convulsing as two delicate hands — one from each side of the Mr. Chen sandwich — slid down each of his hairless thighs. As they fondled and stroked his chopstick and dumplings, they took turns tilting his head toward them and kissing his lips.

Then came tongue kisses and lip-biting, both firsts for Mr. Chen.

Then came a tongue in each ear, another first.

Then came dirty talk, another first.

Then came Mr. Chen.

# 3

---

MR. CHEN AWOKE from a deep sleep in an unknown bed; it was frivolously comfortable, unlike the sad excuse for a refuge of daily slumber that was his bed at home, which came with the apartment. As far as he knew, he had inherited a bed upon which others before him had endured thousands of nights on a slightly more comfortable mattress. What to the gentleman from the fancy SUV with the femme fatales that passed out overpriced trinkets like candy would surely consider an abhorrent block of despicable mediocrity only a degenerate peasant would stoop to sleeping on was, to Mr. Chen, simply his bed.

There never was shame in minor to moderate discomfort in Mr. Chen's family. Such were simply the circumstances of life — settings he'd not in four and more decades so much as considered altering. This peculiar morning was the first time he considered that he might have some choice in beds. If it were possible to wake up in such a comfortable, large, opulent bed once, it therefore must be possible for it to happen again; and again; so on and so forth.

That, he realized, for the first time, must be what it's like to have a better life. Before the voice in Mr. Chen's head had a chance to interject, and remind him that a man like him did not deserve a better life; that to attain such a life would be a vague though unacceptable violation of some sacred commitment he had made to remain persistently content in sequences of perpetual, just bearable discontent... he felt a most unexpected and jarring sensation — excitement!

Excitement, because his body had just touched another body; a lovely lady, sleeping soundly under the goose down comforter, which was also of course far more comfortable than the ratty old blankets on Mr. Chen's from this day forth unacceptably uncomfortable bed. To his right, lied a sleeping beauty whom, as Mr. Chen confirmed with a discreet peek under the covers, was topless, and with another peek — also bottomless.

*Why*, wondered Mr. Chen, *is she in this bed with me?*

Mr. Chen searched his memory for clues as to what had led them to share this most comfortable bed. With some strain, he recollected the raising of thin glasses filled with light beer, and shots of baijiu — a rice-based liquor ubiquitous in the Orient — thus determining intoxication played a role in the forgotten sequence of events.

He struggled to remember details, but suspected with a high level of confidence they had done things together. And for several luxurious moments of silent self-satisfaction, Mr. Chen considered the near certainty that after four decades of involuntary chastity, he had finally discarded his virginity. It was a proud moment, to put it lightly.

A ringing phone on the bedside table demanded Mr. Chen's attention, and simultaneously awoke his first probable lover. The voice on the phone was unmistakable — it was the giver of girls and Rolexes, and apparently his new best friend...

"Did you have fun last night, Mr. Chen? I've not the time to listen to answers to questions I already know the answer to, and I know this is all still rather overwhelming, for which you have my apologies, but evolution is not the slow, steady, gradual process you've been led to believe. Growth is. Evolution though... can be, and for you, most certainly is — sudden and overwhelming. Many do not survive the process. But those that do carry your species forward, as is intended.

"It is my role to accelerate that evolution... to give you opportunities to learn and change. You, Mr. Chen, have been chosen to evolve. Your life will never be the same again. All you need do is go where I say when I say; do what I command when I command it; and all will go precisely as intended. I cannot answer your next, predictable questions about who I am, what will be asked of you, etcetera... but what I can say is if we are in agreement, we are in business."

After a long pause, Mr. Chen opened his mouth, nearly at the point of settling on a decision to obey this most persuasive and alluring stranger, when a sudden and relentless knock at the door was accompanied by the line going dead.

It was at this time, as Mr. Chen noticed the bouncing breasts of his first lover who was quickly affixing her bra and searching for her panties, that Mr. Chen realized he was also naked. It was in that unclad state that Mr. Chen was greeted by three men, who would go on to sternly though politely request he get dressed.

---

THIS DRIVE WAS FAR LESS EVENTFUL THAN THE DRIVE THE DAY PRIOR. NOW MR. Chen sat in the back seat of a clearly marked government vehicle beside a man wearing aviator sunglasses. Whether the man was staring at him or out the window was indeterminable.

Up front, the driver drove and the passenger passengered. A silent box of Chinese men in a long line of boxes of Chinese men and women moving up and down the four-lane highways separated by a cement partition, on the other side of which four more lanes moved in the opposite direction.

Mr. Chen thought of the roads and walkways as the veins of the organism that is the city of Beijing; each individual like a cell; the hustle and bustle of their collective daily routines the capillary movement keeping the urban life form atop the Earth's crust alive and growing. This was an uncharacteristically abstract passing quandary for Mr. Chen: the city a life form. The people a living piece of a giant, ever expanding, ever changing entity guided by forces outside the scope of any individual component.

Mr. Chen took a moment to try again to remember what had happened the day before, after his surreal vehicular meeting, and before he most likely lost his virginity. At once, a headache seized Mr. Chen… a sharp sensation in the center of his brain, that disrupted all conscious thought and brought him into the present moment.

Mr. Chen took a few deep breaths, discreetly, feeling a slight sense of relief; but a second after returning to the surprisingly difficult task of recounting recent events, the pain again returned — this time amplified, as if something inside was urging him not to think about it.

---

MR. CHEN FOUND HIMSELF WAITING OUTSIDE A ROOM FOR WHAT HIS WATCH would have tracked to be precisely 13 minutes, but what Mr. Chen subjectively experienced to be in the range of three to four hours. The means by which he was able to experience this new sense of time dilation was the activation of certain dormant potentials that lied in wait of resurrection deep within his DNA.

These and more potentials lingered, and linger still, in the code shared by the entire human species. Seldom, if ever, however, do such breakthroughs occur within people like Mr. Chen, in times such as these, for the simple reason that getting to this point requires lifetimes of effort, which most people don't feel they have time for.

The reason Mr. Chen seemingly inherited bewildering new powers of an unspecified nature and purpose overnight, is because he was being acted upon by an entity which sought to use him to fulfill an important role in some grander scheme. At this stage, however, Mr. Chen was only just beginning to perceive the magnitude of the changes he was undergoing, and too of the risks associated with going along for the ride as this metamorphosis akin to a second puberty ran its course.

In what Mr. Chen could most closely associate with a dream-state superimposed on known reality, he played with the unseen winds of time... speeding it up and slowing it down. One instant Mr. Chen finds himself waiting to be interviewed by government agents in a boring, quiet hallway, staring at what appeared to anyone else as an unremarkable empty space on a white wall.

The next instant, Mr. Chen is seeing geometrically perfect patterns in flux... intertwined with intersecting, converging, and emerging points flowing and bursting in unpredictable yet pleasingly orderly ways; like some energetic tapestry — patterns that expressed themselves as light, engaged in some intricate dance that was already well underway and would remain active when he took his attention elsewhere.

So bizarre and utterly fascinating was the sight that Mr. Chen was more than satisfied to simply observe and rest in a state of awe. This went on for hours to Mr. Chen, but again, only precisely 13 minutes for everyone else around. While Mr. Chen did not hear any words, or receive any articulable experience beyond general wonder, he did find himself physically charged by it all. He seemed to be drawing energy from the mysterious field surrounding him. By the time the door to the room Mr. Chen was waiting outside opened, Mr. Chen felt fantastic. He put on a pair of sunglasses he did not remember having, without knowing why or consciously intending to.

His eyes opened wide. His pupils dilated. His skin tingled... as if wrapped in a cozy blanket of pure electricity; a warm invisible armor-like new layer affixed to the entire surface area of his visibly weak and universally unimpressive body. His posture too had radically transformed. What had been a seemingly permanent slouch — one that carried the weight of a lifetime of gently aggregated trauma, and the accumulation of fear reinforced with anxiety — had given way to a posture that exuded borderline excessive confidence. Within his lungs, he held thrice the volume of oxygen than before he'd found himself entranced in the alluring patterns on the wall.

Each of his 33 vertebrates was extended and in full alignment. His neck, usually sunken low, like a big spring supporting the weight of a bowling ball in the style of a frightened turtle... was now stretched upward, as if compelled by magnetic attraction coming from above. His breath, tradition-ally shallow and rushed, was now slow, deep, and steady... coming from his nose, rather than his half open mouth, as it had before.

Mr. Chen sat down at the table, opposite one government agent over-looking a modestly thick file. The other agent stood by the door, as if to either prepare to block him from leaving or to make a quick egress should the need soon arise. Mr. Chen sat there with his newfound impressive posture and a highly uncharacteristic smile closer to a smirk than anything else.

What came next was to Mr. Chen more akin to passive observation of astute performance than it was active participation in an interview going about as good as it could. He didn't speak, but words were somehow still coming out. The speech just came to Mr. Chen, word after word; sentence after sentence. The unconscious speech flowed seamlessly and effortlessly, until every last question had been satisfactorily answered.

While Mr. Chen couldn't remember anything he said over the course of the 23 minute interview, he could remember the tone of voice he'd used. It was at once calm and assertive. Inquisitive then declaratory. With each remark came an emotional tone that allowed his two man audience, and the future listeners and viewers with access to the recordings, to feel what he meant, rather than just understand it.

On multiple occasions, he had both men laughing. By the time the inter-view was complete, he was asking his interviewers questions, in a charming way transitioning the dynamic so that rather than treating him as some kind of suspect or subject, they were speaking with him as a friend... or in the least, an admired and engaging new acquaintance.

He had, by all appearances, won them over; and as he shook their hands and bid them farewell, it felt as if he had just gotten away with something. He enjoyed this unspecified sense of achievement only long enough to make it out of the building and into a taxi.

The sound of the car door closing caused a sudden loud ringing in his head, and he clenched tight his jaw, before vomiting on the floor of the taxi and being informed he would be expected to pay a cleaning fee if this drive was to be driven. Mr. Chen exited the unlucky taxi and made his way down the street, the painful ringing and headache pulsating now with varying intensity.

When sufficiently far away from the government building, Mr. Chen collapsed against an alley trash can in total exhaustion and fell quickly into a deep and sudden restorative slumber.

Some time later, Mr. Chen came to again. It was night time, and Mr. Chen had but one thought: *water!* He ambled to the nearest corner store, bought a bottle of water and a citrus soda, then guzzled both as he walked to the street to hail another cab. He found another taxi and got in.

"Where to?" asked the driver.

It was then Mr. Chen realized he was suffering from some form of amnesia because he hadn't the slightest idea where to go; upon further attempts to remember, his head began to ache again.

The taxi driver asked if he needed to go to a hospital.

Mr. Chen left the second cab in a hurry, made his way back to the site where he had awoken, and rested again, soon falling into a deep sleep.

This time, Mr. Chen had a dream.

13 minutes, but th...

experienced to be ...

3-4 hours. The mea...

to experience this ...

dilation was the ...

dormancy. Potenti...

resurrection, deep ...

...Mor...

human species. Selde...

such breakthroughs o...

Mr. Chen, in times s...

planet like this, for t...

to that point require...

# 4

THE CONTENTS of Mr. Chen's dreams are unknown; even to Mr. Chen. Were he to remember his dreams that evening, it would be of no relevance, for to describe a dream in words is as futile a task as describing a painting in scent.

Mr. Chen had up to then carried within his soul a weight of unknown origin that prevented him from knowing well what it is to "be okay". His baseline state was not one characterized by sanguine equilibrium. While also not typically one of particularly intense passion or emotion, it was marked instead by a light though consistent state of depression, punctuated by short bursts of internally directed rage, which transmuted into deeper instances of depression, occasionally culminating in a numbness-inducing sense of general apathy.

To say Mr. Chen woke up a new man is not as far an exaggeration as is typically the case, for Mr. Chen arose from a makeshift bed of packaged trash free of the aforementioned "weight", which had for decades calcified the boundaries of his heart such that new emotions were hard-pressed to make their way in, and old emotions were equally blocked from getting out. Such is and has for much time been the human condition on Earth for a sizable portion of its inhabitants.

The removal of Mr. Chen's blockages allowed a new sense of energetic fluidity he was immediately and intuitively aware of. He quickly rose to his feet with great ease and found himself walking, then jogging, then running, in no particular direction, and with no destination in mind. Intoxicated by this new and thrilling energetic state, Mr. Chen ran faster and faster, darting down an ally to the left, leaping a formidable four-foot high chainlink fence and literally bouncing off the outside building walls in a freeform parkour.

Mr. Chen did not know parkour, which was apparent to the chuckling onlookers, as this small, middle-aged gentleman in business attire darted and leapt about in the manner to be expected of a crack head; though in Beijing, such a sight would be so rare an occurrence it would merit recollection many years after, even if Mr. Chen hadn't become so famous.

Mr. Chen did not realize it at the time because he was so fully immersed in his ballad of exuberant expression, but while running wild he did not care who might be looking. For the first time since very early childhood, Mr. Chen had the simple mindset of a kid having fun; and in this unexpected and forgotten state, Mr. Chen found joy, and even moments of wonder, in the most mundane sights, sounds, and experiences.

The air tasted delicious! Pollutants be dammed; he inhaled the oxygen with the vigor of the aforementioned crack head archetype engaging in the crack head's treasured practice of vigorously smoking crack. He stared for several seconds at his own reflection in a puddle, and found himself infatuated with curiosity about what it meant for light to be reflected or absorbed, why reflections appeared or did not, and what, if anything, his sense of sight might have to do with the creation and interpretation of imagery.

This could have potentially persisted for several moments, if not for a bike tire splitting his reflection in two with a splash which, when Mr. Chen noticed had in part wet his socks through his shoes, only further delighted him. Rather than being the catastrophic minor hinderance sufficient to ruin his whole day an unlucky puddle splash would have been just days prior, now he interpreted it to be an interesting and even inexplicably enjoyable experience with each squishy press of his toes into the soaked cotton of his socks.

Mr. Chen noticed many sights, sounds and sensations that had always been easily available to him but that he rarely found himself consciously aware of, in which rare cases, it was only because he wanted to assign a negative meaning, suspicion, or fear to that which he noticed. Mr. Chen would not be so fortunate to maintain this childlike sense of wonder and excitement for an extended period, but for the time being, Mr. Chen hadn't a care in the world; nor did he find himself for more than a few seconds at a time bored by his surroundings, or in lack of an object of interest.

As in the case of a child, this primordial excitement and uninterrupted clarity of focus on anything and everything around would abate him, and for the same reason. While continuing his directionless bout around the city, Mr. Chen found himself captivated by a sparrow that he strongly desired to get to know; so much so that he ran into a busy street, narrowly missed being hit by a car, and thereby drew noticeable glares of disgust and ganders of concern of others surrounding him.

At once it struck Mr. Chen that the manner by which he had been conducting himself was to blame for the negative attention. He remembered it was not proper to behave in such a way that others cast judgment. Further disruptive behavior, reasoned Mr. Chen, could lead to consequences up to and including imprisonment, and/or the tarnishing of that conceptual thing he'd temporarily forgotten existed, and was to be valued above all — his reputation.

Glancing at the nearby cameras pointed in his direction, it occurred to Mr. Chen the government either was, or could be, watching and judging him. He was at once ashamed of himself, and an all too familiar weight returned, felt primarily in his stomach area. His little heart raced, and he was unable to discern whether this was more attributable to all the running and jumping around, or his increasing feelings of shame and self-conscious paranoia that if he did not acutely curb his enthusiasm, there would be consequences.

Mr. Chen lowered his head and began walking calmly in one direction, blending into the sea of people doing the same... the same way, for the same reasons. With each step, the previously acceptable squishy socks now tormented Mr. Chen.

He felt frustrated at himself for standing so close to a puddle. He was asking for it. He lamented his now disastrous inconvenience with each squishy stride, all the way to the nearest subway station, where he happened upon a merchant whose wares included socks.

―――――

ON THE TRAIN BACK HOME TO CHENGDU, HIS HOMETOWN WITH A POPULATION OF roughly 10 million, Mr. Chen took a moment to discreetly wind his Rolex, setting the proper time and noting an inscription on the back case: MEMENTO MORI.

He wondered what it meant as he drifted to sleep.

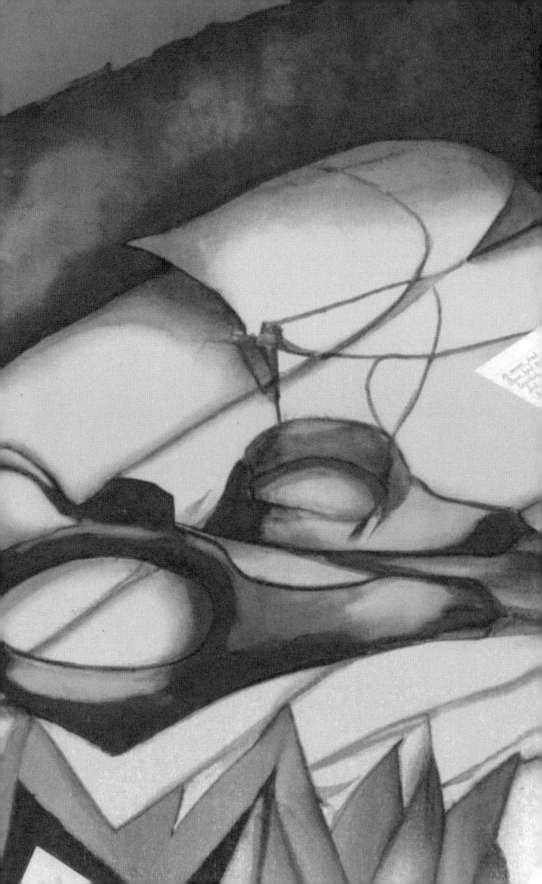

# 5

---

A WEEK and a day had passed, since Mr. Chen had returned from his sojourn to the capitol. He resumed his usual routine. From time to time, Mr. Chen would find himself contemplating the inexplainable events of the week prior, but he grew increasingly apt at pushing from his mind the understandable curiosity that lingered.

He also of course found himself remembering the excitement brought about by his sexual escapades; the latter with great consistency. That he was probably finally a virgin no longer was to him a proud accomplishment, as he had over the past decades gradually relieved himself of the fantasy anyone would, or could, ever find him attractive. He still could not remember the actual event, but the knowledge of it having transpired still sufficed to bring him joy, or in the very least — validation.

Returning from work, he discovered on his pillow a black envelope with his name on it, in bright red ink — handwritten in calligraphy so pristine it looked as if it had been lifted from the Declaration of Independence, not that that was a thing Mr. Chen knew about. Mr. Chen's little heart skipped a beat, and he felt a cold, electric tingle soar from his chest to his extremities. He began to sweat and breathe rapidly.

Mr. Chen sat on his bed for over an hour, just staring at the envelope, afraid to touch it, hoping it might just dematerialize. He lifted it off the pillow and slipped it onto his spartan desk, which had also come with the apartment. It seemed to make a sound too loud to make sense, and Mr. Chen thought he was beginning to hear a familiar, now undesirable ringing in his ear.

The ringing persisted, as he went about his evening routine of rinsing his face of the invisible residue, meticulously brushing his teeth with a brush worn and frayed both from overuse, and from Mr. Chen unconsciously giving expression to buried rage through the most minor forms of self-harm possible — the hard tooth brushing being a sort of release valve for the general anger he felt — the remainder of which was to be converted seamlessly into shame and depression.

Mr. Chen spit the bloody toothpaste into his sink and watched the conglomeration of saliva, blood, plaque and paste form a little vortex that he found soothing. As he stared at the waning vortex in his sink he projected the intention to be left alone.

While as far from religious, or spiritual, as a man could hope to be, Mr. Chen would have to confess what he was doing — projecting a clear intention with the hope, though not expectation, his wish would be somehow granted — was a lot like praying. Mr. Chen had never prayed before, and while he had of course hoped for many things over the years, this subtle act of the heart and mind was by far the closest thing to a prayer he had ever conjured.

He was relieved to find the ringing sound accompanying his thoughts of hesitancy toward opening the letter instantly subsided. The fact that his projection of intention had actually worked would have bothered him more than the ringing, had he the willingness to accept it, but being the hardnosed realist he was, Mr. Chen protected himself from such a dissonance-inducing realization by immediately rationalizing it to be just a coincidence, albeit a strange one.

Mr. Chen went on with his usual nightly routine, changing into his faded pijamas, stretching half-heartedly, eating a small cookie, and turning off his lights, then bedside lamp, then closing his eyes and surrendering to the night. Unfortunately for Mr. Chen, the next part — where the sleep usually begins — evaded him. He tried to calm his anxiety and avoid his usual compulsion to tabulate the time spent not sleeping according to schedule so he could make up for the sleep debt the following night — failing to do so.

He went on trying like this for another hour and a half, when it finally occurred to Mr. Chen that his bed was uncomfortable, and unless he found the courage to open that letter, his bed would only get more and more uncomfortable until he found himself in some casket where he could finally get some rest.

Mr. Chen gritted his teeth as he slipped more and more back into the memory of that comfortable hotel bed and how much he preferred it. Those memories naturally led to associated recollections of the girl he woke up next to, and in particular, the graceful way her breasts bounced when she scrambled to find her clothes. His hands sweat when he wondered what it must be like to firmly grip those hearty milk-makers in the throes of lovemaking.

These thoughts predictably resulted in a deeply unwanted erection, which Mr. Chen pitifully failed to extinguish with both willpower and a swift backhand slap. Mr. Chen felt a need to relieve himself, matched only by the desire to abstain from touching himself. He breathed quickly through his little nostrils and felt as if he might soon roar like a dragon. He felt himself shaking and repeatedly struck his uncomfortable bed, which he soon transitioned from no longer being content with, to hating with a burning passion.

In a remarkably uncharacteristic act of pure unbridled emotion, Mr. Chen got out of bed, went to the desk, wished he had a knife and settled for a squeaky rusty pair of scissors, then proceeded to murder his stupid fucking bed. He stabbed it, sliced it, and tore it with all his nominal might. Nine minutes later, the end results was a now unusable mattress, and tangible proof that he was no longer willing to go on living as he always had.

Mr. Chen picked up the letter courageously. He stared at it and felt special. Still afraid. Still hesitant. But special. This was a feeling Mr. Chen did not know how much he needed to feel. Simply contemplating that someone — off-putting, potentially criminal, and somehow supernaturally inclined as he may be — could care enough about him to write his name so beautifully, was highly poignant to the neglected, obsessive, little angry man.

Tracking him down, giving him a priceless possession, and sneaking into his apartment somehow were all impressive indicators he mattered to someone. However, simply investing the time to write his name by hand so beautifully was amazing, flattering, and kind.

Mr. Chen's little eyes widened. He grinned. His name looked lovely. He found himself imagining the name appearing elsewhere, and on more envelopes… perhaps even in print; perhaps on TV; perhaps on billboards… perhaps people would start recognizing him, smiling at him, waving to him every time he walked down the street. *Significance.*

The thought of being significant, in his own eyes and the eyes of others, gave him energy. He began to hear another ringing sound, but this time it didn't bother him so much. This time it was somehow pleasant. It got louder and more pleasant as he ran his fingers over his name on the envelope, and reached a fever pitch paired by a pulsating, warm, electrical impulse resonating throughout his body as he finally chose to open it.

———

THE LETTER INSIDE THE ENVELOPE WAS REMARKABLE IN MANY RESPECTS, NOT least of which being that it was on a paper unlike any he — or for that matter anyone Mr. Chen had ever met — had ever seen. It was soft to the touch, somewhere between cotton and a flower petal, and the surface was not flat, but textured. It also emitted a spectacular scent, which featured soft notes of vanilla and rose petal, overtaken by the unmistakable heavenly aroma of burning leaves.

The aroma would in fact be mistakable to Mr. Chen at that time, as he had not yet been afforded the privilege of being in the reach of the smoke of crisp, crackling, Autumn offerings from the trees. He had no memories of any close encounters with nature, save for the unpleasant time he was chasing a ball into a small garden in the courtyard of an apartment complex adjacent to his own. There, seven year-old Mr. Chen stepped in the soil of the garden, which led to his tracking dirt into the apartment, triggering a particularly jarring glance of disappointment from his father, and ensuing complaints from his mother. It was terrible. He hadn't set foot in dirt once in the 35 years since the incident.

When he finally opened it, even more remarkable features were to be found. As Mr. Chen looked at the paper, which was black — jet black — he saw words slowly materializing; one letter at a time, as if searing out of the paper with a dull luminescence of a reddish orange hue. The poem was in English, but Mr. Chen somehow understood it in its entirety, despite not knowing more than five words of the language.

GOOD EVENING MY DEAR NEW FRIEND MR. CHEN.
I HOPE MORE TIME TOGETHER WE'LL SOON SPEND.
ANSWER THE RIDDLE TO ACHIEVE THAT END...

YOUR SHIT SHEETS ARE RIPPED, YOUR OLD BED IS DEAD.
DO YOU FEEL THAT FIRE IN YOUR HEART AND HEAD?
TIME TO FACE YOUR FEARS; OVERCOME THE DREAD.

YOU KEPT THAT OLD SHOE; WITH THE SOLE SO WORN?
DISPOSE OF IT; TONIGHT A STAR IS BORN!
YOU'LL LIVE FANTASIES, YOUR LIFE WILL BE PORN!

HIDE NOT FROM THIS NEW ENERGY WITHIN.
HOW CAN METAMORPHOSIS BE A SIN?
FUCK YOUR FEAR; IT'S TIME TO FINALLY WIN!

YOU FEEL WHAT THE WOLF FEELS BEFORE EACH HOWL.
TONIGHT YOU WILL SLEEP AS MUCH AS AN OWL.
WETS AS IT DRIES? WELL IT MUST BE A _____.

THE ONLY DIFFERENCE BETWEEN BEING AFRAID OR EXCITED IS ATTITUDE. WHILE IN most cases Mr. Chen's unconscious preference would lean toward the former, he felt himself then leaning decidedly toward the latter. He decided to solve this riddle and see where this rabbit hole led.

He sat on his ruined bed and thought with all his might. After a few re-reads, the answer dawned on him: *a towel?* As soon as he had the thought, he felt and heard the familiar though still terrifying return of the sound in his head. It seemed to change gradually in pitch and intensity, not unlike a radio caught between stations. Everything began to vibrate with a rumble.

It crossed Mr. Chen's mind that he might be experiencing an earthquake, but a quick glance confirmed the until recently half-empty, now half-full glass of water on his desk remained completely still, eliminating that hypothesis. He looked back down at the letter. Now it only said one word, "Correct."

He dropped the letter, gasping as he stood up, closing his eyes as the auditory and physical sensations continued. The vibration in his head locked into a frequency that created a lasting, overwhelming sound, and the rumbling seemed to concentrate from a singular direction somewhere outside his room. Disoriented as he was by the all-encompassing sound in his head, Mr. Chen intuited it was pertinent he find the source of the quaking, and quickly. He hastily stumbled out of his room like a drunkard and down a hall toward a closet.

Mr. Chen began to feel something like a magnetic force acting on his body, slowing his movements. He glanced at his Rolex, which fit poorly — in dire need of the removal of a few band links, but just tight enough not to fall off. The second hand swept at an increasingly slower pace, confirming he was entering another state of time dilation.

He slowly reached for the closet's doorknob as quickly as was now possible, and he felt his heart slow down, the blood retreating from his peripheries — starting with the toes and fingertips — and regrouping at the sights of his body's most essential organs. He felt an electric charge as his hand made contact with the doorknob and was surprised and relieved to find it was not painful, though not necessarily pleasant either. He threw open the door in slow motion to reveal a portal where he kept the extra towels.

It looked like an electrically charged miniature lake oriented vertically; just large enough to fit a Mr. Chen, who hesitated for a moment to him and several according to his watch — the second hand of which now crept slowly. Even for a man far more on the coward than hero end of the spectrum, his curiosity urged him to abandon his reasonable reservations and enter the portal. Mr. Chen stepped in and felt his foot dissolve. He was struck by the horrifying thought that if he were to pull his leg out, he would find himself shy a leg.

Without wasting any more time on the fence, he committed to a leap of faith into the portal, which instantly caused the rest of his body to dematerialize until all he could perceive was an all-encompassing bright light — so bright it would be blinding if he still had eyes.

That he did not but could still see gave Mr. Chen the impression he might be dead, and that this could be the afterlife — a place he did not believe in.

... for us to directly ...
... some risk. I ...
... the loss for being the ...
... home in the shadows. Do in the ...
understand our in person meeting
... space, and only arranged with ...
... to protect ... physical security ...
... keep yourself and yours as yet unknown
... from being labelled to known associations,
... assured, I fear no one Mr. Chen, but I ...
... avoid excessive confrontation whenever ...
He walked ahead of Mr. Chen, and wore a bla...

# 6

Mr. Chen rose to his feet with a gasp. He found himself in a desolate shipping yard with an aisle of cargo containers stacked like legos, several stories high, as far and high as he could see through the foggy night.

A loud creak from behind made Mr. Chen shudder. He turned to see the cargo container behind him being opened from inside, and heard a slow clap and familiar voice...

"Ah, Mr. Chen — So glad you could make it."

Mr. Chen breathed quickly through his little nose and failed to muster the courage to step forward.

"A journey of a thousand miles begins with a single step. Do you know who said that?"

Mr. Chen did, but considered it a rhetorical question and kept silent.

"That's right. Lao Tzu. You've already taken the first step, Mr. Chen. The second is much easier, I assure you."

Mr. Chen still hesitated.

He looked around, wondering if running away was even an option.

"Do you really want to go back now? Back to your shitty apartment where you wait around until it's time for your shitty job... and that just about covers it. Are you truly so eager to remain such a sad lonely little man? A misfit, afraid of his own socks. Ashamed of his own jizz. A pathetic nobody. Unforgettable, but not because he did something great, because no one knew him to begin with.

"Do you want to waste my time and your potential by leaving without even entertaining my unbelievably generous proposition? If that's your choice, I respect it. I'll not force you to let me hand you the world. If that's your decision, Mr. Chen, by all means, go!

"Go back to being a loser with nothing to give and nothing to show. A man who knows not the thrill of victory nor the sting of defeat. A man on the sidelines of the game of life, content to watch others get everything he truly and deeply desires but is such a fucking coward he's too afraid to admit it out loud... even to himself!

"A man so timid he's too self-conscious to even sing in the sanctity of his own shower. I mean, come on! Is that it, man? Does that sum you up? Is that the life and legacy of Mr. Chen?"

Mr. Chen stood, dumbfounded by the avalanche of truths no one had ever voiced. The man stepped forward and from the shadow of the hood emerged two beautiful glowing blue eyes.

"Or perhaps you'd like to know the life and legacy I had in mind before you pack your little sac and scurry back to what you know."

Mr. Chen clenched his rectum and summoned the courage to ask this man who he was and how he knew so much about him, but the answers came before the questions left his mouth.

"I'm The Man, Mr. Chen. That's the only name you need know me by. And all you need know about me is I'm your new best friend. You've no idea how lucky you are."

The Man laughed. Mr. Chen experienced a powerful influx of energy, accompanied by a high pitched ringing sound in his head and enhanced sense of exhilaration. Mr. Chen's leg trembled as he tried to lift it. But it still felt anchored to the pavement by fear. The Man sighed.

"If you can't obey such simple instructions after a speech like that, perhaps I've chosen poorly. Hmm... so this is what being wrong about something feels like. Interesting."

The door slammed shut.

Mr. Chen stood still for five seconds then slammed his fists on the door and prepared to yell. It squeaked back open.

"Let's try that again — Ah, Mr. Chen, so glad you could make it."

---

THE SHIPPING CONTAINER DOOR CLOSED WITH A CLANK. A SOFT AMBIENT LIGHT engulfed what turned out to be much more than it seemed from outside. Mr. Chen looked up to see he was actually inside a building the height of five shipping containers, and a length thrice that. The Man walked ahead of Mr. Chen and spoke quickly and decisively...

"You see, Mr. Chen, while it is obviously possible for us to directly interact, doing so comes at some risk. You'll have to pardon all the secrecy but I am most at home in the shadows. Our in-person meetings will be sparse and only arranged with great care, to both protect my physical identity and person, and to keep yourself and your as yet unmet allies from being labeled known associates. Rest assured, I fear no one Mr. Chen, but I do avoid excessive confrontation whenever possible."

The space was vast, and well lit, but there didn't appear to be anything or anyone else around. In fact, there didn't even seem to be a clear source of the light.

"The light is in the air, Mr. Chen. To use traditional electricity is to draw from the grid. To draw from the grid is to announce your presence to the authorities; most of whom are allies, or in the least associates of allies, but some of whom are not. As Mark Twain put it, politicians and diapers need to be changed often, and for the same reason."

The joke went over Mr. Chen's head.

"I, on the other hand, am not full of shit. What I am full of is knowledge; some of which I intend to pass on to you, if you possess the eyes to see and ears to listen. Think of me as your new mentor. I am here to guide, help, protect and inspire you."

They reached the end of the grand, empty room, arriving at a hatch on the floor in the back left corner which opened as they neared. Mr. Chen sallied forth down a steel ladder affixed to a plain cement wall, then through a tunnel the width of four subway tunnels. As they walked, the air illuminated a ten foot radius around them in every direction.

"These tunnels were built long ago. Much longer than you'd think. They were expanded and connected over the past century, after being discovered by people in governments here; the type obsessed with war and self-preservation in the event of a massive catastrophe; like a thermonuclear war, for example. In the event the cowards ever do hit the buttons that make Earth go boom, and no one from off planet intervenes this time, rest assured, these halls will be filled with the people to blame, and their chosen minority of survivors. I've seen it happen a number of times. It's never fun."

Mr. Chen continued to follow The Man, deeper into the megalithic tunnels, noting multiple points they intersected with other tunnels of many variations and sizes.

"I of course would be among those averting the destruction above, and thanks to me and your courageous decision to join my team, I'm happy to say you would also survive. I can and will protect you in the years to come, Mr. Chen, from all threats, seen and unseen. Consider me your new guardian angel, albeit an unorthodox one. Here we are."

They stopped at a platform where a parked vessel awaited their arrival. It was ostensibly a trolly of sorts, though unlike any Mr. Chen had ever witnessed or imagined. It was shaped like an egg, and the top half lifted open as they approached.

"All aboard."

Mr. Chen boarded the vessel. The hatch closed. He took a seat. The shuttle launched suddenly, silently, and quickly, reaching speeds two then three times that of the high speed trains he found so impressive. Moments later, the vessel came to a gentle halt at another platform.

"After you, Mr. Chen."

Mr. Chen walked forward, still mesmerized by the simple wonder of the light-filled air, and followed the floor made of giant stones furnished with a type of bright white coating. The latest room was about half a football field long, and just as wide... at the far end of which was a massive staircase leading as far up as the eye could see.

"Don't worry. We'll take the lift."

They boarded an elevator big enough to fit a jumbo jet. The lift silently ascended, and the floor-lit platform dimmed to a pleasant dark purple hue. The duo ascended in silence for nearly two minutes before The Man spoke again...

"I can't tell you how much I appreciate you not bombarding me with questions. If only I chose all my leaders as well as I chose you."

Mr. Chen smiled bashfully. Of all the wild things he was encountering, for some reason being called a leader surprised him most of all. He had as little leadership experience as anyone could, if their goal was to remain a permanent follower, which it was at the time.

The last time he'd led anything was over 30 years ago, when a gym teacher made him a team captain. He nearly had to leave the class because the pressure of even choosing his teammates was so excruciatingly stressful; especially given his choice of players needed to be made on the spot, giving him no time to gather data and make informed decisions. Mr. Chen wouldn't be leading anything if he had a say in the matter; then again, second-guessing The Man was out of the question.

"Just this way. We're almost, almost there."

He followed dutifully, through yet another gigantic empty room, akin to a pristine, high-end warehouse with light-up air and excellent climate control. As they reached what appeared to be a wall, it smoothly slid open with the speed and swiftness of a fine elevator in a modern office building. All this occurred so silently, Mr. Chen wondered if it could be some kind of illusion. It was as if everything was more advanced than everywhere he'd ever been.

"There are many things that have been kept hidden from you, and everyone you knew your entire life... something you are no doubt starting to appreciate. Hidden histories. Hidden technologies. Hidden governments. I consider my operation to be a global consulting firm, moderating the evolution of the species. Helping as I see fit. Intervening as necessary, to ensure the most ideal outcomes. Ideal for you. Ideal for me. Ideal for us."

Mr. Chen took it all in as best he could, filled with a growing sense of shock and concern — a common and natural response to the shattering of so many fundamental presuppositions about reality. Outside, the sun was just setting, over an unfamiliar desert.

Mr. Chen looked around and saw nothing but sand dunes in every direction; save for the direction they were headed, where something was rising out of the sand. It was solid black and pyramidal in shape, with a base length of 33 yards and a height from base to tip measuring the same. It hovered silently a few feet above the sifting arid sands.

"Just up the ramp, Mr. Chen. I hope you don't have a fear of heights."

Mr. Chen did, but he kept it to himself.

# 7

MR. CHEN HAD NEVER BEEN on an airplane. Nor had anyone in his family, for that matter. Needless to say, he had never been on anything like this. He boarded the large pyramidal craft from the center, where a circular staircase descended to just above ground level.

His embarkation afforded him a welcome respite from the desert winds and heat, and an airlock above the stairs and before the entrance to the ship hit him with a quick swirl of air that somehow cleaned all the sand from his clothes, body, and hair.

"The technology attracts silica in the sand, much in the way a magnet attracts metal shavings," explained The Man, who still kept his face concealed under his hood, and his back to Mr. Chen. On a table in the airlock portion of the ship rested 12 matching black robes.

"Please put one of these on."

Mr. Chen obeyed.

They proceeded into the central hull of the ship, which contained a circular arrangement of large, throne-like chairs surrounding a large circle encasing a pentagram made of red light… a visually appealing sight far and away more luxurious than any first class flight available to even the most privileged of the uninitiated masses.

"Please have a seat here."

He pointed to a chair. Mr. Chen obeyed and awaited further instruction.

"See that button on the left arm of the chair, Mr. Chen? The big one. Press it."

Mr. Chen obeyed. It felt as if some kind of seatbelt for his whole body had suddenly engulfed him. He was still able to move in all directions, but when he did, the movement was met with weighted resistance, like one would feel moving around underwater.

"Relax and enjoy the ride."

With that, the ship moved upward, in a silent explosive burst. The shock of the movement startled Mr. Chen, but he soon adjusted to the upward momentum. The sensation of speed being relative, it felt no different than a fast omni-directional elevator. The Man held his hands on the armrests of the chair, from which he seemed to be controlling the ship, despite not moving them or holding any visible mechanism. *Was he controlling it with his mind?* Mr. Chen wondered in amazement.

After a moment, the ship descended. It halted and The Man stood.

"Be right back. Your hood... if you would."

The Man pointed to his hood.

"A precautionary measure for all parties involved."

Mr. Chen gave a thumbs up and obeyed. He affixed his hood and waited, avoiding the tinge of desire he felt to take off his "seatbelt" and explore the ship. Instead, he focused his attention on his chair, which was no thicker than a sheet of paper, yet easily supported his weight, melding to his body exactly — like a gelatin of perfectly calibrated softness.

His ears still rang from the comparatively loud winds of his brief desert sojourn, made noticeable only by the contrast of absolute silence the ship provided. Then he heard the sound of the airlock and voice of The Man in conversation with someone else; they were speaking French. The French guest, whose face was obscured by the prevailing darkness, selected a seat on the opposite side of the circle of chairs and was taught how to apply the "seatbelt".

The process repeated several more times. In the span of roughly twenty minutes, all remaining 10 seats had been filled, each by someone speaking a new language, all of which The Man spoke fluently. It gradually dawned on Mr. Chen they were indeed comfortably traversing the entire planet at inexplicable speeds. Rather than consider how, why, or the innumerable other curiosities such an experience entailed, Mr. Chen turned his focus entirely to what he had going on inside his double layered socks above his rapidly bouncing legs — moving about out of nervousness rather than turbulence. He concentrated on clenching and unclenching his toes, squeezing the sides of his big toe nails into the skin to generate a mild sensation somewhere between pain and pleasure; a meaningless activity that took his mind off the extraordinary situation unfolding and granted him some semblance of relative equanimity.

The ship made a final upward push, then halted completely and The Man began...

"Gentlemen, it is with great pleasure and well-warranted enthusiasm I welcome you to our first conference. I apologize for all the secrecy but assure you it's for your own protection. Here I have assembled 12 people from all around the planet — diverse in many respects; united by a common fate. A fate to moderate, with tact and care, the good people of planet Earth.

"You see, gentlemen, every so often, I select another group... or class... or crop... if you will, to serve as a globally cooperative team that acts in unison, and colludes in secret, to stage manage the politics of the so-called governments of Earth. All you have been led to believe — about your supposed leaders being the ultimate authorities of this planet — are lies. It's all smoke and mirrors. They are more aptly described as customer service representatives that work for myself and a few friends and competitors.

"Earth's governments are the intermediaries between the self-conscious terrestrial resources of earth, i.e. humans, and their exalted overseers, i.e. me. It has been structured like this for centuries — generation after generation — as far as your meager recollections of history can trace, and far beyond. I do have some degree of competition, but it is ultimately I who rule this planet. And I intend to keep it that way."

Mr. Chen looked around at the other 11 men assorted around the center window. They all listened intently as he continued...

"Earth is like a giant refugee camp, mixed with a laboratory, mixed with a playground, mixed with a school, mixed with a business. Your kind was engineered several thousand years ago. Your purpose was, and remains, to serve your gods.

"I've not the ego to force you to get on your knees and worship me. I don't like forcing you to do anything, for a number of reasons you needn't concern yourself with. But make no mistake, in comparison to you, I am divine. I am more or less all knowing, all seeing, and I cannot be killed. I cannot die, and my will is the force that guides the evolution of life on this planet."

The Man looked at the overwhelmed faces and laughed.

"Any questions, so far?" No one spoke.

"Splendid. Now, on to the good news. Yes, you and every man, woman and child on Earth are at my mercy. But you select few exceptional individuals are my direct subordinates. My employees. And should you serve me loyally, which is all I ever ask; should you heed my every order, without hesitation or resistance, this shall be your reward..."

The circle with the pentagram center of the ship began to open — interlocking circular teeth disassembled to reveal a floor window, through which they had a beautiful view of Earth... from space. The planet fit perfectly in the center of the window. It was easily the most august sight Mr. Chen had ever laid eyes on; a sentiment shared by the rest of the group.

He pointed at the blue and green sphere below.

"My gift to you."

A moment of silence ensued. Then the Man continued…

"You are now to be made kings and presidents and the like. You are to become lords of the Earth. Your power will be vast. Your subjects will be all. You will not need to follow the rules and laws and limitations foisted upon your people. From now on, you are above them. You are untouchable. You are to be revered and obeyed by all. You will have whatever you desire until the day you die."

The twelve robed men all sat in silence for an extended period.

"I'm sorry, were you hoping for more?"

Someone across from Mr. Chen began to clap.

His clap was joined by others, with laughter and cheers.

"Yes. Yes! That's more like it, boys!"

The Man lifted his hands and began slowly clapping. His clap resonated louder than everyone else's combined. Mr. Chen joined in, and they all soon clapped in perfect rhythm. As the claps continued, Mr. Chen felt a powerful energy emanate from his scrotum, and into the base of his tailbone. The clapping got louder and gradually faster as the energy — something like an electrically charge surge of adrenaline — worked its way up his tailbone and into his stomach. His abdomen now resonated potently with each clap.

Mr. Chen began to laugh… first quietly, then not so quietly, joining the chorus of this newfound fraternity of bewildered power-drunk men.

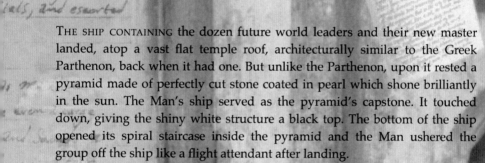

## 8

THE SHIP CONTAINING the dozen future world leaders and their new master landed, atop a vast flat temple roof, architecturally similar to the Greek Parthenon, back when it had one. But unlike the Parthenon, upon it rested a pyramid made of perfectly cut stone coated in pearl which shone brilliantly in the sun. The Man's ship served as the pyramid's capstone. It touched down, giving the shiny white structure a black top. The bottom of the ship opened its spiral staircase inside the pyramid and the Man ushered the group off the ship like a flight attendant after landing.

"Just down the stairs. Stay in a single file line. Your gifts await."

The stairs led to an opening at the base of the pyramid, where the dozen impressed men were greeted by yet another surreal sight — 24 people in red robes, faces concealed, standing on either side of a red carpet spanning the 228 foot length of the temple roof — the perimeters of which afforded a second-to-none view of a gorgeous island sunset.

The procession of The Man's new disciples walked the red carpet. The line leader stopped at the end of the carpet, between the two hooded people, and each behind him stopped between their assigned matches. The Man walked across the temple ceiling slowly, leaving all in anticipation, then finally spoke.

"Gentlemen. I present to you these gifts."

He snapped his fingers and all 24 robes dropped. Beneath each — a beautiful woman. All were topless, wearing only black thongs and matching high heals with red bottoms. They stood perfectly still, staring straight ahead, with blank expressions — their palms all pressed together between their breasts in a prayer-like gesture. The women to the left of the carpet would more aptly described as girls, all in their teens, and from all corners of the world. Those on the right side of the carpet were up to twice their age, also of a diverse set of ethnicities. Mr. Chen stared in shock and felt overcome by a wave of anxiety.

"I've hand selected for each of you a pair of beautiful servants you'll find most eager to please. Each selection is based on your past romantic interests and/or pornographic preferences. They will escort you to your private personalized quarters."

The Man snapped again.

In unison, the "gifts" each took a step toward their assigned man.

"Your gifts are now your property. Feel free to name them if you'd like. They are yours to do with whatever you please. They'll not speak unless spoken to, your wish is their command, and they don't know the word no. Isn't that right, ladies?"

In unison, they said "Yes, Master" and bowed their heads, keeping their gazes affixed on the carpet. "Gentlemen... Do as thy wilt! This is the whole of the law on my island. And, in time, everywhere you set foot on my planet. Eat. Drink. Be merry. We'll meet in the small salon for brunch tomorrow, at your leisure, between the hours of eleven and one, to be followed by a meeting at one thirty. Now please, enjoy the rest of the night! Obey my wishes and I promise it will be but one of many blissful nights to come."

With that, The Man made his exit.

---

To gratuitously describe the sex appeal of these women would be an affront to their forgotten dignity, given the delicate nature of the circumstances. Suffice it to say, they were the most sexually appealing physical specimens Mr. Chen had ever encountered — the type to turn heads when they entered the room. Any room. Show stoppers. Smoke shows. Drop-dead gorgeous. Of such beauty it was easier for Mr. Chen to accept that he had been in outer space and to be given providence over billions of people than it was to accept these two women were his to do with as he pleased.

Mr. Chen breathed heavily and felt his little heart palpitating with unprecedented intensity. He began to sweat profusely as his tall gifts huddled around their nervous little lord. Each held one of his clammy, trembling, tiny hands and both leaned in close. Their exquisite natural breasts pressed into his shoulders, causing his whole body to shiver with increasing intensity. Each gave him a kiss on his beet red cheeks and whispered the same thing into each of his ears, "May we show you to your room... Master Chen?"

Master Chen fainted.

BY THE TIME MR. CHEN CAME TO, HE WAS ON A STRETCHER, BEING WHEELED BY two men, whose complexion suggested they might be native to whatever island they were on. They had deep tans — the type that can't be properly replicated by artificial means. They wore black medical masks, the sort of which had become a staple of many societies, if not a downright require-ment since the outbreak of the first Covid pandemic, which had by now gone from being the focal point of mainstream global news coverage for the past two years to at most a secondary concern, replaced by what was at the time described as the "War in Ukraine" and would in later years be cred-ited as the catalyst for the outbreak of World War III in the European theatre.

The duo transporting the still woozy Mr. Chen also wore matching sunglasses, also black, and carried themselves much like secret service agents. Mr. Chen's thoughts wondered between a disagreement between his memories and what until very recently seemed utterly unlikely, if not down-right preposterous; spaceships, global conspiracies, secret island temples. It all stretched the bounds of what until now Mr. Chen had confidently main-tained were the musings of the mad, gullible, and over-imaginative.

The pleasing scent of coconut butter emanated from the muscular arm of one of the men pushing the stretcher down a paved walkway through the tropical oasis. Mr. Chen found it soothing, and his sense of shock was nomi-nally nullified by the profound serenity of that scent being carried gently into his little nostrils by the soft warm breeze.

"Mr. Chen? Sir, we're taking you to the manor, where you can rest and will receive any medical attention you may require."

*Sir?* Mr. Chen was not used to be recognized, even by some people he knew, and he'd never once been referred to as "sir", or any other title of respect. With that came for Mr. Chen a sense of appreciation that lifted his spirits and significantly downplayed his still resonating sense of general anxiety.

He felt another boner brewing and was struck for the first time by the possibility he was gay. In truth, Mr. Chen was of a bisexual inclination. But he would never admit this to anyone, including himself, even after experi-menting with men years later. To punish himself for the disgusting thought, he bit his tongue.

The confusing boner Mr. Chen was fighting was in fact not attributable to the beautiful women or men of the island. It was actually a rare and peculiar reaction to being treated with respect for once. Appreciation was a thing he had unconsciously craved his entire life, and this sampling of it whet his appetite for more. It was a hunger that would turn into an addiction in the fateful years to come, but at that time Mr. Chen was still a nobody to everyone off that island.

Perhaps if Mr. Chen had been allowed to stay on that island indefinitely, he would have found sufficient fulfillment to never feel the compulsion to force the world around him to offer him respect, attention, and affection — or some manufactured semblance thereof. It is often the case those who are driven to pursue fame, power, and the like, are doing so in an endless attempt to get from others what they cannot find in themselves. Those with the proclivity to break are often those who are themselves most broken. As the saying goes, *hurt people hurt people*.

Mr. Chen's fundamental hurt was not attributable to any particular trauma. The physical abuse he endured growing up was negligible. Mr. Chen's particular brand of hurt was more-so a product of what didn't happen to him. He was the sort of man who was never noticed and easily forgotten. He had nothing special to differentiate himself from the rest of the pack; no apparent talent or skill deemed valuable to society, unless you count diligence, consistency, reliability, punctuality, agreeableness, and the propensity for ceaseless and unquestioning adherence to authority.

To most, those traits were perhaps admirable, but in no way attracted attention, friendship, love, and the other related untasted fruits Mr. Chen silently longed to devour. The Man had for years been shopping for someone just like Mr. Chen; someone who could be fashioned into anyone and would do anything for whoever, or whatever, could notice and fulfill those basic unmet needs; someone no one had ever heard of, who had never made a single enemy or friend… someone who had never done anything wrong, and done enough right to be trusted when suddenly vaulted to a position of great influence and authority. Thus were the designs The Man had on Mr. Chen.

Mr. Chen felt himself capable of walking the rest of the way, but he didn't voice the fact. Truth told, he quite enjoyed being taken care of, and he found the trip to the manor — all the way up a windy road leading up to an epic mansion atop a cliff on the highest point on that side of the island — rather relaxing. Upon arriving at the circular driveway outside the front door, the unnamed, masked, sunglassed men helped Mr. Chen to his feet, did a quick checkup on his vitals, and escorted him to the house.

---

THE SENSORY OVERLOAD CONTINUED AS MR. CHEN ENTERED THE MAJESTIC manor. To describe even a large minority of the sights, scents, and sounds he took in over the next hour is a task incompatible with the goal of concisely recounting the key events relative to our story.

Among such sensations, however, was a sense of awe Mr. Chen felt as he made his way past the largest entrance to a house he or anyone he had ever met had ever seen or imagined. It was the height of three of the doors to the entrance of his apartment building stacked atop one another, which converts to roughly 13.5 feet, or 4.2 meters, and fashioned out of what Mr. Chen assumed to be some type of marble, but was actually petrified wood from enormous ancient trees found in Northern California, transported to the island by way of privately charted cargo ship, and brought to the top of the cliff by means of processes hitherto undisclosed, but that involved the use of concentrated sound and applied thought — the same methods said to have been used by ancient builders who transferred rocks several hundred tons in weight up hills and mountains to construct megalithic structures of mysterious and forgotten purposes; most notably, the famed pyramids of Giza in Egypt.

That the tightly knit "academic community" explained such feats as transferring blocks of stone weighing millions of pounds across vast distances, then stacking them up, as being achieved by primitive people using logs and ropes, and all for no clear reason was testament to the successful work of The Man and his allies and rivals, who had muddled the academic waters with a decades-long deluge of disinformation, leaving modern scholars scratching their heads and propagating illogical and unimaginative theories ad infinitum. Some researchers who escape these biases claim sound-based levitation methods can still be witnessed by monks in Tibet.

Such methods are also believed by some to be the means through which a man named Edward Leedskalnin erected "Coral Castle", or "Florida's Stonehenge," in 1920, using several multi-ton stones. He claimed to have done it singlehandedly, to impress a girl. However bizarre, it is possible; many if not most of man's greatest feats and accomplishments are simply attempts to impress girls. The structure exists to this day and no one was ever able to prove him otherwise.

Furthermore, the prospect of forgotten advanced knowledge and technologies is in no way outlandish. If anything, the inverse is true. Earth has existed for billions of years, and has over the epochs been occupied by a lot of people, from a lot of places; some of whom had mastered abilities and technologies the public has been intentionally left unaware of. This obfuscation too is the handiwork of The Man and his co-conspirators/competitors, who have their own self-serving reasons for keeping the public in the dark.

Also impressive to Mr. Chen was the fresco painted on the ceiling, which featured images of Egyptian and Sumerian deities being worshipped by meager-looking men and women. It depicted occult symbolism he knew nothing about, but found visually appealing. The statue of Egyptian Pharaoh

Akhenaten caught his interest because his head was long and his face looked like an alien.

While curious about the meaning of the iconography painted so majestically on the enormous, domed ceiling — akin to that found on the United State's Capitol buildings, St. Paul's Cathedral in London, the Dome of the Rock on Temple Mount in Jerusalem, St. Peter's Basilica in Vatican City, the Reichstag in Berlin, the Taj Mahal in Agra, and the temple on Little St. James, better known as Epstein's Island — to name a few notable examples, Mr. Chen held his questions; his little brain too full of information he was still struggling to process.

In the center of the room was a large obelisk made from a single piece of stone, spanning the height of roughly two Mr. Chens. He recognized the simple and pleasant structure because he'd seen it in images of ancient Egypt, City of London (not to be confused with London the city), Vatican City, and Washington D.C. — all important headquarters to those who dictate the lives of the masses.

According to mainstream history, the popular design is said to represent penises, which Mr. Chen remembered considering odd, because it looked very different than his own, and fashioning a more realistic, more cylindrical iteration seemed not only within the bounds of possibility, but notably easier than fashioning it to such exact geometric proportions. The only other plausible explanation was Egyptians had much more angular penises than the men of today.

The obelisk nevertheless reminded Mr. Chen of his penis, and he felt a surge of excitement at the recollection he had been offered the services of the women he found so attractive he fainted. His body began to tremble as he recalled their striking beauty. He suffered a sudden heat flash, and stumbled for a step as he reached one side of the large staircase hugging the wall on both sides of the curved foyer, allowing access to all visible floors on either wing of the grand abode.

The masked gentlemen hurried to Mr. Chen's side and helped him instead toward an elevator between the stairways, elegantly set into the wall so as to avoid breaking the room's classical aesthetic. A brief rise to the second floor ensued in an elevator with hexagonal walls coated in gold tinted glass, giving rise to the illusion of infinite reflections within reflections when he looked to either side.

For someone who considered his reflection ugly, beholding an infinite row of undesirable reminders of physical inadequacy was more disquieting than it was cool. The doors opened to a pleasant ding — a universally uniform sound — and to Mr. Chen in that moment, an instant of calming familiarity in this new domain of the extravagant and exotic.

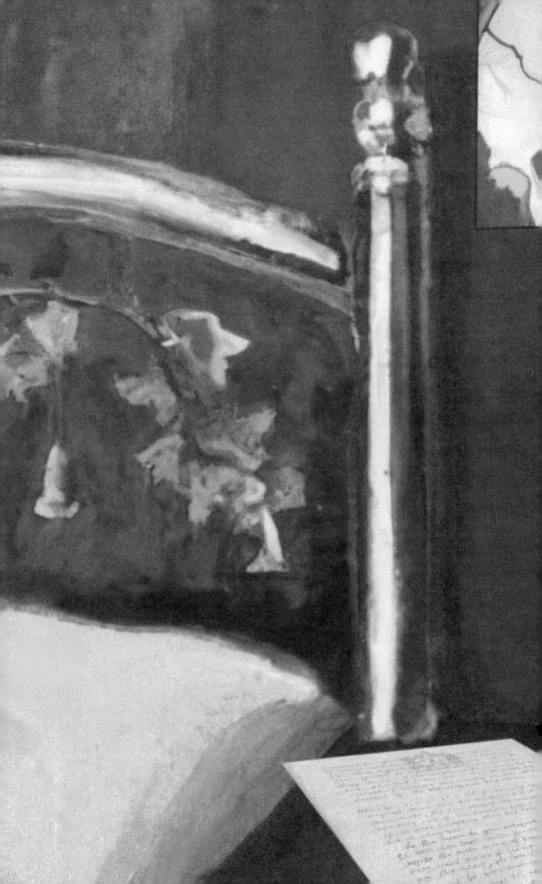

---

## 9

HE ARRIVED at a set of imposing though elegant double doors: ~1.5 Mr. Chens high and ~1 Mr. Chen wide. The two manservants each opened one of the double doors in perfect harmony, as if it was a task they had rehearsed to perfection.

"Is this room to your satisfaction, sir?" one asked.

Mr. Chen took in the surroundings and nodded in the affirmative. Despite the wide array of beautiful artifacts, ornate over-sized pieces of furniture, and priceless paintings, all Mr. Chen saw was the empty spaces he was worried might be occupied by his "gifts". He wasn't in the mood for any more surprises in his fragile state and was relieved when one of the manservants, as if reading his mind, spoke...

"Mr. Chen, the bell on the table beside your bed — should you desire the company of the ladies from outside, just ring it three times and they will arrive momentarily. Should you require our assistance, ring once and we will arrive — any time, day or night."

"Will that be all, sir?" asked the other manservant. Mr. Chen nodded yes. With that, both doors were quietly shut, again in perfect harmony — a detail Mr. Chen quite enjoyed. He looked around and was pleased to finally feel the equanimity of solitude that was his preferred and default setting. He made his way through the multi-roomed room's living room, beheld briefly an ornate painting of Chairman Mao — a historical figure he deeply revered, despite only possessing a passing degree of knowledge about. He opened another large door and was immediately taken in by the mise-en-scène. Every inch of the room was thoughtfully decorated, and clearly modeled after China's prestigious ancient history.

Fine flowing silk curtains graced the giant windows; the windows foisted open decoratively, revealing what could only be a view of the ocean, though not clearly visible in the darkness of the night, lit only by a moon peeking occasionally through streams of dark clouds. The shimmering dots of starlight, even amidst the overcast skies, shone more brightly than any stars Mr. Chen had ever seen through the usually dense metropolitan smog that hung over his home city like a slightly poisonous blanket that had, to his government's deserved credit, ameliorated significantly in recent years.

Twin lamps made entirely of jade, with red lantern tops, gave the large but somehow cozy room a warm, soft, relaxing glow that was just bright enough to light the paintings of mountains and cliffs. He recognized some of them, or in the least their style, and wondered if they were originals. The artists he could not remember were Li Suxen and Qu Ding, and of course they were. The Man would settle for nothing less.

A fireplace in one end of the room gently crackled, and the only other sound came from a sort of fountain built into the wall around the fireplace; a smooth trickle falling on either side of the fire, congregating beneath a stain glass floor with a familiar, flower-like geometric pattern. The water flowed from its pond under the stain glass floor beneath the fireplace area and crossed the span of the room, until it reached the wall to wall windows.

Upon closer inspection, Mr. Chen saw the stream was released out the side of the house itself, cascading all the way down the cliff into the darkness below. This was not only the nicest room Mr. Chen had ever stayed in; it was the nicest room he had ever seen and never could have imagined. If the aesthetics weren't enough, the scents were also there to supplement the room's pristine beauty… a mix of lotus flowers and cherry wood danced with the smell of the strips of cedar wood being slowly consumed by the crackling fire.

After relieving himself in a jade toilet that flushed quietly and peacefully — another small detail Mr. Chen appreciated — he thought about how his bathroom at home was smaller in area than the mirror in this bathroom, and his toilet was a hole in the ground he needed to squat over, hoisting himself high enough to dodge the splash of his plunging stools. That all felt so barbaric now; even after such brief encounters with true luxury, he was already despising his former ways of living.

Mr. Chen washed his face with the warm water that needed no time to heat, in contrast to his home sink which took so long he'd become accustomed to washing his hands and face with cold water — the warm water flowing smoothly from a gold spicket and into a large sink carved out of a single slab of pink marble. Mr. Chen decided he never wanted to go back to the way things were before.

JUST BEFORE LEAVING THE BATHROOM, MR. CHEN NOTICED A LUXURIOUS BATH had already been drawn for him, complete with rose petals and foamy bubbles. The water was perfect temperature, to his delight, and sat atop a heating element keeping it just so. He treated himself to a cleansing and relaxing soak and found the experience exhilarating. Mr. Chen had never been in a bath tub.

He did not have a bath tub. He didn't even have a shower separated from the rest of his dainty bathroom; just a cracked faded tile floor he would clean with the same squeegee he used on his mirror, after the just shy of seven minutes of hot shower water the heater in his apartment could hold ran out. None of these things seemed more than a slight inconvenience at most before; now they would be forever regarded as intolerable, degrading, and pathetic woes fit only for the underclass, amongst which Mr. Chen would never again be counted, and would go on to associate with only as dictated by necessity. He swam in different circles now. Better circles. The Man's circles.

As Mr. Chen laid under the satin sheets of the soft, heavy silk comforter with an innumerable thread count, his head graced the most comfortable memory foam pillow on the market, encased in an even softer silk pillowcase. He turned to his side and took note of the bell on his bedside table.

Tempted as he was to ring it thrice, he proved too tired to go for it. He drifted off to sleep, and within moments the ambient symphony of crackling cedar wood and trickling water were joined by the sound of the surprisingly loud snores of a man who would never emit so much sound while awake.

---

UNBEKNOWNST TO THE SLUMBERING PROTÉGÉ, HIS NEW MASTER WAS AT THE FOOT of the bed, still in his hood, smiling like a proud father. He looked on lovingly at a man who said so little, obeyed so readily, was so easily contented, and slept so soundly after such a wild day.

The Man was pleased with himself and his selection. His radiant eyes glowed.

"Sweet dreams, my little quartz crystal. I have big plans for you."

Mr. Chen smiled in his sleep as he dreamt of sex, luxury, and above all: recognition and significance.

...had a dream he

Every so... the feeling from

...had a feeling of foreboding.

...the bell on the nightstand, and

...ning toward giving it three rings,

could make a final decision, 2

sound came from the other room.

uickly dressed in the sweat drenched dress

worn the day prior, having me alternative.

as the voice of one of the manservants

the tropical accent.

...him, so sorry to disturb you, but I

...instructions to provide you with breakfast

...ince you skipped dinner last night. I'll leave it

...ide the door. Also, please help yourself

...I like to wear. Everything in

...belongs to you. Good day

...heavy double doors to

...is already

## 10

---

MR. CHEN AWOKE with a gasp from a dream he instantaneously forgot. Even so, the feeling from the dream lingered — a feeling of foreboding. He glanced at the bell on the nightstand, and found himself leaning toward giving it three rings, but before he could make a final decision a knock came from the other room. Mr. Chen quickly dressed in the sweat drenched dress shirt he'd worn the day prior, having no alternative.

In came the voice of an unmet chef: "Mr. Chen, so sorry to disturb you, but I have instructions to provide you with breakfast since you skipped dinner last night. I will leave it outside the door. Also, please help yourself to whatever you'd like to wear. Everything in the closet and dressers now belongs to you. Good day, sir."

Mr. Chen opened one of the heavy double doors to give his thanks, but the hallway was vacant. He looked down to see a set of covered dishes and a pot of tea atop a trolly fit with white linens. He wheeled it into the room and realized he was hungry. He rolled the meal beside a table next to the window, the curtains to which opened automatically.

The view was even more breathtaking than Mr. Chen had anticipated. In the distance — a fresh sunrise, no more than an hour old. Between the sun and window was an expanse of ocean that got bluer in color as it reached the atoll below, at the foot of the towering cliff. An assortment of large rocks and tiny islands jutted from the sea with an apparent clear path leading from the base of the cliff to the open sea, the only area that looked safe to navigate a boat through.

The mansion, Mr. Chen now noticed, was also a fortress. The outside walls, from what he could make out, were comprised of massive stone bricks, fit together like one giant puzzle. On the horizon, the sea went on as far as the eye could see, with nothing else in sight.

Mr. Chen devoured the best breakfast of his life, which included eggs, pancakes, and toast, and more adventurous dishes, like crêpes and a salmon salad. The highlight was a delectable croissant — warm and soft on the inside, crispy and flaky on the outside — complete with a saucer holding a ramekin of half-melted fresh butter.

He began slurping down his hot but not so hot it burns tea, then spit some out when he looked again at the majestic portrait of Chairman Mao. It looked different than he remembered; less like Chairman Mao, and more like Mr. Chen! *Impossible,* he thought. But the resemblance was uncanny, and surely he would have noticed it before.

He shuddered as he heard a knock at the door and a familiar voice. "Good morning, Mr. Chen. I hope you might have the strength to accompany me on a morning stroll before brunch."

Mr. Chen hurried to the doors and opened them to reveal The Man, whose face was finally fully visible. He was handsome. Lean. Old enough to have greying hair, but free of the facial wrinkles that typically accompany the entry to senior citizenry. He was fit but not buff, with broad shoulders and a slim waist. A sharp jawline held a picture perfect pearly white smile he wore effortlessly and with great consistency.

Most notable of all were those eyes; framed by dark bold eyebrows and glowing with unprecedented intensity and beauty. His pupils seemed to shine in a hard to place way, and his irises were in a constant state of flux, flowing between sapphire blue and clear green ocean water bathed in sunlight — unforgettable eyes that emitted an entrancing powerful sensation by default; eyes that politely begged you to linger. And the longer the eye contact, the more potent the sensation he was staring directly into your soul — seeing you for who you truly are, rather than who you pretend to be.

Mr. Chen stepped aside and The Man entered. Mr. Chen swallowed the saliva in his mouth, complete with croissant crumbs — an involuntary human response to the arrival of an intimidating presence.

"Well, Mr. Chen. Am I what you expected?"

Mr. Chen worked into a polite smile, and gave a respectful, bowing nod. Holding The Man's powerful gaze, Mr. Chen felt like nothing could harm him — as a child feels while being adored by loving parents. The eyes made one feel safe and vulnerable at the same time. A ferocious predator housed snugly behind a liquid wall of loving admiration. The eyes of a leader; a salesman; a statesman… a man of action who knows exactly what he wants when he sees it, and will certainly get it.

Such determination and poise was exuded from The Man's eyes alone. His charming and eloquent, almost musical way of speaking was superfluous. One look would be enough to convince just about anyone of just about anything. Such was the tremendous force exuded by this rare, fascinating, formidable individual. Mr. Chen was speechless, and without needing to say a word, The Man understood the impact he was having on his new subject.

"There there..."

He brought Mr. Chen into a gentle embrace that filled him with an incomprehensible flurry of new emotions, to include a kind of love.

"Welcome home, my son."

Mr. Chen's eyes began to water and he held in some aspiring sobs. Over his shoulder, The Man smiled. He had certainly made the intended impression. He suddenly pulled away, and Mr. Chen instinctively reacted as if a blanket had just been pulled off and he'd suddenly been caught naked in the cold. Confusion and shame filled the bewildered man-child as he dried his eyes and regained composure.

"I'll meet you downstairs, where you first came in — if you can remember as much... in say, 30 minutes?"

Mr. Chen smiled and nodded.

"Splendid. Attire is outdoor casual."

---

Mr. Chen took a nine minute shower that never got cold, scrubbed himself clean with one of several choices of fine soaps, then dried his portly, compact figure with a fluffy towel that smelled of lavender. After eight minutes of trying on shirts in the walk-in closet, Mr. Chen had narrowed it down to two options... a simple though exquisite off white polo and a silky black T-shirt with appealing little triangles embroidered around the sleeves.

After another six minutes of deliberation, Mr. Chen opted for the former, on grounds the black might get too hot in the sun. Three minutes later, he changed his mind, on grounds despite it being cooler, if he did start to sweat, it would be far more apparent in the white shirt, and thus far more embarrassing. With that in mind, he settled on a new alternative — a silky Navy blue polo with a criss-crossing pattern on the collar. It was a compromise Mr. Chen felt exceptionally content with.

After another rushed six minutes of preparation, Mr. Chen had settled on some khakis that breathed well and luxurious boat shoes. Unsure whether socks were to be worn with boat shoes, he deliberated on the matter another two minutes while staring at the wall. He selected new shoes that certainly merited socks, a matching cream colored soft leather belt, and a spritz of an oud wood based cologne.

For some odd reason, despite craving the sustained approval of The Man more than anyone else ever, Mr. Chen felt less anxious than usual at the prospect of being less than over-punctual... so it was with a slight jog rather than a frantic sprint that he carried himself out of the room, through the hall, and down one side of the wraparound staircase to the foyer, where The Man was waiting, stoically staring out a window.

The Man wore a white blazer with matching trousers and a mother of pearl faced luxury watch of indiscernible make, with a matching white leather band — which Mr. Chen only noticed from his vantage point across the span of the marble floored foyer because it reflected a rectangular glare of sunlight with a most notable brilliance. The Man checked his watch then addressed his eager admirer without turning around, as powerful men are prone to do.

"Precisely on time, my quartz crystal man! That's you, Mr. Chen — Reliable. Dependable. Consistent. A man I can always count on. "

The Whiteness of The Man's wardrobe continued through the rest of his accoutrement — to include a bracelet, ring, and pocket square — with the exception of his belt and boat shoes, which were black — and as Mr. Chen then learned, did not necessitate socks.

The Man turned and watched Mr. Chen walk down the stairs, vulnerably and proudly, grinning and strutting his new style.

"You look magnificent, Mr. Chen. With one small exception... your new Rolex doesn't fit."

The Man promptly ordered a manservant to make the proper adjustments while they took a stroll.

"Even perfect things need modification sometimes."

Two manservants opened the huge front doors, again in perfect harmony, as if they shared a single mind. Mr. Chen found himself smiling as he transitioned to the outdoors, and proceeded on to enjoy a delightful stroll about the canyon top, marked by a serene silence — the sort typically only attained by acquaintances well-acquainted, who are free of the otherwise shared compulsion to fill the void of silence.

For a good 20 minutes, the two continued their walk, down paths carved throughout the jungle overgrowth just wide enough for a pair walking side by side. They approached a clearing on a hill overlooking a hidden garden flush with meticulously planted and maintained flowers of many shapes, colors and sizes.

"This garden, Mr. Chen, is among my favorite places on Earth... a place I come to reflect. It is a place few others have ever been. You see, Mr. Chen, I'm someone who appreciates life. And beauty. I take great pleasure in scouring the lands, assembling collections of trappings and resources — both inanimate and imbued with consciousness of the type you and I most easily relate.

"Among other things, this island is a sanctuary for the life I collect, watch grow, keep safe, and tend to. As is the natural course of life on this planet, no matter how beautiful and admirable the life, sooner or later it is fated to die. Every flower will return to the soil from which it arose. And for as tragic as all that may be to a self-conscious life form aware of its own inevitable demise, mortality is in another sense a most precious gift."

The Man continued walking. Mr. Chen followed.

"The most pertinent reasons for this, to my view, being that it necessarily instills within one a sense of urgency to live before it's too late; and too affords you the freedom to make choices, to include the many mistakes that to the astute are simply lessons. This is a freedom not so easily afforded to those to whom death is optional."

The Man stopped walking and let out a sigh.

"Or worse yet, those to whom death is not an option. Because life can be a curse as much as it can be a blessing. Wouldn't you agree?"

Mr. Chen nodded, at best half following his meaning. The Man took a deep, contemplative breath.

"Infinite possibility without boundary and limitation, as appealing as it might sound, can be rather overwhelming. Exhausting even. And absent the parameters of death... knowing you will go on forever and ever, even long after you have been everywhere you want to go and done everything you want to do... after you have watched everyone else — including those you love — fade into death's embrace, only then to start a new life and go on a new ride, where it all feels fresh and exciting... with so much to learn and experience again, as if for the first time... that, as it turns out, can be a more appealing proposition than immortality."

The Man put a fatherly hand on Mr. Chen's shoulder.

"I don't expect you to understand everything. Or even much of what I'm saying. I suppose all I want is to be listened to. To be heard. And you, Mr. Chen, are the best listener I've encountered in half a baktun!"

The Man looked at his majestic garden sadly then turned to Mr. Chen and patted him on the arm. Mr. Chen smiled, like a dog happy to be pet.

"And while I have your golden ear, Mr. Chen, it would offer me some satisfaction to share with you some general details about my grand project. It is my present intention, as it has been for many years, to shape the current cycle of life in such a way that your kind reaches then exceeds the progress of prior, similar civilizations."

The Man reflected in silence for a prolonged moment, which Mr. Chen did not interrupt.

"You see, I had this thought — how true it is, I don't know — but the thought is intriguing enough to at least keep me busy. Would you like to know what it is?"

Mr. Chen nodded, genuinely interested though thoroughly confused. "The thought is this... what if I could grow from humanity an ascended and evolved being capable of eventually taking my place? What if I could create a form of humanity so powerful it could assume my position and govern itself? Would that perhaps give me the choice to finally retire?"

The Man looked at Mr. Chen and laughed.

"To break apart into a trillion pieces and either fade into a deep sleep indefinitely, or just as appealing, to my mind — experience new life in different forms? Not just human forms. What, I wonder, is it like to be that rock?" Mr. Chen looked at the rock.

"Or that flower?" Mr. Chen looked at the flower.

"Or that tree?" Mr. Chen looked at the tree.

"To start from a new beginning. Then to gradually ascend back to something akin to my current state of being. To wipe the slate clean, as it were. That is to me, for reasons I wouldn't expect you to understand, an endeavor most appealing. And I'm beginning to consider it may be a motivation experienced by higher forms of intelligence I was once and for a long time at odds with. But that's another talk for another walk. Perhaps in another life."

The Man checked his glare-inducing timepiece.

"I'm afraid we must be mindful of the time. I've further preparations to make for this afternoon's activities, which, after much reflection, I have decided to exclude you from. You didn't indulge in your gifts last night, which was a precursor to the activity. But don't feel bad, Mr. Chen. I take your restraint as a sign of great discipline. For now, I suppose I just wanted to give you some semblance of an understanding of what the hell I'm up to. Simply put, I'm orchestrating global affairs in such a manner the prospect of destruction... the perceived threat of annihilation... the fear of death and suffering, motivates mankind to evolve more quickly.

"Man is at his most clever when in fear for his life; and so, by creating an overall environment of fear, the various tribes humanity has come to group itself into can be set against one another, and challenge one another to become more creative, more inventive, and more motivated to learn and grow."

The Man spread his arms, as if the garden below was all of mankind.

"In the short term, this leads to suffering, death, and destruction... which people find rather off-putting. But zoom out, even a mere generation or two, and the results speak for themselves! Pain creates growth, Mr. Chen. And as the prudent gardener cuts off the weaker branches so they can grow back stronger, so too do I facilitate the conditions for humanity to self-harm, from the comfort of the shadows, unheard and unseen... advising the leaders of the tribes to carry out my will, of their own free will — exempting me from consequences that would befall should I take a more... direct and coercive approach. You'll find free will is something I respect dearly."

The Man gave Mr. Chen a well-received pat on the back.

"Before long, you're going to be helping me tend to the garden. In return, you will live a life of great purpose, and you will be remembered as a great leader, who made tough choices, paving the road for future generations to evolve at unprecedented rates, pushing the species to do in hundreds of years what traditionally takes thousands, or more commonly — is never achieved at all.

"Thanks to you and your allies, the species will survive itself; and any future cataclysm that would otherwise restart the game — because humanity will have finally left its nest, spread its wings, and begun to explore the galaxy... and that's just the first leap forward. You will go on to inhabit many planets and form many civilizations... as I've seen happen before, as is already happening elsewhere, and as I am happy to make happen here."

He looked Mr. Chen dead in the eyes.

"As WE are going to make happen here!"

Mr. Chen smiled as he fell deeper into The Man's penetrating gaze, drifting happily into a hypnotic state.

"Isn't that right Mr. Chen?"

Mr. Chen nodded in the affirmative, slowly and deliberately.

"Excellent. Off to brunch we go."

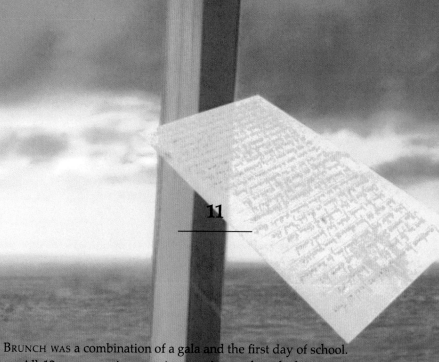

## 11

Brunch was a combination of a gala and the first day of school.

All 12 new recruits were in attendance, though they arrived at different intervals, and excused themselves on various occasions, ranging from trips to the restroom for purposes of relieving themselves, to trips to thrice ring bedside bells, also for purposes of relieving themselves. Though never explicitly stated, there was a general understanding a sort of double life dynamic was to take effect; meaning those in residence would, by unspoken gentlemen's agreement, conduct themselves with the utmost sense of dignity and poise in the common quarters, and in private indulge in their preferred vices.

This would hold true both on the island and back in their respective "real worlds", where each man had an obligation to comport themselves a certain expected way in public, reserving for behind closed doors their more potentially embarrassing and/or criminal misdeeds. The Man was of course fully aware of the various weaknesses and vices of his selections; each candidate had been vetted not only for their talents and abilities, but equally for their vulnerabilities and shortcomings. Whereas Mr. Chen's were more subtle and harder to spot, those of some of the other attendees of that day's brunch wore their Achilles heals on their sleeves.

Signore Stronso Minciata, for example: a middle-aged Italian who served as the dean of a major university in Milan — Politecnico di Milano — whom The Man had plans to elevate to Prime Minister of Italy, was a man of great passion who more than once used his power as a gatekeeper to exchange admissions board recommendations for sexual favors from aspiring students.

As in the case of predecessor Silvio Berlusconi, he could easily be baited into a scandal at any time, evidence of which, when fed to the press with the right timing and incentive, could remove him from his future position with relative ease and surety.

Sir Friederich Shlesshen was heir to a telecom empire, who had yet to work a day in his life, never met a dollar he didn't like, and despite being assured an eight figure inheritance and lifelong allowance equivalent to a top salary every month, for the accomplishment of continuing to breathe, he still ripped off whoever he could. Whether it be leaving contractors unpaid or skimping on the tip expected by the valet, he always succumbed to the temptation to keep or accrue more without working for it. Baiting such a man into a scandal of a financial nature would be child's play.

Every man brought to the island had at least one failsafe. A destruct button The Man could push to ruin the careers he gave them, should they forget who got them there. In fact, he had not just one, but multiple contingencies to keep his underlings in check... the most absolute of which was to be established for all of them in a matter of hours. Such was a major purpose for the impending post-brunch activity to which Mr. Chen had been preemptively excused.

While the others, between rounds of quickies with their new "gifts", and in the case of three of them — recreational drug use (the best of their preferred drugs stocked in their rooms) — the collection of power players networked with one another. Mr. Chen took a plate of food — to include noodles, dumplings, rice, and eggs; all safe choices from the Asian section — back to his room, successfully avoiding any conversations with the other still hooded guests.

He was hardly yet comfortable making eye contact with these new acquaintances of such impressive accolades, and he found the prospect of being questioned and judged by them too exhausting to consider. Besides, Mr. Chen knew exactly what he wanted to do to pass the time. He wanted to take a nap and another bath. Then maybe, just maybe, ring his bedside bell three times.

---

SOON AFTER, MR. CHEN WAS ALONE AGAIN IN HIS BIG BATHTUB, FEELING LIKE HE was getting away with something, just for the fact he felt too happy. He held the fine China plate above the slowly rising bath's surface, from which he ate his food with his hands... an innocent, primal thrill brought about because he couldn't hold his plate with one hand and successfully navigate his chop sticks without dropping food into the bath.

That each morsel he ate was delicious was not a trend that got old for Mr. Chen. Not then. Not ever. He was a man descended of humble ancestry; and his parents, and more-so, their parents, truly knew what it was to be hungry. They had survived periods of famine and starvation, brought about through a mix of bad luck, bad policies, and the remarkable capacity for humans to obey authority, even when it's against their own interests, and to convince and police one another to do the same.

Starvation, like any threat to survival, leaves its imprint on the genes. Mr. Chen's genes were deeply imprinted in this regard. For as tragic as the circumstances his underfed relatives faced all those years ago were, the bright side is it brought Mr. Chen immense satisfaction to slurp down his tasty noodles with wild abandon, to an extent that might not have otherwise been possible.

His brunch plate had been licked clean, save for the stray rice grains that had drown in the tub early into his meal, and the mini corn cob bit and two bamboo shallots that had been tragically lost to the jet-stream of the Jacuzzi feature, which he'd activated by accident. He set the plate on the floor and let out an unrestrained burp followed by a laugh, followed by another burp, followed by another laugh, followed by a bubbly fart.

There were over a dozen men in this house, and Mr. Chen was fairly certain most, if not all of them, had been having sex. But thus far, he had yet to hear a sound. This gave Mr. Chen the confidence he needed to burp and fart without the usual restraint he required of himself. Smacking his thin lips with his tiny tongue, absorbing the final flavors, he turned his gaze out the window, where far below, he could just make out the silhouette of a small black speedboat zipping around the rocky harbor, island bound.

Mr. Chen thought nothing of it and closed his eyes, farted once more, then fell asleep in the bathtub.

The speedboat was not 2 rentally but it was
necessarily stolen, so much as it had been bo
without permission, from an orthodontist w
for the sea, who was waiting for a judge to
would get it in the divorce, after havin
in an affair with one of his assista
two men on the speedboat, which
safely navigated to this island
the Bermuda Triangle, became
after having met the Scorne
faithful orthodontist by h
orcer, and lear
marri

## 12

---

THE SPEEDBOAT — The S.S. Bright White — was not a rental. It wasn't necessarily stolen, so much as it had been borrowed without permission, from an orthodontist with a passion for the sea, who was waiting for a judge to confirm he would get it in the divorce after having been caught in an affair with one of his assistants.

One of the two men on the speedboat, which had just been safely navigated to The Man's island in the heart of the Bermuda Triangle, most miraculously, became privy to this fact after having met the scorned wife of the unfaithful orthodontist. They convened by happenstance, at a bar two weeks prior; and it was from her he learned about the artifact of their imploding marriage floating in the harbor a short drive from his house in the Florida Keys — a famed archipelago on the Southern-most tip of the peninsula state.

Finding himself in a rare position to both secure the keys to said boat and make a quick trip to a nearby Walmart, where he could quickly and conveniently make a copy of the key. This was all to occur unbeknownst to the aspiring divorcee, who slept alone in the bed she'd recently begun sharing with sufficiently attractive, hopefully disease free younger men she met at bars in the hopes they could fuck the sadness out of her. Luke was one such gentleman. He took the opportunity and secured the copied key.

Having drunken unprotected sex with strangers then stealing their husband's boat was excitement-inducing, and reminiscent of the thrills he had become addicted to following his brief though eventful career in the U.S. Military. After several deployments, Luke had received in exchange for his service three medals, a GI Bill that would pay for a four-year college degree anywhere he could get in, and rather severe PTSD, with a side of clinical depression.

Despite making an honest attempt to carve out a new life for himself in the civilian sphere, starting with a college degree in an as yet unchosen discipline, Luke found the classes so boring, and the prospect of ever finding an occupation that didn't involve guns and secret missions so dull, that he was utterly incapable of taking the educational charade seriously. Thus, he compensated for the dearth of excitement with cheap, fast thrills, whenever and wherever the opportunities arose.

One such opportunity was with the aforementioned aspiring divorcee, whose name he thought might be either Simone or Sandra. His drunken haze, compounded by his religious adherence to his VA supplied opiates "for his back" made it harder to feel and easier to forget. It was hard to feel affection for the lady, and also hard to feel much from the sex, due to the numbing side-effects of the pills, without which he stood no chance of sleeping.

Luke's friends called him "shooter", on account of his savant-like skills with a rifle, which were detected early in life and nurtured with care by his father — a veteran of the same military, who also quietly suffered from the same addictions to pills, drink, and cheap thrills of a precarious variety — though not once had the two ever discussed it; both shared an unspoken understanding that real men kept secrets instead of sharing problems. It was an ethos reinforced by the military culture that permeated their psychology to the point neither could make a clear differentiation between what they believed and what they'd been taught.

Luke was not a prideful man, but he was a man who aptly assessed his own skills as masterful; at least when it came to hitting targets from long distances with bullets, so he was not intimidated by the challenge presented to him by his eccentric, possibly mentally disturbed younger brother, Mark. Both had been named after New Testament biblical figures by their mother — a born again Christian who instilled in her children what moral compass she could and taught them conflicting ideas like that God loved them with all his heart, but will also condemn anyone who didn't love him back to an eternity of suffering in hell.

Like millions of people holding the same mutually exclusive beliefs, if held to the scrutiny of basic logic, they chose to accept by faith rather than question the incompatibilities of their inherited dogmas. This was in part out of a humility to accept there were simply things that could be true without making much sense, and also because the ramifications for getting it wrong were so incomprehensibly dire it seemed wise from the perspective of self-interest alone to give it all at least a half-hearted amen and think about something else instead.

Luke hadn't borrowed the unfaithful orthodontist's boat just for kicks.

He'd done so for the mission. He did his best to navigate it slowly and carefully into a cavern beneath the cliff, where the shiny black boat could be left with minimal chances of being stumbled upon in the brief 24 hour window he had agreed to give Mark.

Theirs was a deal he was beginning to think was a lot crazier now that he had sobered up during the several hour trek from the keys to the island. Unbeknownst to Luke, the trip had been extraordinarily dangerous, and would have almost certainly been a failure culminating in yet another disappearance in the foreboding Bermuda Triangle had the seas not been so uncharacteristically calm that particular night.

Such synchronicities were integral to the success of this suicide mission that they gave Mark increasing confidence theirs was a righteous quest and they were being protected by divine intervention. Whether or not this was truly the case, Mark's faith in the notion was sufficient to give him confidence enough to convince his half-sober, half-suicidal, risk-prone older brother to join him on the mission.

The mission was to gather incontrovertible proof of the existence of a Satanic cult that was part of a longstanding conspiracy to dictate global affairs to the benefit of a global elite that saw mankind as their slaves. Mark was known to what few friends he had back home in Indiana, where he and Luke were born and raised, as a conspiracy theorist; though whenever he was called the demeaning term, he would invariably counter with: "No, I'm a conspiracy factualist!" ...often then proceeding to go on a rant about how if conspiracies weren't real they wouldn't have the RICO statute codified into law.

He was referring to the Racketeer Influenced and Corrupt Organization act, which he mistakenly thought stood for the Racketeering and International Conspiracy Organization Act. Mistakes like these made it all too easy for anyone at risk of buying into Mark's crazy ideas to discredit him and go on with their day. But despite his tendency to slip up on details, much if not most of the wild things he claimed did in fact check out; or would eventually, though few ever cared to find out.

He was correct, for example, that the explanation that the very term "conspiracy theorist" was minted by the CIA for the explicit purpose of creating a blanket phrase that could be employed by the various news and media outlets they influenced to demean anyone attempting to reveal information damaging to the agency and its various secret agendas. The term was successfully integrated into the lexicon to become a scarlet letter people would seek to avoid for legitimate fear it would destroy their reputation and credibility.

Mark was one of few people in possession of the energy, patience, and intellectual capacity to get to the truth buried under so many layers of carefully orchestrated misinformation and obfuscation, while at once being immune from the fear of reputation assassination, for the simple fact he'd never built a reputation worth protecting. This was because the eccentric demeanor with which he conducted himself, to a good extent thanks to his bipolar disorder which was never successfully treated in such a way that he could remain "normal" enough for long enough to establish for himself an identity or reputation worthy of defending.

Objectively speaking, at least in the eyes of society, Mark was just a mentally ill person obsessed with crazy ideas, whose one-man crusade for truth was a futile endeavor brought about by an incurable madness. Luke, however, who had remained close to Mark over the years, indulged his brother's manic rants — about 9-11 being an inside job, or fluoride being put in the drinking water, or there being evidence of a breakaway Nazi civilization in Antarctica that was in league with wicked reptilian aliens — with more curiosity than judgment. He found the stories entertaining, without giving much thought to their veracity, and granted his brother more benefit of the doubt than anyone else Mark knew, because having served as a piece of the tip of America's spear, he himself had become increasingly disillusioned by what he saw firsthand.

There had been no discovery of weapons of mass destruction in Iraq, and Al-Qaeda, even according to the mainstream narrative, was not an Iraqi terrorist organization. The attackers on 9-11 were of Saudi nationality, yet not only had Saudi Arabia been left out of the crosshairs from the start, Luke knew the U.S. Government had been aiding, protecting and conducting major business with the Saudis before, during and after the invasions and occupations of Iraq and Afghanistan. If anything, he was sent to protect the inhabitants of the terrorists' place of origin.

Stranger still, Bin Laden himself was a Saudi royal and a CIA asset when the Russians had their go at conquering Afghanistan decades prior, and the agency quietly funded, trained and supplied Bin Laden directly. And so, while Luke found himself bored in the desert, waiting for his next order to go shoot vaguely defined bad guys, he indulged in Mark's frantic, exclamation point filled emails where he drew associations and proposed theories as to why his brother was "really over there" and what they, whoever *they* was, were "really up to".

One thing was for certain, there didn't seem to be much moral high ground from his sniper perches, where Luke found himself picking off dozens of young men who never stood a chance and seemed thoroughly convinced they were just defending their homeland. Nor did he detect the presumed moral compass of Uncle Sam when ordered not to intervene in protecting children from being sexually abused by older men, because it was "off mission" and "part of Afghan culture". Nor did he understand why his

unit was used to protect the poppy fields that grew the opium used to manufacture drugs like heroin, which his countrymen would eventually presumably be imprisoned for using if and when the final product reached home.

He would have found it even more tragic if he knew he was protecting
the drug ingredients that would also be used in the pills "for his back",
which would go on to contribute to far more deaths of American soldiers —
through suicide and accidental overdose — than the vaguely defined technically not wars they were being used to fight. When considering the deaths
the same drugs also brought the civilian population, to great extremes in
states like Indiana and Florida, where they were from and now lived, respectively, the realization of how his skills as a shooter and propensity for
courage were being misused, it might have been enough to give him that
final nudge into joining the tragic statistics.

It was only due to Luke's near suicidal attitude that he agreed to embark
on Mark's proposed "operation" to infiltrate the island in question, get proof
of whatever was going on (if anything) and leak said damning proof to the
world. Mark's escapade had been inspired by the brazen mission of a similar
nature, in which now infamous conspiracy aficionado Alex Jones had
successfully infiltrated the secret gathering of elites at Bohemian Grove,
where he obtained unprecedented secretly recorded footage of powerful men
gathering for a mock human sacrifice to a giant statue of an owl representative of the pagan god, Moloch. Members of the Bohemian Grove included
Presidents George H.W. Bush and his son George W. Bush, who were among
the more notable of the powerful regular attendees of the strange annual
gathering.

Videos containing Jones' footage were still available online. That Jones
became the first target of the big tech cartel's enhanced censorship
campaigns of recent years was to Mark proof a single man with a camera
could expose a powerful sect of people to the world in such a devastating
way they sought to make an example of him when the opportunity arose
nearly two decades later. Mark hoped to make a similar impact. Luke knew
nothing of the significance of giant owl statues or secret summer camps for
rich white men, but upon finally reviewing the footage of the odd ceremony,
he did consider it proof enough some weird shit was going on, and his imag-
inative little brother might not be fully delusional.

That his misfit brother had also made a small fortune as a member of the
Wall Street bets subreddit, which had made global financial news for
temporarily catapulting the value of the stocks for AMC, Gamestop, and
other companies being shorted into dust by ruthless traders didn't hurt
Mark's recruitment efforts. He'd been smart enough to close a sizable portion
of his positions before his brokerage, Robinhood, betrayed retail investors
and froze their ability to buy the targeted companies, while allowing them to

sell, intentionally triggering a crash and wiping out most of the retail investors' gains. Had they not, people like Mark would have become multi-millionaires while crashing greedy hedge funds betting against their favorite companies; hedge funds like Citadel, which owned a good chunk of Robin-hood and held substantial short positions against the meme stocks.

The message was clear: playing the markets is for the 1%. Normal people are not allowed to win big at the expense of the elites; if they do, the game board shall be flipped over.

In exchange for accompanying his brother on the fool's errand, Mark had offered to buy Luke any guns he wanted to protect them in the case of an emergency; guns he could keep or sell when they made it back. Luke agreed, because Luke loved guns more than safety.

Luke unloaded from the now anchored boat a rucksack filled with basic survival supplies and extra ammunition, Mark's camera bag, and a sling attached to the brand new long range rifle. To be safe, and capitalize on Mark's offer, he'd also added to the tab a new sidearm, a combat knife, and what was technically not a short-barreled shotgun, to satisfy ATF (Alcohol Tobacco and Firearm) rules forbidding such weapons — and instead consid-ered a long barreled handgun "with a brace", not stock. For all intents and purposes, it was obviously a short-barreled shotgun... a fact everyone knew but couldn't admit.

Luke finished unloading the cache and exchanged his waterproof vest for a bulletproof vest. He opted to leave the not a sawed off shotgun where he stored their waterproof vests, in a compartment under the seats. As he stepped off the boat, Mark literally jumped for joy.

"We're really here! We're really doing it! This is so fucking cool. The detectives have arrived!"

*Great*, Luke thought, sarcastically — he's manic. Luke was hoping his brother would slide more toward the depressed side of the spectrum, perhaps just enough to leave him thinking this was a bad idea and wanting to go home. To the contrary, despite not sleeping in over 24 hours, Mark was wide awake and ready to confront the forces of evil head on. To him, it was Christmas morning. Nothing excited manic Mark more than going on an adventure with his big brother... akin to their childhood woods explorations in their youth; only much, much more dangerous. Luke sighed and said, "Alright, let's get this over with."

---

THE CAVERN IN WHICH THEY SET ANCHOR WAS A SLIT IN THE CLIFF WALL JUST BIG enough to fit the boat. A discreet parking spot they were lucky, or fated, to find. Before disembarking to continue the mission on foot, Luke wiped the throttle, wheel and radio of the boat with a wet rag to cover their tracks if the boat were to be found in their absence.

Luke set a countdown on his watch — a solidly built Bell & Ross with a black face that featured both an analog and digital display, the latter of which read 23:59:07, as in their deadline to leave — a deadline he had every intention of meeting, no matter what Mark said. The watch also relayed the time, of course... 14:24.

Luke did not consider himself to be a particularly smart person; nor was he, by most standards. He was far from stupid, but in possession of no rare intellectual gifts like Mark, who had excelled at school when he applied himself, but that had only been about 20% of the time, and strictly in classes he found interesting. But Luke didn't envy his bipolar brother. For as nice as it would be to speed read and retain or write without planning in flow states, as Mark did with ease, Luke would never voluntarily trade places with him.

Luke had never called his brother crazy — to his face or behind his back; nor did he consider him to be. But there was no denying he pitied him for being unable to turn his overactive brain off and relax. He loved his brother and never left his corner, to the point their mother occasionally accused Luke of enabling Mark's madness by indulging his paranoid fantasies about all the cover-ups and conspiracies.

Luke was smart in his own way. He was very good at recognizing incongruences... disruptions of patterns... or, as he would in most cases call it — bullshit. He was also extremely observant and attuned to his environment, which was both a predilection that would make him well suited to become a sniper and a skill further refined through his brief but intensely eventful military career.

Before he knew why, he was covering Mark's mouth with a gloved hand and listening closely, simultaneously crouching to the floor of the cave. After another 47 seconds in this frozen state, he felt safe again and took his hand off Mark's mouth and said, "Mark. Brother... listen. I need you to shut the fuck up. In general. For the duration of the mission. We are not supposed to be here and no one will know what happened to us if we go missing. Do you understand?"

Mark retorted, a few notches louder than Luke found acceptable.

"Yeah yeah—" Luke cut him off with a soft but deliberate slap.

"I'm serious, Mark. You brought me here to get us in and out safely. Right or wrong?"

Mark raised his eyebrows dramatically and a finger to the air in an expression of sarcastic confirmation.

"You're right. I forgot. I thought I—" Luke interrupted what he correctly presumed to be the start of a lame joke only Mark would have found funny with a harder slap.

"Ow! You just said you're here to protect me!"

Luke started loading the gear back onto the boat.

"Fuck this. We're going home."

Before Mark could argue, a noise came from deeper inside the cavern — a feint echo followed by a sound that could only come from something alive. Luke motioned for Mark to hide behind a rock as he quickly and quietly drew his knife in one hand and gun in the other.

The gun was an Israeli-made semi-automatic pistol that cost a pretty penny, and in Luke's hands shot good enough to hit said penny dead on from 20 yards out. After a tense moment, Mark slipped, giving their position away, then whisper-yelled "fuck me," doubly so doing.

Luke crouched, perfectly still, pistol outstretched, paused between breaths, senses elevated… waiting for the threat to reveal itself. Then they heard a voice from the dark… the rarely heard but still familiar hoot of an owl. Then came the subtle sound of the owl taking flight, followed by a glimpse of its imposing silhouette flying over the duo's head and out the cave entrance.

"Weird," said Mark, and thought Luke.

"Luke, do you think you could have shot that owl if you tried? I remember you shot a hawk after it grabbed that rabbit and flew off. Remember? That was awesome! Hey Luke—"

"—bro! Seriously. Shut the f—"

"—front door. Watch your mouth man. There's owls around."

Luke took deep breaths to prevent himself from snapping. Mark picked up on the fact he'd pushed Luke too far, something he was marginally improving at, thanks to his therapist.

Luke took the gear back out of the boat, slamming Mark's camera bag into his chest.

"You're manic. Calm the fuck down. Seriously. Enough bullshit."

Mark nodded in agreement then muttered, "Bird shit."

Luke let out an exhale that amounted to a hint of laughter, making Mark smile. Maybe mom was right. Maybe he was an enabler.

...e natural cover of the jungle foliage provided

...e shade for the majority of the hike the 11

...look) moving across the island slowly and in

...roup) like a boyscout troop made of grown

...ithout a pack leader) as the man why

...he activity was conspicuously

...t escort) the men were

...make their wa...

...he islan...

# 13

THE NATURAL COVER of the jungle foliage provided ample shade for the majority of the hike the 11 men took, moving across the island slowly and in a tight group — like a boy scout troop made of middle-aged men, but without a pack leader, as the man who had scheduled the activity was conspicuously absent. Without apparent escort, the guests were following their instructions to make their way, on foot, to the highest point on the island, where they could expect to find The Man and further instructions.

In contrast to the fraternity house party vibe present the night prior, now a more somber demeanor had seized the group. All were still in a shared state of exhilaration, understandably so, following their impending appointments to seats of power and newly adopted understandings they were in some way superior to the rest of mankind; which, on some level, most of them had already believed. The only difference now is they weren't without justification, and thus fated to develop such a narcissistic demeanor that their already over-inflated egos would balloon to unprecedented heights.

An interesting thing happens when several men used to taking the lead go somewhere in a group. There is a tendency for all of them to intuitively presume themself to be the rightful leader of the pack, giving rise to a subtle jockeying for the lead that results in the group as a whole getting where they're going faster, regardless of who happens to be in front when the group arrives.

This is something The Man, who called the shots on the island, and to a broader extent, the rest of the planet, understood deeply. For as evil as his means and methods might appear to the outside observer, to include Mark, there was a rhyme and reason to his approach. The Man's means of motivating people — by setting them up for conflict, the resolution of which, by way of competition — was one way to motivate people. It was not the only way; nor was it necessarily the best way. But this is something The Man was not, for all his genius, yet aware of.

The Man looked down from the highest point on the mountain on the far side of the island, perched upon a bolder that had been carved into the form of a giant owl — roughly nine feet in height, and just wide enough for The Man to sit on comfortably, cross-legged. It was from this vantage point The Man watched his bumbling flock of power hungry men power-walk through the winding jungle trails, quietly racing to be the first to the summit, which was unique in that it featured the mouth of a massive active volcano, belching steam and smoke with great consistency.

The owl statue was elevated to the highest position possible, buffered by about five feet of solid rock that gave way to the mouth of the seemingly hungry volcano, which from time to time, spritzed from beneath the rising flames streams of molten lava shedding brilliant trails of sparks. The volcano was a most formidable expression of nature's restrained power. The Man liked his volcano for a number of reasons, to include metaphorical significance. He contemplated the manner by which lava can drastically reshape a landscape through fire and fury, then solidify into new formations on which the survivors could safely build anew.

Among The Man's competitors was a cabal of people simply called The Cabal, who were intent on applying this principle to the world at large. They sought to push mankind to destroy itself in a mass apocalypse, for which they would be prepared and escape, and from which they would emerge the only game in town.

The Man reflected on whether he should allow their plan to succeed. He was being pressured to do so and foresaw war with them if he refused. He smiled at the predicament because he appreciated competition. He liked having a foe to defeat. It kept life exciting. His meditation was interrupted by the arrival of the group, save for his star pupil, Mr. Chen, who was, per The Man's wishes, still asleep in the manor, enjoying his treasured and as of late, neglected, sleep.

---

ON THE OTHER SIDE OF THE VOLCANO, LUKE AND MARK WERE DILIGENTLY HIKING their own way up the formidable rocky mountains at the quickest pace Mark could muster, which to Luke was annoyingly slow. He had grown used to rapidly ascending and descending similar landscapes in Afghanistan, and under similar conditions. Luke stopped his climb for a moment to let Mark catch up. Being a Sniper, Luke would never dare light up a cigarette in potential enemy territory, but he did find himself craving one.

A man of contingencies, Luke did have handy a vaporizer; he took in a deep drag, let it marinate in his lungs a few beats, then let it creep out of his nose in a dragon-like fashion. Ever the multitasker, he also took the recess to relieve himself, drenching the adjacent landscape in what remained of the night prior's Michelob Ultra.

Already at the mercy of nature, on his way toward some allegedly evil island, Luke thought it proper to discreetly indulge in one last booze cruise, though he hadn't extended the offer to Mark, who responded unpredictably to alcohol, even in moderation… it sometimes pushing him into mania while drunk, and twice as often pulling him into depression when sobriety finally struck again.

Luke was baffled by the fact his brother could so rapidly fluctuate between such disparate emotional and cognitive states. He could wake up ready to take on the world full force, brimming with enthusiasm and his unique brand of humor and charm, then go to bed the same night genuinely wishing to never wake up again. Given their genetic similarity, Luke always counted himself lucky to have not been born fated to duel the same demons, and would from time to time thank God for not making him the same kind of crazy, then feel guilty and recant the prayer before ruling God had never heard it to begin with, so there was nothing to be sorry about.

Luke hated these kinds of mental gymnastics and did his best to avoid overthinking, fantasizing or remembering. Luke much preferred to experience the present with such clarity and intensity all else faded into irrelevance. This is exactly what happened whenever Luke looked through a scope. Ironically, what had for Luke evolved into a violent profession had begun as a method to calm himself. Over time, life just nudged him so the cans and bottles became chests and heads, and the BBs bullets. Luke was never driven by some dark desire to end life. He just liked shooting. But it stopped being fun the first day the targets became people, and for as celebrated as he was back in the army for his skill to kill, the more he was made to do it and the worse he felt about himself.

One day, he started drinking to make himself feel better. He just never stopped. And the truth was, even in this dangerous environment, mid-mission, he was still thinking about how much he was looking forward to washing down a small handful of Vicodins with an ice cold beer… or what he had begun to affectionately refer to as a "Vico-dinner".

A HALF HOUR LATER, THE BROTHERS HAD REACHED A HIGH ENOUGH POINT TO make out the terrain atop the mountain, which they were just now realizing was an active volcano. They took cover between some rocks and overgrowth. It gave decent cover for now and a clear view of the summit.

"Holy shit! Amazing! You seeing this, bro?"

Mark handed Luke his set of astronomy binoculars he used to watch UFOs that no one ever believed he saw. As Luke confirmed the giant owl statue sighting, Mark excitedly went on with *I told you so's* until Luke succeeded in hushing him. Setting the acceptable volume for their whispers, Luke asked: "So what is this owl thing?"

"It's Moloch — an ancient Canaanite god people sacrificed babies to. Super fucked up. Even back then. The Bible even says 'fuck those guys,' basically. Like multiple times, in multiple books."

Mark went on about it resembling the one in Alex Jones' famous Bohemian Grove footage, then something about the writer Hunter S. Thompson having a similar statue at his house, where he supposedly committed suicide, while writing… mid-sentence.

Mark then connected that to the testimony of a former child sex slave named Paul Bonacci who had reported witnessing atrocities committed against kidnapped and murdered children too grotesque to recount, in a forest with tall trees, next to a giant owl statue. Mark went on about how the countless cases of child abuse from Boys Town, Nebraska, the investigation and trials that were sabotaged by powerful elected officials implicated in the atrocities and the mysterious last minute quashing of a BBC documentary on the scandal.

Luke shushed him.

"You see that guy on top of the owl?" he asked, handing Mark the binoculars. Mark took a look.

"Nope. What are you talking about?"

Luke took the binoculars back and looked again.

He had seen someone in a robe with a hood sitting on the statue, Indian style. But now, Mark was right, there was no guy. Luke scanned the rest of the horizon for a trace of the figure. His eyes had never deceived him in such a way. *Weird.*

"Alright, Mark. Stay quiet. Start filming. I'll keep an eye out."

04.11.2022 24

...he Summit was an ▓▓▓▓▓. He was

...figure who was easily one of

political figures in the United States,

... He occupied the far end of one side of

reason the United part had become a

American political spectrum, which was as bipolar

as Mark, who had long followed the smarmy smooth

talker's career during his all-nighters drifting through

an avalanche of Wikipedia articles and blog posts

on fringe websites that looked as if they hadn't had

a style update. Some the earliest days of the

internet...yet they were fast becoming the only avail-

-able depositories of conspiracy fodder escaping the

-dal waves of online censorship only because they didn't

reputable enough to take seriously and would be

obscure a source for any whitehat Mainstream

to dare cite as a source.

... politician trying to make it devious

...he unspoken face to the top of

...pearing to be discreetly

...the constant dam...

...his jo...

# 14

THE FIRST TO EMERGE TO the top of the summit was a prominent American politician. He was an easily recognizable public figure back in the United States, and a major reason the United part had become a misnomer. He occupied the far end of one side of the American political spectrum, which was as bipolar as Mark, who had long followed the smarmy smooth talker's career.

The governor was one of many nefarious characters Mark got to know during his all nighters drifting through an avalanche of Wikipedia articles and blog posts on fringe websites that looked as if they hadn't had a style update since the earliest days of the internet... yet were fast becoming the only available depositories of conspiracy fodder, escaping the tidal waves of online censorship... perhaps only because they didn't look reputable enough to take seriously and would be far too obscure a source for any journalist to dare cite.

The American politician trying to make it obvious he had won the unspoken race to the top of the mountain, while appearing to be discreetly humble — the constant dance of any good political athlete — let his jog unravel into a walk, shoulders broad, chest forward, chin up, as he approached the mysterious avian shrine. His rise to The Governorship of the great state of California had been meteoric. He was the youngest governor in U.S. history and by a good margin... in terms of voting mandate, age disparity, and looks.

Despite having stirred up some trouble in his personal life, having been caught in an affair with his own campaign manager's wife, he made it out relatively unscathed, thanks in no small part to the mainstream media's coddling approach to covering him. Rarely would a negative word be printed or aired about the man, no matter how hard he fumbled, how many campaign promises expired on inauguration day, and most pertinently — no matter how aggressive he was in bringing to bear the full power of the state to enforce his increasingly invasive and coercive agenda to control the population.

The mass hysteria that carried the virus of fear that masqueraded as a respiratory infection was amplified to its zenith in his state, and The Governor never passed up an occasion to somberly remind the public of the severity of the virus, and the need to use any means necessary to enforce a widening series of dictates penned by a council of unelected "health experts". The epithet "recommendations" was applied carefully, but they were in truth dictates. The Governor had served his role well, and was lauded by the echo chamber media as a shining example of how every governor should govern.

Obedience = Safety.

That is what his and the media's general message had ultimately boiled down to. Over time, people largely became accustomed to sacrificing their rights, comforts, and general way of living — to include things they had never before considered privileges, such as not needing to wear a mask, or not being told where you could and couldn't go, or not being coerced into accepting experimental medical treatments. While The Governor oversaw the closure of countless small business and enforced the new mandates with Gestapo-like vigor, he attended maskless parties at five-star restaurants with the elites.

The man who had been The Governor's largest donor, and behind the scenes powerbroker that had architected the ambitious and handsome young man's rise to prominence was the man seated atop the owl statue before him... *the* The Man. The Governor had enjoyed The Man's substantial donations over the years, but this excursion had marked their first face-to-face meeting. While The Governor didn't know who The Man was, he knew lobbyists and advisors who worked for him, and if he simply granted their requests and obeyed their "recommendations" money kept flowing in and doors kept opening. So he did. No questions asked.

He, like most politicians, much preferred the lifestyle afforded to him when he only truly needed to answer to a small handful of ultra-wealthy masters, rather than millions of constituents. It freed up a lot of time and energy that would otherwise need be spent begging people for donations to fund the next election and addressing the many conflicting grievances of the people. Far better to just obey a few big donors.

Besides, The Governor was convinced The Man was smarter than him, and it all seemed tied into some grander plan... which he hoped with all his heart included him as the next president of the United States. Nothing less would be enough. And so it was with great tact he had worked his way to the front of the pack. He waited until the final stretch to really kick it into gear and wanted to make sure his latest accomplishment, nominal and inconsequential as it was — was duly noted by the big guy who could make it all happen. The Man indulged his puppy so eager to please.

"Ah... Governor! Right on time. I hope the rest aren't too far behind."

The Governor flashed his famous smile.

"They should be here any second, sir."

As The Governor offered his master small talk about how beautiful the walk was, how perfect the view was, etcetera, the rest of the pack arrived, doing their best to appear less tired from the hike than they were. It was with unparalleled excitement Mark watched the governor turn to face the camera. Luke gasped at the sight through his scope.

"Mark, you were right. Holy shit. I can't believe it. That's the fucking Governor of California!"

Mark stared at The Governor through the camera, zooming in close on his face to confirm. Mark smiled.

"What was that first part again?"

Mark had been waiting to hear that for a long time — *You were right.* It was a great relief to hear it coming from his brother, and as he continued collecting the evidence, he joyfully anticipated soon hearing that phrase from everyone else who had dismissed him as a loon.

"You're recording, right?"

"Of course."

"Okay, stay still. Stay quiet. Keep the camera lens out of the sun. No reflections. We wait. We record. We egress. Stick to the plan."

"Sir yes sir," Mark responded, in a flow state of his own, recording every instant as perfectly as possible. Now it was Luke having a tough time keeping silent...

"Holy shit. Look at all of them!"

The men gathered around the owl, with their backs to Mark and Luke. The Man stepped off the head of the owl statue and descended by levitation, or a very effective illusion to that effect.

"What the fuck... Did you get that Mark?"

Mark didn't reply, locked in. But he had. And it was terrifying. Mark slowly and quietly retrieved another device from the camera bag without moving the camera — a dessert plate-sized satellite dish encircling a microphone the length of a pencil. Mark plugged it into a pair of earbuds and hit the little red record button.

"Got sound."

The Man, still hooded, walked up and down the line of men. As soon as he'd given them all a once over, he finally spoke...

Author's note:

It's worth noting that this
would be instantaneous

langue most easily
interno listener. R
address an unlimited
as ma languages as
which this was ma
by way of modern sc
— or the phenomenon g
benefit to the mans e
by his tendency to turn

# 15

It's important to note that when The Man spoke, his intentions would be instantaneously transmuted into the language most easily comprehensible to the intended listeners. In this way, he could at once address an unlimited multitude of people in as many languages as necessary. The means by which this is made possible is not explainable by way of modern science but is sure to include the phenomenon of telepathy.

An added benefit to The Man's elusive demeanor, characterized by his tendency to turn his back to his audience, or "speak" from beneath the shadow of a hood, is a reduction of the cognitive dissonance to be experienced by anyone hearing words that did not match the movement of his lips. While the concealment of his present visual identity was the chief priority, this was an added benefit.

It is, unfortunately, the case that the secret footage being captured from the other side of the mouth of the volcano would be rendered inherently suspect for this reason. It's far easier for a viewer and listener to accept that the footage has been doctored, or voiceovers have been dubbed in, than it is to accept the unlikely reality what is being sensually interpreted is only one of multiple potential interpretations.

When staring for more than a few seconds at quickly rotating car wheels, the viewer will begin to "see" the wheels going the reverse direction. The human mind is constantly employing little tricks such as these to create a sense of reality congruent with our presuppositions. In truth, blue ink on paper is only blue because the eyes — which are direct extensions of the brain itself — are filtering out all the other shades of light being reflected off the surface of the pigment.

When scanned and printed, the intervening devices will convert the aspects of the image into a code it can process to recreate, to the nearest extent possible, a replication of the original image — calibrated to appear as such to the human sense of sight.

The blue words written in blue ink do not necessarily look blue to the bird, bug, or dog. In this way, The Man's ability to "speak" with a thought that could then be interpreted several different ways was no more unusual than what the dog sees when he sees what we call blue.

---

THE SOUND CAME THROUGH CLEARLY AS MARK LISTENED IN ON THE MAN...

"Gentlemen, I thank you for making the hike to this most special place. It is a special place not only because of the lovely view and majestic volcano; it is a special place because it is here that I assemble my new allies to undergo a most unusual, albeit necessary, ritual — the completion of which will serve as your official initiation rite to become part of a longstanding hidden community responsible, by in large, for the effective management of this lovely little planet and all its resources, mankind included.

"The ritual you are to partake in, bizarre and unconventional as it may seem, has been undertaken by each of my understudies; and I can assure you that while you will never forget this day, in time you will be appreciative of my insistence you carry out my wishes. It's best to just do as I say with as little hesitation as possible, even though you might feel naturally inclined to abstain."

The men exchanged bewildered glances as their leader turned around and faced the giant owl effigy. With that, he lifted his hands and the owl's eyes lit up with fire from inside, which served as a cue for a procession of people dressed in black robes, with hoods covering their faces, to emerge from the jungle. There were 22 total, and they populated the ridge in a crowded semi-circle, face to the owl, back to the brothers capturing it all on camera from across the ridge.

Two manservants holding marching band sized drums added an ominous undercurrent of percussion to the proceedings — BOOM BOOM BOOM BOOM — in regular intervals, for the duration of the proceeding. The Man's voice boomed even louder than the drums, with an unnatural echo that made it feel like he was all around you at once.

"There can be no progress... no evolution... without sacrifice. Each of you will inherit the Earth, under my guidance, and together we will usher humanity into a new age. This will be our shared legacy."

The Man thrust his arms down and lightning suddenly filled the air.

"Remember, you are going to die. MEMENTO MORI! Let this be your mantra. Death is your fate. But before you die, in accordance with my will and grace, you shall first know what it is to truly live."

The Man lifted his arms slowly, palms up. The drum beat hastened, sound expanded, and lightening and thunder intensified. The hooded figures handed each man a torch. The Man snapped his fingers and a single bolt of guided lightning lit them all in an instant.

"In exchange for all this, I require two things: loyalty and obedience. I am the mind. You are my appendages — my hands and feet and ears and eyes. Each of you serve a vital function. But any appendage that stops working will be cut off and thrown into the fire."

The Man suddenly blasted one of the men with a burst of telekinetic energy, knocking him off the ridge of the volcano and into the lava below.

The men gasped in terror, some pissing their pants.

"He betrayed me. I hope none of you were too fond of him. But rest assured, he can and will be replaced. As will any of you if the need arises. So too will be the fate of any who oppose you!"

A sonic boom filled the air, causing all to tremble... even Luke.

"To ensure each of you understand this fully, I will test you, here and now — one by one. Prove your loyalty by sacrificing something you loved. Traditionally, I'd request a a child or loved one. But in the interests of convenience and as an act of benevolence, I've chosen that thing for you. It's something each of you have loved but haven't had time to get too attached to, so you're welcome."

The Man turned his palms down. As he did, the hoods of the caped figures flew back, as if struck by a sudden gust of wind, revealing the faces of their "gifts".

"Governor, since you like being first so much, let's start with you. Kindly select a gift to sacrifice."

The Governor stood motionless. He hesitated another second and fumbled for words of protest.

"I'm sorry, Governor. Did you not understand my instructions?"

The Man walked closer, until he was only inches away from The Governor, and lowered his hood, finally giving Mark a clear visual of The Man's face — creating the only known footage of The Man in existence.

"I need a president who understands and follows instructions. Are you my president? Or have I misjudged you?"

The Governor stared into The Man's mesmerizing eyes and swallowed; he took a deep breath then stood at attention.

"No sir! You have not misjudged. I will do as you command."

With that, he pointed to the younger of his two gifts — a Thai girl with long black hair and tear-filled pleading brown eyes. A look of terror overtook her. The Man pointed at her, snapped his finger, and all traces of fear instantly disappeared from her face. Her eyes rolled back and her facial expression became apathetic… clearly under some form of trance. The Man patted the Governor on the back, making him shudder.

"Don't worry, governor. They won't feel a thing. But you will."

This caveat emboldened The Governor, who reached for the girl with a trembling hand. He had done a lot of things with a lot of women. But nothing like this. And he had hurt a lot of people in a lot of ways. But never so directly. He never actually had to see the damage left in the wake of some of his more ruthless decisions. The Man pointed toward the edge of the volcano.

"Just give her a little push. It's easy."

The Governor took his most recent lover's hand and she mindlessly followed his direction until she was standing at the edge, toes hanging over, a tiny shove from certain death. Pebbles fell into the bubbling lava below. The Governor took his last breath and let out an animalistic roar as he moved in for the kill.

Then came a sharp thunderous crackle immediately followed by a scream. But it was not the scream of a girl. It was the scream of a man. And it was not the sound of thunder. It was the sound of the hammer of a gun igniting a bullet. Luke finished cocking another round into the chamber of his rifle before it even registered…

He'd just assassinated The Governor of California.

enough time to break
before he sunk in the
at risk of getting shot
however
must the the shot at
of surprise,
the scene throug
the primary target
ledger was. But it
He now where to be
likely have only secon

# 16

WHAT ENSUED WAS a wave of confusion; as when a fire alarm goes off and people start looking at one another to gauge whether they are in danger. This, Luke recognized from experience, meant he had enough time to bring down another target or two before it sunk in to the aristocrats that they were indeed at risk of getting shot next.

Luke was discerning in his targeting, however, resolving in an instant to make the next shot count while he still had the element of surprise. He deftly scanned the hectic scene through his rifle scope in search of the primary target. He didn't know if a bullet could kill him but was intent on finding out.

Try as he might, Luke couldn't find him. Despite being so clearly visible just seconds prior, he'd somehow already fled the scene. Luke aborted the target acquisition attempt and flipped over on his back, then slid quickly behind the closest full cover — a boulder just big enough to conceal him and Mark, who rolled clumsily from his vantage point, camera in hand, and hunched up against his brother.

"You just… I just… we just…"

"Yeah. Now let's get the fuck off this island."

Mark nodded in agreement.

"On my mark, run for the jungle. From there, we work our way down to the cliffs. Then hug the walls around to where we left the boat. Okay?"

Mark swallowed and nodded.

"Okay."

Luke scanned the sky and each direction with his field binoculars.

"Alright, go!"

He gave Mark a head start and continued scanning for incoming threats, avoiding the temptation to look over the ridge and hope for another shot at the primary target. The main objective had been met. All that was left was to escape with the footage.

About 20 yards out, Mark turned around to urge Luke to join him. Luke waved him off and kept scanning the environment, knowing with certainty how long it would take him to catch up. Just before making the dash, Luke saw the black pyramidal roof fixture atop the imposing temple in the distance detach, hover briefly, then suddenly, and with no apparent means of propulsion, ascend directly upward at faster than rocket speed, disappearing into the firmament above.

"What the fuck?"

Luke then noticed something less unexplainable and more terrifying — a drone swarm assembling... dozens of them, coagulating into a spiral, holding formation as their numbers grew.

"Fuck."

Luke broke out into a full sprint, soon catching up to Mark, who was just making it to the tree line below, kneeling over, panting in exhaustion... exhaustion that was far too premature if he had any hope of making it off the island. Luke calculated they had two, maybe three minutes before those drones, which he correctly assumed were equipped with infrared cameras, would be overhead, where they could easily detect them, even through the densest tree cover. He explained so much to Mark in as few words as possible...

"Drone swarm! Infra-red. Fucking run!"

With that brotherly advice, Mark summoned unknown speed and barreled his way like a linebacker through the poking tree branches, slicing thorns, tripping vines, and disorienting bushes, using the trees for balance as he skid and rolled down a sharp decline, dropping his sound recorder. He frantically searched for it but it was nowhere to be found in the dense growth of the jungle floor.

Luke shouted, "Leave it!" as he grabbed Mark by the sleeve and jerked him back on track.

Mark realized protecting the footage was priority number one. He was lucky he hadn't dropped the camera, and it occurred to him that if they got caught, the camera would be a lot easier to notice than the memory card. He pulled away from Luke, opened the camera bag, removed the camera, and opened the compartment containing the memory card.

Before he could protest, Luke was yanking him again by the sleeve, with such force and unfortunate timing that it made Mark drop the memory card. It bounced off a rock, fell several feet, then slid off a ledge and into a crevice between the rocks. Mark screamed and threw a flurry of punches Luke's way until he let go of him.

"What?"

"The memory card! The fucking memory card! Fucking fuck!"

"Where'd it fall?"

"There!"

Mark pointed at the hole he was running toward. Suddenly, he tripped on the root of a tree, slamming his head into a rock. He came to only seconds later with a brutal headache and amnesia enough to forget where they were. Luke slapped his face repeatedly and poured water from his canteen on his head.

"Mark. Mark. We have to go now, Mark. Mark!"

"Ow! What the… Where am I?"

"We have to go!"

"What? Go where?"

Luke yelled *fuck* through his closed mouth, gritting his teeth tightly, as he tried to figure out what to do. A feint buzzing sound became audible. Luke looked up and through the trees could make out the visual of a line of a drones, evenly spaced, combing the landscape in unison — like a big tractor in the sky, harvesting video from a field. They were maybe a minute out, on a trajectory sure to reach their location.

Luke abandoned the hope of escorting Mark another 300 yards, then down a cliff, then for a swim around the island between Mark's questions about where they were, why he was bleeding, if Luke brought bug spray, and what they were doing for dinner.

Their only hope, Luke reasoned, was making it down to wherever that memory card had fallen. That plan had the added benefit, with some luck, of not making this whole fiasco a failed mission. The only problem was the hole it fell into was at most wide enough to fit a leg through.

Luke opened his rucksack and retrieved a folded up trench shovel — the type of shovel originally created for soldiers during World War I to dig trenches, as the name suggests. Luke had only used it once, to help bury the bodies of a family killed during a midnight raid on a suspected terrorist's home back in Iraq. He slammed the shovel into the soil on the perimeter of the opening with the ferocity of a man trying to stab Mother Earth to death in a blind rage.

Seven swipes in, the soil started to give way. Rocks fell, loosed by his constant shovel slams, and made a splashing sound. Water. A good sign. As the sound of the incoming drone swarm ominously loudened, Luke didn't take his eyes off the only thing that mattered — widening the hole just enough to squeeze Mark through.

A large rock finally broke through, falling with a loud sploosh, followed by a sandtimer-like trickle of sediment. Mark instinctively began to shimmy down the hole, feet disappearing first, followed by legs, torso, and with Luke's weight on his shoulders, finally chest and the rest. Mark landed with a resonating splash.

Luke immediately followed, hanging on to the edge with one arm, desperately trying to cover up their entry point with the shovel. In the final seconds before the drones were overhead, he yanked a nearby bush hard enough to unroot it and covered the hole to some effect as he fell through and landed into a pool of cool water in a dark cavern.

Luke's next priority became keeping his rucksack dry enough to ensure his lighters would still work as he doggy paddled away from the hole to ensure a barrier of Earth crust between him and the drones, which he could now clearly hear overhead. Their buzz permeated the cavern and echoed against the solid rock walls, giving Luke some appreciation for the size of wherever they had landed.

"Pst! Hey. Over here."

He swam toward the voice until his hand made contact with rock. He reached up to feel a flat surface, large enough at least to toss his gear on, climb up, sit down, and finally catch his breath.

He rummaged through his bag until he felt the familiar smooth texture of the packaged, army issued glow stick. He tore at the edge, unsealing it, retrieved the plastic tube inside, and cracked it by pushing and pulling both ends simultaneously. As the cracking sound subsided, the soft green glow from the stick came to life — a sight that never ceased to impress Luke.

He stood, cautiously, and held the glow stick before him with one hand, clutching and unsheathing his combat knife with the other. He made out the perimeter of the platform they were standing on then heard another cracking glow stick and turned around to see Mark crawling to his feet, extending the exploration in the opposite direction.

---

THE CAVE WAS SO QUIET EACH FOOTSTEP CARRIED AS THE ONLY CLEAR SOUND IN the space. They spoke in soft whispers that echoed intensely. Mark answered the question on Luke's mind…

"I know what this place is. It's called a cenote. Fresh water, natural sink-hole formations."

The brothers continued surveilling the cavern, hugging the walls, meeting at the middle point where they started. Luke sighed and spoke: "Walls all around. No exit. So unless you can jump all the way back up there —" Luke pointed up at the hole they'd fallen through; a good 30 feet up. "— we're fucked."

Normally Mark was the bleaker of the two, but Luke's pessimism was starting to seep through. Mark felt oddly comfortable with their futile situation, having an inexplicable general sense that despite appearances, things were going to work out.

"You know, if you think about it, we just stumbled on the perfect hiding place. Didn't we? I mean, what are the odds of that?"

Luke knew this tone of voice. It's how his brother sounded when he was on the verge of sudden religiosity. The range of his perception was such that not only did Mark fluctuate emotionally, so too he seemed to fluctuate spiritually; depending on when you asked him, his views ranged from "of course there's no God" to "I am God and God is me," and all points in between the extremes.

At times, it escalated to messianic delusions, where Mark genuinely believed to be endowed with spiritual gifts that, when awakened in himself and others, would save mankind from itself and foster in a new age of heaven on Earth. But his grand and peterbingly certain prophesies would invariably fade back into a depressive state, in which he would feel ashamed for having been so arrogant and foolish, accepting once again his own limitations and overall insignificance.

However, in this particular instance, Luke welcomed any form of hope that could take his mind off wondering if they should shoot themselves now or wait to starve or be found and killed. All paths seemed to lead to an unfortunate demise in the near future. Mark's hopeful enthusiasm in the face of certain death was inspiring, and so without a plan to get out, Luke opted to help his brother find his precious memory card.

At least, Luke figured, if they died down here and weren't found for a long time, or by the wrong people, they could leave behind for some explorer proof of the existence of this group — whatever it was, their sacrificial traditions, and maybe it would somehow make the world a better place. Luke had almost sacrificed his life in the past for causes he believed in a lot less. If nothing else, he'd gone out taking down at least one tyrant, and extending the lives of all those girls who didn't deserve their intended fate. Luke's cognitive preparation for death was interrupted by Mark's excited voice...

"Wow! This is awesome!"

illuminated the spectacle that [...]. It was clearly the outline of a [...] human in appearance, save for the size. It nearly 2, maybe 3x larger than the usual expected size. Strangest of all, the hand print looked as if it had been pressed into wet cement that cried, ala a Hollywood star on the pavement. But it clearly wasn't cement. This hand print was incredibly cast into pure, solid rock. Mark commented -

So it's said leaving a hand print in stone was 2nd I guess, maybe still is, a rite of passage for Mystics. Like those monks in Tibet. They first meditate hardcore on whatever, then he like think the rock get soft, put their hand in, then he like think that shit out. I'm a fucking beast! Can you believe it?!

No mark, I can't. But I've seen a lot I don't believe today. So who knows. Mark carried on, talking too loud for Luke's tastes.

I know. I just told you. It's quantum mech- -anics shit, man. x-men shit. How else you going to explain that? what, they just carved it? why? I'm telling you bro, all this magic shit. It's real. You saw that fucking leader guy levitate

## 17

THE GLOW STICK illuminated the spectacle that had Mark so excited. It was clearly the outline of a human hand, save for the unusually large size, and presence of a sixth finger, by the looks of it. It was easily two, if not three times larger than a usual hand, but held the unmistakable form. Strangest of all, the handprint looked as if it had been pressed into wet cement before it dried, ala Hollywood stars on the pavement. But it clearly wasn't cement. This handprint was indelibly cast into pure, solid bedrock. Mark added his commentary...

"So it's said leaving a handprint in stone was, and I guess maybe still is, a rite of passage for mystics. Like these monks in Tibet. They just meditate hardcore or whatever, then like, quantum alter the molecules in the rock to make it get soft enough to press their hand into. Then they pull it out and let it go back to normal. Presto. Handprint. Like a mystical master's version of scratching Steve was here into the wall of a bathroom stall. Can you believe it?"

"No. I can't. But I've seen a lot I can't believe today. So who knows..."

Mark carried on, talking too loud for Luke's taste —

"I know. I just told you. It's quantum mechanics. Mind over matter. Thought power. How else you going to explain it? What, they just carved it? Why? I'm telling you bro... a lot of this magic sounding shit is real. You saw that fucking leader guy levitate off the owl, right? Lighting the torches with lighting. Fucking... wizard shit."

Luke held his head in frustration.

"Just shut up for a minute and let me think."

Mark granted his request, for 14 seconds.

"I mean think about it—"

"Enough, Mark. Primary mission objective is to escape. The memory card recovery is a secondary objective."

"Oh, okay. Thanks for explaining that, bro. Also, fuck that. This is my operation and we're going to switch that order. And tac on a bonus objective: figure out magic shit and unlock latent godlike powers within."

"Please just shut the fuck up and stay focused. Play time is over."

Luke gave the perimeter another once over. Nothing but solid rock all the way around and the pool of water in the center. The light seeping through the bush half-covering the cenote entrance he'd broken open lit the space enough to see the surface of the water, but not into the depths.

Luke hoped it was shallow enough to reach the bottom. If there was any hope of finding the memory card, or, more importantly, a way out, it was in the water.

"We have to go in," Mark decided.

As Luke contemplated his approach, Mark jumped in, cannonball style, as always. He doggy paddled to the center of the cenote.

"Cold. But not freezing."

Mark let himself slowly sink toward the bottom, rotating so he was facing downward, glow stick in hand, outstretched.

Another splash. Mark looked up to see his brother's leg. Bubbles ascended as he chuckled at his impulse decision to grab Luke's leg, which earned him a deserved kick to the head, which hurt more than usual, given the recent concussion. Mark came up for air.

"You trying to give me another concussion?"

"Sorry. Forgot. You shouldn't be in here. Rest up there. I got it."

Mark ignored the advice and re-submerged. The combined light of their outstretched glow sticks and what sunlight was offered from above was just enough to reveal a sight that caused them both to let out a gasp of bubbles. Before them, on the cenote's floor, was a skeleton.

Mark immediately swam back to the surface. Luke continued to face his fears head on, as was his personal rule. Anything he feared, he ran at, rather than away from. Luke continued scanning the cenote floor, where skeleton after skeleton lay scattered. Based on their state of decay, the remains appeared to be hundreds, if not thousands, of years old.

Even for Luke, who was no stranger to corpses — particularly the several he'd created — this was something else. Something about soaking in the remains of so much death made him sick to his stomach. He came up for air and joined Mark back on the side of the cenote, vomiting in disgust.

The two sat in silence for at least two minutes — an exceptionally rare accomplishment for manic Mark. Luke finally broke the silence.

"These glow sticks have another five, maybe six hours left in them. And we only have one more left. They're getting duller by the minute, so our best bet is to get back down there now. Give me your glow stick."

Mark considered arguing with Luke and insisting on keeping it a team effort, but found his body in strong agreement with Luke: *rest*. He dutifully surrendered his little green cylinder of chemical light and laid down on his back. Luke warned Mark not to fall asleep; not that it was going to be a problem. Wet, in terror, and manic to boot... sleep wasn't an option.

Following a series of preparatory breaths, Luke dove back in, headfirst, kicking his way back down into the bone-laden aquatic abyss, focusing exclusively on matching the visual he had in his memory of the missing memory card. After a few minutes of failed efforts, he returned to the surface for another oxygen top off.

He heard Mark quietly singing to himself: "I wish they all could be California girls. I wish they all could be California girls..." A stark juxtaposition to the immediate circumstances and an endearing demonstration of the man's ability to retreat into his own mind, for better or worse. Mark noticed Luke had resurfaced.

"Any luck?"

"No."

Luke continued his preparatory breathing, flooding his body with fresh oxygen.

"Hey Luke, you ever think about how *I wish they all could be california girls* could be interpreted to mean the guy wishes more girls from other places would move *to* California. Like he doesn't want to leave home. He wants all the girls to move to where he lives. Who wrote it? You think—"

Luke re-submerged. As he went down for another attempt, it dawned on him that the card contained evidence the governor had been shot. And if Mark were the one coming forward with the footage, and his brother happened to be a sniper, it would be obvious who the shooter was. It might not be in his best interests for this video to get out.

Considering the imminent threat of death in general, and the cons to finding the fumbled evidence, Luke resolved to put the memory card search on pause and redirect his focus on the primary objective: escape. He resurfaced for another refill of air, heard half a verse of Mark's rendition of "All Star" by Smash Mouth, told him to shut up, then went back underwater, this time hugging the walls, looking for any potential underwater caverns... their only hope.

Luke's sense of urgency was only enhanced by his sudden remembrance he'd forgotten to drop his rifle down the sinkhole, meaning as soon as it was found, it would be a matter of time before their pursuers discovered where they'd absconded. On the other hand, if they took them alive, the rifle misplacement could turn out to be their salvation — at least in the short term.

It was in this moment Luke realized that despite his cavalier attitude toward danger, and his general sense of apathy toward life, he didn't want to die. Not here. Not like this. And so it was with increased urgency and resolve he swam in circles around the cavern, one hand against the slick, cool, rock wall, feeling for any break in continuity.

After another refill of air, and half verse of song from his potentially delirious brother, Luke swam back down with great determination in his eyes, which were thankfully safe to open in the fresh water.

Luke smiled bigger than he had in years when his hand gripped an opening in the rock easily large enough to swim through, if not for the skeleton in the way. He pushed it aside, doing his best to pretend the bones were just rocks.

He came up for one more long oxygen refill, this time sitting on the ledge with Mark for a quick rest and strategy session...

"Alright, I found an opening."

"Awesome. What about the memory card?"

"Don't worry about the memory card. Right now we need to get—"

"Nooo! If we leave it now we're never going to get it. What, do you think we're just going to come back next fucking weekend? Like we left our wallet at the gym? We can't fucking—"

"Listen! I'm going to see where this hole goes. Hopefully there's an opening on the other side. If I don't return after say, ten minutes, I joined the skeletons, in which case, it's been an honor. And while you're welcome to give it a try yourself, you've never come close to beating me in a breath-holding competition, so I'd advise you not push it."

"But what about the memory card?"

"Jesus Christ, Mark. I'm trying to save our lives here. First we find a way out. Then we worry about the card. Okay?"

Mark shook his head in discontent.

"There's something else I need to tell you. I forgot the rifle outside. And your sound recorder's not far off, either. Someone will probably find them, and then find here. Maybe in a few minutes. Maybe in a few hours. Maybe days. If I don't make it back, I recommend waiting here and yelling for help. With your gift of gab, maybe you can blame it all on me and talk your way out of here."

Luke took a deep breath, realizing the gravity of the situation. Mark stared ahead in silence, also grasping the same.

"Mark — For what it's worth, you were right about a lot of things. I'm sorry I got us in this situation. But it wasn't for nothing. We took down a bad man about to do a bad thing. We saved lives. That's all I ever signed up to do."

"Beautiful speech, man."

"Shut up."

"Stop talking like you're going to die. We're going to make it out of here. I can feel it. I've been right about everything else. I'm right about this too. While you work on finding a way out, I'll look for the card."

"Bad idea but I know you're going to do it anyway. If you start losing consciousness, get back out. You hit your head pretty good."

"Deal."

The two clasped hands and Mark prepared for a long trip underwater. He began breathing in and out in equal intervals, through his nose, doing what yogi call "Breath of Fire". Luke always considered yoga to be too effeminate for a man like him. He'd never taken a class or learned anything about it, other than that he was thankful for girls in yoga pants; but a friend in the service had taught him this technique, and it worked.

He continued the Breath of Fire for 100 breaths then stopped.

"I love you bro," said Mark, matter-of-factly.

"Love you too," said Mark, unexpectedly crying just a little.

Luke took a few more deep breaths then jumped as high as he could, making a dive with some momentum behind it, accelerating underwater with powerful kicks and a frog stroke — both glow sticks in hand illuminating the water just enough to see what was directly in front of him.

Through the opening in the wall he went, thanking the God he didn't believe in there was some depth to it, and it opened wider rather than narrowed, as he proceeded deeper into the aquatic unknown. The path split to the left and right.

He chose left.

He continued to swim forward through the underwater alley, striking a careful balance between physical exertion and oxygen retention. Too slow and he could drown. Too fast and he could drown. To prevent any negative cognition from depleting oxygen supply unnecessarily, he narrowed his conscious focus to mentally humming the chorus of "I Wish They All Could be California Girls", as he ventured further and further into the dark waters.

He'd hummed without humming the whole of the song at least once, and there was no end in sight. He began to wonder if he could swim back still, or if he was past the point of no return. Then he remembered an early lesson the army had taught him:

*Indecision is a decision. Hesitation gets you killed.*

So, with that in mind, he spent no more than two seconds in deliberation before opting to carry on, with one slight adjustment — he started focusing on the ceiling rather than the wall.

As he completed a second rendition of the song, Luke felt his head tinging, and he began seeing tiny specks of light. *Not good.* He kept calm, deciding if he were to drown it would be at the last possible second, and with as much dignity as possible. He felt a tingling sensation in his arms and legs and an increasingly burning, desperate urge to inhale, surrendering to which at this point would mean certain death.

He continued moving, but became disoriented, and could no longer tell if he was going forward, backward or in circles. His vision began to fade as he continued to fight the urge to inhale. He lost feeling in his fingers and toes, which caused him to drop the glow sticks. The specks of light he saw in the darkness extended into stripes, then coagulated into a kaleidoscopic pattern that spun, as if on a wheel, faster and faster...

Then, he felt nothing. For an instant that felt longer than it was, Luke clearly saw a face he'd not seen in many years. It was the face of his high school sweetheart — Jessica, whom he'd left behind when he joined the army after 9-11, in response to the perceived new threat of foreign terrorists.

Luke saw Jessica on the beach... warm brown eyes glowing like blazing fragments of amber, and a big, bright, carefree smile... the kind smiled by people comfortable enough around someone — someone they love — to be their truest, most joyful self... the smile that lingers after a forgettable joke... in that state of being where there is no thought other than appreciation for the beauty of a fleeting moment of complete peace... the sort of which can only be found in union with someone feeling the same way, at the same time... the type of moment a person can forget is worth more than anything that can ever be bought, earned, or stolen; a state of joy, gratitude, and togetherness that costs nothing but the attention of your spirit — which, in most other moments, lives in a cage of thought, cemented shut with fear and anxiety, and for many, if not most, stays locked in that cage — barred from love — until finally set free by death.

And so, as Luke's connection to his body continued to sever, and his bones sank into the cold rock floor to join the remains of all the others, his last bit of control over his body came in the form of a twitching grin on the right corner of his mouth, and a blink that dropped, as a final offering of a spirit longing to be freed by love, a single tear, into the dark cold waters of fate.

# 18

MARK GENUINELY BELIEVED he and his brother were going to make it out of that cenote, off that island, and back to Florida with the unbelievable footage in hand. He held on to these beliefs long after the 10 minute deadline expired and his brother didn't return.

He dedicated himself to the task of finding the lost footage for hours. Dripping wet and wheezing in exhaustion, he collapsed his body back on safe ground and briefly slipped into that halfway place between sleep and wakefulness... as found in the sprinkles of sleep you get on a flight, where flashes of dreams dance through the slumped heads of passengers. He saw a plastic boat floating on a lake. It was a boat made of memory cards.

Mark woke from the micro-sleep with a gasp and game-changing realization: memory cards float.

He started and promptly ended the search against the wall of the rocky ledge. There it was, bobbing gently on the surface of the still waters. He clenched it safely in his wet grasp, kissed it, laughed, then blew it dry, said "please God", and slid it into his camera.

He flipped the switch to turn it on. "Come on baby... come on."

A pleasant ding accompanied the cracked viewfinder turning on. He played back the last video and there it was. Exactly what they had seen. Perfectly filmed. Sound and all.

"Got you, you son of a bitch."

Mark began laughing, covered his mouth, and continued, while kicking his legs in the air in joy then promptly drifted into a well-earned nap.

WHEN HE OPENED HIS EYES HE SAW NOTHING. TOTAL DARKNESS. TOTAL SILENCE. Nightfall had arrived.

He imagined Luke must have by now made his way out of some exit, and be finding his way back to the hole in the ground above, presumably with a rope, or long piece of bamboo, or some clever means of fishing him out. Luke always found a way. Luke always made it back.

But alas, unbeknownst to Mark, this time, Luke did not find a way. This time, Luke was not coming back to save him. His lifeless body was slumped against the far side of a dead end; even the most heroic among us can fall victim to dead ends.

It was not Luke's fault for choosing to hug the left side of the wall instead of the right. Sometimes right can be wrong. Had he chosen right by choosing right, just a few feet down the corridor that had ultimately claimed his life, he would have discovered another hole that led to a walkable, water-free path to an exit.

After one of the most uncomfortable nights of a life full of uncomfortable nights, Mark found hope in the sight of the sunlight from above. It made him think of an early scene in a Batman movie, when the hero is imprisoned in a similar environment... underground, with an opening high above. In the film, through hard work and determination, Bruce Wayne eventually gains the strength to make the arduous climb and death-defying leap to freedom.

But this place was worse. Because there was nothing to climb. No way to even get close to the exit. Just a tauntingly out of reach hole to salvation in the roof that was once ground. Mark spent a torturous morning waiting for Luke to appear above or emerge suddenly from the water to explain he'd gotten lost.

He sat completely still, listening closely for any sound; praying over and over and fighting the growing need to confront the very real possibility his brother wasn't coming back, and with that possibility, so too the possibility he was fated to die down here too. Mark felt sad, cold, and alone... all things he was used to feeling, but drastically more so now that the causes for his suffering were extrinsic, rather than a symptom of his bipolar disorder.

---

SOME TIME LATER THAT AFTERNOON, MARK DECIDED IT WAS TIME TO FACE THE music and see what Luke saw on his way out — literally or metaphorically. The water felt much colder this time around, now that his body wasn't running on the same level of adrenaline it had been the day prior. Using the last glow stick for illumination, he swam through the known hole, constantly feeling in the little square pocket inside his front right jean pocket to confirm the memory card had not strayed.

He'd chosen to leave most of the supplies behind but had stuffed his pocket and waist band with the handgun, knife, some vacuum sealed beef jerky, and a small seashell with a little hole drilled into it that Luke always traveled with and refused to discuss; reason being, it'd been the final gift his high school sweetheart Jessica gave him before his first deployment.

She said it would keep him safe. It was a fantasy he indulged; wearing it on his dog tags every time he went behind enemy lines. He still traveled with it, long after their breakup. She said he came back different than he'd left.

Combat had changed him. He was riddled with PTSD and new addictions, including an addiction to not demonstrating weakness or admitting he needed help. There was too much yelling, too many broken dishes, and not enough love left in him, so she left. Every week he thought of calling her. But each time he had opted for a Vico-dinner instead.

---

MARK MADE HIS WAY DOWN TO THE OPENING LUKE HAD FOUND. CONFRONTED with the same choice of which side of the wall to use for guidance through the dim, murky water, Mark chose right by choosing right. He came out of the water with a gasp. His emergence was only mildly relieving, because as great as it was that he survived the plunge, it begged the question why Luke hadn't returned as planned.

Mark immediately went to work on a satisfying *what probably happened. What probably happened is Luke had taken the same path and continued without going back to tell him first because...* he struggled to invent a reason, but still told himself Luke must have had one. He refused to seriously entertain the idea his invincible big brother had drown.

Mark set off down one of the cave paths alone, dismissing the voice in his head suggesting he go back in the water and swim further in the other direction... just to confirm there was no body to be found. *Waste of time,* he thought to himself; *Anything I can survive, Luke survived.*

This ability, or depending on how you see it, weakness, Mark had — that allowed him to win arguments with himself when the outcome less preferred, or in this case, severely dreaded, seemed objectively more likely — is a defining human trait. It's a talent we have — to fool ourselves into believing what we wish to be true is the case... our preferences weighing the scales in favor of the preferred outcome; what we hope to be true. Hope is a powerful thing.

Hope can give us faith; faith that emboldens us to take necessary chances. Hope can, and does, lift the spirit out of negative states, in which we cannot garner the strength to even try. Hope is a force so powerful that it alone can put the twinkle back in the eye and the dance back in the step... hope can, in many respects, imbue one with life. But hope can also be an intoxicating force that blinds one to unfortunate realities that linger beneath facades of idealism — that optimistic fairy dust that makes the room sparkle until you choke on it.

Hope can bring a great hero to his knees, and keep him there, worshipping the illusion that despite appearances, in the face of facts, and against all odds, if he just doesn't lose hope, eventually everything will work out just like he hoped it would. But sometimes, if not most times, the things we hope for evade us to the very end.

Hope is a speculative strategy.

Perhaps hope's only job is to give us that extra push... or that mirage that can offset our fated disappointments and sorrows long enough to survive. Hope can give us the strength to take the next step when realism would keep our feet planted firmly in the quicksand of dismal odds, reducing our chances from slim to none to just none.

In Mark's case, hope served that motivational function. Without it, he would have surely taken Luke's gun and shot himself on the spot... if he could figure out how to work it. And so, on that particular day, it could be said hope saved Mark, when it so deftly talked him out of exploring more seriously the possibility it was too late to save his brother.

On the other hand, it could also be said it was Mark's hope that got his brother killed because if he wasn't so hopeful all would improve, and justice would be found, if only he could prove the veracity of his "conspiracy theories", the two would have never come to the island in the first place. If Mark's sense of hope for a better world he could personally help bring into being hadn't been so exuberant, he never would have dared take on such an insanely futile mission... much less pull his brother into it.

Mark did not think another negative thought for the next two hours as he randomly explored the winding caves under the island in search of Luke and an exit. Hope's effects were so potent on him that day that he forgot how tired he was and didn't notice how much pain was waiting to be felt. He just marched on, thinking *one step at a time, for as many steps as it takes.*

Hope kept Mark going all afternoon, lost in a vast serpentine cave... all the way to a dead end. But this dead end had a door: a modern, metal door, with a handle and everything. Beneath the door was a line of bright light, meaning this was either an exit to the cave, or an entrance to somewhere else.

In any case, it was a door that needed to be opened.

04.13-14.2022

...he door in the Cave
...to knock, or check to
or, he began to think, maybe
...he Labrynth. But in search
...expected is still a door.
...more appealing than a door
... in a cave. So it was with
...rom Mark slowly turned the
...or knob... tried to, rather, because
...and slid open. Just like that, the
Sliding into the rock... like a
...essible door opening after hitting
...on with the wheelchair on it. It
...uncanny grace, not making a sound.
... remembering he had his
... wasn't sure
...deciding

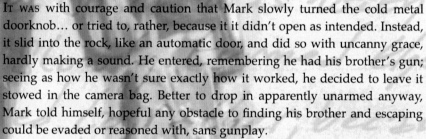

# 19

It was with courage and caution that Mark slowly turned the cold metal doorknob... or tried to, rather, because it it didn't open as intended. Instead, it slid into the rock, like an automatic door, and did so with uncanny grace, hardly making a sound. He entered, remembering he had his brother's gun; seeing as how he wasn't sure exactly how it worked, he decided to leave it stowed in the camera bag. Better to drop in apparently unarmed anyway, Mark told himself, hopeful any obstacle to finding his brother and escaping could be evaded or reasoned with, sans gunplay.

He surreptitiously crept through a hallway which was walled and had a ceiling of unusual height; so high he could throw a baseball with all his might and it wouldn't make it to the top; and it was a throw from 3rd to 1st in width. A hazy light lingered in the air, giving it all an odd glow. No visible light bulbs. No clear source of the light. Just a floating pool of ambient light, like some luminescent vapor. The floor beyond the door was perfectly level and very clean, in contrast to the natural cave filled with dirt and rock.

At the far end of the bewildering installation were two opened hangar doors that expanded the full height of the building. Wary of being detected, Mark quickened his pace to a run, another 50 yards, until he reached the threshold between the spartan futuristic domain and tropical oasis outside. Mark appreciated the sensation of sunlight on his skin in a way he never had, having spent nearly 48 hours underground.

He took only a brief moment to indulge in the exquisite beauty before him. He listened to the singing birds. He inhaled the oceanic aroma. And he lamented the fact that such evil could hold claim over such paradise. Then, far off in the distance, towering over the tree line, he detected movement. He retrieved Luke's field binoculars, which were slung around his neck, and gave it a closer evaluation. It was a giant robot, moving through the jungle with the swagger and size of a T-Rex.

Continuing to scan the horizon, he detected another robot. Then another. At least four in total. Then it dawned on Mark, as he noticed several giant imprints in the ground, leading from where he stood to as far as he could see — the structure was a hangar where these mechanical nightmares must be stored. He noticed the outside of the hangar doors were painted to blend in, very convincingly, with the natural surroundings. Above each robot, and scattered throughout the air in every direction, were what he first mistook for flocks of birds, then realized were all drones. *Not good,* Mark admitted to himself.

The sound of footsteps from the other side of a nearby hill of Earth and stone alerted Mark in time to abscond into the crevices between some boulders. From cover, he saw six men in a single file line quickly making their way into the hangar.

He stealthily made his way out of hiding and peered around the corner, just in time to see and briefly film the men — who were clad in camouflage, bulletproof vests and helmets, each carrying military grade weapons — as they filed into the same door he had just come out of. Had he taken just two minutes longer to find his way to that door, he would have surely been confronted by the squad.

Mark racked his memory for any recollection of landmarks that could help him find his bearings. After a brief though stressful hike upwards, he reached a spot from which he could see the most obvious and memorable point of reference — the volcano at the highest point of the island. It was miles away, giving Mark an appreciation for how far he'd traveled. Recalling the direction from which they had arrived in the speedboat — South by Southwest, he recalled hearing Luke say — he pieced together a rough estimation of where they'd left the boat.

It was only a matter of minutes before Mark attracted the watchful eye of a drone. He ran as fast as he could through another patch of jungle to evade it, and found a hiding place beneath a collapsed tree — the result, by the looks of it, of having been stepped on by a giant robot. In the distance, through the chirps of birds and insects, he heard a hydraulic mechanical movement and the foreboding hum of inbound drones.

He shifted his priority from escaping to hiding the camera somewhere he could later find it. Following the advice of an iguana shooting up a tree and laying leisurely on an overhanging branch, Mark found the nearest climbable tree and mustered all his remaining strength to shimmy his way up he trunk where he could just reach a tree branch thick enough to hold the weight of his camera bag indefinitely. He successfully tossed it over and tightened strap, securing it snugly against the tree — invisible to the drones above and impossible to spot from the ground below.

Leaving the camera behind was about as easy as leaving a son. But Mark's hope was not too grand that he couldn't accept his dismal odds of making it to the boat now, given the proximity of the impending search party, and his extreme exhaustion, which was finally starting to get the best of him. He had the idea to leave a marker for himself, or whoever may be able to one day return and find the camera.

It couldn't be too obvious, or too close to the tree holding it... so he decided to face the direction of the volcano, and count 20 trees in that direction, where he stabbed Luke's knife into the base of the 20th tree, handle facing the camera bag. This would have to do. With that, he sprinted as far as he could in a random direction to get as far away from the hiding spot and marker as possible before getting caught.

This would prove to be a series of shrewd decisions, as soon-after Mark found himself stuck in the back with an electric dart that instantly brought him down and into convulsion. When the shocking finally ceased, a half-conscious Mark looked up to see the approaching legs of one of the giant robots. It was bipedal, with thick metal legs, like telephone poles on hydraulics.

Above the two legs were four armlike appendages stemming from a dark center shaped like an egg that housed the pilot. One arm held rockets, another a gatling gun, another a 10 foot serrated dagger, and the last a four-fingered hand, which gripped him firmly by the torso and lifted him twenty feet off the ground.

Mark felt thankful to be alive more than he did angry about getting caught. Well aware there was a very real possibility this would be the last time he ever saw the beauty of nature — which he was only just beginning to appreciate since arriving at this wonderful, terrible place — Mark took in the view and smiled as he began to cry while a gathering swarm of drones flew in a circle around him like a giant mechanical halo.

As the robot marched him across the island, toward the manor, Mark tried to focus on the positives: (1) They didn't have the camera; (2) They didn't know about the camera; and (3) Luke might have been captured under similar circumstances, given the fact he had been apprehended rather than killed on sight.

A good 20 minutes later, the robot, now also accompanied by six men on foot, approached another giant hangar door disguised just the right color. It smoothly and quietly opened, then closed behind them. The robot gently lowered a few feet above the smooth black floor then released its grip, dropping Mark with a thud, knocking the wind out of him and bringing a wave of pain to the site of his recent concussion. His head throbbed, his vision blurred, and he flailed his legs as he desperately awaited the return of the ability to breathe.

The six men encircled him. They each wore sunglasses and emotionless faces. All were large and strong, and 100% focused on making sure he didn't escape. For hours, Mark laid like this, half-asleep. No one spoke. No one even moved. Not a single sound. Not a single step.

The stillness was bizarre to the point Mark began to wonder if these people were cyborgs, robots, or something stranger. The silence was finally broken by the sound of two high healed shoes clacking on the floor behind him. With this, the six men lined up and faced the direction of the incoming sound. The deliberate pace gradually got louder; the sound from each step bringing a little extra pain to Mark's throbbing head.

He kept his eyes down and didn't turn around — not in the mood to make any new friends. An unmistakably feminine voice — soft and raspy — casually issued a single command...

"Take him to B-4."

# 20

---

THE STOIC, android-like men surrounding Mark spoke in unison, as if controlled by a single consciousness, and used as few words as possible to convey their intentions.

"'Walk. Stop. Turn right."

Mark's thoughts were now with Luke, who he resolved not to mention when questioned. He began preparing himself for the excruciating pains of torture he anticipated to be on the evening agenda and tried to form a strategy to obscure as much as possible while appearing to cooperate. He thought of all the times he had wished to be dead; he remembered the handful of times he'd flirted with self-inflicted demise, and he began to focus on reframing his doom in a more positive light.

As soon as end of day, he could find himself relieved of the burden of living. *No more suffering*, he thought. *Just a little more pain, then no more suffering.* Sure, as of late, he had been on an upward spiral, and he'd found purpose in his recent renegade quest, but so much of his life was listless. Boring. Dull. And filled with disappointment after disappointment. Like a long-anticipated exit on a full bladder — death would be a great relief.

While a major factor, he couldn't attribute all of his problems and dissatisfactions to the mood disorder. He was simply a man in his early 30's who had failed to carve out for himself a life that gave him a compelling reason to get out of bed in the morning. No job he loved. No family of his own. No wife or girlfriend. No children. No pets. No one back home, save for his parents, to whom he often considered himself a burden... and his brother, who for the first time, he was starting to realize, might have already died... all thanks to him.

The cloud of sadness that so often accompanied him had returned, and in short order he felt himself succumbing to an increasingly weighty state of depression. He forced a smile and thought: *Good. That's more like it.* Better, he reasoned, to not want to keep living going into the torture session. Maybe his captors would lose interest and kill him fast. Ahead of him and out of his body, he assumed, awaited either a new life, somewhere else, perhaps as someone new... or else an eternal slumber. Disillusioned as he was with the current life, and tired as he was of the burden of living, either sounded just fine.

He challenged himself to simply appreciate the passing moments, no matter how uncomfortable they might prove; each endured instance one step closer to the solace of his long awaited demise. But alas, fate had other plans.

———————

They reached the room labeled B-4. It had a white marble door, with a beautiful albeit ominous statue of a cobra head jutting out of the center. The serpent was made of gold, with two sparkling rubies for eyes and a delicate looking tongue made of either emerald or green crystal — forked and outstretched in a formidable manner. One of Mark's captors opened the door. A terse but not violent shove accompanied a command...

"Go inside."

He took a deep breath in anticipation of whatever horrors awaited, which came out with a stream of relief when he saw not bars, chains, or instruments of torture, but the furnishings of a luxury apartment. It was impeccably clean, featuring all black and white furniture and paintings.

Everything in the room seemed themed around the juxtaposition of those colors. A black sofa with white pillows. And a white sofa with black pillows. A black fireplace with white wood. A white desk with a black chair. A grand piano. Black and white floor tiles formed a chessboard pattern matching the centerpiece of the room — a large circular bed with a comforter depicting a yin-yang symbol... the two contrasting dots made by round pillows.

Mark turned around to see an empty room. He stood there, in shock, confused out of his mind. Then a very plausible possibility entered his mind. It made him laugh aloud. *I'm already dead! This must be... heaven?* Perhaps. Or, he thought with a tinge of terror — *hell*. Or, he thought, with slightly less terror — *purgatory*.

Decent theories. But in addition to having no memory of dying, paired with a full memory of everything leading up to this point, and the fact he was exhausted and in the same physical pain he'd been before didn't jive well with the already dead theory. Neither did the fact that he smelled terrible.

Mark realized if he was here, Luke could be nearby; possibly even within earshot, so he called out to his lost brother from different parts of the room. He knocked on the walls, to no avail. Then he approached the window he still had not drawn the black and white Venetian blinds from and threw them open. Behind the curtains was a large window that spanned the length of one of the walls, beyond which was ocean. The B in B-4 stood for basement. He was indeed underwater.

In another context, this might be an exciting feature — like a novelty in a Dubai hotel — but to Mark it only had the effect of making him feel more trapped. He continued calling out for Luke, in tones of increasing desperation and elevating volume... still to no avail. He finally gave up and slumped to the floor, prostrate and dripping with tears. He wanted to sleep, but the stench from his own body wouldn't allow it.

He helped himself to the much-needed hot shower in a generously-sized walk-in shower with black and white tiles stationed beside a separate stand-alone bathtub — true to theme, black with a white faucet. He tested the water on his left pinky toe for a full minute, just to confirm it wasn't acidic or poisonous.

It was neither. The flowing water made Mark realized how incredibly thirsty he was. He darted for the sink and gulped the stream of water from the faucet — too much too fast — causing him to cough droplets all over the pristine mirror containing his filthy, bloodied and bruised reflection.

He went into the shower, sat on the floor, and stared at the water flowing down the drain, adding to the stream tears of both sorrow and gratitude. Once he had finally purged the emotional overwhelm, he proceeded to cleanse with a black bar of charcoal soap, gently lather a creamy white shampoo into his hair, and carry on with the most appreciated shower of his life. Eventually his thoughts faded and emotions dulled to the point he found himself deliriously humming "Hakuna Matata".

Mark exited the steamy bathroom in a black robe with a white belt and found a dresser filled with fine clothes, just his size, to include nightwear — black satin pajama pants and a white shirt of the same material. Finding them not to his tastes, he opted instead for black boxer shorts and a plain white V-neck T-shirt of exceptionally soft cotton.

Mark laid on the yin-yang bed slowly, half expecting it to be booby trapped. Nope. Just the most comfortable bed he'd ever laid on. Mark propped his head up on the white pillow and stared at the ceiling, which had a layer that encased gelatinous blobs of white goo, floating in a transparent liquid against a black ceiling— one giant lava lamp that spanned the whole room. He stared at it for only five blinks before falling into a deep and sudden sleep.

That night, Mark was bombarded by a vast collage of dreams — a storm of the unconscious mind of a sleep deprived, manic, recently concussed brain. He slept a full 12 hours and woke up from the surreal dreams in the sleep realm to the even more surreal dream that had become of his waking life.

Mark slid the soft, warm, weighted blanket aside, and rose to his feet, suddenly aware of an array of minor injuries his adrenaline had hitherto denied pain the freedom to announce.

On his way to the toilet, he noticed a black envelope, perched on a stand on the bathroom counter; an envelope with one word on it, written in elaborate calligraphy, in a shiny white ink: Mark.

———

MARK STARED AT THE DEEP BLACK, GLOSSY ENVELOPE ON THE BATHROOM counter, racking his frazzled mind for a recollection of whether he might have overlooked its presence the evening prior. He was almost certain he had looked at that part of the counter, and even laid a towel in the precise spot it now sat, perched on what appeared to be a letter holder.

Something about the thought of someone coming in while he was asleep bothered him tremendously. As a child, Mark had once called the police on Christmas Eve because there arose such a clatter he hopped out the bed to see what was the matter, remembered all the talk about an obese intruder giving gifts, and didn't trust the mother fucker.

Even then, Mark was wary of conspiracies… and Santa Claus is one of the greatest conspiracies. Mark didn't like having the wool pulled over his eyes — even if there were presents under it. He hated being lied to more than just about anything, and much of his depression came from an unending awareness he was living in a world infested with lies of all shapes, sizes and implications and everyone seemed to be fine with it. To others, Mark was crazy.

To Mark, the world was. But alas, he had no room to complain. He was a prisoner in this place. And like many a fresh prisoner, he had designs on escape… even if it was from the nicest room he had ever stayed in.

He finally worked up the gaul to open the letter. He grabbed it swiftly and assertively, as if to telegraph he wasn't afraid of any hidden cameras he suspected might be present, and opened it. He looked at the paper, which was blank black, until it wasn't. The words appeared as he read…

MARK,

·  ·  ·

While admittedly not under ideal circumstances, I hope you enjoy your stay on the island.

I leave you in good hands and look forward to meeting next year.

Make yourself at home in the meantime.

Sincerely,

The Man

---

Beside the signature was a sketch of a pyramid with an eye in the center and the words FATI CREDERE.

It was a lot to process.

Mark had plenty of time to process.

Frank had always possese[d]
Since early childhood he had [?]
what was beneath him, i[n] [?]
given moment, and too it [?]
possible to do so. At a [?]
old people don't like dig[ging]
the ones to prematurely end
They were very sensitive a[bout]
want anyone moving it. Th[?]
the dirt and they did not
to be a shared belief am[ong]
that no one is allowed to d[?]
Frank disobeyed.

## 21

FRANK HAD ALWAYS POSSESSED a strong desire to dig. Since early childhood, he'd thought it only natural to wonder what was beneath him in any given place; and felt it only natural to want to find out. So he dug holes. Lots of them. In doing so, Frank also learned at a young age that old people didn't like digging. Because they would always prematurely end his exploratory excavations and close his dig sites.

They were very sensitive about "their land," and didn't want anyone moving it. They didn't know what was under the dirt and did not want to find out. There seemed to be a shared belief amongst the grown up class that no one is allowed to dig here… here being anywhere.

Frank disobeyed.

Frank dug where he pleased, opting always to ask forgiveness instead of permission. He had followed his inexplicable passion for unearthing relics of the past from roaming forests, trusting his general intuition to just start digging in some spot — happening on the odd arrowhead or fossilized trilobite — to formally studying ancient history and archeology in college.

He had intentions to learn all he could in the halls and journals of academia but always found himself utterly underwhelmed by the lack of imagination and open-mindedness of the so-called "experts" in the field, who seemed far more interested in defending their vague explanations of everything in history being a chronologically convenient ascent of humanity from simple minded hunter gatherers to modern man than they were in entertaining new theories and making discoveries.

The prevailing orthodoxy seemed to maintain that history was a story that gets increasingly boring the further you look back, and that we'd already figured out everything worth looking into. Better now for the field to churn out a steady stream of adherents who could join the chorus of boring and defend the sacred consensus that told a linear story about organisms that randomly emerged from a primordial goo, randomly developed brains and bodies somehow imbued with conscious awareness, and arose from the oceans, gradually evolving into ape-like creatures who somehow came up with technologies and languages and started forming societies that warred with one another over superstitious beliefs and control over resources until unguided evolution produced logical, rational beings, from whom we all descend.

*Random? All of it? Really?*

Frank felt there to be something very off about the story. He didn't like how so many interesting possibilities were dismissed out of hand as foolish mythology; claims like people who came down from heaven once shaped the fate of humanity, ruling over our ancestors, teaching them how to survive and thrive... a remarkably common claim by cultures everywhere. Frank also found it very peculiar so many cultures depicted giants in their histories, both as friends and foes. He felt it odd they all happened to tell stories of a great flood and claimed to have received help from revered beings from the skies and/or seas to rebuild in the aftermath.

Frank's penchant for the exploration of the work of historical apostates like Erich von Däniken, Graham Hancock, and Randall Carlson and his choices to cite the writings of he and his fringe contemporaries in his research projects earned Frank some bad grades he didn't deserve. Despite knowing what his professors expected and required him to parrot back to them to pass their classes, Frank couldn't help but push back at every turn.

When he started arguing some kind of grand conspiracy was at play, keeping the true history of modern man buried and the focus of the field off uncovering anything new, his grades got worse. It became clear to him that if he jumped through all the hoops to earn his PhD as intended, he would be asking the adults for permission to dig for the rest of his life; and he knew they'd always say no because he couldn't provide enough evidence he would find anything.

Frank's approach was to simply dig until he found something, somewhere he suspected there to be something... and if he didn't, to either keep digging until he did or start over somewhere else. He was all about finding buried treasures; not confirming boring historical narratives. The final straw that ended his academic pursuits was his fascination with the fact people had been finding giant bones, right in his home country of America, for centuries; and these stories had gone unshared.

His professors uniformly dismissed the topic, often with scorn... even when he included in his research photographs from old newspapers not retrievable online — painstakingly discovered after countless hours in many different towns and cities, looking through library microfilm archives of local papers — of what were clearly giant human-like skeletons, along with huge objects proportional to their size. To Frank's great dismay and surprise, without exception, rather than providing enthusiastic support and suggesting a path forward to pursue related research, his professors snarkily wrote off his findings as clear hoaxes. Not only did they not believe him or give the evidence he'd meticulously accrued anything close to due consideration, they had no interest in even debating the matter. Worse still, they all dismissed him with a seemingly uniform tone of intellectual superiority, often laced with condescending chuckles — as if he was a cute child proposing the Easter Bunny was real.

In his frustration, Frank went so far as to go to the Smithsonian museum and make an unannounced visit to the head curator's office to directly request he be shown giant skeletons that had appeared in that very museum years ago before being quickly removed and never shown to the public again for no apparent reason. He knew the skeletons existed because he had read articles about and seen photos of the exhibit. Photos and articles before the era of photoshopping and special effects. Stuff that would be damn hard to fake.

He also continually came across reports in which people who came forward with the giant skeleton discoveries claimed government agents either arrived to confiscate the bones and relics, or people claiming to be from museums like the Smithsonian acquired them under the pretenses they would be put on display. But they rarely were. The artifacts and "officials" alike then just disappeared without a trace.

Who do you complain to about something like that? Who would even believe you? The Smithsonian curator not only bade Frank leave without answering his questions or granting his request, he contacted the dean of his university to complain. Following the episode, Frank was promptly dismissed from the program, marking the end of his formal academic studies and the start of his renegade endeavors.

The episode came as a shock, but it only served to enhance Frank's suspicion there was some conspiracy going on to keep those particular discoveries hush hush, and to make it a toxic subject for serious academics to pursue. Armed now with a sense of burning indignation for red tape and cover-ups, Frank decided that no matter the cost, he would pursue the discoveries he felt destined to make and share the truths he found with the world.

He had his four word creed — *Find truth. Share it.* — tattooed on his chest, using the Latin word for truth: VERITAS, with the *find* and *truth* encircling it in English. Thus, Frank became, in effect, a renegade archaeologist. At present, he was putting the final touches on his most daring artifact heist yet.

He was going to secretly excavate what he was nearly certain to be a structure, if not city, once inhabited by giants... at a mysterious site just outside of the city of St. Louis called the Cahokia Mounds.

The Cahokia Mounds are comprised of millions of pounds of dirt and said to have been created by Native Americans, anywhere from 500 B.C. to 1,650 A.D. It's surmised the uncredited creators built the structures manually, using simple handheld baskets to carry the dirt. A tremendous undertaking! While Frank did not take issue with the possibility such a project could have been accomplished by such primitive methods, the bigger question than the *how* was the *why*.

Why the hell would so many people work so damn hard for so damn long just to make a big mound? Was it just to build some simple little structures on? Could it be someone ordered them to? Or was it to bury something they were afraid of? Perhaps something they wanted to hide from future generations... and if so, what could they fear so much it would be worth all that hard work to cover it with dirt?

The existing clues were sparse but one uncovered artifact put Frank's curiosity into overdrive — the *Bird Man Tablet* — a stone tablet uncovered at the site depicting a being with the head of a man, wings of a bird, and diagonal lines crisscrossing on the back of the tablet, like a reptile's skin. What could be gleaned from the puzzling object? The only proposed explanation Frank could find was that it was symbolic of the sky world, our world, and the underworld; he certainly considered this an interesting possibility that if correct shed light on the beliefs of ancient Native American people. But Frank was a first-principles thinker and if it is to be believed baskets were the height of these people's technological advancement, perhaps a more literal interpretation should in the least also be considered.

Whoever created the tablet was obviously making a correlation between reptiles and flying people. *But why? Was it just art? A work of the imagination?* Perhaps. *But what if they were commemorating literal interactions with people who could fly like birds with reptilian features? Or even people who had beaks and wings as well? Why rule those possibilities out and jump straight to metaphorical interpretations? If we really evolved from primitive mammals, why couldn't other species also possess levels of intelligence on par and in excess of our own? Does all intelligent life in the universe mirror us exactly? Or might there be some variation worth taking into consideration?*

*Could Cahokia be another ancient monolithic site of unknown purpose and origin that was intentionally buried, ala Göbekli Tepe, in modern day Turkey?* It too had been found beneath what turned out to be an artificially constructed mound, long mistaken for a natural hill. The literal meaning of the phrase Göbekli Tepe itself is "potbelly hill," or "hill with a navel". The latter translation intrigued Frank as it could imply a point of connection with that which created life, as in the case with the umbilical cord that extends from the navel.

Göbekli Tepe is a site that even mainstream archaeologists and historians were finally conceding served as undeniable proof intelligent civilizations date back about a dozen thousand years. That's over twice as old as had been taught by the field for many decades!

But it didn't surprise Frank. Because Frank had good reason to believe history featuring intelligent human beings like us went back way further than that. A substantial amount of artifacts have been found, in several locations, deep in the ground, that were carbon dated as far back as hundreds of thousands of years.

Sometimes "the experts" are wrong. In truth, most are clueless. They just memorized stories they repeat unless and until incontrovertible proof finally puts their long-preached theories to rest. Overnight, one guy like Frank could flip the whole discipline on its head with the right discovery. He longed for that day and believed himself fated to reach it.

For some reason, Frank was convinced the Cahokia Mounds off the Missouri River, which provided a nice view of the St. Louis Gateway Arch — one of the seven modern architectural marvels of the world, had another Göbekli Tepe underneath it, hiding in plain sight... a forgotten chapter in human history. Frank knew he'd never get permission to attempt a dig, most predictably on grounds that it's a sacred site to Native Americans.

The conquering of the Native Americans amounted to one of the largest recorded genocides of all time — some 110 million people having perished through disease and in the many forgotten wars waged on them by European settlers and their descendants. They didn't get much sympathy for a long time, but when it came to defiling land they no longer inhabited hundreds of years later, potentially offending the sensibilities of some of their remaining ancestors — few if any of whom would even notice or care — that comparatively laughable offense constituted moral outrage. Something about it seemed disingenuous to Frank.

It didn't make sense why those mounds were there. It didn't make sense no one had since bothered to check and see what's under them. And it didn't make sense that just beside them was a celestial calendar built to track the solstices — this one out of large trees curated into a perfect circle, with another tree right in the middle. It was the same kind of "calendar" found at megalithic sites worldwide, such as Stonehenge and Adam's Calendar in South Africa.

The mystery bothered Frank so much he concocted a most daring plan to lay his undying curiosity to rest.

4.21.2022

...nched down on the roof of a
...He was promptly greeted
...e woman named ~~Tiffany-Rife~~ who info-
...r the man by subtly revealing to Mr.
...— the all too familiar mark of the man, on
...which she showed him with the same degree of
...have her wrist. The sight aroused and
...now smiled with ever increasing
...in terms of height, and large
...everything) but her attire was
...the line between
...r. She had black
...leaving
...n small

## 22

THE HELICOPTER CARRYING Mr. Chen touched down on the roof of a skyscraper in the heart of Guangzhou — a historically significant city on the Southeastern coast of the Chinese mainland, with a population close to 15 million.

He was promptly greeted by an attractive Chinese woman named Ting Ting, who informed him he had a new assistant named Ting Ting. She hinted that she worked for The Man by subtly revealing to Mr. Chen a tattoo of the all too familiar mark of The Man — the eye in the pyramid — on her left breast; her areola the iris and nipple the pupil. She flashed her breast like a badge then dropped it back in the hardworking bra. Mr. Chen understood the implication and became observably aroused, which Ting Ting pretended not to notice.

Ting Ting was short in terms of height, and large in terms of bust. She wore tight everything, but her attire was still professional— carefully tight-roping the line between successful corporate executive and porn star. She kept her silky black hair in a tidy ponytail, leaving her beautiful round face in full view. Her porcelain skin was flawlessly smooth and her eyes were unusually large — as if the eyes of a Persian princess had found their way onto a Chinese princess.

She blinked slowly — a subtle extra pause when her eyes closed — as if even her automatic movements were somehow deliberately seductive. The same applied to the way she breathed. Everything about her demeanor was purely feminine; save for her walk, which was deliberate and fast — the walk of a perpetually busy lady; though thoroughly measured and in no way frantic.

Ting Ting ushered Mr. Chen into the building and onto another elevator, not mincing words. Mr. Chen hadn't a clue where he was going or why. His faith was fully placed in the hands of The Man, and he was just along for the ride — exactly as The Man liked it.

Mr. Chen's smile returned as he saw Ting Ting open the back door of a high end Mercedes Benz — black with matching rims and a burgundy interior he sunk into, promptly affixing his seatbelt, then questioning that choice as he noticed Ting Ting hadn't done the same. He wanted to take it off to impress her with his courage but didn't want her to know that was his intent. Mr. Chen had a longstanding tendency to alter his behavior constantly in an unending attempt to appeal to everyone. This habit of his — to constantly try to appear as others expected him to be, and to obsess over whether he was getting it right — is yet another talent The Man saw in Mr. Chen, as what he had in mind for the naïve, unassuming man would require he remain pliable and able to appear in an ideal way to whoever he would later need to convince to go along with his recommendations and suggestions, which would gradually become orders and commands as he rose through the ranks.

His first raise in the ranks, Ting Ting informed him, over tea in the Mandarin Oriental Hotel lobby, was to Deputy Minister of Virus Control for the Sichuan Province — a territory covering several major cities and home to hundreds of millions of people. She informed Mr. Chen he could expect further instructions periodically, advised him to go with the flow, and asked if he had any questions. He did, but chose not to voice them.

She gave him a room key, said she would be in the room to his left if he needed anything, and would reconvene with him the following morning, at a time of his choosing. Mr. Chen, though a huge fan of being told exactly what to do, appreciated the flexibility. Being allowed to decide when to show up to something is a power he had never experienced. To be waited on. *Wow!* He liked the feeling. He liked it a lot; though it also still gave him a minor sense of anxiety, knowing he would need to make a decision in the morning.

The hotel room was a suite, and five-star quality, but still a big step down from his lodgings at The Man's island. This gave Mr. Chen yet another impetus for a smile, because it meant one of the best hotel rooms at one of the best hotels was a roadside motel compared to the luxuries he was privy to on the lowdown.

This sense of appreciation for his new elite status — the contentment he felt knowing he had access to places and people 99.999%+ of people never would, no matter how successful they became — was intoxicating to a man of such humble origins and low expectations. No one Mr. Chen had ever met could claim anything like he could; and for some reason, knowing no one else got to have what he had, or do what he did, was more exciting than the experiences themselves.

Mr. Chen, like countless others, lived for many years unnoticed, uncelebrated, and unappreciated. He was left no choice but to watch in bitter silent envy as others got it all in front of him. This made Mr. Chen a quietly angry and sad man, despite his genial outward demeanor.

Sometimes, late at night, consumed with dissatisfaction and jealousy, Mr. Chen would wish he could know what it would be like to have it all... to be a real winner... to be the one everyone else looked at and thought... *He's so damn lucky. I wish I could be him for a day.* In short, he wanted to know what it would be like to be The Man.

Mr. Chen never shared these thoughts and feelings — these desires and ambitions — to anyone. He never spoke a word of discontent with who he was and what he had — or, more accurately — who he wasn't, and what he didn't have. But before meeting The Man, sometimes he thought to himself, in the privacy of his lame room, on his shitty, hard, old mattress, and worn thin sheets, hardened by his lonely midnight messes, that he would give anything to know what that would be like... it's something he wanted so badly he'd trade his soul for it.

Thus The Man had first become aware of Mr. Chen.

---

FRANK'S ASSETS WERE WELL SPREAD ACROSS THE BOARD. FROM TRADITIONAL bank and credit union accounts in his home country of the United States, to off-shore stock brokerage accounts, to crypto exchanges and wallets, to precious metals buried in the woods, to money orders, envelopes of cash in several currencies, and billfolds inside suit pockets with slender stacks of hundred dollar bills.

He'd never been able to pin down a clear net worth, given the ever-changing values and difficulties associated with logging into accounts, which he would never do on his personal computers, and only with a reliable VPN; preferably running a military grade TOR browser that served as the strongest protection, but at the price of tormentingly low speeds and constant trouble establishing a connection — something also often an issue in his personal life.

But at present, his net worth ranged between $200,000 and $300,000. This so, he had plenty of money to survive — especially off the grid in a foreign country in South America or Southeast Asia, where between digs, while waiting for the heat to cool down, he would take jobs teaching English under an assumed identity. This, in addition to providing cover and survivable, untraceable income, also afforded him consistent opportunity to expand his linguistic repertoire, which currently included fluency in Spanish, Italian, and French, along with passable Mandarin, Vietnamese, Portuguese, and limited Arabic and Farsi.

He avoided using translation apps entirely to evade generating evidence that could one day be used to catch or convict him for his many victimless crimes. He'd never stolen so much as a candy bar, though he had come close as a young boy on at least two occasions — both involving a good deal of peer pressure and strong hunger for sweets — but he had in the eyes of certain self-proclaimed "authorities" stolen millions of dollars worth of artifacts from long dead, and until then, completely forgotten people.

His personal ethical code exonerated him from the crime of theft when the "victims" had been dead for at least 500 years; and while he did respect the stated authority of governments, he limited their valid jurisdictional claims to the surface of the planet. Anything below that they had taken no interest in before, and would have taken no interest in unless someone crept in and found it... not so much.

That someone would be him, and he was never surprised by a government that would find out someone had made a discovery under their soil and express interest in learning and discovering more. But they inevitably also expressed outrage, referring to his discoveries as "sovereign historical property theft", and they sought payouts and the forced surrender of whatever he found — which they rarely even knew how to describe, much less assign a value to.

Frank had lost count of how many governments, historical societies and interest groups had opened some form of case or lawsuit or investigation against him. But so meticulous was he in covering his tracks, and so lucky was he with each close call, and so discerning was he with each interaction with locals and cash-in-hand dealings with tour guides and local descendants of ancient cultures (who often lived at odds with their present governments and held far more legitimate claims to the finds than them) that he had never once been caught; nor had he ever been betrayed by a contact... not that he left them much to go off of in the way of tracking him down later anyway... often no more than an encrypted email address he would only check a few times a year, with the proper security protocols followed to a T.

Frank's discoveries too were spread out across the globe, finding their largest caches in crates left in old cargo vans in long-term parking lots or behind never visited buildings in neglected cities and in shipping containers with well soldered steel doors. Still other stashes rested under blankets in the basements of billionaires' second or third mansions. The true goal wasn't to acquire the physical relics so much as to upload pictures of them to his website — *franksfinds.com* — which was freely accessible worldwide. The sale of the artifacts were simply a means to fund the next expedition toward the ultimate aim of accruing a vast library of thoroughly-documented historical finds for all to see, thereby amending the history books without needing to join any stuffy academic clubs or have a certificate or two that said he was smart enough to be taken seriously.

Frank's latest customer had been referred to him by an existing client — a billionaire who swam in elite circles. This mysterious buyer was interested in having a first look at any new discoveries, most specifically OOPAarts, which stood for *Out of Place Artifacts* — objects deemed too advanced to be found where they were according to established historical theory. The collector expressed a keen interest in anything having to do with giants — especially ones with elongated skulls. Frank trusted the aspiring buyer's legitimacy, both because of the quality of the initial referrer and the immense knowledge the gentleman demonstrated concerning ancient civilizations — including a refreshing lack of guarded language in referring to historical theories at odds with mainstream orthodoxy.

His first purchase had been a Mayan calendar made of solid gold, about the size of a large dinner plate. No more than 24 hours after Frank confirmed he had the relic in hand and was willing to sell it, he'd opened his hotel room door to find a duffel bag filled with $100,000 in cash and a handwritten note in beautiful calligraphy that read, "Consider this a downpayment. Request delivery in person where we can discuss our next project. Please email me to confirm a time and receive coordinates. I look forward to funding your next giant discovery." The letter was signed only with a simple drawing of a pyramid with an eye in the center, reminiscent of that found on the $1 bill.

Frank recognized the handwriting because the buyer's correspondence was done by way of a digital photo of a developed film photo of a hand-written letter — a clever though arduous way to obscure his messages from digital traceability. The method provided protection against intelligence agency bots running through all the text of everyone's emails, flagging keywords and phrases of their choosing, and tagging hidden lines of code to every digital photo sent or accessible through the various cloud backup services, using AI tech developed and implemented directly through the tech giants producing all the devices and digital infrastructure for global commu-nication.

The incident startled Frank because it meant whoever this buyer was, he knew who he was, and he knew where he was. He'd not actually finalized the deal, but the "downpayment" was double the price he himself had suggested. More troublesome still, the wording "giant discovery" seemed a coded allusion to Frank's next project, through which he anticipated he would unearth proof of the existence of giants. It was a project he hadn't said anything about in their correspondence.

Intrigued as Frank was, it all seemed too convenient. He smelled a possible trap and resolved to keep the money somewhere safe, take extra precautions, and avoid further correspondence with the menacing buyer until he figured out how to proceed.

# 23

HUMANS ARE capable of altering their perceived sense of reality in several ways, some of which include the cultivation of medications. As the word itself implies, the task for the medication is to make it so it is *me* who *dictates* how I feel. There exist better alternatives to pharmaceutical solutions for many, if not most, of the ailments they currently address, but those have of yet not been made available to the masses. And Mark, like many of the 70% of Americans reliant on daily pharmaceutical remedies, depended dearly on his medications to make it from each sunrise to sunset.

Obtaining the pills for his ills required a tedious series of steps, none of which could be carried out from captivity on an island. Mark had brought at least two weeks worth of his prescribed medications — antidepressants, mood stabilizers, anti-anxiety pills, sleep aids, and amphetamines prescribed for ADD — each had a specific job to do to keep Mark mentally and emotionally fit enough to make it through each day.

Each was also dependency-inducing or habit-forming, or, candidly put: addictive. With the exception of the anti-anxiety pill — a little blue guy who could sedate his fear away, nudging him quickly to sleep — Mark had taken each practically every day, for the past dozen years. In addition to the strife the whole being imprisoned on a mysterious island owned by a supernaturally inclined sex and death cult leader obsessed with global domination posed, which was considerable, Mark too had to contend with the woes of quitting a barrage of sanity candy cold turkey.

He had kept his pills in a heavy duty ziplock bag in the front pocket of his camera bag and hadn't thought to take them out before stashing it in the tree. Surely the pills for the footage would be a reasonable trade from his captor's perspective, but it would come at the price of sacrificing the whole goal of the ambitious mission, surrendering his only leverage.

In walked two sunglassed troopers, holding futuristic rifles, followed by the face of the voice he had heard the day before, commanding he be taken to B-4. It was an alarmingly beautiful face with a set of warm brown eyes and free-flowing black hair — the sort to be found on a Japanese, Chinese, or Korean girl. But the face was not Asian, for her eyes were big and round, set behind a sharp nose that connected to lively lips perched into a mischievous, knowing charismatic grin... the kind that says, *I have you. And I know it. And I like it.*

But what the voice through the grin said was, "Hi Mark!"

Her grin opened into a smile to reveal glistening white teeth and prominent dimples, the sight of which sent a jolt of warm excitement through Mark's veins, making his leg tremble. It was the most entrancing smile he'd ever seen, bar none.

"I'm Hope."

She continued walking to Mark as if they were old friends, invading his personal space without protest from the bewildered man reduced to a boy with an instant crush, as she moved in for a tight, warm embrace that felt like a cloud of affection that lingered far longer than most hugs that don't culminate in kisses.

Mark found himself most pleasantly paralyzed in her grasp and did nothing to protest. This hug felt to Mark like the home he never knew he didn't have. And he much preferred it to anything he could remember feeling for a long time.

Hope's scent was unplaceable but perfectly intoxicating. Since she seemed to be in no rush to put the prolonged greeting to an end, and Mark had nothing to lose by reciprocating, he wrapped his arms around hers and gently ran his hands along her upper back, which was exposed, to his surprise and excitement, save for her long flowing, silky, soft hair.

The guards moved in, perceiving it a potentially hostile maneuver, causing Mark to let go and pull back. She looked over her naked shoulder to the men and laughed.

"Please, guys, Mark's not going to hurt me!"

She transitioned the hug into a single arm around his shoulder, resting her bare left underarm on Mark's slumped right shoulder. He felt from it a radiating warmth that turned him on almost as much as her soft hand, running surreptitiously through his messy hair.

He felt her fingernails dig playfully into the back of his neck, and another jolt of energy ascended his spine to meet the sensation at the top of his backbone and base of his skull, where the pads of her fingertips now gently massaged his head — casually — like she'd done it a hundred times.

She had. Just not with him.

"Isn't that right, Mark?" she asked, playfully, turning to Mark, in kissing range, throwing him a soft wink that — considering the seductive allure of those eyes and their sparkle — melted his heart.

"No. No. I'm absolutely not… going to hurt her."

He looked at the guards, who were standing down, then back at her; she was smiling even brighter and pushed into his formerly personal space even further… looking at him coyly.

"Not going to—" he took a deep breath and stammered on, absolutely mesmerized, "—hurt her. We… we're cool. It's… it's all good."

Hope turned her attention back to the guards.

Mark instantly missed it.

"Leave us," she commanded.

They obeyed. The door locked with another pronounced CLACK. With that, she took her perfectly manicured hands off him and walked cross the room, her red bottom shoes making a sound much like the door lock as she strode spryly toward a sunken level of the room that contained couches and chairs, each black and white, tying in seamlessly to the room's theme. He watched her calf muscles flex as she descended five carpeted steps down into the living room area, where she playfully fell onto the couch, causing her perky breasts to bounce and tumble about without the limitations of a bra beneath her top — red, silky, and thin enough for her hardened nipples to be slightly visible through the cascading fabric.

She turned on the couch, into a perch on her bare smooth legs, and slipped off her shoes, dropping them to the floor nonchalantly. She slid herself elegantly to the center of the couch, then pat the now available space to her very immediate left.

espective ( ) ies with
spon... up global Comm
Mr... who clocked in
been ... med of the gov
of ... rre Sacrifici
L... ell timed bulle
(ra... dy moved w
and ... ce, Mr. Ch...
some... off the E
he ... a more fo...
... er. But it
... een. Black

## 24

THE PYRAMIDAL CRAFT Luke had seen taking off from the volcano was the evacuation of The Man and his VIP guests. They'd swiftly absconded through a portal behind the owl statue to the temple, boarded the ship and departed. The Man apologized for the unforeseen interruption and deployed each of his newly drafted disciples to their respective countries.

Few words were spoken on the global commute... fewest of all by Mr. Chen, who clocked in at exactly zero. He was never informed of The Governor's assassination or the bizarre sacrificial ritual he had been excused from. After a few hours in the craft, Mr. Chen was deposited on another island, somewhere off the East Coast of China, from which he boarded a more familiar form of transportation — a helicopter.

But it was unlike any helicopter he'd ever seen. Black, unmarked, and combat ready — judging by the array of missiles tucked discreetly beneath the cockpit, and the slightly less discreet gatling gun protruding from the front, like a phallus of destruction.

It was very quiet for a helicopter, but very loud compared to The Man's spaceship. Mr. Chen began laughing under the noise cover. He had ridden on a spaceship. That happened. He had been anointed a future viceroy of his nation. That happened. He stopped laughing as he contemplated what hadn't happened — copulation. He now found himself regretting his abstinence, as he returned to the "real world" where he had no expectation similar opportunities would await.

His expanding mind bounced from thought to thought — from sexual to social fantasy — a vision of himself basking in the uproarious applause of crowds as far as the eye could see, all gathered to see him. *Mr. Chen! Mr.*

*Chen! Mr. Chen!* Never before had he dared imagine mass adulation, or the feeling of completion he expected it would afford.

Mr. Chen enjoyed his two hour helicopter commute, exploring the corridors of imagined possibility for the first time available to him. Something about the unceasing sound of the rotary blades chopping the air relentlessly put him in a higher state of mind where new and original thoughts seemed to manifest.

What he was experiencing was the same thing people often do when driving alone, radio blaring, windows down, blazing down the highway... or in the shower... the constant cover of sound and presence of vibrations putting the experiencer in a protective bubble where no one is listening, no one is watching, and no one is judging. It was an experience Mr. Chen had never had.

He did not own a car, so he had never known the simple pleasure of singing "Sweet Child of Mine" or "Bohemian Rhapsody" uninhibited, speeding down an open freeway. And while he did of course have plenty of hours logged in the shower, being so closely surrounded by neighbors, and always conscious of the thin walls, he always settled for half-assed renditions of his favorite tunes, if not just hums. Where he was from, alone was not a thing. Feeling alone was a constant. But actually being away from everyone physically is something Mr. Chen had never experienced.

His was a culture where privacy was not a right or expectation. It was a collective-minded culture, where people closely shared space. Such were the reasons Mr. Chen derived so much pleasure from the privacy afforded to him in the sky with no one to see him be himself so brashly.

He began to sing "Sweet Child of Mine" in his head and was tempted to vocalize it while the sound shield kept it safe enough to do so, but held off, just in case the pilots could hear him through their headsets. That would be embarrassing. He would lose face.

Then, on the horizon, Mr. Chen saw the lights of an unknown city... and was struck with a very unusual thought...

*One day, this will all be mine.* Stranger still, he meant it.

04262022

Mr. Chen awoke the next morning at dawn, then went back to sleep and awoke at 8:00, then went back to sleep and awoke at 10:24. He underwent his usual morning ritual, then changed into the same clothes he had been wearing the day prior, not having packed for the unexpected journey, nor having had time to take any of his newly provided clothes before evacuating the island the day prior. When he opened his hotel door, he was surprised to see Ting-Ting, his newly provided reminder/assistant, already standing right there, holding a bag from supermarket. He wondered how long she had so patiently been waiting outside his door, like a cute but formidable dog, then why she hadn't set the bag down if she had been waiting, then heard her answer his next question, which would have been "what's in the bag?"

New clothes for you, mr. Chen. She handed him the bag with a polite bow of the head, which he took back into the room and excitedly changed into - growing even more excited when he noticed the extravagant price tags - easily two months wages based on his old job's salary, which was frankly. He wondered what the new salary would be, then for the first time in or entity,

## 25

MR. CHEN AWOKE that next morning at dawn, then went back to sleep and awoke again at 8:00, then went back to sleep and awoke at 10:24. He underwent his usual morning ritual, then changed into the same clothes he had been wearing the day prior, not having packed for the unexpected journey, nor having had time to take any of his newly provided clothes before evacuating the island.

When he opened his hotel door, he was surprised to see Ting Ting already standing there, holding a bag from Emporio Armani. He wondered how long she had so patiently been waiting outside his door, like a cute but formidable dog, then why she hadn't set the bag down if she had been waiting, and then he heard her answer his next question, which would have been: *What's in the bag?*

"New clothes for you, Mr. Chen."

She offered him the bag with a polite bow. He took it back into the room and eagerly unpacked the contents. It was a full outfit — suit, shirt, pants, underwear, socks, a belt, and shoes. He felt the smooth fabrics, admired the lovely colors, and rejoiced in the fact that this is how he got to dress from now on.

He felt a joyous tingle as he gazed at the still affixed price tags and considered how few people could ever afford such exorbitant and luxurious garb. Exclusivity, for Mr. Chen, bred feelings of superiority that fed his steadily growing ego, despite his still monumental insecurities.

He wondered what his new salary would be as Deputy Minister of Virus Control for the Sichuan Province, then, and for the first time, wondered what he might do for his mother with the extra funds surely coming his way.

Perhaps a new apartment. Some new clothes. A bigger TV. Definitely a new bed.

Mr. Chen examined the black dress shirt's buttons, which were sewn snugly with generous amounts of fine thread — buttons that wouldn't ever pop off, as they tended to do with his peasant clothes of the past. He looked like a million bucks, or roughly 6.5 million Chinese Yuan.

He admired his reflection in the large, un-cracked mirror — a first for Mr. Chen. He was feeling better about himself and his life than ever before. After dressing, he returned to the hallway housing the ever-patient Ting Ting, who greeted him with another polite bow, asking if he was ready to start the day. He responded with a grin and nod and they were on their way.

Ting Ting went over the day's itinerary, which mandated a brunch with some associates of The Man, then a dinner meeting with his soon to be superiors (and later to be subordinates). The rest of the day could be spent however Mr. Chen deemed fit. Ting Ting explained he could now travel anywhere… anytime, as long as it was first class. Per The Man's orders, Mr. Chen would always receive the highest possible luxury accommodations; cost was irrelevant.

Ting Ting held the door open for Mr. Chen on the way out of the hotel, and back to the black Mercedes, which sparkled subtly, like Ting Ting's eyes. Each favor she did for him came with another respectful bow, and each bow made Mr. Chen stand up a little straighter and puff his chest out a little more. His transition into his intended persona was well in effect.

The brunch was held at a 5-star restaurant on the top floor of a particularly striking skyscraper overlooking a sea of buildings as far as the eye could see through the hazy horizon. The guests were two executives from a major pharmaceutical company based in the United States that was looking to extend its global operations into the closely guarded, highly coveted, notoriously exclusionary Chinese market.

---

NOTE: THE NAME OF THE PHARMACEUTICAL COMPANY WHOSE REPRESENTATIVES Mr. Chen had dealings with will be kept out of the story, as it is an entity sufficiently powerful to prevent the publication of this book. Their profits sprung from the suffering of the Covid-19 and ensuing Covid-20 virus like a geyser, so from this point on, the unnamed corporation will be referred to as Geyser Pharmaceuticals (not to be confused with another six-letter company it may or may not rhyme with).

---

THE TWO GEYSER EXECUTIVES WERE EXTREMELY POLISHED. NOT A HAIR OUT OF place. Not a cent spared on their impeccable professional attire. Not a misspoken word, though Mr. Chen wouldn't have noticed if there had been, as he didn't speak English. The role of translator was played by one of the executives, who was from America but of Chinese descent, and spoke nearly perfect Mandarin.

Mr. Chen had only met a few white people over the years, spoken to none of them, and never heard one speak more than a mistake-ridden sentence or two in his native tongue, so he found the sight entertaining and endearing. The Geyser executives spoke with clarity and certainty about the unfortunate inevitability of more variations of "the virus", and the sad inevitability that the world was in for more pandemics. They paused after each sentence, leaving time for translation. Mr. Chen astutely detected a beguiling glimmer in their eyes as they spoke on the upcoming storm, and a subdued pretense of a grin.

The unfortunate inevitability was really a welcome expectation from a business standpoint. This made sense, as they went on to articulate in increasingly hushed tones, that their company had been leading the charge in developing, proactively, an array of new vaccines for exactly such potential threats. They had done so by means of a controversial and technically, under American policy, legally forbidden form of novel virus production referred to as "gain of function research".

The term was a misnomer. Who would oppose gaining functions? A lot of people, if they understood it meant reengineering harmless animal viruses so they become contagious to humans, able to kill us and capable of causing pandemics. The deceptive term had only entered the public lexicon thanks to outspoken American politicians like Rand Paul, who ranted and raved about the fact the United States government had been indirectly funding the forbidden research through something called the Eco Health Alliance, in partnership with the Chinese government.

Such funding had been used toward the purpose of manufacturing novel corona viruses in the now infamous Wuhan Institute of Virology, widely suspected to be the point of origin of the pandemic, though the public narrative parroted by Chinese and American propaganda outlets remained that it came not from the lab making the same exact kind of viruses, but from bats sold in the wet market nearby.

The Geyser executives informed Mr. Chen they no longer use the term "gain of function" to describe their research. The methods — creating viruses then figuring out how to stop them in case they happen to organically arise down the line — had been rebranded "creative protection" research. Public relations studies had indicated the largely unaware public was more in favor of the terminology, with focus groups rating "creative protection" research as more than twice as acceptable as "gain of function".

The name change also helped alleviate potential future legal ramifications. It was the equivalent of renaming blackmail as "leveraged persuasion". Same shit, repackaged to mislead. When it comes to controlling a planet where free will is a thing, words matter.

The third executive was introduced as a representative of the American government there on "unofficial business". His function was to ensure Mr. Chen that regardless of what he might come to hear in the international media — even if being said by duly elected public officials — what they were doing was perfectly legal. He advised that anti-science types and competing firms sought to muddy the waters and give the impression the American government would not permit the continuation of the same research falsely attributed to the creation of the Covid-19 virus.

Mr. Chen scowled at hearing this, correctly assuming he was being lied to. This not lost on the executive, he leaned in and, as if revealing a secret, explained that he had worked many government jobs over the years, while also working for many corporations, and that he understood how it really worked.

The so called government of the so called United States was not really in control. Unlike in China, the separation between private industry and public oversight was an illusion. In America, the elected officials themselves knew they were not really in control; they were more accurately understood to be customer service representatives for the top 1% — the financial elite that truly ruled the country.

Ting Ting translated this to Mr. Chen as…

"America's government crazy. The government just customer service for rich people."

Mr. Chen remembered The Man using the same terminology and considered it further evidence this guy was an ally to be trusted. The customers were the people. The politicians were intermediaries, relating the concerns of the customers to their donor overlords and helping the latter smoothly enact their agenda with minimal resistance from the former. The public was allowed to retain a mirage of democracy. But it was bullshit. And everyone in D.C. knew it… if not before arriving, soon after. He went on to say…

"Despite all the talk of democracy, rights, etcetera, those in power recognize the necessity for there to remain a stable, permanent, long-term minded central government to ensure the safety, peace, and prosperity of the people… a government not vulnerable to the easy sway-able whims of the ignorant underclass, which of course greatly outnumber the ruling class."

Ting Ting translated this to Mr. Chen as…

"America's government trying to be same as China."

"I come to you as a reliable liaison between the Chinese Central Government and the real American government — which exists beyond the scope of the United States alone. We are controlled by what is in effect an international government made of powerful families, institutions, and individuals from many countries. You see, Mr. Chen, I'm not here to tell you I speak for the people elected by the American people. I'm here to tell you those people aren't who you're really dealing with. They're powerless puppets with our hands up their asses."

Though he did not fully follow, Mr. Chen laughed gratuitously at the remark. To clear up any potential confusion, Ting Ting leaned in and whispered…

"They work for The Man too. Make viruses. Sell vaccines."

"The world is in for a storm, Mr. Chen. And it's essential your government maintain strong ties with the true government. I urge you to simply avoid directly engaging any publicly elected or officially appointed Americans falsely claiming power as we endure this common crisis. Ignore what they say on TV. Don't take their calls. Don't respond to their public statements. Understand they are just playing a role to keep the people who voted for them happy and ready to vote for them again.

"Unfortunately, you can expect to hear increasingly hostile rhetoric from politicians looking to make China out to be the big bad guy across the lake. They may criticize you. They may blame you — for the virus; or your extreme policies in response to the virus, but rest assured — the real government of the West wants to, and will, come to resemble your form of government more and more. It just takes time.

"We too monitor all of our citizens. We too control what information is allowed in and censor what circulates. We too swiftly silence dissenters and enforce necessary restrictions to ensure the public safety. We just can't do so as swiftly and decisively as you can here because we must respect the formalities of our chaotic political process, as well as ease the public into accepting a future that's very different than the past.

"But rest assured, Mr. Chen, we expect to successfully enforce enhanced measures of control during the next pandemic. And we expect to see increased compliance with vaccine mandates worldwide."

The first executive cut in…

"Mr. Chen, I'd like to just be direct and now articulate exactly what it is we want from you. First, we want to ensure that if and when the time comes to produce, sell and distribute billions of doses of our new vaccines, that China can and will without issue accommodate the orders in terms of manufacturing and shipping, regardless of international affairs. Even in the face of… war."

Mr. Chen nodded in a way that conveyed that sounded reasonable.

"The point is, you will receive credit for finding the vaccine we invented. You will profit from the manufacture and sale of the vaccines we require back West, and you will be given the means to replicate our patented vaccines to ensure the health and safety of the great people of China."

Mr. Chen stared at the men stoically because he was trying to understand. Instead, they interpreted this to mean he was nonplussed by the proposition, so after an uncomfortable silence and another discreet and quick nonverbal conference between the Western executives, he sweetened the deal:

"What if we credited you as the man who discovered the vaccine?"

Mr. Chen was suddenly struck by the gravity of the scenario to come. He would be the hero who found the vaccine to the next virus. He would be the one responsible for saving both China and the rest of the world.

His eyes opened wide as he looked out the window, imagining the adulation, seeing his face on TV and on magazine covers and newspapers worldwide. The executives misinterpreted his daydreaming to indicate he still was not sufficiently pleased to accept the offer.

"Of course, we would need to transfer the patent to a company you own, then buy it back when the time comes. We would be willing to pay, say a hundred million dollars for the privilege. To you. Personally."

Mr. Chen smiled and nodded in approval.

"After all, this path would ensure the prompt and willing adoption of the vaccine here in China... suspicious as some in your government are of Western pharmaceutical companies. As for the West, well, we're used to everything being made in China anyway, so it should be an easy sell. Perhaps we can frame it as a team effort."

To that, Mr. Chen held up his mimosa for a toast.

The executives rightly considered that to be an indication he had accepted their offer.

## 26

RANDY IS the type of guy who's only thinking of one thing: and it starts with Randy, and it ends with Randy. Randy is a man who had many problems, if you asked Randy.

If you asked Sheila, in confidence and without fear of reprisal and ample assurances no one was secretly recording, she would tell you Randy's only problem was being born so rich he knew nothing of the plight of everyday life. How could he? He'd spent his early decades going from one fancy building to another — everything always prepared by someone else.

School had been a breeze. He went to private schools in different countries that prepared him for admission into ivy league prep schools that deposited him snugly in his ivy league college where he cheated and partied and skated by, checking the boxes necessary to acquire his prestigious unearned credentials.

Work too was never a concern. He received an annual annuity payment in the amount of $500,000, which was a pathetically low sum to Randy, who hailed from a prominent American family with major interests in global chemical companies and explosives manufacturing... a family that goes back hundreds of years, and you might say: *That name sounds familiar. Where have I heard it before?*

Families like Randy's are few and far between. Easily in the top 1%, based on their known legitimate holdings of stock ownership alone. He was from a family where there were a lot of cousins marrying cousins. It got a little weird. It got a little awkward. But it was always of supreme importance to Randy's parents that he "consider the bloodline" in making his choice of who to marry, which, at the moment, was a tossup between Sheila and his own cousin... unbeknownst to Sheila.

Had Sheila known Randy didn't love her, because he was a psychopath incapable of love, she would have understood why he did not show her any affection — verbally or physically — unless it was either a public display of affection in front of flashing cameras or lackluster romantic foreplay. The entire foundation of their relationship up until recently had been novelty and excitement. Exotic vacations at the world's finest resorts, parties and raves fueled by enjoyment enhancing drugs, and a thorough exploration of her bisexuality with hedonistic club girls... with Randy then, and only then, fully appreciating and paying attention to her.

Sheila had met Randy in a box suite at a professional football game, back when she was a cheerleader for the New England Patriots. It was common practice for the cheerleaders to visit the VIP spectators in their private alcoves during and after the games, to take pictures and be objectified in the tradition of a stripper, but without the tips and touching... save of course for the occasional hand slipping casually to the small of the bare back and beyond if they didn't politely and discretely move forward a step to convey to the opportunistic high roller she wasn't "that kind of girl".

This cheerleader was not "that kind of girl", but she was the kind of girl who considered becoming that kind of girl because since her breasts came in at 16, men had always given her the kind of devious glances that said things like, *I'd throw away my marriage for a night with you.* Sheila was a natural beauty who made up for the dearth of love shown to her by her loser father — who was always too busy drinking, gambling and philandering to take interest in her life — via exhibitionism.

Her father's apparent indifference had predisposed her to a certain vulnerability readily seized upon by the type of men who picked up on it, and since she was 17, she'd found herself in scandalous relationships with older, more mature men, starting with her high school principal — whose wife never found out, despite a few very close calls, which Sheila would be ashamed to admit, she found very exciting.

Strapped for cash in college, she'd taken a job at a restaurant called Twin Peaks, which was a play on words, alluding to the breasts of the sexy girls in tight tank tops who served patrons beers and chicken wings and let them ogle them in exchange for tips. Something about it felt shameful to a certain extent, especially when the patrons got a little too drunk and started trying to get her phone number or to convince her to go out later... offers she (almost) always turned down. But it was fun. And the money was good. So she did it.

She eventually began modeling. A short career emerged organically, after she started posting fun, sexy pictures of herself on Instagram and playful Tic Toks in which she happened to be scantily clad. She knew at any given moment there were arenas worth of men jerking off to her; a fact she found at once despicable and flattering. In any case, it seemed like harmless fun, the attention was extremely validating, and it only grew by the day — to the point she had literally millions of followers and hundreds of thousands of fans bombarding her with an endless cavalcade of likes and posting mostly flattering comments on each and every post.

She started getting modeling job offers from people through her social media apps. They were usually unpaid, and often pornographically suggestive. Everything from calendars to lingerie and swimwear to artful nudes to photography school projects came her way on a regular basis. Once in a while she would get a legitimate enough offer from a photographer with enough pre-existing work to prove he wasn't just another opportunistic creep with a not-so-well hidden agenda and she'd consent.

The photo shoots were fun, and gave her some extra spending money, along with an increasingly large catalogue of work that in turn drew in more offers. She was eventually making more from the social media payouts and freelance modeling than she was at Twin Peaks, so she quit the job, and eventually college too, and began calling herself a professional model with decreasing levels of embarrassment and increasing levels of confidence.

Sheila elegantly toed the line between confidence and arrogance, paying little mind to the compliment avalanches and inevitable digs from jealous girls and mean spirited guys who would deal with their own envy and frustration with a comment about her boobs being fake (which they weren't) or her nose being crooked (which it wasn't… well, just barely) or whatever other creative demeaning jab they could come up with. She came to accept that she was professionally desirable, and choosing to be looked at in lieu of working a real job, like ugly and average looking people had to, naturally drew envy and ire.

Sheila had other skills and talents, of course, but they were largely unexplored and fully overshadowed by her looks. The big blonde hair and dark blue eyes. The perfect tan. The ideal everything, to the point no one ever found her unattractive, even if they tried. Her personality too was generally upbeat and playful, if not downright flirtatious. Most of the men that could have loved her properly were too intimidated to even talk to her or cutely pathetic when they tried.

Sheila found herself readily asked for the time by nervous men, for directions by people who damn well didn't need them, and where she bought that shirt or necklace by interested ladies. She was attracted to men who could approach her calmly and confidently and feign just enough disinterest to challenge her, concealing just enough about themselves to maintain an aura of mystery. But even so, she typically just enjoyed the attention and sport of flirting, rarely taking them up on their date invitations, which always came, sooner or later.

Sheila had found Randy alluring because he was classically handsome, tall, a sharp dresser, and he treated her like a normal person... which bothered her, because she wasn't. Obviously. His apparent indifference to her looks made her feel a strong unconscious desire to earn his attention... insecurities no doubt inspired by her indifferent father.

The way he chatted with her while focusing on his phone, grinning as if whoever he was texting was more important than her, even though she was leaving any minute and this was his only shot at a real NFL cheerleader, drove her crazy. Such was the scenario upon their first meeting at the football game in the private box.

These unusual feelings of self-doubt Randy was giving her bothered Sheila so much that she was relieved when, just as she was leaving, Randy casually mentioned they were going out for drinks after the game and she could drop in if she felt like it... still focused on his phone as he made the emotionless take it or leave it offer. She said "yeah, maybe"... then, in an upbeat tone, offered him her number, which he promptly punched into his contacts while saying, "cool," and dismissing her with "take it easy," not even bothering to watch her strut out.

And so Sheila waited for a text or a call as she got ready to go out that evening, and was disappointed when the new suitor never reached out with a time or place, and bewildered as to why he hadn't given her his number back when she had so generously proffered her own coveted digits. That had never happened to Sheila.

---

NINE DAYS LATER, SHEILA GOT A TEXT FROM RANDY APOLOGIZING FOR forgetting and telling her she could "tag along to a gala" that night.

As the date ensued, Randy continued to treat her like someone he wanted nothing from and was used to being around; like a little sister... and his focus was always on the people he kept running into, who all seemed to be very rich; a theory confirmed when a charity auction ensued, following the three course dinner and tiramisu.

Two and a half million dollars was raised for some charity that night, with Randy buying his mother a painting for $16,000 and Sheila a fine necklace of pearls and sapphires for $3,500. It was a gift far too extravagant for a first date, but Randy bought it for her as if insisting on paying for the movie tickets. It was no big deal to him. Just like her. And all of it was a big deal to her, especially the not being a big deal to him part.

That's why Sheila was so thrilled when he ended their first date with a passionate kiss, most unexpectedly, before casually departing without looking back... even though she was half ready to invite him in! She slept alone, wearing the extravagant new necklace that meant so much to her and so little to Randy, and suddenly felt very lonely. She thought about what his bed must be like and how lame hers would have been to him.

Sheila wondered if maybe she wasn't enough for a man like Randy. And she felt a burning sudden jealousy when she went on his Instagram to find some very recent posts of him at the gala with various people, none of whom were her and some of whom were other women... women clearly less beautiful than her, but what if, Sheila began to worry, for the first time in a long time, she wasn't so beautiful anymore... or not attractive enough to Randy specifically... or worse still, he was embarrassed, rather than proud, to be seen with her in public given her boring backstory, perhaps shameful profession and lackluster lineage.

She found herself further enraged when Randy continued to post pictures of himself at a high end downtown night club, surrounded by yet more "friends"... some of them actually pretty hot! Questions raced...

*Why didn't he invite me? Is he dancing with those bitches right now? Is he taking some club slut to bed?! Instead of me?! WTF. Ugh!*

Sheila knew she had no claim to Randy, and knew he hadn't actually done anything wrong. He'd been a perfect gentleman, taking her on a fairy tale first date. He'd even bought her the nicest gift anyone had ever given her... and the money had gone to charity, meaning because of her, someone was being helped.

Sheila went to bed with a pouty face that night and had a dream she was a child again, looking up at her father standing above her with her hands wrapped around his legs, which felt sturdy as tree trunks. He was talking to Randy in the dream, deep in some engaging conversation.

Sheila tugged on her dad's jeans to get his attention, but he ignored her. She tried again, with both hands, but it only made him kick her away. Randy, also towering above, looked down with a look that said *pathetic*. Then he and her father turned their backs to her.

She woke up to a text from Randy: *had fun. brunch?* She went to brunch with Randy that day, and over the course of the next six months, had gone out with him, on average, once a week. He rarely spoke of work but never seemed to be doing nothing. Sheila appreciated the time Randy gave her, and the sex turned out to be good... though increasingly kinky, in ways she found both sadly degrading and oddly arousing.

Foreplay consisted of him shoving his cock down her throat and gagging her with it until her eyes watered, at which point he'd take it out; not because he thought she'd had enough, but because the tears messed up her makeup. After fucking her face until she nearly passed out, he would order her to lick his ass until he was hard enough to fuck his little slut. He would always spank, slap, and choke her while in the act, and he spit in her mouth far more than he kissed it.

He expected her to give him head on command — like while he was driving a golf cart, or in fancy restaurants with long tablecloths. He pressured her into trying new things like anal, and letting him finish on her face... she even let him piss on her once, but found the act so humiliating she asked him to never do it again. They settled on an agreement he would only be entitled to anal access and piss privileges on his birthday.

Randy was rough. But Sheila still felt safe. And for as harsh as it all sounds, the sexual deviance actually made her feel special. Because she was the only one he ever explored this dark side of himself with; because he loved and trusted her in a way he never had anyone else. That's what he told her at least. She tried to believe it, but on some level she knew he was lying. The only question was to what extent.

For fear of losing him, she never tried too hard to find out. For his part, he went out of his way to keep her comfortably in the dark, constantly and convincingly assuring Sheila she was his one and only with grand romantic gestures made possible by unlimited funding: like having her name written in the sky with a heart around it with a plane on her birthday, or having the flower store deliver her all the flowers in the store to apologize after an argument... the type of gestures that would make any girly girl like Sheila blush for days.

All the while, he was doing everything he did with Sheila with other women every chance he got. And he got a lot of chances. The truth was, Randy enjoyed deceiving his gullible girlfriends as much as he did fucking them, and his myriad indiscretions with innumerable partners lead him to pass on to his loyal girlfriend a number of infections.

Evil as he was, he gaslit her into believing she had always had the STDs from all the men she'd been with before him, and that she must have passed it on to him! There were only five other men before Randy. But he was able to convince her that was a despicably high number, and her lack of control had made them both sick.

He would later brag about the episode to his equally psychopathic trust fund baby friends, adding that his "body count" was more than the Spartans had to work with. In the event they didn't catch on, he'd ask them what that movie about the Spartans starring Gerard Butler was. And if they still didn't get it he'd say...

"I've crushed upwards of 300 pussies. And counting."

Randy was, objectively speaking, a very bad guy.

But to Sheila, he was a complex, classy, mysterious powerful man who brought excitement, fun and prestige into her life. She tried to appreciate it for whatever it was. But something about it all had started to feel contrived. She felt a lot of things for and because of Randy, but love was not one of them. And so it was with both great pain and great relief that she responded to his sudden "we need to talk" that ended in a breakup… which happened while she was wiping cum of her face with a Starbucks napkin in his Lamborghini.

A month later, Sheila received an invitation to Randy's wedding to his cousin. The sick fuck was marrying his own cousin… who wasn't even remotely attractive. In his shitty handwriting it read…

*would be hot 2 fuck @ my wedding ;)*

The note made Sheila gag, as Randy always had.

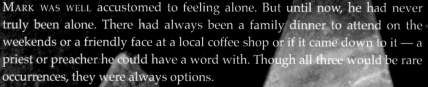

## 27

MARK WAS WELL accustomed to feeling alone. But until now, he had never truly been alone. There had always been a family dinner to attend on the weekends or a friendly face at a local coffee shop or if it came down to it — a priest or preacher he could have a word with. Though all three would be rare occurrences, they were always options.

Now, after over four and a half months in luxurious captivity, in the underwater basement of The Man's island mansion, his only interaction with anyone had been his encounter with the vivacious and mysteriously intentioned raven-haired beauty, Hope.

Strangely, she had in no way treated him like the prisoner he was; rather, she had embraced him — both figuratively and literally — as if he were a long lost friend… or even a boyfriend, back from a long voyage. Had their encounter occurred a week or so later, Mark would have likely convinced himself he'd imagined the entire affair and dismissed it as either a vivid dream or startlingly realistic delusion, byproduct perhaps of his withdrawal symptoms for having abruptly gone off all his medications — something that had gotten him briefly committed to a mental institution the last time he tried it.

The first two months had been hell for Mark; the unavoidable effects of both his bipolar disorder running rampant without the nullifying effects of his resented yet required pharmaceuticals, and of course the added stressors of his given situation — which seemed bleaker and more hopeless with each passing day. He spent most of the typical day and night in bed — exhausted and buried under a black and white blanket of sadness, impressing himself with how many tears he was capable of producing.

At times, he would snap into fits of rage he had nowhere to direct but at himself, which had resulted in his damaging the only clearly breakable thing there — the bathroom mirror, which he'd fractured with a single punch of his sullen reflection; but the mirror returned the favor, giving him a hairline fracture on a hand bone, a week of profuse swelling, and a permanent reminder of the incident in the form of a substantial discomfort when he clenched his hand into a fist.

The destruction of his mirror had been his only achievement in that period, and being trapped in the prison of his mind in the solitary confinement of the prison of his room had been enough to lead him to the brink of suicide. He awoke the afternoon after his lost fight with the mirror sufficiently motivated to give it a shot, using a mirror shard to slit his wrists; but to his added dismay, when he went into the bathroom to find his makeshift instrument of death, he was met by nothing but his own reflection; unbroken; the mirror somehow having been replaced in his sleep. If not for the proof offered by the lasting pain in his broken hand, he would have thought that too to have been a product of a dark and unconstrained imagination leading him into the depths of insanity.

One day, he awoke to a knock at the door, which, while a normal knock by all standards, reverberated as loudly as a gunshot to the man who hadn't heard a single sound he didn't himself make in over a third of a year. He heard her voice — the voice of the siren…

"Mark? Baby? Can I come in?"

Mark jumped out of his bed in a panic, quickly opting to make a run to the bathroom to fix his hair and rinse his face of the residual tears of his latest crying spell. Finally, as she knocked again, Mark granted her the permission they both knew she didn't need, in a long unused voice that cracked, most embarrassingly.

"Come in!"

She entered, spry as ever, with the same pep in her step. A trooper mindlessly followed her into the room, rifle slung over his back, hands full of a large stack of big, hardcover books — aged and on the verge of tatters. She told him to put the books on the table. He obliged, passing Mark casually, secondarily vulnerable to a sneak attack as he bent over to place the pile of literature on the oversized marble yin-yang table.

Mark balked at the unexpected opportunity, lamenting Luke not being there to wrestle away the gun and lead an escape. Mark was not a man prone to violence, save for the occasional self-inflicted. But even if he could somehow defeat the clearly stronger opponent, he couldn't even imagine pointing a gun at something as beautiful as Hope, who was approaching him for another long-craved hug.

This time, Mark was unrestrained in his requited affections, holding her tightly; so much so that he could feel her heart beating through her soft, warm chest. His heart slowed, in pace with hers, and she stroked his hair, as she had done before, spreading a wondrous tingling sensation through his head and down his spine, as their hearts came to beat in perfect harmony.

"There there, Mark—" Her whisper in his left ear spread goosebumps, which became electric when she granted him a few generous smooches on the cheek "—I missed you too, baby!"

She walked to the table, her high heals clacking with each step, and placed a well-manicured index finger on the top book.

"Figured you might be a little bored."

Mark tried to discreetly wipe away a tear of gratitude and overwhelm as he nodded yes, unsuccessfully, because Hope hurried back to him and wiped it away, kissing where it had fallen, then where it had not — directly on his lips.

The kiss proved as sensational as it was unexpected, and after a few seconds of passive acceptance in utter paralysis, he participated in the kiss with great intensity for several heavenly seconds, until she pulled away, putting her hands over her mouth in a show of embarrassment.

She looked at the trooper, who was watching apathetically.

"Leave us."

He obeyed, closing the door behind him, which locked with the pronounced CLACK sound.

"I'm so sorry, Mark. I don't know what came over me. I know, we hardly know each other. But I feel like I know you so well now."

She looked at his puzzled face bashfully.

"I confess, I'm a big fan."

"What?!" Mark asked, genuinely bewildered.

"Yeah—" She continued, walking around the room slowly, twirling her silky hair in a smooth swirl with her finger, "—I kinda stalked you after our date the other month—"

*That was a date?*

"I did a little snooping. Found your podcast. Your website. Read your blog. Everything I could find that you've made over the years. Just... amazing work, Mark. Wow. Frankly, I don't know how you're not famous. Your thoughts. Your ideas. The way you explain things. It's so... SO good, Mark. YOU are so good! I'm beyond impressed."

Mark stared suspiciously. He'd never told her his last name, but his gratitude exceeded his need for explanation.

"I just... I know it's probably totally inappropriate, in so many ways, but I took it all in while I was traveling and feel like I got to know you through it all. And I just have this feeling I get when I'm with you. I don't know what it is. I know it sounds silly, Mark, but I'm such a big fan of yours, and I—"

She covered her mouth, then assumed a more decisive stance, with a hand on her hip, like she was finally finding the courage to get something big off her chest, "—I have a crush on you."

She laughed and put a hand over her eyes, then smiled, crossed her legs, shook her head and sighed.

"Full disclosure Mark, I'm not supposed to be here. I'm just supposed to make sure you're fed, pretty much... until The Man returns to meet with you. I vouched for you. I told him you didn't shoot that governor guy. I told him everything you told me — that you don't know anything about it. And he trusts me. Before long it will be water under the bridge. He just has to meet you. He's a good judge of character."

That is what Mark had told her when she brought up the topic last time. She had done so in a kind of "oh, by the way, I'm supposed to ask you..." tone, and Mark suspected it was all part of some trick to get him to talk, so he had held his ground and confessed nothing of his brother or the footage. Surprisingly, she didn't press the topic beyond the single, polite inquiry, or even ask him to explain basic things like how he had gotten here or why he came, which Mark also found suspicious.

But he was relieved because he had no good cover story anyway. He still didn't. Everything he'd thought up so far was stupid, so he had decided, when pressed for more, he would simply claim he didn't know how he got there. He had amnesia — a bad cover story, but at least it didn't invite unanswerable questions.

Mark was not stupid. He knew this was all too convenient. And he didn't believe a girl like her would ever truly be into a powerless guy like him. But he was very lonely, and his basis for what could and couldn't be true had been so thoroughly turned on its head that if so many outlandish and terrifying things could turn out to be real, why couldn't this?

Regardless of the futility, that kiss felt realer to Mark than life had for a long time; so, he reasoned, even if she did have ulterior motives unconfessed, and even if she hadn't been genuine at the start, maybe, just maybe, she really was falling for him. Truth be told, he felt the same way about her. Maybe they'd look back on this as a crazy way they met and go on to to live happily ever after.

There was of course the added component of her claim The Man had taken her in as a helpless orphan, and she had grown up on the island, content and well cared for... but also lonely — her only company being The Man's occasional guests, who with limited exception had been rude, entitled and objectifying. She was sure to add that she was in no way a sex slave, escort or concubine... and that The Man was, despite his eccentricities and undisputed power, at heart a kind and gentle man who had never taken advantage of or mistreated her or made her do anything against her will.

She had even claimed he would let her move whenever she wanted if she chose, and while she did love to travel, this island was the only place that felt like home to her and she had everything she could ask for, so she chose to stay and remain in the general employ of The Man, who asked little of her, and found value in keeping a trusted cohort to help manage the epic estate. Occasionally, she'd said, people try to assassinate or kidnap The Man, which he'd assumed Mark had come to do; hence the reason for his captivity. She was confident he'd let him go as soon as he realized that wasn't the case.

It was a story Mark was skeptical of and at once desperate to believe. And so, taking all that into account, Mark chose to let himself put some hope in Hope, and to appreciate the power and joy and excitement that Hope had to offer. After all, a lonely hell was his only apparent alternative. At least Hope gave him something to look forward to, and now too, something to read to give him a vacation from his hated self.

The projects of Mark's she'd referred to, which she claimed to have loved, were by all accounts little more than outlets for an overactive mind to find expression. While manic, he would be seized at times with a Caesarian sense of destiny for greatness and attribute great value to his work — believing he was on the cusp of becoming a voice that would be heard… that his musings and offerings to the world would one day suddenly be received by the masses with the kind of enthusiasm Hope had just expressed. Then he would snap out of it and remember he was just an eccentric, delusional, annoying loser.

Fantasies of fame and riches and influence resulting from his years of unpaid labors of love suddenly manifesting — the long awaited light at the end of the tunnel of the American Dream — where glory would rain upon him and everyone would finally recognize his value and it would all prove to have been worth it and it would feel like he was on easy street from there on out, still struck from time to time; they were intoxicating, inspiring and enabled tremendous creative output. But such fantasies left him feeling worse when they faded because of the vast chasm between his intoxicating expectations and the cold, harsh reality that he was a nobody… and the odds were well against that ever changing.

And so it was with great effort Mark avoided letting himself take Hope's compliments to heart. *She must just be there because she wants something,* he admitted to himself. What, he did not know. But it was the only realistic explanation. He possessed some bit of truth she needed to hear so she could go on with her life and forget about him again, just like the rest of the world surely had by now. That's why she was here. Once she had whatever she was truly after, she would disappear for good.

Whatever the true motive, and whatever price he ultimately paid for the encounters, the fact was Hope did offer him hope. And that hope was enough to not only get him out of his big empty, tear soaked bed... it was enough to make him literally jump out of it.

---

BEFORE EXCUSING HERSELF, IN ADDITION TO THE BOOKS, HOPE GAVE MARK GLASS jars filled with ink, a quill with a fountain pen style tip, and a large stack of parchment paper.

She said she was busy and on the go, but looked forward to reading anything he might want to write her. If he slid his work under the door, the servants would be sure to have it scanned and sent to her. Like this, he could keep busy while she traversed the globe working for The Man. It was a way to still spend time together, separated as they were by space and time.

She hadn't said so specifically, but Mark was left with the impression for some reason that if he wrote enough, and it was good enough, that would be the key that unlocked the door to the room... and the catalyst that unleashed the potential he and Hope had to experience an exciting, joyful, loving relationship. Mark wanted more than anything to be with someone like Hope, who elevated him to a higher state of being through her presence alone; someone who had the power to excavate from beneath his shell of calcified sadness the unexperienced capacity he had to love and be loved.

There lingered somewhere within this loser a king uncrowned. Well hidden, beneath all the neuroses and insecurities and shortcomings that had come to define him to the outside world was unlimited potential. He had no one to teach him how to access this hidden potential, rays of which shone through while he was in the act of creation. The thousands of pages of unread writings and hundreds of hours of amateur content that constituted his legacy were no more than random samplings of what he was capable of conjuring into being through applied thought alone. What could he do with Hope in his corner?

*Anything; Everything;* he thought, finally able to smile again.

What Mark felt he needed, in addition to his freedom, was someone to remind him of what he was capable of; someone to challenge him to rise to the occasion and apply his talents in some meaningful specific way that could have a lasting impact. He didn't know or even trust Hope, but he accurately assessed she possessed the rare ability to bring the best out of him... through the application of her attention alone. His desire to do whatever necessary to please and impress her knew no bounds, and he imagined himself capable of empowering her in some similar fashion... of contributing something to her growth and experience of life.

Then there remained the obvious possibility of starting a family — something he had also always wanted. His recent brushes with death and prolonged solitude had brought the subject to the fore. Mark suspected the responsibilities of being a husband and a father would prove another force multiplier, imbuing him with new energies, affording his life lasting clarity and direction.

No longer a young man, these thoughts of having a family seemed to be arriving of their own accord in recent years. Hope had to be of similar age. Was she not experiencing something similar? On an instinctive level, was there not a primal urge to find the right partner before the clock ran out? Had she already resolved to dedicate her remaining years of fertility working for The Man? Why? What fulfillment could be found in her work that could supersede the joys of romance, love, and motherhood?

Sure, Hope would always have options. Down to the last egg.

*But how many of those suitors would prove better than me?* Mark thought. *Is it all in the timing? What role does chance play? Fate? Destiny? Why do I feel so confident it could work? Why have I fallen so easily under Hope's spell? Is it just because I'm lonely? Is it mere coincidence she happened to show up when she did? Or could it be she was meant to?*

Mark had no good answers to any of these questions, nor would he ever find them. But his drive to discover the potential between them was more than sufficient to fill him with an energy that required some form of expression. Mark wanted desperately to impress Hope; to make it so spending time with him became a top priority rather than a passing fancy or work-related task.

Even if she was faking her affection for him, that could change. But the riddle of how to accomplish such a feat was a puzzle that to Mark seemed unsolvable. How could he impress such a well rounded, intelligent, beautiful woman? Or was it a futile endeavor not worth pursuing?

Mark had nothing to offer Hope that she did not already have. But she said she liked his writing. Perhaps that much was true. She would not be the first. And he now had paper. And ink. And a head full of thought, heart full of desire, and absolutely nothing to distract him.

And so it was that as soon as Hope left the room and the door locked behind her, punctuating her visit with that dreaded CLACK that Mark sat at the desk, picked up the quill, and dipped it in the ink. He had no idea what to write. But he was going to write. He was going to pour everything he had into whatever this was to become.

Mark was a genius. But like most geniuses, he'd never been made aware of this fact. He'd never before found himself under the conditions necessary to truly force that genius to the surface. He'd spent his whole life running from who he really was in order to adapt to a world that rewarded conformity and made no place for men like him — men blessed and cursed with such unusual minds.

The powers that be seemed intent on beating Mark's genius out of him. Through church and school and work he was expected to play a role that felt to him unnatural. He was fed medications designed to normalize his behavior to meet cultural expectations and convinced there was something wrong with him; that he was somehow defective.

Like most geniuses, his latent potential had long been sealed away in the vault of self-doubt and perceived limitations that kept his brilliance at bay, burning him from the inside out. This occasion marked the first time he truly had nothing left to lose and everything to gain. He did not know it, but these were precisely the type of conditions The Man sought to foster to push people to reach their full potential. It was the reason he wanted to inflict suffering.

The instant the first drop of ink soaked into that first piece of paper Mark decided he was going to devote the entirety of his focus and ability toward making something perfect. He was going to write as if it was the last thing he was ever going to create. Because it just might be.

There was no such thing as the past or future. There was only now. He knew on some primordial level that all he really needed was opportunity, desire, and a willingness to take action in the face of fear, doubt, and any other obstacle that might dare try to keep him from his goal of creating something worthy of Hope's attention. Something that would make him worthy of Hope. Something that would make him worthy of love.

Mark decided he was going to hunker down and by any means necessary call into being letter after letter, word after word, sentence after sentence, page after page, and chapter after chapter; and he wasn't going to stop until he died or birthed a fucking masterpiece. His intentions for doing so were pure and simple: impress a girl. Little did he know, this book forged in the infinite passions of his heart toward the end of capturing Hope's interest and gaining her favor would soon become one of the most valuable books on the planet.

Mark didn't know if he would ever make it off that lonely island. He had come to accept the very real possibility he would spend the rest of his life at the mercy of The Man. And he didn't know if it was even possible to write his way out of a prison or into Hope's heart.

But he was damn sure going to try.

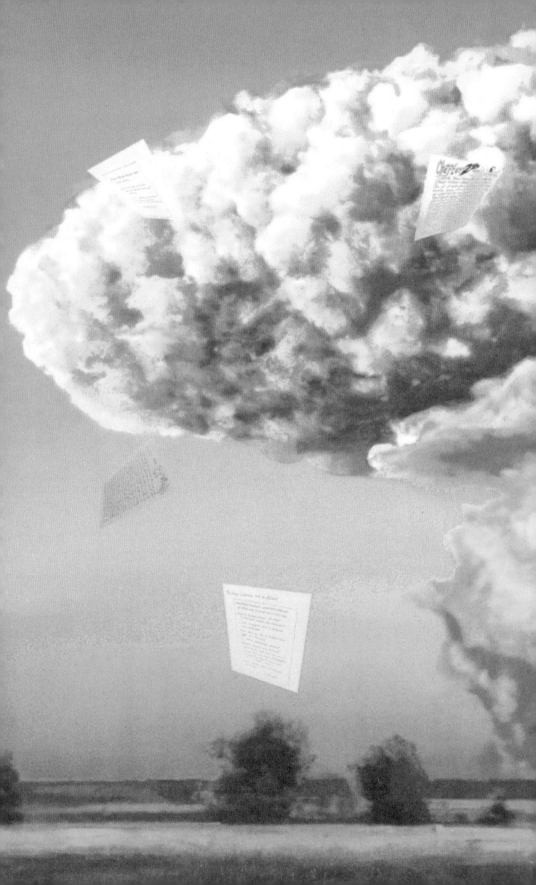

## CHAPTER 59

# 28

FRANK HAD JUST ARRIVED at the Georgia Guidestones — a site on a long list of places to visit. It's only natural for thousands of years of hazy, if not lost, history to shroud giant stone structures in intrigue; the peculiar thing about the Georgia Guidestones is they presented the same aura of mystery despite having only been built in 1980 (AD). That mystique endured until they were destroyed in 2022 (AD).

Many questions remain unanswered.

The Georgia Guidestones was a monument comprised of four 16 foot high solid granite stones with a capstone resting on the top. The massive slabs were precisely constructed and arranged to track astrological and solar cycles, just like so many ancient examples, to include, among many others — Stonehenge and the tree iteration beside the Cahokia Mounds outside St. Louis. The Georgia Guidestones were nearly twice as tall as the far better known Stonehenge and weighed almost a quarter-million pounds in total.

Inscribed on the stones are ten guiding principles, much like the 10 commandments of Judaeo Christian tradition. But the contents of the advice is rather different.

The Georgia Guidestones read as follows...


MAINTAIN HUMANITY UNDER 500,000,000
    IN PERPETUAL BALANCE WITH NATURE


GUIDE REPRODUCTION WISELY —

IMPROVING FITNESS AND DIVERSITY

UNITE HUMANITY WITH A LIVING
   NEW LANGUAGE

RULE PASSION — FAITH — TRADITION
   AND ALL THINGS
   WITH TEMPERED REASON

PROTECT PEOPLE AND NATIONS
   WITH FAIR LAWS AND JUST COURTS

LET ALL NATIONS RULE INTERNALLY
   RESOLVING EXTERNAL DISPUTES
   IN A WORLD COURT

AVOID PETTY LAWS AND USELESS
   OFFICIALS

BALANCE PERSONAL RIGHTS WITH
   SOCIAL DUTIES

PRIZE TRUTH — BEAUTY — LOVE —
   SEEKING HARMONY WITH THE
   INFINITE

BE NOT A CANCER ON THE EARTH
   LEAVE ROOM FOR NATURE —
   LEAVE ROOM FOR NATURE

———

THE GUIDING STATEMENTS DO NOT SEEM TO BE AN ADAPTATION OF SOME religious text or philosophical discourse or legal tradition, but rather a unique and modern collection of advice... advice deemed important enough to not only preserve in stone for posterity but also to have translated into 12 different languages: English, Arabic, Chinese, Hebrew, Russian, Sanskrit, Spanish, Swahili, Classical Greek, Egyptian hieroglyphs, and Babylonian cuneiform — all ten being inscribed on the stones.

Frank found the last two choices very puzzling, as both are considered long-dead languages, and the oldest written languages, with the Babylonian cuneiform predating the Egyptian hieroglyphs. The goal of translating the message into so many languages seemed obvious enough. But why include languages we no longer speak? Why go through the immense work and pay the exorbitant expense required to translate into those languages and give them precious real estate on the stones?

A slab on the ground titled ASTRONOMICAL FEATURES gave explanation to the calendar function; it read: 1. CHANNEL THROUGH STONE INDICATES CELESTIAL POLE. 2. HORIZONTAL SLOT INDICATES ANNUAL TRAVEL OF SUN. 3. SUNBEAM THROUGH CAPSTONE MARKS NOONTIME THROUGHOUT THE YEAR.

Beneath that it reads: AUTHOR: R.C. CHRISTIAN (A PSEUDONYM).

Beneath that, it reads: TIME CAPSULE: PLACED SIX FEET BELOW THIS SPOT ON [empty space] TO BE OPENED ON [empty space].

Most presume the empty spaces imply no time capsule was ultimately buried. What is known about the origins of the monument is substantial, in terms of who literally built it. What is deliberately obscured is who R.C. Christian was. The man who initiated and funded the expensive one of a kind project went by that pseudonym in the few direct dealings he had with those involved.

It is known R.C. Christian insisted on both lifetime confidentiality agreements and commitments to destroy anything that could be traced back to him, and such conditions were met and honored.

Frank had his theories. He suspected the R.C. was a reference to the Rosecrutian Order, otherwise known as The Ancient and Mystical Order Rosæ Crucis — an ancient fraternal secret society Frank believed to be an offshoot of the Ancient Egyptian Mystery Schools, whose known notable alumni included such prominent fathers of Western philosophy and science as Pythagorus and Plato's ancestor Solon — who reported learning about the lost civilization of Atlantis from the Egyptian mystics.

The Rosecrutian Order tasked itself with preserving the so called *Mystery Teachings*, and very little is known about them to this day. They went to great lengths to conceal their identities and encode and disseminate their elusive wisdom in various ways. One surprisingly likely possibility is that the famed Sir Francis Bacon was among the most notable Rosecrutians, and the true mind behind the most famous writer of all time — Shakespeare, whom evidence suggests was just a frontman.

The wording of the first guiding principle, to cap the human population at half a billion, led many to conclude it was a proclamation of plans to massively depopulate the planet by nearly 95%. While that implication is a rational possibility, Frank was not in this camp. The year the monument was constructed — 1979-1980 — was the height of the cold war between the United States and Soviet Union. With the threat of nuclear war on the periphery, it was plausible a group might take it upon themselves to prepare the remnants of human society that might survive the man-made apocalypse some guidance that could lead to the eventual creation of a new global society that would avoid repeating the same mistakes of the past.

The monument was apparently left incomplete, with plans to extend its scope and contents being abandoned in 1980 and the time capsule instructions being left unfinished. If nothing was buried, a possible explanation might be the R.C. Christian group determined the prospect of a global catastrophe being imminent dissipated, and the gloomy and expensive undertaking was deemed no longer necessary.

Frank thought that unlikely. He estimated there must be some kind of coded message with an explanation and had a gut feeling someday something buried under this thing would be dug up.

*But what? And by who? And for what purpose?*

Frank had no intention of digging for a possible time capsule here, as it was not within the parameters of his own personal ethical system not to violate anything that hadn't been found for at least 500 years. This place was hardly past 50 years old. What Frank found valuable here was the line of thinking it sent him on... the question:

*If this is why someone would make a modern day stone monument with celestial calendar features — to equip future generations with knowledge that would endure an upcoming extinction event — might the builders of the past have done what they did for the same reason? Did they know something inevitable was coming? Were they evacuating? Dropping clues for anyone who might survive what was to come?*

It gave Frank a lot to consider, which is great, because Frank really came for another reason. He wanted to preemptively establish a provable alibi, should his now underway Cahokia Mounds project run into any snags. Frank asked a tourist to take a picture of him standing before the monument on his phone, generating pictorial proof of where he was that would be linked to the metadata from the phone — proving the time and date of his presence at a sight a two hour drive from Atlanta (a city that's name also suggests the existence of Atlantis, along with the ocean its state borders) — the closest airport with commercial flights to St. Louis, just miles from where his archaeological heist was officially underway.

From his various scouting expeditions, stakeouts and drone surveillance missions, he had determined the mounds were rarely busy and unguarded by anyone or anything but humble signs asking people to stay on the paths and avoid climbing the mounds. But the easygoing Midwest folks were unlikely to give a damn if someone did. The only real security to contend with, so far as Frank could gather, were local police and highway patrolmen... people not specifically tasked with protecting the mounds from trespassers, but who would have the authority to intervene if they happened upon something suspicious. They would also be the most likely to respond in the event some random person might call in to report someone disobeying the signs.

What would not go unnoticed, however, would be large quantities of dirt being removed from the site. Frank had explored several options and decided on a clever plan that would allow them to hide the dirt removed from the giant mounds on site, while being able to remove it in phases... the best of both worlds.

The plot was to erect, overnight, an inauspicious dumpster enclosure... like the sort you'd see behind a gas station or any number of commercial establishments; the type of sight so common no one would think twice about seeing it, and people who had seen the new structure appear, if they even noticed it at all, would just assume it was some low level city project. Frank's crew could then dig at night, under cover of darkness, when the site was closed and completely unpopulated.

They could load the dirt into the back of a pickup, drive the truck a few hundred yards to the fenced enclosure they built, where your standard dumpsters would quietly hold truck beds of dirt and well-compensated Mexican immigrants with shovels. When these were full, it would just be a matter of renting or otherwise obtaining a proper garbage truck to go to the site as needed, emptying the dumpsters and dumping the removed mound dirt somewhere in the woods.

It was a clean, simple operation. All he needed to really worry about is someone stumbling on the hole leading into the ground, which would be well into an already roped off and overgrown area. To counter that, he built a discreet hatch-style entrance to be covered by a blanket that matched the rest of the tarp covering the forbidden area.

He'd locked that up too, so if some other rule breaker stumbled on it, they'd be dissuaded from messing with it. He also thought to include the words "hydro-offset valve" so anyone who might step on it would get bored and assume it had something to do with the water supply.

It was a simple plan. It was a good plan.

the least of his concern
...not to mention...
...were with like...
Preparing himself for the excruciating pain &
torture he anticipated to be on the evening's
agenda, and tried to form a strategy to deter
as much as possible, while still appearing to
cooperate. He thought of all the times he had
wished to be dead; He remembered the
# of times he'd flirted with self-inflicted demise,
and began to focus on separating his doom in a
more positive light. As soon as that Some day he
could find himself relieved of the burden of living

**29**

WHILE THE LUNCH meeting with the pharmaceutical company executives had gone swimmingly, Mr. Chen's dinner meeting with the new boss was a different story.

The dinner began with Mr. Chen's characteristic early arrival, upon which he was guided up a staircase, down a hallway, and through a door manned by two government security guards, who politely greeted him and showed him to a room with a large circular table. They took he and Ting Ting's coats, hung them on a rack in the corner beside a window overlooking another hazy skyline, bid they wait there, then returned to their post at the door.

A waitress arrived with a fresh pot of green tea, pouring a cup for he and Ting Ting. On the ride over, Ting Ting had advised Mr. Chen to never say anything he wouldn't want everyone to know anywhere other than the locations she had arranged for him to be, like the cars she would summon or hotel rooms she booked, which she or someone else — an ally, as she referred to her unknown, unseen associates — had thoroughly swept for bugs. Anywhere else he went, she advised, he should assume there were always people monitoring and recording anything and everything he said or did.

Mr. Chen was now an important government official, and any concept of privacy he might have once enjoyed was now officially extinct. She told him especially anything he said into a phone not provided by her, or even around anyone's phone or computer, anywhere, would automatically be saved and would remain accessible to government officials and others for the rest of his life — to be used against him, sooner or later.

She said their government would certainly have access to all these recordings, and often too intelligence agencies of foreign powers, especially the

Americans, who had pioneered full spectrum global surveillance and tech-based subterfuge as national policy — practices that had been first frowned upon then replicated by other nations as a natural consequence, and were constantly being improved. Information, Ting Ting had expressed, is power. She assured him that so long as he never provided his unseen existing and future enemies anything that could be used against him, he would remain untouchable and maintain the full protection The Man's extensive network and clandestine alliances provided; but that if he slipped up, he could lose that protection and be left to face the consequences.

Such were the stakes, and he understood that, for the first time he was aware of, his extreme introversion could prove an asset. Mr. Chen was the type of person who wouldn't even say "hi" when a nod would do and would never utter a sentence without overthinking whether it was necessary and all the possible ways what he wanted to say could be misinterpreted or lead to some sort of unwanted confrontation. Such neuroses once made him an offputtingly shy man, considered by many to be unintelligent, lacking in confidence, or even mentally retarded.

Now the same predilections would start being interpreted as signs of sophistication and power. All Mr. Chen knew, and all he needed to know, was he was now a chess piece on The Man's global board, and like any good chess piece, his sole responsibility was to go where the hand guided it, in service to the king. His only job was to obey — something that came as natu-rally as breathing to Mr. Chen.

The meeting began 15 minutes later when his new temporary boss entered, followed by an assistant of his own and two other colleagues — all of whom shook hands with Mr. Chen and paid brief respects to Ting Ting before sitting down to fresh cups of steaming tea. The new boss' name was Jung Wen Fei, or Mr. Fei — an elderly statesman who was humble and reserved in demeanor and unconcerned with the vanities of appearance. His suit was old and worn, like his teeth, which were a light shade of yellow from too much tea and not enough toothpaste. His voice was a loud whisper that seemed to struggle to make its way through wheezes, product of his being a lifetime smoker.

Mr. Fei was frail by appearance, but his eyes burned with pronounced lucidity, and he commanded respect by way of reputation. He was a lifelong public servant who had loyally served with limited personal ambition and boasted a legacy of involvement in large scale public works projects, like roads and infrastructure generally. He was a well-oiled cog in the vast machine that had become of the Central Government, and had faithfully served his role with discipline, consistency and commitment — traits all admired by his compatriots, and deemed essential in this new global pre-occupation with the enduring war against "the virus".

Mr. Fei was not privy to anything he was better off not knowing concerning government culpability in the creation of the threats he was now tasked with combatting, but he remained wary of those who stood to benefit from the prevailing conditions — particularly those coming from the Western corporations, like Geyser Pharmaceuticals — whose greed had showed no bounds historically, and which he rightly considered a dangerous brand of bedfellow. All this was conveyed to Mr. Chen by Ting Ting on the ride over, along with general instructions to simply gain Mr. Fei's trust and favor while avoiding challenging or contradicting or triggering him in any way — a vague though palatable set of goals. Also of vital importance was that he not utter a word about that afternoon's meeting with the Geyser executives.

Mr. Fei spoke glowingly of the government's successful endurance in the face of the virus over the past few years. He lauded how across the land people had united to obey a quickly construed set of responsive measures to contain and control the spread, and claimed their decisive actions had spared countless lives. He spoke highly of the effectiveness of a well-directed Central Government and of the importance of maintaining a harmonious relationship between it and the myriad municipal and regional governments that would now report to Mr. Chen. He slurped up a hearty helping of noodles from a large bowl of soup and told anecdotes of how soups like these were all his family could afford his entire childhood, and though so many options were now on the table — he said, emphasizing the literal large selection of plates on the round table, which rotated constantly, allowing each participant to take what they pleased and add it to their personal plate — he still found the simple noodles to be the only food he needed or desired.

He seemed to exude a certain sense of pride in his own humility that bordered on vanity, a relatively common irony not lost on Mr. Chen who met each and every statement of opinion and fact and anecdote with a respectful and submissive nod of agreement, sigh in solidarity or generous laugh — whatever seemed most appropriate.

As the meal progressed, Mr. Fei maintained the spotlight, and true to his word, ate no more than the simple noodle soup, leading Mr. Chen to eat with restraint as well, taking only half the food he otherwise would have. Periodically, Mr. Fei would turn the floor over to his colleagues, who would delve into the numbers and data — the nuts and bolts — of how they measured and quantified their successes, and some of the means by which they intended to contain and even extinguish the remnants of the Covid-19 virus through avoiding the temptation to go back to business as usual. Mr. Chen liked and understood the data, still far more comfortable trafficking in numbers than words. It was clear by their analysis, paired with the affirmative demeanor of Mr. Fei, that their vision of the future necessitated sustained control over the population, with plans to enhance those means as necessity dictated in the years ahead; all contentions Mr. Chen took no issue with.

The dinner concluded with a series of toasts — to the Central Government, to Chairman Mao, to Secretary Xi Jinping, and to their new friend and colleague, Mr. Chen. Each toast was followed by a shot of Baiju — the ubiquitous rice based liquor that burns like gasoline, tastes vaguely of foul grape and black licorice, and lingers in the gut and throat, leaving a residual taste Mr. Chen — not a drinker — found putrid. But he didn't neglect his duty to fit in, so he drank each time... three shots of baijiu, then another two short glasses of light beer.

Though the dinner was through, and Mr. Chen had somehow skated by without saying a word, as Ting Ting had warned, this next bit was what the meeting was really about. She said a common tactic he was sure to encounter was the practice of pressuring new associates into drunkenness — a state from which they could more easily extract and assess his true motives, intentions, views, ambitions and personality — hidden typically under the veneer of his chosen face in sobriety.

Confronted now with the onset of this feared state of intoxication, Mr. Chen felt himself being overtaken by anxiety, a fact his body expressed with profuse sweating and an obvious reddening of the face, which Mr. Fei brought direct attention to.

"Your face is red as the flag, Mr. Chen. Are you feeling alright?"

Mr. Chen forced a smile that excreted a most embarrassing burp, which triggered a small rumble of laughter, led by Mr. Fei, who found the little man's antics most amusing. It reminded Mr. Fei of being with his nephew the first time he got drunk, and he voiced as much. As humiliating as waiting out their hazing was, Mr. Chen was grateful for it, as the bellicose laughter overtook the sound of a sharp fart he couldn't hold in. Mr. Chen felt his stomach churn and began breathing erratically. Mr. Fei turned away, allowing his new second in command to save face.

"Perhaps you need to use the restroom, Mr. Chen?"

Ting Ting came to Mr. Chen's aid, taking him by the arm and escorting the dizzy man-child down the hall and into a private bathroom; she locked the door behind them, led him to the sink, and turned on the water, just in time to cover the sound of Mr. Chen regurgitating a small river of alcohol, teeming with chunks of fish, miniature corn cobs and fragments of rice. Ting Ting watched patiently until the worst of it was over, then leaned against Mr. Chen, standing in solidarity with the ashamed and pathetic reflection in the mirror.

"When you go back out there, they are going to test you. They are going to decide if they like you. And if they trust you. If both don't happen, The

Man will be very disappointed. And it's very bad news for us. You need to succeed."

Mr. Chen's breath came fast and he felt the onset of a panic attack. He fell, catching himself on the sink, then stumbled to his feet, knocking over the trash can with his slipping foot, struggling to maintain balance in the fast spinning room.

Ting Ting gave Mr. Chen a moment to collect himself and cracked open the bathroom door. Down the hall, she could see Mr. Fei and his men all talking quietly, in a more serious, less jovial tone. One of them checked his watch and gazed at the bathroom. Ting Ting quickly shut the door, sighed, then approached Mr. Chen, who was now splashing water on the back of his neck with one hand while slapping himself in the face with the other — which didn't help the redness — while struggling to end a stubborn string of drool with a series of increasingly forceful spits. Ting Ting took a deep breath. She knew what to do.

"Relax and trust me, Mr. Chen. It will all be better when you wake up tomorrow. Just let go. Surrender to the experience."

Ting Ting dropped to a sturdy squat position with the precision of a heavy lifter then quickly and decisively unbuckled his belt and unzipped his pants. Before Mr. Chen could understand what was happening, he felt himself inside Ting Ting's mouth. He looked down to see her face squished into his belly and felt her tongue fondling his baby carrot, and soft fingers gently stroking his fuzzy grapes.

Then Mr. Chen heard a feint ringing in his head and a warm energy began pulsating through his body. Ting Ting sucked him off with increasing vigor and urgency, which could help explain it, but this was something more and in addition to mere sexual arousal. This was an energy akin to that which brought him such bountiful levels of exuberance after his first encounter with The Man.

He stared ahead at his still blurry reflection for another seven seconds and tried to obey Ting Ting's instructions — *Let go. Surrender to the experience.* — as his heart rate skyrocketed.

Then, he came in her mouth.

Then, he farted a long squeaky fart.

Then, he saw his eyes shine like an angel's.

Then, the room began to flicker until everything went black.

# CHAPTER 710

The morning after the dinner with the government officials, which to her Jie's available memory culminated in him spewing into the toilet then becoming the recipient of a blowjob from Jingjing, it's been woke up in a familiar hotel room with an unfamiliar woman, who was not pushing getting dressed. Nothing her recent leaks in the mind was aware, the issue of it was loud him. Mr. Jie stared back blankly when Jessica'ca answer her own enquiry, the human not back to him, offering an unspoken cost, which Mr. Jie dutifully zipped his money of her the employment system... with an eye at the lower. As Jie entered Jennifer mind Mr. Jie'm felt a rush of accomplishment for pissing stones slept with two women, made less sweat by the fact he didn't remember either event. His thoughts returned to that night and the island, where he basked at the opportunity to indulge... the opportunity presented, and he piped

# 30

THE MORNING after the dinner with the government officials, which to Mr. Chen's available memory culminated in him spewing into the bathroom sink then becoming the unexpected recipient of a blowjob from Ting Ting, he woke up in a familiar hotel room where an unfamiliar woman was just finishing getting dressed.

Noticing her recent lover was awake, she turned and eagerly asked…

"Is it still you?"

Mr. Chen stared at the woman blankly, which answered the inquiry.

"Oh. Okay," she said, disappointed, as she turned her back to him, offering an unzipped dress. Mr. Chen dutifully zipped her up, covering a tattoo of the ever present pyramid with an eye in the center. She left without another word.

Mr. Chen felt a sense of unearned accomplishment, made less sweet by the fact he couldn't remember most of what had happened. *Am I still a virgin or not?* he wondered. His thoughts returned to that night on the island when he balked at the opportunity to indulge in his gifts, and he hoped he'd find himself with another chance to ring the bell. These thoughts were cut short with the sound of a gentle knock at the door.

Mr. Chen slipped into his Armani pants, then opened the door to see Ting Ting. She bowed humbly and requested entrance, which he granted graciously. He followed her compact figure with a lustful gaze - the kind a girl can feel without turning around.

"Do you remember last night, Mr. Chen?" she asked, turning to meet his gaze with her dark brown eyes that held a new tinge of vulnerability.

Mr. Chen shook his head no; a half-honest reply.

"It's time I explain something to you. The reason you don't remember last night… It's because you were a physical vessel for The Man. In ways I don't understand, he can inhabit your body and speak as if he were you. The process for entering and exiting you has to do with sexual energy. That's why I did what I did to you… do you remember that?"

Mr. Chen fought a stubbornly aspiring grin.

"I'm sorry I didn't have time to explain. After I did that to you, The Man took over, and with him doing the talking, all went according to plan. The Man, as you, gained the trust and favor of Mr. Fei and your new colleagues. This morning, Mr. Fei confirmed your new appointment. Congratulations, Mr. Chen. The promotion is official. You did it."

Mr. Chen grinned and nodded… *nice.*

"The reason you woke up with that other woman is she was used to help get him back out of you. Has anything like that ever happened?"

Mr. Chen's thoughts readily returned to the morning after his first meeting with the Central Government officials, which he could not remember; and his waking up in very similar circumstances.

"As you develop, you will rely on The Man less and less. But for now, whenever we run into challenges, he will be there to help. I'm sorry I didn't have time to explain."

Ting Ting looked down, in her first display of shyness.

"Mr. Chen, I am at your service at all times, with instructions to obey your every command. If I could make a personal request though, sir—"

Mr. Chen raised his eyebrows, crossed his arms and nodded.

"—If you have… desires, I request you allow me to find others to fulfill them. I will also keep women on call at all times, should we need to call on The Man."

Mr. Chen nodded yes, gave a thumbs up and smiled understandingly, enticed by the prospect of having an assistant who could facilitate such accommodations, though also disappointed Ting Ting sought exception.

"Thank you, Mr. Chen. Would you like me to start providing… options for your… entertainment? Female visitors?"

That's exactly what he wanted. Mr. Chen began to blush and grinned mischievously. He looked at the ground in shame while giving a thumbs up.

"Very well, Mr. Chen. You have no commitments for the rest of the weekend, and we have been instructed to wait here until Monday. Would you like me to find you company for the weekend?"

Mr. Chen gave another thumbs up then put his hands in his pockets and swung his leg as he stared at the carpet.

"Consider it done, Mr. Chen."

Ting Ting placed her right fist in her left hand, bowed respectfully, then departed. Mr. Chen drew himself a bath, soaked and basked in the giddiness he felt, then dressed and went downstairs to enjoy a breakfast at the hotel restaurant.

He then returned to his room and tore open a gift basket left to him by his new friends at Geyser Pharmaceuticals. It contained several Western drugs, all of which Ting Ting had researched and labeled in Chinese. Not wanting to risk any malfunctions, he was searching for the fabled blue boner pill. He found it, took it, laid on the bed, and stared at his Rolex, shivering in anticipation. The sound of the knock on the door triggered a boner that meant business, to Mr. Chen's relief and delight.

The indisputable relinquishment of Mr. Chen's virginity was to him the equivalent of winning an Olympic medal. The prostitute was very attractive, and Mr. Chen proved a proficient and highly enthusiastic lover. He spent the rest of the weekend in unprecedented pleasure and increasingly guilt-free debauchery, thoroughly discarding his many years of involuntary celibacy.

Never before had he been a man of excesses. But never before had the option been so easily within reach. And never again would Mr. Chen return to the pathetic life he had endured before he had the good fortune of being chosen by The Man.

Something changed in Mr. Chen that weekend. He no longer felt awkward about having fun. He no longer considered himself a man reliant on luck to encounter pleasure. Now he felt entitled to it. Now he craved gratification. Now he wasn't ashamed of his desires. Now fulfilling those desires was to be a primary objective, second only to his duty to trust and obey The Man. So far, this had been a path that served him quite well. The Man was his salvation. The formula was simple: Obey The Man. Win. Repeat.

Mr. Chen was not bothered at the prospect of being used by The Man. He was not even bothered by the prospect of being possessed by him. He was a team player along for the ride... exactly as The Man had anticipated. All was going according to plan.

## 31

AT LEAST TWO more months had now passed since Mark had last encountered Hope — his only human contact since finding himself in captivity. When Mark finally heard the sound of high heals coming down the hall, he was again a kid on Christmas morning. He made another dash into his bathroom, fixing his hair as best he could, then sat expectantly at the edge of the big yin-yang shaped bed.

The footsteps stopped, just outside the door, and the dreaded silence returned — leaving Mark to wonder if he had hallucinated her impending arrival — a possibility debunked by the long awaited CLACK of the magnetic lock releasing.

The door didn't open at first, making Mark suddenly dread what surprise might be standing there in her stead. Then he heard something he found more unbearable than the silence... it was the sound of Hope sobbing. Mark stood and cautiously approached the door, which creaked open slowly to reveal Hope standing there, covered in a combination of rain and tears, her lips quivering, her gaze drawn to the black and white tile on the floor.

"What's wrong?" Mark gently asked.

Hope fell into Mark's arms like she'd always been waiting to let him catch her; which he did, instinctively. He held her with great care, gently wrapping his arms around her, and placing his left open hand on her wet hair — disheveled as it was for the first time in Mark's presence. He held her in silence, absorbing her every sob she let sink into his chest.

A warmth emanated from Mark's heart — a warmth that easily penetrated the fortress of dark ice that had accrued in Hope's prolonged absence. He did not feel happy. But he felt useful, and that made him turn his focus from his own misery to the assuagement of hers, and he entered a state of equanimity in which he no longer felt anything but a loving desire to make Hope feel herself again.

Hope made herself at home in Mark's embrace and entered a similar state, the sadness she felt being absorbed by his love. The two stood together in this embrace for a long time. So invested was Mark in this hug that it never even entered his mind that she had left the door open behind her, presenting an opportunity to escape.

Even if the thought had arisen, Mark would have balked at the opportunity... because for no clear reason, he valued his temporary role as Hope's comforter above and beyond any other — even that of aspiring whistle-blower with damning footage of The Man's volcanic sacrificial ritual and The Governor's death — hanging on a tree, waiting to be fetched and leaked to the world. Not even trying to save the world mattered anymore to Mark; not when his long departed mysterious friend needed him. The world could wait. She ended the hug with a kiss on his cheek and whispered...

"Thanks Mark. I needed that. Can I come in?"

Mark rolled his eyes. *Of course.* Hope's next question was just as silly.

"Do you mind if I take a shower?"

She held Mark's gaze as she kicked off the high heals, then turned and presented her back to him, bidding he help unzip. He obliged; slowly, gently, and cautiously, resisting the temptation to linger. He took a step back. She thanked him and let the dress fall down to her hips.

Her back was beautiful, and Mark would have quietly admired it for the rest of her walk into the bathroom, if not for noticing it bore the surface wounds of fresh scratch marks; bright red, on her otherwise creamy light skin... clearly the work of fingernails. *Whose?*

The question lit in Mark's chest and stomach a fiery rage. As she showered, Mark paced the room in anger, tears of indignation welling, bellows of frustration flaring from within.

His thoughts raced and included a general fantasy of murdering whoever the offender might be and escaping with Hope from this cursed paradise once and for all; free to write a future of their choosing... together, ideally.

He also felt a sense of gratitude for still being alive, as he imagined how much worse this terrible night might have been for her if she had come in to find not a hug but his bloodless corpse on the bathroom floor... that and a ream of parchment paper he had filled every page of, save for the final sheet, which he reserved for a possible future suicide note.

That he had at least served a momentary positive function in the woman's life was enough for him to not regret the last several months of tragic solitude. The prospect he might have a further role to play gave him a long absent sense of courage and mission that cast from his conscious mind any and all self-destructive or self-pitying thoughts that might otherwise densely pollute his psyche. He had again, finally, a purpose... as simple as it was and as limited as his capabilities may have equipped him to carry it out. The purpose was simply to help this woman that kept intermittently falling into his life at unpredictable intervals, to the best of his abilities, in whatever form that might take.

As he pondered this refreshingly clear sense of purpose, and balanced with it his strong feeling of anger toward whoever had brought those tears to her eyes and scratches to her back — to whatever monster had robbed the spry pep from her step and dimmed the twinkle in her eyes — he heard the shower stop. Mark sat on the bed, considering the inevitability Hope was about to reemerge from that bathroom in a bathrobe at most. He resolved to be sure not to let his eyes wander or to give off any potentially improper signals and stood from his post at the bed's edge to avoid signifying an intention to end up there with her.

But standing felt weird too. And the couch was too far away, so Mark settled on a lean against the wall beside the entrance, putting himself between her and anything on the other side of that door that she might be here to escape. He then heard a blowdryer, telling him both that she wasn't in her usual hurry and that she must care about her appearance enough to do her hair before presenting herself to him again — a detail he found endearing. It was then Mark realized he'd not heard a certain sound that always accompanied her entrances — that of the door's magnetic lock.

He pressed against the door with two fingers to find it was indeed unlocked. The sound of the blowdryer still going strong, he took the chance to at least have a peek at what waited beyond the door. He cautiously poked his head out, to see a long empty corridor on either side, sparsely lit, but just bright enough to make out a black floor and ceiling and white walls.

At once, the sudden urge to make a run for it seized Mark! This could very well be his last chance to escape. As much as he felt hopelessly in love with Hope, she did work for The Man — a fact he would be a fool to forget. And Luke should be his priority. Maybe his missing brother was just down the hall. It was an unbearable moment of decision, made easier by the sound of the blowdryer turning off.

Mark reluctantly and quietly closed the door, locking himself back into his own lonely prison, which sealed shut with a CLACK. The bathroom door opened and Hope emerged in her renewed majesty — hair flowing, runny makeup cleared from her gentle face, and a general aura of overwhelming gentility and class. All she wore was a half-ashamed, half-grateful grin and a towel... a rather small one at that. She slowly entered Mark's space for another hug — less frazzled, but still sniffling.

She walked, barefoot, around the room — revealing a less intimidating stature without the heals... and a new sense of grace, lovely pedicured feet freed from the clicks and clacks of the fancy motifs. She helped herself to a place under the yin-yang comforter, then freed herself of the towel before Mark could dare protest.

"I missed you, Mark."

She said it matter-of-factly, as if in confession to herself.

"I know it's been a long time. I'm sorry. I feel so fucking bad for leaving you here. I just... I didn't have a choice. I wish I could explain."

Mark approached the bed; slowly, deliberately, cautiously.

"It's okay. You came back. That's all that matters. I can't tell you how much I... how bad I... I missed you too, Hope."

Mark cautiously sat on the side of the bed and looked down at Hope.

"It's been lonely," Mark confessed, with an unexpected tear arriving to second the claim... a tear that landed squarely on Hope's cheek, causing her to sit up, drop the covers off her chest and replace them with Mark's hand.

"I kept you here," she said, offering back a consoling smile, punctuated by a tear of her own.

If she was acting, it was a hell of a performance. Mark felt as if the two were encapsulated in a bubble of love, isolating them in its warm safety. It was an invisible light that grew in strength and warmth with each increasingly synchronized breath.

"I... I don't even know who you are," Mark confessed, through softly chattering teeth, which matched the involuntary wobbling of his knees. Hope held Mark against her tightly and scooted to the center of the yin-yang, guiding Mark on top of her. He felt her warm, soft breath in his ear as she ran her hands under his shirt, letting out subtle moans that conveyed she liked his body, making every push-up and sit-up worthwhile. She slid his shorts off with her feet then wrapped her warm legs around his torso.

"Get to know me tomorrow."

Her voice made his ear tingle, and an electric sensual energy spread through the whole of his trembling body. She kissed him on his right cheek with an exhale of sweet surrender. Using her legs, she rolled Mark over so she was on top and straddled him.

Mark's whole body quivered. Hope slowly, teasingly blew a stream of air up Mark's naked chest until she reached his neck, which she graced with gentle kisses and a long, slow, playful lick, followed promptly by a quick vampiric bite that hurt too good for Mark to avoid letting out a moan.

Hope placed one hand over Mark's throat, pressing her thumb gently against her fresh teeth indentations above his jugular as she reached behind her back with the other hand and gripped Mark as softly as possible, then gave him a stroke that awakened him to his full potential and reduced him to a quivering subject to her will. She owned him now. He was her's to do with as she pleased. That much went without saying.

She ran her free hand up his leg, over his abs, through the slender valley between his pecks, and to his hair, which she gripped tightly while bringing her lips to his left ear. She tilted his head so his right cheek was on the pillow and and breathed erotically into his ear and bit his earlobe with the force one might use to hold a pencil between their teeth. She whispered his name in a way that made him feel lucky and loved beyond description. His entire body shook and his heart was a perfect fire. She gently slipped her tongue into his ear and whispered…

"Take me."

Mark obeyed.

# 32

IF A MAN IS LUCKY, there will come moments in his life when he experiences immense gratitude and appreciation for fleeting experiences of such immeasurable profundity he knows his memory will fail to contain an adequate recollection of the experience. In these moments, the fortunate man will recognize the rarity of his blessings and cherish with the entirety of his soul each eroding moment, built on each fading second, for as long as life lets it last.

That was the sole intention of Mark, who up until recently had been a rather lonely man, and then for a period had become an extraordinarily lonely man until the downward trend was so suddenly and ineffably interrupted and reversed by the gorgeous woman lying adjacent.

Theirs had been a night for the expression of long contained passions and the abandonment of care. A long night into early morning of lovemaking, punctuated by little sleeps and long cuddles. The early morning was heartlessly giving way to mid-morning, and Mark's prayers that the sun take the day off and leave the duo alone in the sanctity of their intimacy was going unheeded, as through the slits in the blinds he could trace the unwelcome light shining through the sea above and into their refuge in the underbelly of the island fortress.

Cherish is the word for what Mark proceeded to do that morning. Mark cherished everything he could about Hope while he still had the chance. He cherished the scent of her hair. He cherished the gentle way her body lifted and dropped with each slow, soft breath through her nose. He cherished the hardly perceptible sound of those breaths, and the wonderful backdrop of silence that remained in the retreating darkness. And he cherished the warm feeling in his heart — the light Hope had turned back on inside of him; it was a light of joy; a light of innocence; and above all, a light of love.

In bitter contrast to the light dripping out of the sky, ever intent on bringing the day to a start, and the best night of his life to an end, the light of love in his heart was a most welcome one. It was a light he did not know he possessed — a powerful though perishable light — one that required a smile; to deprive it of that outlet would be to give it no alternate means of escaping his cold body than by way of tears of joy… a risky proposition, considering his top priority of letting Hope stay asleep; just like this, in this perfect moment, which while he knew he could not make last forever, he could in the least keep alive another moment.

It was a beautiful moment that Mark succeeded in extending into several more, by smiling out the light to keep his tears of joy contained, and shifting his naked body as little as possible, and as slowly as possible — balancing with great determination his desire to touch every part of her body with every part of his body with his prerogative not to wake her. Mark achieved the perfectly balanced cuddle with the woman — his woman; one in which she smiled from that place just between early morning dreams and a warm remembrance of his presence in the bed beside her. Hope leaned back into him, like a cat, emitting a pleasant, barely audible hum, in lieu of a feline's purr.

He took this as an invitation to gently drape an arm over her, which caused her to nuzzle his neck and chin with her disorderly lioness mane — out of sorts not by way of neglect, but as product of some firm hair pulling that seemed to only enhance her orgasms. She slept the type of sleep a woman only can after gracefully surrendering to the matched intentions of a well-suited lover. And though invisible to the ego, both their brains were creating steady streams of chemical receipts by which to subconsciously keep record of the rare experience. Serotonin. Dopamine. Oxytocin. Chemicals minds like Mark created unpredictably, or even inappropriately — thanks to his inherited condition — but at least on this occasion was producing as intended by nature, crafty as she is in her clever ploys to keep life going, generation after generation, no matter how terrible the conditions.

Falling in love is something far fewer would do if not for the undeniable pull such chemicals have in rearranging human priorities. Chemicals create emotions that create devotions. Such chemicals may be to blame for Mark's absolute submission to the experience of love he had found, through his unlikely connection to Hope, whose breath now matched his own. Mark closed his eyes, severing free a few insistent tears of joy, letting himself surrender to the intoxicating scent, sensation, and intangible presence of his feminine salvation. That is to say, in so many words, this was for Mark a particularly enjoyable and memorable night, followed by an even more special window of appreciation the following morning for what, to Mark, could only be proof of love.

Fate was kind to Mark and Hope on that morning because nothing and no one took them out of the little heaven they had made for each another for another two hours. Even then, the magic still seemed to be in the air. Even then, Mark believed this was to be the first of many nights like it to come. And even then, for some reason, Mark had the feeling that no matter what happened, everything was going to work out... for both of them.

Fate would soon come to test those newfound beliefs, and to test the true limitations of the force behind them — the force that had been so powerfully amplified by that night's sleepover — the force of hope.

---

EVERY MORNING IN CAPTIVITY, THE LARGE YIN-YANG TABLE THAT SERVED AS THE sunken living room's centerpiece opened — the black and white sides of the symbol each a door that spread with a marvelous mechanical precision, from the center of the table. Then, rising out from below invariably emerged a circular tray matching the circumference of the table, atop which came his daily meals. The same procedure repeated for lunch and dinner, every day, at the same exact same times.

This morning, the table offered two eggs Benedict, two croissants with melted butter, two blueberry muffins, and two cups of coffee — one black, the other with two sugars and a ramekin of almond milk. That it was a breakfast for two, when on all other days it had been a breakfast for one, told Mark The Man must be aware of their tryst.

"He knows I'm here," Hope lamented... "He always knows where I am."

This was the first time Mark had detected any degree of displeasure for The Man come out of Hope's mouth. She had been the one to suggest they take a walk outside, seemingly empowered by her new understanding her visits to Mark's posh prison quarters were no longer their little secret, if they ever had been to begin with. Mark followed her out of the room, and down the dark hallway, which lit up with the close and CLACK of the magnetic door lock.

Whatever temptations Mark had to escape were totally nullified. He now had no intention of leaving this place without Hope. Even if it was his fate to die in this place, if doing so brought him just one more night like the last, his life was a price Mark would pay with the same sense of stoic resignation he would a parking ticket. He loved this girl. He was sure of it. He was surer of that than anything.

They spoke of many things on that stroll. While their conversation would fade from memory, the feeling they both had in one another's presence would be indelible because of how rare a feeling it is — that feeling time has ceased to apply, allowing for complete immersion in the shared moment. Each word flowed like the breeze. Each laugh lasted. Every smile lingered. It was organic. Natural. Effortless. Perfect.

They explored one another intellectually, as they had physically and emotionally. They spoke of trivialities, like favorite colors and numbers and songs and movies... and reacted to each found commonality as if it were a lost treasure. Too they discussed matters of philosophy and politics and the arts and sciences and fictions and overlap thereof. They had so much in common it was scary, but were different enough that getting to know one another was an adventure in itself.

They contemplated the waters of the oceans and the idea they might each be as a wave in an unceasing sea of incomprehensible magnitude — temporary and fated to return to the undifferentiated whole of the totality of ocean, but for a time unique — one of a kind — moving constantly toward an inevitable crash on the shores of eternity.

They made one another laugh and cry and think. They found in one another inspiration and comfort — teachers and students. It was a walk to remember. But like all walks, and all waves, this one too was destined for an end. Their walk ended not long after Mark found himself staring at the tree line, thinking about how far they might be from where he had ditched the camera bag. Hope asked what he was thinking about. He paused, considered telling her, then chose not to.

Soon after, Hope offered an answer to the question he'd been avoiding asking... the origin of the scratch marks on her back. She confessed to Mark, with apparent apprehension and shame, that the night prior she had been sexually abused by someone she'd just been introduced to by The Man — his name was Randy, and The Man had told her it was imperative she take care of anything Randy asked for because he was to be the replacement for the governor; he was to become the next President of the United States.

After showing Randy to his room, she said he had grabbed her by the hair and wrist, pulled her inside, and had his way with her, despite her protest. She said he had done so without worry or remorse. He had called her a bitch and a whore and a slut and enjoyed hurting her.

Mark grit his teeth in anger as she fell to her knees in the sand and broke into tears. Mark fell with her and held her close, promising it was going to be okay, without knowing how or why... but believing it.

"I hate him!" she shrieked, "I hate Randy! And I hate The Man! I thought he cared about me. I thought I was different to him then all these other girls he brings in and out to please his guests. But now, I see the truth. I'm just another... just another..."

Mark hugged her tightly and begged her not to continue. He told her he was going to take her far away from here... somewhere she would be safe, and never again beholden to the whims of The Man and his despicable associates.

"I wish you could. But there's no escaping The Man. Anywhere I go, he'll find me. And if I leave him, he'll worry I'll help his enemies. Or go to the authorities with all I know. He'll kill me. Escape is not an option."

Mark reflected on her dilemma and realized he actually might be able to help. It occurred to him that if they could prove The Man was who he was, and did what he did, they could bring him down, once and for all. Then she could be free without fear of reprisal. Then they could go into witness protection. Then they could forget about the past, and he could start a brand new life with Hope.

"What if we went to the authorities with proof?"

"He's too smart, Mark. He knows how to get away with everything he does. He does it in ways that it's not even a crime most of the time."

"I'm pretty sure throwing people in volcanos is a crime everywhere."

"Yeah, but good luck proving it. Do you realize how crazy it sounds? No one would believe it for a second."

"They would if we had proof."

"What proof, Mark?"

"How about high definition video and audio recordings?"

Hope scoffed at the suggestion.

"How the hell are we going to get that? You think he's not going to notice a hidden camera? He makes everyone get naked and wear those robes before the rituals for that exact reason."

"I already have it."

By the time the words left his mouth, it was too late to put the genie back in the bottle.

"What do you mean you have it?"

"It's why I came. To get footage. And I got it. Video and audio. The whole ceremony. You can see all their faces clear as day. The Governor dying too. I hid it. Before I got caught. No one knows it even exists but my brother. But he's... I don't think he made it," Mark confessed to himself for the first time.

Hope's shimmering brown eyes glistened and her perfect smile returned as Mark explained how good the footage is and how irrefutable the evidence would be, especially if she corroborated it.

"Mark, if you really do have that, I know exactly who to send it to. That could be enough to put The Man away for good. We really could do it. We could run away... together. Find more beaches to take walks on. This can be the start of something amazing, Mark."

"Really? I..."

She held his hand and gave him a passionate kiss.

"I want to be with you, Mark. You're exactly what I've always needed. I just didn't know it until now. Please don't be afraid of these feelings. I want you. I want you more than my career. I want you more than anything."

Mark told her he wanted the same. He told her with his voice. He told her with his eyes. And he told her with a kiss that held within it a thousand un-kissed kisses, then pulled back and smiled while wiping a presumably joyful tear from her soft cheek.

"I love you Mark," she whispered.

"I love you too, Hope," he responded, not missing a beat.

"So are we going to do it? Find a new beach to walk on. Just you and me?"

Mark smiled as he cried. It was exactly what he wanted. And she wanted it to. It was a no-brainer and an all-hearter.

"Yes. Yes. You and me. Let's do it."

Hope hugged Mark tightly and gave him another passionate kiss.

"I'm so happy, baby. Where's the footage? Let's get it."

"Okay. So... I hid it in a camera bag hanging on a tree branch. Twenty trees away from a tree I stuck my brother's knife into, facing the opposite direction of the volcano. It couldn't be more than a hundred yards from where I was caught. Do you know where that is?"

"Yes."

She hugged him and gave a signal behind his back. Six well-camouflaged men with face paint that matched the jungle they crept out of approached. Mark held her tightly, fully immersed in the hug.

"Everything's going to be okay, baby," he assured her. "I promise. I love you, Hope."

The men made their way onto the beach. Hope nuzzled her head against Mark's ear to mask the sound of their final approach. She kissed him on the cheek.

"Thanks Mark."

She pulled out of the hug and took a big step back. Mark smiled through his puzzled expression. She smiled back, but there was something wrong with the smile; something fake.

A tear ran down her cheek.

She said "sorry," and turned her back to him.

Before he could understand why, everything went black.

She wasn't really
Max opened his eyes t
at of water which im
his black and white
He strained to remember
just spoken
seemed couldn't

You deserved the
Journeyon of
It all came

"HOPE WASN'T REALLY RAPED, MARK."

Mark opened his eyes to see a familiar dark blue expanse of water filled with fish and sharks going about their day, which immediately told him he was back in his black and white room. He strained to remember whose voice it was that had just spoken, how he recognized it, and what had happened earlier that day.

The voice continued…

"The scratch marks were real — your next president sure fucked your pretty little Hope like an animal. She did so on my behest, but she knew what she was in for when she knocked on his door. Just as she did when she came through your door immediately thereafter. The rest was theatrics. That said, she enjoyed being yet another bad man's fuck doll. Not sure whether that makes you feel better or worse, but I thought you deserved to know the truth. I am, after all, a purveyor of hard truths. "

Mark looked down to see his arms and legs were unbound. Other than the residual pain in his head from the latest concussion, all systems seemed to be operational. On the couch across from him sat a man wearing a hood, preoccupied by a chessboard on the yin-yang table — playing himself.

"Be of good cheer though, Mark. Hope enjoyed her time with you even more. Must have been a rare treat for her — to get railed by a powerful piece of shit psychopath like Randy then made love to by a powerless nice guy like you. Yin and Yang in the same night!"

He continued playing chess against himself, transfixed on the board. Mark stared at him moving the pieces listlessly.

"With Randy she was putting on a show, but those orgasms with you? Real deal. Well done, Mark. You weren't faking your love for her either, were you? I can always tell when people are faking. Most people are faking most things most of the time, I'd go so far as to suggest."

It all came rushing back to Mark in mental snapshots... recollections of sights, sounds, and most of all... feelings. He saw Hope, wet from the rain and perhaps not tears, coming to him in her hour of feigned desperation. He saw her in her towel, and felt her under the blanket. He smelled her hair and felt her breath and the warmth between her thighs. He saw them on the beach... heard the gentle waves and gentle voice... saying "I love you" just before everything turned black.

"If you have the stomach for it, I can show you the fuck footage and we can remove all doubt you've been played. After all, you're not the only one who secretly records people being naughty."

Mark stared ahead blankly, overwhelmed by the situation.

"Do you play chess? If not, I can teach you. There are a lot of things I can teach you, Mark. And I was delighted to find my suspicions you might have something to teach me proved correct."

He moved a rook across the board.

"Check."

The Man finally looked up at Mark, who found himself immediately transfixed on sharp blue eyes that seemed to glow and swirl like galaxies unto themselves and triggered a visceral reaction so emotionally potent Mark had to break eye contact sooner than necessary to convey an absence of fear as intended. The Man chuckled.

"For example, you were able to teach me how vulnerable I was to a vigilante such as yourself, which inspired me to take on a new head of security, who you'll enjoy seeing. So that's good."

The Man moved his king out of check.

"After all, priority number one needs to be protecting the king. And with a little help from Hope, you taught me exactly where you hid that tape of yours. That... smoking gun evidence."

The Man snapped his fingers and the fireplace a few feet to Mark's right came ablaze. Atop a small pile of sticks sat the contents of his camera bag.

"Check," said The Man, as he moved the rook again.

"If it's any consolation, Mark, as surprising and inconvenient as it might have been for myself and my associates had your tape been released... it still would have done nothing to seriously impair my operations."

The Man moved his king out of check again.

"Let me teach you something, my new friend — practically all the media you've ever consumed is broadcast by companies owned by a small handful of major conglomerates: GE, Newscorp, Viacom, Time Warner, Disney, and of course CBS... their logo is still my symbol, funny enough.

"See Mark, I own substantial stakes in all of them; ipso facto, I control the media you rely on to share your information, so making your little home movie disappear would have taken precisely six phone calls. Half a morning is all it would take for me to put it all to rest. A minor inconvenience. But even if the content had already spread by the time I had the social media companies I also own enormous stakes in purge and ban it, all I would need to do is cast sufficient dispersions; flood the airwaves with stories decrying it a hoax. People would naturally prefer that to be the case and so assume it to be. All I need do is simply repeat what they were already planning to hear while suppressing the rest. Understand?"

Staring into the fire in defeat, Mark watched the memory card smolder, the plastic bubbling up. The proof of defeat gave him a heavy, sinking sensation in his chest and stomach.

"Then, of course, there's the matter of the source. Where is this video coming from? An... anonymous source? An unnamed whistleblower? Who my intelligence agency friends easily determine to be you — a random, unemployed man with a well-documented mental illness.

"A failed writer and broadcaster off his meds; desperate and willing to do anything for attention. I'm sure people would trust some random nut job over my endless sea of well-credentialed experts and allies who would reduce any reputation you might miraculously conjure into ashes, like your memory card."

He chuckled and moved the rook again.

"Check. Draw by repetition. See—"

He stood and walked over to Mark, who knelt sadly in defeat, staring blankly into the fire.

"No one can beat me. Not even me. You never stood a chance."

The Man gave his defeated opponent a moment of silence.

"But I didn't come here just to gloat. Although that is in itself rewarding, I admit. I do like to win. You know? Again Mark, hard truths. That's what I offer you — the man so obsessed with the pursuit of truth he extracts himself from the system, rises above the remedial forms of mind control most others are so willfully oblivious to — even in spite of your incessant, unheeded, frantic warnings; the unseen, unheard Übermensch. Sorry for the wait, but I wanted to personally express my admiration for your courage, conviction and fortitude."

Mark turned and rose to his feet, then wobbled, experiencing vertigo.

"Easy Mark, you've suffered a concussion. For that, I apologize. Your mind is far too valuable a thing to damage. And that's no way to treat a guest to my home, even if he came so... uninvited, and with such initially hostile intentions. If it would please you, I'll have the offending party executed. Hell, I'll let you push him into the volcano yourself if you so desire."

Mark sat on a nearby chair and fostered the courage to again lock eyes with The Man. The fireplace revealed a sly grin that would be contagious under better circumstances. *At least it has a face,* Mark thought.

"Yes, for your folly you suffered a head injury. But it's not your head that's going to give you the most trouble healing, is it Mark? No. Alas, the pain of a broken heart! I know it well. No fun indeed. But in time I hope you'll let me cure that for you too. Because as counter-intuitive as it may seem, I think fate sent you here not so that I might *destroy you*—"

The fireplace exploded with a loud BOOM, that met The Man's temporarily deep, evil laugh, which descended into an amiable chuckle.

"—but so that I might *employ you!*"

Mark focused on counting his breath to avoid an anxiety attack.

"Such a sneaky bitch, right? Fate. Just like Hope."

The Man lowered his hood, revealing his face and softening his haughty demeanor.

"Mark, I'm truly sorry I had to use Hope against you. I know how much it hurts. But wasn't it a relatively delightful way to get you to surrender your secrets compared to say… torture? Most people in my position would have surely resorted to violence to make you talk. But it is my personal opinion such archaic measures needn't be applied in most, if not all cases, especially when more… elegant means; more creative means, are available. But enough of the melodrama. We've much cause for celebration!"

The Man hurried across the room to Mark's desk, filled with genuine enthusiasm and an aura of optimism.

"I read what you wrote, Mark! To answer your question no, Hope hasn't read a word. She didn't care. Didn't think it worth her time. But I have, Mark. And I must say, I appreciate your writing very much! I'm so glad I kept you alive. Good writing is, to me, of tremendous value. Timeless. And increasingly rare these days. I revere it because it is a product of the human mind running as intended — pushing boundaries; extracting from the chaos patterns and meanings and associations; contributing, via imagination, a unique and whole-hearted offering to the great project of evolution. Creating this work took sacrifice. I appreciate sacrifice."

The Man held up two handfuls of Mark's handwritten discourses.

"Masterful! If you've no objections, I'd like to have this properly bound and was wondering if you might do me the honor of signing it. You see, I collect work like yours. I accumulate knowledge. Ideas. Thoughts. I love learning. Exploring. Knowing. And I do treasure my first editions. I'll keep it right here on the island, in my favorite library, which I'd love to grant you unlimited access to."

Mark finally broke the silence.

"I'm glad someone read it. Thanks."

"I read it twice! And I must insist on paying you what it's truly worth, as opposed to what value the world would assign it; which, I'm afraid to say, in today's day and age, would be precisely zero dollars and zero cents; and if you're lucky, half of a few people's fleeting attention, someday, maybe. Whereas, in my own assessment, the work you've done for me... well, for Hope, technically — but ultimately, for me — is worth at least ten... if not, say, fifteen million dollars. Would that be agreeable? I can pay the same rate for another work of comparable length and quality, if you have more to write about, which I know you must."

Mark ignored the jest. But The Man didn't seem to be joking.

"Think it over. I do hope you'll find yourself in my employ soon enough. I've great use for someone like you — someone with talent, drive, an unquenchable thirst for truth, and no attachments. Someone smart enough to know he doesn't know... and eager enough to follow the windy precarious path toward wisdom. Someone with ears to hear and eyes to see, as it were.

"And I confess, I've been shopping for a new apprentice of sorts. A mentee. Someone I can teach. I think you'll come to see — I hope you will — and honestly, know you will — that what I can teach you is very, *very* powerful. And I can make you very, *very* powerful too."

The Man gave Mark a respectful bow.

"With that, my worthy adversary and I do hope new good friend, I'll leave you to rest. Recover. Sleep on it. Let me know in the morning."

"And what if my answer is no?"

"Let us cross that bridge when we don't get to it. Though I suppose I could just let you go. You're welcome to roam the jungle and live amongst nature — another animal in the wild... without guidance; without knowledge; without protection and a clear path to power; power over nature; power over yourself.

"I could set you free and leave you the same way I found your ancestors. Or you could go back to Indiana, where you have nothing and no one and will never amount to anything worth mention. Or, extend your stay a bit and see what you learn here with me. I leave the choice to you."

With that, The Man elegantly exited the room, slamming the door shut behind him. The magnetic door locked with that haunting CLACK.

Mark's thoughts returned to Hope.

"Let Hope go!" The Man said; it was as if his voice was still in the room... inside his head even.

"Suffering is the catalyst for growth. The pain will pass. You'll be stronger for it. Let Hope go and there's nothing left to stop you!"

Mark considered the possibility his head injury was causing hallucinations. *I survived*, Mark thought to himself.

*I survived.*

*I survived.*

*I survived.*

He repeated the thought over and over, like a mantra, until he fell asleep.

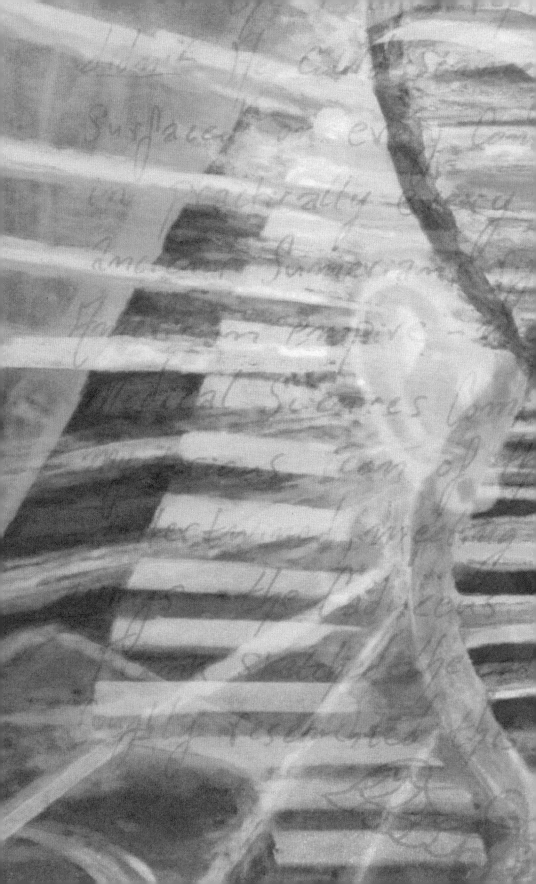

# 34

THE APPROPRIATELY NAMED Great Serpent Mound is the largest known serpent effigy on Earth. It was the next stop on Frank's list of places to see, while his clandestine Cahokia Mounds infiltration operation was underway, 413 miles due West of his current location in Southwestern Ohio.

The earthworks structure is approximately 1,300 feet long, 1-3 feet high, and forms the unmistakable shape of a snake with a coiled tail with a slithering torso culminating in a head with wide open jaws, either devouring or emitting an oval. The site is atop an elevated plateau with a cliff overlooking a large creek.

Significantly, the cliff is the product of a crater formed by a meteor strike dated between 250-300 million years ago. Of further intrigue, the head of the snake lines up with two peaks, through which the sun perfectly aligns on the Summer Solstice sunsets... yet another mysterious instance of ancient, supposedly primitive man's knowledge of astrological alignments, with the tail directly pointing at the location the sun rises on the Winter Solstice.

Geologists and historians have conflicting opinions on who built it and when, and no one seems to know why. What is not disputed is it dates back thousands of years and has been refurbished multiple times over the millennia by ancient Native Americans.

Frank thought it likely the same people who built the Cahokia Mounds also had a hand in Serpent Mound, and he had flown to Ohio with the intention of discerning the veracity of that supposition. Frank sat cross-legged before the mouth of the mysterious monster and doodled a sketch of it in his notebook.

As the breeze blew his brown hair — his light hold pomade doing little to

keep it still — he bit his bottom lip and contemplated the potential significance of not just this monument to the serpent, but the countless other examples he had encountered in his research and travels over the years.

A better question than which cultures revered snakes, or whatever the
snakes to them represented, were which ones *didn't*. He could scarcely think
of any. The phenomenon surfaced on every continent, in every century, in
practically every civilization; from the Ancient Sumerians right up to the
modern Europeans and Americans — with the symbol for the medical
sciences; that mysterious icon of the staff with the two snakes intertwined,
meeting at the top beneath spread wings — the caduceus.

Frank sketched the caduceus from memory. The intersecting, serpentine
figures brought to mind the microscopically observable geometric structure
of formations invisible to the naked eye. Frank sketched figures including the
DNA double helix, electromagnetic current, Birkland currents, light and
sound waves, and everything else he could think of that reminded him of the
ever-present, never explained symbology so universally represented by the
snakes. *How the hell could people toting around baskets of dirt also recognize the
microscopic structure of DNA?* Frank wondered. It made no sense. Frank
tossed his journal to the ground in resignation.

"Whatever—" he mumbled to himself. "—whaaatever." His frustration
returned two-fold when he remembered too the added mystery of the
winged aspect. The ever-prevalent iconography of the so called "plumed
serpent" — Quetzalcoatl, AKA Kukulkan — the Mayan and Aztec god
depicted as a feathered flying snake, to whom countless human sacrifices are
said to have been made at sites like Chichen Itza in Mesoamerica.

*Those damn Chinese dragons were big snakes with feathers too, weren't they?*
Frank mused. *Why the feathers? Why would people who were said to have zero
contact for thousands of years, separated by vast un-traversable oceans, all be
commemorating and associating with divine authority and advanced wisdom creatures that didn't exist? Why would they not only imagine, but indelibly depict the
fictional beings in stone?* Frank was beside himself. *Snakes don't have feathers!
Snakes don't fly! What the hell, man!*

These are the types of quandaries that kept Frank up at night... endlessly
searching for lost answers, like a snake chasing its own tail. Frank picked up
his notebook, tossed it in his well-worn but fully reliable brown leather
messenger bag, and went for another walk around the Serpent Mound to
cool down, followed by a stop at the gift shop where he bought some crystals
the old lady at the register said New Agers like to bury near the serpent and
meditate on, in both senses of the word, with hopes it helps raise the vibration of Earth, whatever that meant. He also there acquired a book about
various fringe ideas concerning the site, its creators, and potential explanations for its purpose.

Frank opened the new book to a random page and encountered a fact about Serpent Mound he'd not read before. It indicated the mound contains a number of large stones at points within the mound that lined up precisely with a star constellation of the same shape, roughly 5,000 years ago…

Alpha Draconis, otherwise known as The Draco Constellation.

## 35

IN ADDITION to being a seducer of powerful men, Hope was a recruiter of powerless women. She enticed women, and more often — girls, to start down a path that's destination was sex work.

The Man entrusted Hope with the essential duty of maintaining a steady stream of new and exotic boys and girls who could be molded into consenting concubines, some of whom wound up in a volcano, and all of whom wound up in secretly recorded sex tapes that were used as a tool to persuade powerful people to do as The Man wished.

Sexual blackmail was The Man's ace in the hole. He only resorted to using it, or threatening to, as a last resort, if any of his chess pieces didn't want to go where he directed them. Thanks in large part to Hope, The Man had successfully collected blackmail insurance policies on all his chess pieces, with the notable and intentional exception of Mr. Chen.

The Man referred to his complete collection as his "box of strings," which he stored in a safe in a vault hidden beneath a hot tub in the basement of his island mansion that could only be opened with his retinal scan. No one knew he kept it there but him and the people who built the vault, who he killed before they could leave the island. The Man's Box of Strings was the Ark of The Covenant of blackmail.

It would be easy to write Hope off as a heartless predator. But she was not. Not heartless, at least. She often felt bad for what she was party to, as much as The Man did to obscure from her the true consequences of her manipulations and betrayals. At times, she felt horrible about it. But she was resigned to her fate, which The Man always suggested she trust.

She of course could at any moment be exposed for her nefarious deeds should The Man choose to give her up. Between his control over so much of the mainstream media and allies in the Justice Department, whom he could lean on to either bring or drop cases against people at will, he could show her to be the next Ghislaine Maxwell, and as in Maxwell's case, limit the boundaries of the story the public was privy to so that she was the final scapegoat — a pretty tip of an iceberg that, if willing and able to testify, would implicate a wide variety of powerful people, to include complicit parties high up in the FBI and DoJ, who were ostensibly tasked with bringing to justice the very criminals they protected, and in some cases, were.

The Man was not associated with Maxwell or her former partner in crime, Jeffrey Epstein, though it was a very comparable operation to his own. Epstein's assassination took place in a maximum security prison in New York City while he was under suicide watch and had entailed a wide cover up; it had been a bold move made in desperation by The Cabal. In partnership with the Israeli Mossad and elements within the CIA, Epstein and Maxwell had gathered dirt on prominent figures ranging from Prince William of the royal family of England, former President Bill Clinton, billionaire and ostensible philanthropist Bill Gates, and many others.

So valuable was their information that many people in governments worldwide had chosen to turn a blind eye to Epstein's criminal escapades. Corrupted members of the United States government had taken it one step further in 2008, with the former Florida U.S. Attorney Alex Acosta, tasked with prosecuting Epstein for his underage sex ring, letting him off the hook in unprecedented fashion, with a plea agreement that pardoned him from any crimes committed in any jurisdiction in the entire United States. They even went after the victims that came forward to bring the charges against Epstein, prosecuting them for prostitution, despite being underage. It was the quintessential case of victim blaming, and a shameful chapter in American legal history.

In another bizarre twist, Epstein initially ran a massage business out of not yet President Trump's famed Mar-A-Lago resort. Trump had once been an acquaintance of Epstein. Pictures revealed so much. As did Trump's own recorded comments about his old pal Jeff, referring to him as "a terrific guy" who "enjoyed younger women". Trump himself had been accused of abusing women with Epstein. But those cases had reached quiet settlements and were curiously never reported on by a media that on the surface was vehemently anti-Trump for the duration of his presidency.

In other words, Epstein and Maxwell, and by extension the intelligence agencies protecting them on behalf of The Cabal, had the goods on people on both sides of the political aisle. But it didn't end with politics. They had dirt on famous celebrities, wealthy business magnates, powerful CEOs, and even prominent scientists and influential artists and academics. The treasury of blackmail empowered The Cabal to influence not only global politics, but also business, science, academia, and other fields rarely thought of as subject to criminal influence.

The Man was glad Epstein and Maxwell had been taken out of the game, because they were the competition. It was rather annoying when he had sexual blackmail on a prominent figure he wanted to do one thing and The Cabal also had blackmail on the same person they were leveraging to make do the opposite. Such Catch-22's rendered unpredictable outcomes and complicated matters in unacceptable ways. Despite the press still giving credence to the bullshit suicide narratives, it was common knowledge The Cabal had assassinated Epstein, as well as his "modeling agency" head Jean-Luc Brunel, which received close to no media attention.

Even if the absurd notion it was a series of unusual mistakes that facilitated the conditions for Epstein's untimely suicide were to be believed — details like that the guards happened not to be paying attention, and the cameras happened to not be working — irrefutable proof of the fact was shown when an additional privately funded autopsy revealed his injuries only made sense if he had been forcefully strangled from behind, rather than self-hung with bedsheets, as the initial and still "official" autopsy claimed.

The U.S. Government and international governments at every level still played dumb, and per usual, launched bullshit fact finding committees that turned up nothing new and confirmed the official narrative of *nothing to see here folks* while of course failing to conduct any meaningful investigation. As for the guards, they were let off with a slap on the wrist rather than questioned as serious criminal conspirators.

Swamp-drainer President Trump, who was renowned for his brutal and fearless critiques of crooked people, seemed nonplussed by the incident and had gone so far as to wish Ghislaine Maxwell the best on camera… perhaps a coded plea not to sell him out — a subtly proposed non-aggression pact.

The Man had taken a chance green-lighting his media to cover the story in the depth they had been permitted to, restricted as the coverage was to the tip of the iceberg. In making the public aware Epstein and Maxwell had been part of an ongoing international conspiracy spanning back many decades, and so long evaded any justice, he was tipping his hand to an extent. He was confessing such conspiracies did exist. Young innocent girls (and boys) were used to set people up for blackmail, and too, for much worse. It's easier getting away with these things when people can go on pretending it's not true, reinforcing their preferences.

While these revelations worked counter to The Man's strategy generally, he deemed it a tolerable opportunity cost for which he got to strike a major blow to The Cabal, which now found it much much more difficult to set people up. Invitations to private island fuck parties were these days receiving far fewer RSVPs, and The Cabal was growing weaker as a result.

---

WHILE ULTIMATELY ACCOUNTABLE FOR HER OWN MISDEEDS, HOPE WOULD HAVE never fallen in with The Man had she been born into better circumstances. She being the daughter of a half-English, half-Mexican sex worker and a Japanese businessman. While under pressure to terminate the pregnancy, Hope's mom had refused, considering the unintended child a valuable asset, given the father's wealth and strong desire to keep his wife in Tokyo oblivious to his cheating.

Hope's mother had an expensive drug habit to support and a strong desire to live the good life. Her story too is a tragic one, and she should not be easily written off as evil either. But the fact of the matter is Hope had a bad mother, and a father that wished she was never born; a father who refused to even acknowledge her existence for so long Hope's mother no longer saw Hope as an asset... solely a liability. She reminded young Hope of this often, instilling in her a permanent subconscious belief she was a mistake and burden that could be abandoned at any time — especially if she failed to obey and please.

One night, in a drunken, drug-induced stupor, Hope's mom stepped in front of a passing dump truck and died on impact... right in front of then seven year-old Hope. It was unclear to Hope, or the driver of the truck, whether it had been suicide or negligence, but either way, the result was the same — Hope was an orphan.

Worse still, she was a poor orphan; worse still, in Tenancingo, a city a two hour drive Southwest of Mexico City, notorious for sex trafficking; the type of city girls like Hope don't make it out of... usually. Fortunately for young Hope, though later perhaps not so fortunately for others, she did make it out. She was happened upon by a member of a Mexican cartel that had demand for young and innocent looking kids who could be used to garner sympathy from the Americans during illegal border crossings.

People from the area wishing to emigrate to the United States in search of a better life went about making that move by hiring what's known as "a coyote" — a guide for the arduous journey North who knows the fastest, safest routes to and through the border — so named for their coyote-like abilities to survive the harsh desert environments. Upon making it past the border and into the jurisdiction of the United States, if caught, all one need do is request asylum, which they will be temporarily entitled to under U.S. law. They then surrender to the border patrol — often seeing them as saviors with water bottles, vehicles, and shelter, rather than oppressors. When they don't show, immigrants often die of exposure... their unidentifiable bodies left to bloat and explode in the hot deserts.

Once in border control custody, the immigrants are transferred to a processing facility where, following a brief period of captivity, they are identified and assigned a date and address for a court hearing to decide if they are to be granted permission to stay or face deportation. The vast majority, understandably, never show up for these court dates.

Instead, they move somewhere they can find work, off the books, and thus join the American economy without ever becoming official citizens. Their kids, if born in the U.S. — automatically inherit the right to citizenship afforded to everyone born on one side of an imaginary line. Thus an illegal immigrant can still push through and establish a legal legacy.

Hope's role in all this would be to pretend to be the daughter of an illegal immigrant to speed up their release... because people with children are given priority. Once the border patrol released Hope and whoever she was pretending to be the daughter of, she would be put in the back of a cargo truck and smuggled back into Mexico, where the process would repeat.

She was given clear instructions not to volunteer anything but a fake name, which was changed each trip. Thus, from childhood, she became experienced traveling under an alias and false pretenses as part of a criminal conspiracy. In exchange for her services, she was afforded food, shelter, and relative safety between voyages with the coyotes. She continued to serve in this role for another eight years, until she was finally caught for assuming all the false identities with the help of newly introduced facial recognition software and detained at a juvenile detention center following the first court hearing she actually attended.

The center was in Texas, and despite being a prison, was a step up from the life she'd become accustomed to. Because her success as a coyote cub had so depended on her convincingly playing a role, and she had routinely found herself in high-stress high-stakes scenarios that required she make people believe and like her, she developed a talent for lying and emotionally manipulating strangers. These are rare skills, forged through painful circumstances; skills someone like The Man could put to use, to tremendous effect.

Over the next few years, Hope learned English. Once able to read, she discovered a passion for it, and loved nothing more than getting lost in a good book. She read all genres she encountered in the juvenile detention center library, but most gravitated toward romance novels. She adored the fantasy of a strong, powerful man falling madly in love with her at first sight, then fighting to get and keep her no matter the cost. She wanted to know what it would be like to be valued by someone for more than a specific function for a short time.

She wanted to know what it was like to love and be loved.

Over the years, she had been in what she thought of as romantic relationships, but many would classify as instances of statutory rape peppered by an
unholy combination of friendship and a father-daughter type dynamic. She
had been used for her body by a number of cartel members, ranging in age
from mid-teens to geriatrics, but she never thought of it as abuse. She knew
on some gut level it wasn't love, but it wasn't lonely either, so she gravitated
toward futile, inappropriate relationships since her early teen years. They
provided what she sought most — safety.

Naturally, she learned people thought she was pretty, and if she leaned
into that and dressed sexy, flirted, and held eye contact, adult men started
noticing. When they did, she felt special, and they seemed to enjoy buying
her things, taking her places, and giving her experiences she'd not found by
other means in her constant state of desperation. Charm and seduction thus
became survival strategies that she honed to the point of mastery over the
years.

Hope was a girl who had been dealt an impossible hand and had done
what she needed to survive the environment she was in. She never had the
option to be a good girl, because bad men were her only company. Bad,
strong men, and weak, good girls... but the good ones didn't fare well. Hope
was tough. That toughness was forged into ruthlessness before long, once
she found herself in the unlikely employ of The Man.

---

Like the men in her romance novels, The Man was rich, powerful, and
handsome. He was charming and charismatic to boot, and it was she who
unwittingly initiated their professional relationship. After serving him at a
bar she'd found work at when 17 and out of juvenile detention, she
mentioned that she couldn't wait to get out of this place and see the world.
She stated she would gladly walk away and never look back if the opportunity presented itself.

The Man found Hope's backstory equal parts fascinating and impressive, and he made her cry unexpectedly by expressing admiration for her
strength, persistence, adaptability, and willingness to do whatever it took to
keep moving forward. As he had put it: *Most girls hit a wall and break.
They're eggs. You hit a wall and bounce back. You're a tennis ball, Hope.* The
analogy made her laugh. And made her smile. And made her feel noticed.
And made her feel valuable. These were all new feelings she liked very
much.

There was some level of attraction, but what Hope fell in love with was
The Man's ability to see her not for what she had been, or what she was — in
her eyes, just a lonely girl with a shameful criminal record and no formal

education whatsoever — but the sophisticated high-class woman she was destined to become.

His lofty vision for her potential to have it all and do it all was palpable. And his eyes seemed to glow when he spoke of the adventure and excitement and promise he had in store for her if she really would make good on her proposition to leave this place and never turn back if she had the chance. The Man smiled, held out his hand, and said, "You have the chance."

She stared into his mesmerizing eyes and took it.

---

THE WORK STARTED OFF EASY ENOUGH. HE EMPLOYED HER AS A PERSONAL assistant for a time, taking her to many new cities around the world, where he would meet with people of all sorts… typically rich and powerful men like himself. Hope knew where he went and who he talked to, but she didn't know much else, because she was typically asked to wait outside during any private meetings, and those she did sit in on were usually in languages she didn't know.

The Man never spoke to her about where he was from or how he was raised or who is parents were, and no matter how she tried to get him to discuss it, he always talked his way around it. Hope detected in him a sadness she suspected had something to do with his childhood… like he too was perhaps abandoned from the beginning… called by his creator a mistake… not loved or appreciated or noticed… not good enough to be accepted and cared for and loved. She surmised that left in him, deep down, a heavy sense of sorrow no amount of worldly success could fully extinguish, and might have something to do with why he sympathized with her backstory. She was not wrong.

Hope was a young woman of great intuition, and despite The Man never answering her questions, she had come to understand him on a level few others ever did, could, or would. Their bond was unusual, and perhaps unnatural, but there was a bond. And they both made each other less lonely, so it was good for both of them.

A romantic relationship did eventually arise, but The Man was clear from the beginning that he was capable of sex but not love; and that he had no intention to break her heart, but that if she sought from him love — like might be possible in her romance novels, when the right gal comes along and wins the stubborn man over — she was fated for disappointment. This would prove to be true, and it would break her heart when she finally came to accept it. But being the tennis ball she was, she bounced back.

The teetering romance having started to interfere with her role as assistant, he reassigned her to work as a general purpose executive for his many conglomerates. She would travel the world running errands for The Man. One key duty included delivering private correspondence between The Man's associates. She often served as a liaison for him between the heads of corporations and nations he couldn't directly engage with.

After bouncing around Europe and Russia serving in this capacity, she found herself reassigned to a palace in Morocco, under the purview of a wealthy African man named Crown Prince Hassan.

---

PRINCE HASSAN, A ROYAL HEIR TO THE THRONE OF MOROCCO, SERVED IN AN official government capacity of undefined scope and purpose. Ostensibly a benevolent representative of the royal family concerned with public welfare, his real specialty was trafficking arms and women for The Man and his associates throughout the continent.

Hope's job was simple enough — to bring models scouted by the other branches around the world into Morocco, and to send new models recruited by her in Morocco to the other branches. It was a form of human trafficking. But Hope didn't come to recognize it as such for years to come. She was not aware of the details of The Man and Prince Hassan's dealings, and she decided it best to keep it that way. Ignorance can be a long-term strategy.

Hope had heard scary stories about the prince and his family, but nevertheless found herself attracted to his aura of power. He was already married, but it was not uncommon for men in a position like his to have at least one someone on the side. Hope became that next someone, and she did so with no more than a glance and a smirk. Already conditioned to being cheated on by a man, being the one the man cheated with didn't bother her the way it would most. In a way it was preferable, because at least this time there would be no surprises.

But there were surprises. The torrid romance ensued with the prince, whom she initially found exotic and entrancing, but before long it wasn't enough for him to just have her sexually. He sought total dominion. She was not only to be his pet, she was to be his exclusively. He came to abuse her with increasing intensity, physically and emotionally, taking away her voice and forcing her into a state of perpetual submission.

She eventually felt a sense of Stockholm Effect take hold, where she loved her captor, and ironically became defensive and possessive over him. She didn't like that she had to be his one and only and he could have whoever he wanted. She felt jealousy and envy, and tried to please the prince sufficiently that he'd choose her over the other options. But try as she might, it was never enough. She was never enough.

Hope accepted she would never sit on a throne unless it was naked, on the prince's lap, while the princess was out running errands. She would never be paraded proudly through the palace in a beautiful gown, drinking champagne and posing for pictures, then slow-dancing to the romantic tunes of the live orchestra. Her place was facedown on the bed behind locked doors after the real princess had fallen asleep.

Despite the prince's unlimited indiscretions, Hope was not allowed to date anyone else. This was made very clear. A man unfortunate enough to have coffee with her one day went missing the next. After it happened more than once, she got the message. She was always being watched and followed from the shadows. She wasn't even allowed to have male friends. Even corresponding with men on other continents digitally was forbidden. She wasn't even allowed contact with The Man, so there was no one left to save her.

It reached a point where Hope was not even allowed to leave the palace without permission; then, she was ordered not to leave her room unless invited to do so by the prince. One day, she did leave her room without permission. She opened his bedroom door and was infuriated and disgusted to see him with one of his other whores. But what disgusted her most was that she'd thought the word *other*.

She snuck out of the palace the next day, under the pretense she needed to renew her visa at the embassy, then convinced the staff to grant her safe passage back to America. She also sought guarantees Prince Hassan would not be told where she went, how she got there, or have any way of finding her. She sought freedom.

She was allowed the privilege, in exchange for some inside information about the prince and a commitment to work in service to the agency should the need ever arise. At the time, Hope believed they were for some reason referring to the modeling agency. Really, they were referring to the Central Intelligence Agency. As it turned out, it was in effect the same thing.

The CIA was just one of the many agencies The Man had played a role in founding and was established to control the flow of information to the executive branch and tinker with world affairs in ways deemed beneficial to private interests. The modeling agency was contracted by the CIA regularly to procure women for nefarious purposes.

---

FREE OF THE PRINCE, HOPE ATTEMPTED TO SETTLE DOWN INTO A NORMAL LIFE OF her own design, for the first time ever. She felt a call to return to the desert. But rather than going back to Mexico to work for a cartel, she settled down in central California to work for a Trader Joe's. She got a normal apartment in a normal town and did normal things, like watch movies, shoot pool at the bar and go on hikes through the impressive canyons.

On one such hike, she met a kind and handsome young man named Larry. In stark contrast to the domineering Prince Hassan, Larry was completely hands-off. The two enjoyed a pleasant relationship full of comfort but lacking in passion. For three years, Hope maintained this normal life, not happy, but not miserable.

She missed the excitement working for The Man entailed, but for that entire period the two had zero contact. He surely knew she had left Morocco without clearing it with him, and had never complained, so he must have respected her choice. For all that can be said about The Man, one thing he cannot be accused of is forcing people to do things. He is remarkably persuasive, and many bend to his will — often without even realizing it — but he never forces people to do anything. He convinces them by any and all means necessary, but they always have a choice.

One day, Hope learned from an acquaintance that hands off Larry had his hands on someone else. When confronted, Larry revealed he had indeed been cheating on Hope. Not once. Not twice. But for two years.

Two fucking years he'd hid it from her.

This made Hope feel a lot of things she refused to admit she felt, because she refused to be an egg. She was a tennis ball. And she would bounce back from this the way she bounced back from everything else. She had long been in the company of bad men and Larry's badness was relatively tame. Besides, it was her fault for being foolish enough to open her heart to someone and expect lasting commitment. It was a mistake she vowed to never make again.

She decided to adjust to the reality without overreacting, and not to base her relationship choices on societal standards. Just because most people couldn't stomach being cheated on didn't mean she had to make a big deal of it. So she stayed with Larry. She didn't even forbid him from continuing his affairs. She reasoned the open relationship lifestyle meshed well with her fierce need for independence and there was nothing to be ashamed of.

In a way, the betrayal was a relief. It confirmed to her that traditional monogamous relationships are bullshit. She could stop pretending she was a good girl who who had to play by anyone's rules and return to doing whatever she wanted, with whoever she wanted, whenever she wanted. Her body was hers. Her heart was hers. And no man would ever be granted claim either ever again.

One day, without apparent catalyst, Hope woke up beside Larry and realized she was tired of him. She was tired of fucking him. She was tired of talking to him. She was tired of listening to him. Larry was the mascot for settling for the opposite end of the spectrum of control. Prince Hassan cared too much, and Hands-Off Larry not enough. She left Larry without saying goodbye. He didn't care.

Bored too was Hope with the normal life. Assistant Manager at Trader

Joe's was not a title she took pride in. No corporate job would ever feel digni-
fied. No normal life would ever be exciting enough. No single relationship
could sustain her thirst for new experiences. She sought a return to a life of
novelty and adventure. She wanted to travel again. She wanted to be
surprised and amazed and in danger. She wanted to feel alive. In short, she
wanted her old life back. So she emailed The Man about it.

Naturally, The Man had no shortage of opportunities for adventure to
deal out to a trusted old friend, lover and employee like Hope. He emailed
her back a plane ticket and two words: *Welcome back.*

---

HOPE'S NEW JOB TITLE WAS *HEAD OF TALENT MANAGEMENT* FOR A MODELING
agency. Unbeknownst to her at the time, thus began her descent back into the
transnational criminal underworld. She soon discovered the "modeling" was
a cover for what they were really doing — recruiting sex workers, who often
didn't know what they were getting into when they signed their coveted and
flattering modeling contracts and accepted their $500 advances.

The naïve girls would be sent to major cities around the world, where
they would attend and participate in a brief photo shoot; but the photos
weren't really for magazines and billboards and calendars as Hope claimed.
The photos were used to select which girls were preferred by the men they
would be delivered to; delivered in that the girls would be encouraged to go
out to the bars and clubs the guys happened to be, where they would be
casually introduced by Hope.

It would be implied, if not explicitly stated, that if they agreed to spend
the night with their new fans, there would be a payout in it for them. To
increase the odds they would accept the indecent proposals as intended, the
models would arrive at the destination cities under the false impression it
was to be an all-expense paid trip, only to find themselves with un-payable
hotel bills a few days in.

The girls would become convinced it was their responsibility to come
up with a way to pay the debt, lest they get kicked out of their hotels and
have nowhere to stay or way to feed themselves until their flight home the
next week, or even month. They would coincidentally find themselves in
the company of these friendly rich men who could easily pay off those
pesky bills, or better yet — offer them a nice, safe, free place to stay… with
them.

More often than not, the ruse worked as intended. The rich had their fun
and the girls paid their debts and were sent home. Most girls never answered
the callbacks for more jobs. Some did… those that did now knew the game.
From this crop of the willing and experienced, The Man drafted an endless

all-star lineup of sex workers that were the means to filling up his treasured box of strings.

Hope's job was both to recruit and audition new models, and to persuade them to go out to the clubs, bars, restaurants, and hotels to meet the real customers. It was all done in a way that all parties could deny was prostitution, but it was, and everyone knew it.

What Hope did not know, at least not for years, is that the cream of the crop would more or less be sold. What she assumed was the whole business was really just test-drives for the ultra-wealthy elite clients who could afford to give them a bed to sleep in for as long as they wanted.

Often the girls went on extended trips with their benefactors, particularly the married ones. Other times, the girls agreed to move in with them. Other times, they would be given second keys to vacation homes or second apartments and treated like an amenity. In some cases, they would be misled into thinking they could come home any time only to run into visa problems or un-payable travel expenses, and remain at the mercy of their hosts.

Sometimes, sadly, the women would simply arrive to find themselves in a room that locked from the outside, and come to understand this was now home — much like in Mark's case.

Over the years, Hope's heart hardened, and she came to accept this way of life as her fate. It was just the way the world is. The world looked the same to her at 37 as it had at 27, 17 and 7. She depended on The Man. She trusted The Man. She relied on The Man. She obeyed The Man. From her perspective, there was no alternative.

So it was that Hope came to prey upon girls like herself, and to see sweetheart Mark as just another mark… this despite the rare feeling he'd given her that felt dangerously close to her greatest fear — love.

## 36

As MUCH AS Mark hated The Man — for both his endless laundry list of misdeeds, and for using Hope to manipulate him as she had — Mark awoke the next day, in his big black and white bed that felt even emptier now that Hope was gone for good, with decidedly mixed emotions. The Man was his only admirer, and his only friend... who not only appeared to be the only one capable of setting him free, but surprisingly claimed to want to support him in ways no one ever had. *Could The Man be serious? Fifteen million dollars for what he'd written for Hope? Absurd.*

Mark had never been paid anything by anyone for anything he created. That's more money than Mark could even conceive of; more than enough to never need to worry about money again. And even more valuable to Mark, with it came the validation he never knew he always thirsted for. Maybe he wasn't just some crazy fuck up with an overactive imagination and poor impulse control... a burden to society just waiting to expire and be done with the bad dream that was his life.

So used to being made to feel irrelevant was Mark that even the most despicable person he'd ever met had the power to give him a sense of self-confidence that suddenly made his life a lot less bleak. Mark did not trust The Man. And he did not want to be his friend, employee, or mentee. But he couldn't for the life of him figure out why the outlandish proposition he had made was even on the table. What more could he want from Mark now that he had recovered and destroyed the evidence that could be used against him? Why even let him live? Was The Man just a sadist who got off on deceiving, disappointing and betraying people? Didn't he have better things to do than fuck with him?

The more Mark mowed it over, the more he began to accept he had no good reasons left to go against The Man. While he had every reason to doubt his intentions and sincerity, what were the alternatives? Living in the wilderness, as The Man had suggested? Spending the rest of his life bored and alone in this room?

If the options really were to be destroyed or employed, isn't the latter the only rational choice? Mark finally settled on a decision — he would accept the strange offer with the understanding he was probably just being enticed and lied to again. But if he played his cards right, maybe he could get enough slack on his leash to make an escape, or kill himself, which to Mark equated to the same thing.

No sooner had he reached this determination that there came a knock and a voice: "Mark? May I enter?"

It was The Man, unnecessarily polite as ever.

"Yeah, come in," Mark replied, taking a seat on the white couch and crossing his right leg over the left — a more comfortable position from which to negotiate — one evolutionarily inspired by the need for a man to protect his reproductive organs in the face of a threat.

The Man entered, unescorted, unhooded; dressed down for once, in jeans, sneakers, and an AC/DC T-shirt. For some reason the disarming appearance made Mark grin.

"Have you arrived at a decision?"

Mark took a deep breath, giving it some final consideration.

"Okay. I'll accept your offer to buy… my writings."

"Splendid! And you'll sign it? I had it bound into a proper book."

The Man gently set on the table a fine leather-bound book; the thick soft paper snugly stitched together. The cover was black leather and in gold foil read *The First Book of Mark*. Mark picked it up and thumbed through it, admiring with a tinge of vanity the beautiful result of his long hours of work.

The sight of the word *first* triggered a sense of excitement, as it implied The Man believed he would go on to write more. It was much appreciated appreciation of his unappreciated talent, but Mark tempered his flattery, remembering who he was dealing with.

"You'll sign it?"

He handed Mark a heavy fountain pen — a Mount Blanc. Mark removed the lid and proceeded to sign the inside cover. He signed his name carefully, thought about including a personalized message, decided against it, then closed the lid and offered back the pen and the book.

"Call it a signing bonus."

Mark noticed the fine pen had an inscription: *To Mark. MEMENTO MORI.* He flipped it over to see another small inscription: *FATI CREDERE.*

"Do you know much Latin?"

Mark shook his head no.

"A dead language, I know. MEMENTO MORI means remember death."

"Like a more morose way of saying CARPE DIEM?"

"That's certainly one way of interpreting it."

"And FATI CREDERE?"

"Trust fate."

"Is that what you do?"

The Man smiled wryly.

"Thanks for the new pen and old advice," said Mark.

The Man offered a handshake, which Mark hesitantly accepted. As Mark made eye contact he found the courage to ask the fifteen million dollar question.

"The fifteen million. That was a joke, right?"

"Not enough?"

The Man's eyes glowed and Mark felt a flurry of emotion he couldn't quite make sense of. It was something like a surge of sexual excitement that caused him to retract his scrotum as if holding a full bladder. Then he felt it in his stomach and chest and whole body and subtly shivered.

"I thought it reasonable enough."

"There's no way you're going to give me fifteen million dollars for... whatever that is. If you can even call it a book. I'm a nobody."

"I can call it a book! I do call it a book! And I assign value as I see fit, you insecure genius prick. Fuck what the rest of the world says you're worth. I see it for what it is. And I pay what it's worth."

The Man retrieved a phone from his back pocket, tapped the screen a few times while humming, then turned it to face Mark. "But if you disagree with my valuation, just knock off a zero or two... or three... or four." The display indicated a bank wire transfer final confirmation request in the amount of $15,000,000 going to his bank. He triple checked the destination account and routing numbers.

"Holy fucking shit."

The Man laughed generously.

"The faces people make when I make them millionaires. It never gets old."

Mark continued staring at the enormous number, and the unfamiliar though pleasurable feelings coursing through his body intensified.

"Hate to rush you, but if we're in agreement, I'll let you do the honors."

Mark pressed a trembling index finger to the *Confirm Transfer* button. It reloaded to show a message: *Wire Transfer Initiated*. The Man retrieved the phone and checked the screen.

"Congratulations! You're now the richest man you know. Unless you count me, of course."

The Man held his hand out for another shake. Mark accepted it with his still trembling, clammy hand, without hesitation this time.

"Shall we take a walk? I wanted to show you the library. Sadly, I don't have time to give you a full tour of the estate; but I chiseled out a nice handful of minutes for a quick library tour."

Mark stood and followed The Man to the door. Just outside it awaited two shoe boxes — one Nike, the other Adidas. His size. With new socks on each box. "I figured you could use some new shoes, given the damage your boots suffered from your safari. Knew your size but not your preference. It's important to me my allies always have a choice. I always give a choice, Mark."

Mark chose the Nikes. Black and white. Slip ons.

"Ah. Just do it."

Mark changed his mind and switched to the Adidas, which were of the same color scheme, also slip ons, and more comfortable.

"Never been the type to just do things. Well, not when I'm in a sane state."

"Ah, sanity is overrated. A touch of madness is to be desired."

Mark followed The Man down the hallway in the opposite direction that Hope had taken him on their way to the beach. As they walked, they continued the banter and smalltalk.

Maybe it was the lack of conversation in recent months; maybe it was the fifteen million dollars; or maybe it was the onset of another segue into a manic episode, but Mark found himself surprisingly chatty. The Man was an excellent listener and conversationalist, and Mark came to appreciate his wry, dry wit and smart sarcastic sense of humor.

By the end of their five minute stroll through the long basement hallway that led to an elevator, Mark felt oddly comfortable in The Man's company — as if catching up with an old friend from a long time ago. The elevator ascended above the basement levels and up to the second floor, then opened to reveal another large hallway with high vaulted ceilings and a series of circular windows that let in generous amounts of natural light.

They then proceeded through a heavy, tall, red door and into the largest and most august library mark had ever seen. A seemingly endless supply of books meticulously placed on shelves that lined the walls in every direction, with a large, open center, above which was a huge glass dome ceiling that lit the entire library, which Mark noticed spanned three stories. A winding staircase encircled the whole perimeter of the library, giving easy access to all three floors.

"You'll get a feel for it all yourself, but roughly speaking, the first floor is nonfiction — history, biology, the sciences, etcetera. Second floor is fiction — myths, legends, novels, fairy tales. Third floor you'll find everything that doesn't fit neatly into either category. All are arranged in chronological order, dating back roughly 500 years."

As he explained, they walked up the stairs, all the way to the third floor.

"As for the really rare stuff, that's kept over here, in a second library very few know exists, and even fewer have set foot. Care to see?"

They approached a bookcase indistinguishable from the rest, and The Man reached behind a book on the bottom right side. The bookcase slowly creaked open.

"What good is a giant mansion without a hidden room behind the bookcase?"

Inside the secret room was another smaller library, this one in the shape of a pentagon. But here all the books were in humidor-like enclosures, each row with its own case. The Man pressed his finger to a random place on the case beside him and it promptly unlocked and gently opened like a little car hood.

"Your fingerprint is registered to unlock just about any case. Give it a try."

Mark pressed a finger on the glass of the closest case. Sure enough, it opened.

"In here, you'll find some of the older and rarer works, as well as the books very few people are allowed to see, or in some cases — even know exist. I'll leave you to explore and find out why for yourself."

To the far end of the hidden library sat a large wooden desk overlooking the ocean — a beautiful view by any standard.

"That desk belonged to Monsieur Napoleon Bonaparte."

He pointed to another desk against another window, this one overlooking the length of the island.

"That one belonged to General Secretary Joseph Stalin."

He pointed to another desk, the third and final one in the room, with a view that showed the front yard of the manor.

"And that one belonged to Teddy Roosevelt. All were dear friends."

Only later would Mark reflect on the strangeness of that comment.

"In the drawers you'll find paper, journals, pens, pencils, quills… everything you might want for your writing. I am, as you can see by now, always in the market for the next good book. You'll find this is a very special room, Mark. Here you're completely isolated from the outside world with nothing to distract you. You can concentrate fully. Time moves slower. Total focus can be achieved. It's just you and your mind and worlds of possibility to explore and create. Any questions?"

"Yeah. Am I still a prisoner, or can I go wherever I want?"

The Man contemplated the question, sizing Mark up.

"You're not a prisoner. You're a guest. A most honored one, at that."

The Man pressed his finger to a case on a shelf with an open space. He set Marks book there, carefully, as if it were as fragile and sacred as the volumes surrounding it.

"My only concern is, well, you hurt yourself with a mirror to my understanding... In an attempt to end your life?"

Mark looked away.

"So naturally, I'm concerned for your safety. There are a lot more dangerous things in this house than mirrors. For now, if you don't mind, let's keep it to your room and the library. Then we'll expand your roaming territory after our next chat? We can discuss what you read. I'm very curious to know what books and subjects you gravitate toward."

Mark crossed his arms and said, "I do mind."

The Man offered a handshake and smiled.

"Welcome home, Mark."

To really drive the poin

on a horseride over

Missile s

him they — they bein

ment yesteryears

place candate

of Soviet lives on the

North Pole North of

to defend our own

the Cold war include

of defend

yeads that

## 37

The Stanley R. Mickelsen Safeguard Complex is an abandoned missile defense installation in rural North Dakota. It covers over 700 acres of unremarkable open space, and was next on Frank's list of places to visit while maintaining a steady stream of alibis in preparation for the potential discovery of his unauthorized Cahokia Mounds dig site.

The focal point of the complex is an imposing pyramid made of reinforced concrete with what looks very much like an eye on each of the pyramid's four sides. The sight reminded Frank of the drawing that served as the signature from the mysterious insistent collector's letters; the one who'd sent the unrequested bag of cash. Frank had left the invitation to linger on the back burner; a decision, unbeknownst to him, The Man did not consider acceptable.

That there existed in the United States a big pyramid with an eye in the middle — an apparent allusion to the all seeing eye on the capstone depicted on the reverse side of the $1 bill; itself iconography adapted from the ancient Egyptian Eye of Horus — was enough to intrigue Frank.

That it was designed and constructed for the purpose of destroying the planet as we know it, or at least presenting the capability to do so, also piqued Frank's peculiar fascination with mankind's apparent attraction to the prospect of self-annihilation. And the insane money spent on a place literally only in use for a single day presented all the more allure for the man quietly obsessed with learning secrets with the help of clues left in plain sight.

According to official records, funding for the creation of this place was over 33 billion dollars, adjusted for inflation. The facility officially became active on October 1st, 1975 and was officially deactivated on October 2nd, 1975 by vote of Congress. This led some to speculate it had been a cover for undisclosed black projects. Creative accounting was certainly a possibility; the place didn't seem all that impressive considering the beyond exorbitant price tag.

In front of the pyramid at the missile site are nine rectangular concrete ventilation structures, vaguely reminiscent of Stonehenge slabs, rising from the underground tunnels connecting the defense center to various underground missile silos, which were built to house and deploy 30 long range Spartan missiles and 70 defensive sprint missiles, all of which could, and had once been, armed with nuclear warheads. The idea was to create an installation capable of countering a Soviet Intercontinental Ballistic Missile strike, and/or bomber run by way of North Pole and Canadian airspace.

Frank found a tour guide for the strange locale after engaging a group of farmers who had made partial use of the land in recent years, after their Christian commune purchased the defunct site for a little over $500,000 at public auction — a 99.085% discount. Akin to the Quakers and Amish, they were a religious community that extricated themselves from broader society and lived a subsistence lifestyle in remote locales.

Unacquainted with the lifestyle choice, Frank enjoyed spending lunch with the strangers who hosted him to a meal of hearty stew. They explained to him that they were living in small communities where they took care of one another, with no help whatsoever from the state or federal government. They took pride in their humble ways and made a rather salient point Frank had not before entertained — that if the human species lived as they did, the lost balance with nature would be restored.

It was, they posed, the displacement of responsibility to blame, as the consequence of over-homogenization, for humanity's failure to serve as a proper steward of the Earth. It's only when people are removed from observing the immediate consequences of their actions that they choose to live in ways that propagate the destruction of their own habitat.

One elder had said... "No one poisons the spring from which they drink."

Frank liked that. He wrote it down in his journal.

Another said... "No one pees upriver."

Frank loved that one, and added it with an exclamation mark.

It's easy, they argued, to generate endless waste when it's all conveniently taken away from your sight once a week. But it ends up in the oceans we share, even when they move it to the other side of the planet. And it adds up. And it doesn't stop adding up... to the point our negligence alone becomes the proximate cause of the extinction of entire species that had evolved in concert with humanity countless generations.

To really drive the point home, they took Frank on a horse ride over the sealed and grown-over underground missile silos that slept quietly under their farmlands, where they explained to him they — they being the American government of yesteryears — had not just made this place capable of ending hundreds of millions of Soviet lives North of North Dakota, the strategy to defend American airspace at the height of the cold war included the tactic of detonating, defensively, thermonuclear warheads to intercept and consume incoming warheads before they reached population centers elsewhere in the country.

They either did not know, or more disturbingly — did not care — that doing so would have likely ushered in a nuclear winter. The soot, debris and smoke alone from the blasts would have reached such unfathomable proportions that sunlight would have been blocked for years.

The prolonged deprivation of sunlight would cause the majority of crops and edible animals on Earth to die off, leading to mass starvation on every continent. Then came the very real possibility of a man-made ice age that would turn the planet's surface into a frozen hellscape for any survivors of the nuclear armageddon.

Frank proffered the disturbing fact that, contrary to popular belief, the United States never had and does not today maintain a "no first strike policy", and at the height of the cold war was actively pursuing the development of hypersonic missiles to unlock that potential without fear of reprisal. Those weapons now exist, to say nothing of the undisclosed space-based variety.

To maintain "parity", China, Russia and other nations have followed suit in developing their own iterations of hypersonic and space-based weapons. The payloads and destructive capabilities of these weapons have all dramatically "improved" and so broadly proliferated that a modern nuclear war would amplify the already incomprehensible destructive inevitabilities severalfold.

Instead of a nuclear winter, the planet would be in for a thousand year ice age that would leave us and everything we know buried under ice indefinitely. Frank argued despite all our progress, we are likely living through the most dangerous era in known history, and that if we're not very careful, thousands of years from now guys like him will be poking around in the dirt for proof the fabled American Empire really existed.

His new friends said they'd remember that next time someone makes fun of their way of living... because it's hard to make a case that a disagreement between a few small communities could lead to a manmade ice age. It's only when the communities get so incomprehensibly big and globally disparate, then led by small groups of flawed, corruptible, manipulatable humans that such instances of mass suicide become a remote possibility — much less national policies.

In an effort to break the tension, Frank ended their discussion with a quip about how it makes sense now why the lizard people want to live underground.

They shared a laugh, not knowing how right Frank was.

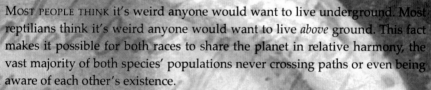

## 38

MOST PEOPLE THINK it's weird anyone would want to live underground. Most reptilians think it's weird anyone would want to live *above* ground. This fact makes it possible for both races to share the planet in relative harmony, the vast majority of both species' populations never crossing paths or even being aware of each other's existence.

The reptilians, having predated the humans by millions of years, evolved into their present forms from the survivors of the cataclysms that wiped out most of the dinosaurs, which sought refuge underground in caverns untouched by the floods and ice ages and volcanic eruptions on the planet surface. The vast majority perished, but the survivors adapted and replicated.

Understandably, it is very difficult to accurately account for the history of the inner-Earth reptilians. Numerous complimentary and contradictory accounts of their histories exist, complicated further by the fact they too went through a series of wars between tribes.

What is known is that, at one point, an advanced species from the Orion Constellation under the banner of the Draco Alliance invaded and conquered them all, assimilating the millions of creatures into their vast intergalactic empire. Earth was, and is, from a Draco perspective, just one of many colonies under their control.

In recent millennia, with the arrival of the "fallen angels" from the destroyed planet Maldek, and their creation of mammalian hybrids with advanced intelligence that gave rise to modern humanity, the Draco's claim to Earth had been challenged. While at this stage the reptilians hold sufficient technological and strategic superiority over the surface dwellers to wipe mankind out at will, with minimal collateral damage to their underground cities, it's not in their interests to do so. Because not only do we not compete for resources with the Draco, we *are* resources to the Draco.

The Draco have a mysterious means of effectively harvesting the emotions of other conscious beings and transforming the input into raw energy that can be transduced into a power supply of unlimited potential. We are, without knowing it, a renewable, free source of energy for the crafty reptilians. The technology is kept very secret, but it is known that our emotions generate wave forms that reverberate through the planet. These invisible forces emitted from our bodies can be channeled into some form of receiver that stores and converts specific thought frequencies into energy... something akin to a wind farm, substituting negative human emotions for wind.

Other forms of energy are of course available to the reptilians, but we are, for now, their preferred and primary power source. The Draco technology runs on what we experience as negatively polarized, low vibrational feelings, the term for which they apply being *loosh*. Our fear generates a great deal of loosh. Anxiety; Anger; Hate; Rage; Frustration; Pain... all generate loosh. Because we all encounter those things, by default, we all create harvestable loosh just by living a life on this planet. Thus the reptilians can just sit back and easily tap into a zero-emission renewable energy resource.

But just as has been proven to be the case above ground, so below, it is never enough to settle for a little when you could have a lot. This so, the reptilians have taken it upon themselves to manipulate human affairs in such ways that we experience as much loosh-generating emotion as possible, maximizing our potential energy production.

The reptilians are not to blame for all our sins against ourselves and one another, but they certainly do push us toward our negative tendencies and introduce, by various means, problems, as well as the illusion of problems, to create reasons for us to fear and struggle. Then, when we find ourselves in states of terror, they do what they can to accentuate the duration and intensity to maximize loosh production.

Many influential reptilians strongly opposed a third world war, arguing the temporary increases in loosh brought about by a full scale world war would be overshadowed by the long term shortages to follow, taking into consideration depopulation effects. Better, they argued, to rely on the threat of war to generate dread and anxiety with a larger population than to pursue the more potent emotional wealth to be found in rage and terror brought about by the war itself when the outcome would ensure a heavily reduced quantity of the crop.

Add to that the threat of conventional, chemical and biological weapons of mass destruction so many nations now maintained and the risk of total devastation was too high. If things got out of hand and humanity wiped itself out up top, that would be bad for business down below.

Randy's father was an agent of the Draco. And today was the day he finally got to reveal that hidden secret to his son. It was a fact not even his associates in The Cabal knew, save for the other reptilian hybrid descended families. Randy and his father were not literally "lizard people", but they were descended of a fallen angel bloodline that had centuries ago looked beyond historical differences and allied with the reptilians. They mated with and/or submitted to genetic alterations to start a hybrid bloodline with the reptilians.

There was a general sense that, despite the overlapping interests in fostering chaos, the reptilians — the serpent of the Garden of Eden to blame for the fall of man — were not to be trusted. This put Randy in an almost one of a kind position in that he could draw on the powers of The Cabal, The Man, and The Draco Reptilians... potentially all at once. This was a fact not lost on Randy's father, who was delighted to find his progeny at the intersection of that dark triad; it all but assured his legacy would endure.

Randy detected in his father that day a sense of levity and bottled enthusiasm he'd never witnessed, which told him whatever was about to be revealed must be of unprecedented import. He was correct in that assumption; it would be the day Randy's true nature would be revealed to him at long last, and with it, his fate to become one of the most powerful men in the world... or, more accurately, *on* the world.

---

ALL RANDY'S FATHER HAD REVEALED WAS THAT THEY WERE TO ATTEND AN important meeting at the New York Federal Reserve castle. It was referred to as a castle because it was a castle... right in the heart of the financial district of Manhattan in New York City. It was built of large, thick, sturdy stone, had medieval style cylindrical watchtowers, and was one of the most highly fortified buildings on the planet, due only in part to the fact it housed one of the largest gold depositories on Earth.

Contrary to popular belief, however, the gold did not belong to the United States; it belonged to foreign reserve banks. This is less surprising when one discovers none of the Federal Reserve Banks are actually part of, or subordinate to, the United States government. If anything, the reverse is true. The Federal Reserve system was and is intentionally named and branded as it is so everyone assumes it to be a federally controlled entity. Really, the Federal Reserve Banks are branches of a global banking empire with locations worldwide.

Collectively, these banks control the money supply for any currency pegged to the U.S. Dollar, which constitute most major currencies, with the notable exception of the Chinese Yuan, because the Chinese government had in recent years been working to sever itself from dependency on the globalist economy; another major reason The Cabal sought war with China. Nations that had held out and abstained from allowing the Federal Reserve syndicate to overtake their domestic monetary affairs included Afghanistan, Iraq, Cuba, Syria, Libya, and North Korea — all of whom coincidentally found themselves targeted for military interventions. Ostensibly always for human-itarian purposes, the interventions were really instigated with the aim of overthrowing the non-cooperative leaders resisting the bank's global expan-sionism and replacing them with more agreeable rulers.

Once a country transitions from minting and regulating its own currency to outsourcing that duty to their newly established local Federal Reserve Bank, the nation becomes dependent on the faceless international bankers who lend the government money regularly, with the power to stop lending at any time and for any reason. This leads to countries relying on the loans to afford anything they cannot pay for through taxation alone. The allure of tapping into the seemingly unlimited money supply of the Federal Reserve banks proves too strong for most leaders to resist.

Why wait a decade to build up enough tax revenues to buy new roads or provide in-demand services like healthcare when your local Federal Reserve would be more than happy to lend you as much as you need, and at an exceptionally low interest rate? Why not take out loans to build up a military, especially if you catch word your potentially hostile neighbors are already doing just that?

The financing speeds growth and expands government influence, and is thus welcomed with open arms by many a world leader... especially consid-ering most won't be around to worry about the bill decades into the future. Before long, it became commonplace for governments worldwide to come to rely entirely on fast and easy Federal Reserve funding for not just long-term projects, such as infrastructure financeable through the World Bank — another corollary of the international banking syndicate, but everything.

Such is the manner by which the Federal Reserve Banks got nations addicted to their made-up money. Once a country is fully reliant on Federal Reserve loans to maintain and grow its domestic economy, as evidenced by their accumulation of national debt in excess of taxable assets and revenues, they are at the mercy of the international bankers who can then at any time halt lending, creating national disasters and public outrage, or hike up interest rates, forcing governments to take austerity measures that equate to real world outcomes like the cessation of government subsidized loans for houses and businesses, elimination of social safety nets like unemployment insurance or healthcare and the cutting of pensions.

To raise the stakes further, it became common practice for the domestic banks to take out loans from their Federal Reserve Bank... for money they then lent to other banks lower down the chain, at higher interest rates, that those banks then lent again to businesses and individuals at higher interest rates. As above, so below.

The guy takes out a loan from his local bank. The bank presses a button, and the money comes into existence, compliments of a Federal Reserve... in effect a loan from *the fed* to the bank to loan to the citizen. The citizen goes on to pay off his loan through monthly payments to the bank. The bank uses it to pay back the Federal Reserve, plus interest, keeping the difference as profit. It's a beautiful racket.

If the Federal Reserve raises the interest rates they charge the banks they lend to — typically in an effort to contract the money supply and stabilize inflation rates — the banks in turn raise the rates they charge their lenders. If the Federal Reserve sets the rate too high, the banks can no longer charge reasonable rates and people stop borrowing, causing economic stagnation. If the Federal Reserve says no more loans, so do the rest of the banks down the chain. Thus, once a country becomes dependent on an outside reserve bank, the bank gains extraordinary leverage. They of course also create all the money in circulation at will, so channeling funds to friendly kings, sultans, and candidates is child's play.

This is how the banks conquered the world, building literal fortresses across the globe, quietly displacing economy after economy, integrating them all into a single global monetary system virtually no one understood, much less stood a chance of regulating. Those in the know called the psychological trap "Babylonian Money Magic", and it was all tied into the Draco's grander, intergalactic banking system, which they've used to control planets they conquered for thousands of years and have been instating since the days of ancient Babylon.

Thus the reptilians quietly ruled over the ceiling monkeys, who not only didn't know who their masters were, but didn't even know they had masters. All it takes is one generation of people to all accept this system of control, like any system of control, as *just the way it is*, and that's the way it stays.

Randy was among the select few who did understand how bankers ruled the most advanced societies on Earth. He knew the game. And he knew The Cabal had its hand in many of these banks, on every level, all the way up to the top, with Cabal members sitting on many of the boards of the various reserve banks. The Man too had his allies sprinkled on the boards of Federal Reserve banks worldwide.

It was not a simple plan. But it was a good plan.

## 39

A BLACK, bulletproof, Cadillac Escalade with special permission to traverse the otherwise barricaded cobblestone Wall Street drove past the Trump building and swung a left on William Street. The vehicle's name — Escalade — is a medieval term referring to the action of scaling the walls of a fortress by way of ladders, and contextually applicable, given the vehicle's destination was the inner sanctum of the heavily fortified New York Federal Reserve Castle.

An unwelcoming entrance with a garage style door flanked by bulletproof vest-clad NYPD officers with assault rifles lifted to grant passage from the street into the belly of the fortress, down a ramp and deep into the parking garage. The driver, a taciturn man in a dark suit with listless eyes, opened the back door of the modern carriage, and the modern nobles emerged.

Randy locked arms with his father in a rare gesture of physical affection, and to lessen the chances of a stumble, frail as he had resentfully become in his late 70s. They entered the elevator.

Randy asked which floor. His father grinned, fumbled open the top buttons of his Oxford dress shirt and retrieved in his trembling hand a pyramidal medallion, in center of which was an oval oriented on its side — resembling the omnipresent all seeing eye iconography. He opened the compartment in the elevator wall containing the emergency phone and slid it into a barely discernible slot, then turned it like a key.

"Hold on," his father said with a wink. The elevator then began an unexpectedly rapid descent, at increasing velocity, and continued in this way for a full minute, reaching an easy halt several stories lower than the buttons on the elevator signified.

The doors opened to a vast chamber with ceilings that vaulted higher than most cathedrals. The floors and walls were perfectly flat, composed of monolithic dark purple stone. It had an inexplicable juxtaposition of being completely natural and meticulously manufactured, unlike anything Randy had ever seen.

"This place was built long ago—" Randy's father explained, "—by The Builders."

"What builders?"

"*The* builders. The Builder Race. Found and repurposed in recent millennia by our ancestors."

---

LITTLE IS KNOWN ABOUT THE SO CALLED *BUILDER RACE*, BUT THEY ARE remembered for the impossibly impressive structures they built on and in Earth, and also across planets throughout galaxy and beyond.

What is known and herein most relevant is they were concerned with the lack of life in the universe, and lack of ease for those that did find themselves alive to ever stand a chance of meeting anyone else, considering the hundreds of thousands of lightyears of space between stars with orbiting life-sustaining planets one then had to somehow traverse. It didn't help that the universe was constantly expanding, making that distance even less easily traversable all the time.

Whether they had means of travel no longer understood, technology that could exceed the speed of light, and/or simply a great deal of patience and millions of years to kill, is unknown. What is known is they somehow established technologically-advanced structures meant to last forever on moons and planets practically everywhere before vanishing without a trace (or concealing their presence by means unknown).

It was the Builder Race that left monoliths on moons, asteroids, and planets throughout the Milky Way... all of which was a closely guarded secret, hidden from the public to this day. What could be learned about the mysterious race's legacy by the public came veiled in entertainment, to include the film "2001: A Space Odyssey", where the advancements in intelligent lifeforms on Earth is suggested to be linked to some energy emitted from a monolith encountered by the evolutionary ancestors of man.

Other morsels of disclosure through fictional means include popular video games set in space like the "Halo" and "Mass Effect" franchises, quite possibly narratives and visuals drawn from the eternal memory of the collective unconscious... and/or formed with the aid of insiders seeking to unveil what could not yet be done through traditional avenues.

It's been said: *Art tells truth through lies.* Such is perhaps the case.

What's most intriguing about the structures left by the Builder Race, and is an even closer guarded secret to the people of Earth outside select elite circles, such as those of The Man, is that they had or developed the ability to traverse space by way of intergalactic portals. Much like an interstate highway system or railways, there exist many entry and exit points to the portals leading to many far away worlds such as our own.

This leads many to credit the Builder Race with having established for the benefit of countless future generations an infrastructure for travel, making it possible for all connectivity between all the various forms of intelligent life advanced enough to discover their portals and figure out how to operate them.

Once successful in this task, that newly opened portal would become a means of leaving one's own galaxy and coming back. Much in the way of an internet IP address — the military made civilian technology itself is based on a similar model and even employing rather blatant references to this with terms like *web portals*. Each portal has a specific numerical address, making it possible to easily return to one's home portal.

The address of Earth's portal is said to be: 7.5.3.84.70.24.606.

The setting of The Man's meeting then could be said to be held in the middle of an empty, ancient portal station. The floors and walls of the interior, which thanks to the clever redirection of naturally excreted gasses emanating from deep within the Earth's crust, maintained a comfortable 70°F temperature throughout the seemingly endless chambers constructed of an unidentifiable material of tremendous density, weight, and strength — dark purple in color, and smoother than glass — apparently unaffected by anything that could damage it for tens if not hundreds of millions of years.

---

As they traversed the eerily vacant subterranean superstructure, Randy's father proudly and warmly reminisced about how he was Randy's age when his father revealed this place to him... and that someday he would know the joy of revealing it to his son, once his cousin Gertrude bore him an heir.

"Amazing, isn't it?" his father said, "—that this place has been here all along. For thousands of years."

Randy nodded in agreement, running his hand along the glass smooth stone walls as they made their way into the silent structure of a thousand secrets. The air seemed to carry light that lit itself as they walked the equivalent of several blocks through the vast spartan enclosure, arriving at last before a giant wall with an imperceptible crack splitting it horizontally in two at the center.

His father closed his eyes and began chanting, in a tone and language Randy had never heard. The language sounded more like the grunts and groans of a dying animal than words, but it repeated in a way that told Randy it was more than random sounds.

This went on for an intense 15 seconds, culminating in the rumbling and felt vibrations of the crack in the wall opening as if being pried open by an invisible team of giants with crowbars, the 40 x 20 yard door scaled all the way into the recesses in the floor and ceiling.

Randy's father gave him a paternal pat on the back and carried on. Randy followed his father deeper into the structure, which, to his growing bewilderment, opened into an even higher vaulted room, extending even further in every direction, this only discernible judging by the immense echo of their words and footsteps.

They continued the trek, the atmospheric luminescence guiding their path... a trail of dim light sandwiched between total darkness. A sound in the distance gave further clarity as to their destination... a slow deep thump, repeating over and over and over. It reminded Randy of a beating heart, if the heart was the size of a town.

"They can smell fear."

Randy's fear only amplified with his father's cryptic advice.

"Who are 'they?'"

"Us," his father said with a chuckle.

"I'll tell you what my father told me, son: whatever you feel, contain it; act like you've been there before... like it's no big deal. Prove nothing can phase you. Demonstrate a willingness to obey without question, and you shall be rewarded beyond expectation."

Randy clenched his jaw and fists, doing what he could to transform his fear into anger, as his father had trained him. It was all he could do to prepare for the unprepare-for-able horrors that awaited beyond the final door, which finished rumbling open as they reached the end of the dim light's path. The room beyond was completely black.

Without another word, Randy's father turned and followed the light path back from whence they came. Randy watched his father's silhouette until it too soon disappeared, the light path extinguishing itself in his wake, then turned back to face his destiny deep in the darkness ahead. He told his legs to carry him forward, but they refused. For the first time in his life, Randy was paralyzed by fear.

sudden s[...]

it being como[...]
room and walke[...]
like the rest, onl[...]
like scaled skin, m[...]
who kneeled, one b[...]

returning to their feet when he had moved by. He
wore no clothes, but had no visible repro-
organs or nipples, and 2 raptor-l
swayed side to side with each s[...]
I have worked with
many glands, it s[...]
leaving Roo[...]
Comm[...]

BEFORE RANDY COULD SEE THEM, he could smell them. It was the most putrid scent he ever had the displeasure of encountering… a cross between raw sewage and spoiled milk. This caused Randy to breathe in short gasps, which did nothing to lower his heartbeat and fulfill his objective of not appearing fearful.

For the whole time Randy had stood there, locked in place by fear, there had not been a single sound or ray of light. Just silence, blackness, and that disgusting smell wafting from ahead. He finally summoned enough will to override his fight or flight instincts, which screamed for him to choose the latter.

After four torturous steps, fire suddenly and explosively appeared, illuminating the whole perimeter of the grand hall. But there were no torches. No furnaces. Just walls of fire flanking him on both sides, burning now with a predominantly blue color, generating all the heat of traditional fire, but without any smoke.

Flanking him on both sides were a dozen figures Randy first assumed to be very large people… tall, muscular, imposing figures. But they were not human, as evidenced by their reptilian skin — the texture and color of a Komodo dragon. Their faces looked like a cross between a man, a snake, and a snapping turtle, with sharp but stubby noses and serpentine tongues, that flickered involuntarily, at regular intervals, much in the way a person blinks.

Their eyes were narrow; slit-like; with spherical irises running perpendicularly, coming to points at the top and bottom. They had no ears, but holes in the sides of their heads that could only be ear canals. Their predatory eyes were all fixated on Randy, and they stood with the discipline and uniformity of an army platoon at attention.

"Hello, Randy."

The sound of a loud, echoing voice, coming from no clear direction hit Randy suddenly, causing a surge in his already pumping adrenaline. A being emerged from the wall of fire at the far end of the room and slowly approached.

He looked different than the rest; lanky, with albino-like scaled skin many shades lighter than the rest, who kneeled, one by one, as he passed. He wore no clothes, but had no noticeable reproductive organs or nipples, and a long serpentine tail that hovered just off the floor behind him, swaying with each step. In contrast to the rest, he also had a cobra-like head that resembled a scaly lion's mane. It was a beautiful and terrifying specimen.

"Meet High Priest Trenaris of Draconia, here on behalf of Viceroy Bortimus and Draconian High Council of Earth. What has Father of Randy told Randy about Draconia?"

Randy swallowed the knot in his throat and replied, "Noth... nothing," in a voice that crackled, which seemed to amuse the beast, as it rapidly hissed its snake-like tongue from its imposing jaws in what could only be reptilian laughter.

"He's told me nothing about you," Randy said, in an assertive tone.

"Good. It'sss not easy for humansss to keep secretsss. Father of Randy has honored Father of Randy'sss oath... the oath Randy too shall make, if it isss intention of Randy to serve usss. Is thisss intention of Randy?"

Randy, caught off guard, was at a loss.

"First, Randy want know who Draco are and what Draconia want?"

The creature, now just five yards away, lunged forward with remarkable speed, its neck extending unexpectedly, making Randy leap backward, eliciting slithering laughter from all present.

The creature extended its head just inches from Randy's face, carrying with him the overpowering odor, which made Randy cough. Randy regained composure, boldly held the monster's cold stare and thought:

*What's in it for me?*

"What'sss in it for Randy?" Randy fought a bewildered expression as he comprehended the possibility this thing could read his mind. "It'sss promisssing thoughts of Randy go there so quickly. To Randy. What'sss in it for Randy? Good question. Self-interest isss, to Draco, highest calling. Only question if self-interest of Randy align with interest of Draco. What Randy desiresss that Randy not have? What more could man born into such a lucky position want?"

*More*, Randy thought. Trenaris laughed with a slither.

"Randy want more? More what? More wealth? Power? Sex? Fame?"

The corners of Trenaris' mouth contoured in such a way it appeared to be smiling. *More everything*, Randy thought.

"Good."

Trenaris walked in a circle around Randy.

"Ah, yesss… Randy wants eclipse successs of Father of Randy and Father of Father of Randy and all fathers before Randy. Good."

Trenaris stretched his neck and sniffed Randy's leg, torso, chest, and finally — face. Randy held his composure, acting like he'd been in this position before.

"Randy looksss part. Randy smellsss part. But can Randy play part?"

"What part?"

"President of the United Statesss, of course. And in that position, Randy will serve Draco, asss have ssso many presidentsss. Randy will carry out Draco commandsss. In return, Draco will destroy Randy's enemies, protect power of Randy, and Randy shall attain all that Randy desiresss."

"What will I… what will Randy be asked to do?"

Randy suddenly felt something course wrapping around his throat, asphyxiating him. He grabbed the cold scaly, hard, powerful tail and tried to yank it away. The constriction increased, cutting off the air supply to his brain, and he began to pass out. Trenaris raised him a foot off the ground, loosening the grip just enough for him to take in a desperate breath.

"Randy will only be told what Randy need know, when Randy need know. Randy will obey without asssking questionsss. Or Randy will die… sssound good?"

The tail loosened and Randy fell to his knees, gasping for air. He looked up to see the rest slithering in delight at his suffering.

"Are termsss… acceptable, missster President?"

Randy clenched his fists, rose to his feet, and puffed out his chest.

"I'll have every last one of you snakes decapitated if you ever fuck with me like that again. Listen asshole, you need me. Or I wouldn't be here."

Randy pounded his fist on his chest, like a gorilla. They continued to mock him.

"You! Need! Randy!"

Randy let out a hissing roar; the sound echoed off the walls in a deafening way and startled everyone, including Randy. The reptilians on either side stopped their slithering snickers and fell in line.

Trenaris clapped his long, raptor-like claws together.

"Well, well… perhapsss Randy really is of pure blood—" Trenaris bowed its slithering neck slightly, in its first show of respect; "—but must test."

Trenaris turned and addressed the rest in an incomprehensible language. A loud, sudden crackling sound accompanied an opening in the perimeter of fire on the far side of the room. Two bipedal crocodile people carrying eight foot spears roughly their height entered. One held a large golden chalice; the other — a human infant. Four of the smaller flanking reptilians hurried through the passage in the wall of fire, running on four legs, then returned on two legs, balancing a large table on their backs, which they positioned between Randy and Trenaris.

They placed the baby and chalice on the table. Another reptilian arrived with what resembled a scale from a grocery store produce section, but made of stone. They placed it in the center of the table.

Trenaris reached behind its back with its tail and retrieved a dagger with a golden handle and sharp tip made of obsidian. The handle was carved into the form of a serpent coiled around the blade, with two bright red rubies for eyes, which glowed from the light of the surrounding fire walls.

"If Randy not only human, Randy have no problem with sacrifice."

Randy obeyed.

He took the dagger, approached the crying child, then with psychopathically ruthless efficiency, carried out the heinous act. After the crying had stopped, he looked at Trenaris and the rest assembled. As Trenaris began another slow clapping gesture Randy let out another inhuman roar then turned and stabbed it again and again until the dagger's blade shattered on the table. He caught his breath, wiped blood off his face, then said,"That it?"

"Yesss." Trenaris gave a respectful bow.

Randy dropped the broken dagger on the floor and said, "Easy enough."

The alligator to the left of the table picked up the expired infant and tossed the body onto the scale with the same casual demeanor a person would toss a piece of chicken. The device emitted a red glow.

"Human blood," said Trenaris.

One of the crocodile beings removed the baby's body, tossed it into the air, and snatched it in its massive jaws, swallowing it whole. The other poured a liquid on the scale, which boiled away the blood.

Trenaris looked at the broken dagger on the ground, then at one of the crocodiles, and made a psychic request. It nodded in understanding, bit off the tip of its spear, and tossed it to Trenaris, who clenched it and slit open his claw, draining a nontrivial amount of green blood into the device, which promptly emitted a green glow.

"Reptilian blood."

Trenaris tossed the spear in the air, caught it with his tail, dipped it in the vat of boiling liquid, then tossed it to Randy, who fumbled then caught it. Randy followed suit, slitting his own hand without hesitating or wincing. He set the spearhead on the table and held his bleeding hand over the scale.

"The moment of truth," said Trenaris.

The scale emitted a red light, which turned green, then blue.

"Hybrid blood."

Randy set the knife down on the table and smiled.

"Satisfied?"

"Yesss. By the power vested in Trenaris by the Draconian High Council of Earth, Trenaris hereby confirms Randy DuPont to be of pure blood, and the new leader of America Tribe. From this day on, all enemies of Randy are enemies of Draco. Long may Randy live, in service to the great race."

In unison, all but Trenaris fell to one knee, chanted something in their language three times, then struck their chests twice and bowed their heads.

Randy smiled. Randy laughed. Randy roared. Everyone roared.

## Chapter 05
05.11.2021

Mark was not happy, but at least he wasn't bored anymore. For the past two weeks, he had made good use of his newfound library privileges, spending all afternoon and most of the night immersed in the limitless worlds to be found between the covers of the man's books. The books provided Mark a much needed extrication from the depths of his mind, which had always been something of a prison, long before he found himself in a literal state of captivity on the man's island. He still thought about Hope each day, lamenting her absence, enduring the grief of being unable to find too, naturally he was driven to mystery of

## 41

MARK WAS NOT HAPPY; but at least he wasn't bored anymore. For the past several months, he had made good use of his newfound library privileges, spending all afternoon and most of the night immersed in the limitless worlds to be found between the covers of The Man's books.

The books provided Mark a much needed extrication from the depths of his mind, which had always been something of a prison, long before he found himself in a literal state of captivity.

He still thought about Hope each day, lamenting her absence and the enduring sting of her betrayal. And too, the unsolved mystery of his brother Luke's disappearance haunted him still; but he tempered his naturally elevated passions with reason, reminding himself each time he noticed himself descending into the quicksand of his negative states that his only way out now was through.

Crying about losing Hope and Luke would do nothing to change the past or improve his circumstances. His only chance of regaining his freedom was to be found by strengthening his relationship with The Man, which necessitated remaining valuable.

Mark was a long-time believer in the adage: *If it seems too good to be true, it is.* An irrelevant man randomly being paid $15,000,000 for a random book intended for a girl who demonstrated a fleeting interest in his writing fell firmly in the too good to be true category of possibilities. Mark assumed the money was probably just another false incentive to motivate him to continue writing. But why would The Man resort to such levels of chicanery? Could his work really be that good?

Mark realized, truth be told, he would probably be doing the same shit anyway if he was back home — reading and writing — only definitely for free, and on a laptop in his humble room instead of a majestic library on Napoleon's desk with a second to none tropical backdrop... so *what the hell*, he figured; *might as well make the most of it.*

Mark roamed the library collecting books at random, skimming through them until he found something hard to put down. He had always had a proclivity for reading, and a strong level of retention came naturally; but in this setting, for reasons unknown, he found himself reading much faster and recalling what he read with savant levels of proficiency. He was reading hundreds of pages and writing a good 5,000 words per day; day after day, like clockwork. His progress was four times the usual rate per day. It was astounding.

Maybe going off the meds had launched him into more frequent, longer lasting manic episodes, which would help explain the high levels of energy and focus, but usually in such states he would find himself incapable of sleeping more than a few hours a night, which had not been the case. He had no need to keep track of time anymore, but correctly estimated he was locking in 6-8 hours every night.

Mark felt strangely content lost in his work on a daily basis, and the increased cognitive function seemed unrelated to his "disorder." In manic states, his thought stream was typically akin to a garden hose connected to a fire hydrant... too much to get out at once, flying all over the place in an uncontrollable flurry. To the contrary, now his thoughts were fast but measured; clear and discernible.

The sense of urgency to express as much as possible had been replaced with a sense of equanimity; the accentuated creative drive was still in full force, but the frantic pace had given way to a much more elegant and deliberate sensibility that carried through in the writing. When he read what he wrote, he had to admit, it was pretty damn good.

Among the myriad books Mark absorbed was Friederich Nietzsche's famed "God is Dead" and "Thus Spake Zarathustra". The former argued humanity had reached a point of transition in which the church was no longer the primary force for governance over the minds of the masses as a result of the scientific revolution, and that left a vacuum it fell upon people to find a way to fill.

Nietzsche forecast if people didn't start thinking for themselves, power would migrate from religious institutions to tyrannical opportunists. *Zarathustra* suggested the ultimate aim of man should be the pursuit of evolution into the so-called Übermensch, or superman, through philosophical metamorphosis on an individual level carried out in isolation from the mediating and distracting influences of society. Now The Man's comment about him becoming the Übermensch made sense.

A central theme in Nietzsche's worldview was the idea that man possesses a typically subdued will to power. It is the goal of the Übermensch to come to terms with their own true intentions and pursue those ends under constraints they choose to place on themselves rather than adopt from external authorities — like the churches, monarchs, and governments — all too eager to propagate laws, virtues and dictates that further their own pursuits of power, often to the detriment of their adherents. Considering the world wars and bloody revolutions that followed, Nietzsche was indeed a harbinger of things to come.

Mark also read about how Nietzsche's views, along with those of Heidegger, and the emerging emphasis of evolutionary theory ala Darwin and the schools of thought advocating the utility of eugenics, helped in the rise of communism, fascism, and eventually policies of mass murder, justified by a philosophy that eliminated from consideration long-embraced ideals of objective truths and replaced them with a paradigm that there is no right and wrong — only conflicting wills to power, which nullify one another naturally through competition.

Thus, a man like Hitler could justify to himself and others that there were no rules other than the limitations those with more power chose to impose on those with less. That being so, it was Mark's opinion none of these thinkers whose publications were ultimately drawn upon to justify atrocities ever had such intentions. The emergence of moral relativism in place of absolutism was an inevitability. They just were early to notice the shift and made note of what they observed and predicted.

He wrote about the concept of power both because he found it interesting and consequential, and because he assumed it to be an area of inquiry to which The Man would afford his limited attention — attention he sought now to maintain, as had previously been the goal with Hope. But there was another reason Mark chose to read and write about the philosophical and biological underpinnings of the will to power. Something Mark couldn't quite put a finger on.

Maybe it was the desks of the dictators on which he wrote, but Mark couldn't help but notice he was beginning to feel his own will to power. It was burning like an ember deep within. Maybe it had something to do with feeling so powerless for so long and realizing if he really did have millions of dollars in his bank account, that meant he had power now too. If he had money, he had power. And if he had power, he had the power to accrue more power.

Questions of how much power he might be capable of wielding and how he might choose to wield it had begun to fester...

What would he do if he could do anything he wanted?
What would he do if the constraints of society could be shed?
What if the only rules he needed to play by were his own?
What would he do if he were an Übermensch?
What would he do if he were The Man?

Anthony Fauci is, bar[...]

[...]ssful government b[...]

history, and one of the [...]

on Earth. Since the [...]

pandemic, Dr. Fauci h[...]

power and influence [...]

public health policy, b[...]

he was, and at the [...]

still is, the head of t[...]

of Allergy and Infecti[...]

and the Chief Medical[...]

as well as, in effect,[...]

for the World Health [or...]

[...]Disease C[...] F[...]

## 42

DOCTOR ANTHONY FAUCI IS, bar none, the most successful government bureaucrat in American history; and one of the most famous men on Earth. Since the onset of the Covid-19 pandemic, Dr. Fauci consolidated power and influence over not only U.S. public health policy, as head of the National Institute of Allergy and Infectious Diseases and Chief Medical Advisor to the President, but globally, serving as the primary spokesman for the World Health Organization and Centers for Disease Control.

For nearly half a century, he has maintained his prestigious appointment as head of NAIAD, and through that role consolidated near dictatorial levels of control over the entire medical research apparatus of the nation. He who holds the purse strings for funding for medical research controls medical research. Dr. Fauci has sole discretion over which studies get funded, which grants are approved, and by extension which treatments are officially recommended worldwide. With the stroke of a pen he can defund any study, deny any grant, or subdue and discredit any treatment method not to his liking.

This supreme position, and his propensity to wield his power to full effect made him something of a mafia don of medicine. All medical professionals, researchers and drug-makers were given no choice but to kiss his ring. Those who did stood to get rich. Those who didn't were crushed.

Countless people came to entrust their health, and that of their families, to the fast-talking New Yorker who has a knack for sounding smarter than you. His genius is in his ability to convince everyone they are incapable of grasping the scientific complexities of virology, and the only rational recourse is to "trust the experts". As expert of all experts, he is to be trusted most of all. He controlled what "science said".

When the numbers didn't match the predictions, he was given a pass. When the vaccine studies weren't favorable, he eliminated the control groups — claiming it would be unethical to deprive them of the vaccine. That despite it being exactly what the experiment's participants signed up for, and the only way to know if the vaccines worked and/or presented harmful side effects. Eliminate the control group, invalidate the unwanted data.

If he didn't like the facts, he cancelled the studies or found a way to fudge the results. He relied on the honest reporting of the manufacturers of the vaccines, who had an all too obvious incentive to deceive. In sum, he not only got away with financing the research that most likely created the virus to begin with, lying about its origin, concealing potential treatments, and profiting off the drugs approved to treat it, he did so while maintaining a reputation for being the Western World's most revered public health expert.

Dr. Fauci is not of the opinion there need exist a barrier between those responsible for setting regulatory oversight over the private sector and those profiting from the same entities they are tasked with overseeing, as he had for his entire career found ways to financially benefit from the same drugs he approved and recommended. The drugs he did not profit from, especially if they competed with those he did, tended not to get approved for one reason or another.

On top of his substantial undisclosed private income streams, he happens to be the most highly paid government employee of all time. Over the decades, he became a millionaire many times over, based on his official reported salary alone.

Dr. Fauci, like most rich and powerful men, desired more riches and more power. But what Dr. Fauci adores most of all is attention. He has a naturally narcissistic personality and curries the favor of the media with great enthusiasm.

This proclivity for the spotlight served him well for the duration of the Covid-19 pandemic, as those who controlled the media's interests — to include of course The Man — were fully aligned with Dr. Fauci's constant messaging that the world was in the midst of a terrible pandemic, and our collective survival depended on everyone complying with the increased constraints on freedoms and rights, to include and of supreme importance: agreeing to accept into their bloodstream whatever he recommended.

The media welcomed the opportunity to generate mass hysteria through blanket coverage of the pandemic to the exclusion of all other news. It was a means of regaining the viewership, listenership, and readership over an audience that had grown fatigued and suspicious of them in recent years. They also gladly generated the sense of fear that had made them so popular following the September 11th attacks, and 20 plus years of war that followed, thanks in good part to their many lies.

The media grew reliant on the propagation of fear and creation and sustainment of polarizing political controversies. The pandemic offered tremendous fodder for both, and the framing of the coverage was done in such a way that they politicized every stage of the emergency and fostered a continuation of the contentious right versus left, conservative versus liberal narratives that had come to dominate news cycles.

The media had gone to tremendous lengths to not only canonize into sainthood Dr. Fauci, but to protect his reputation at all costs. They never cared to mention the relevance of the reality he had himself signed off on funding the illegal gain of function research carried out at the Wuhan Institute of Virology. They never popularized the fact he stood to gain personally from the proliferation of specific drugs like Remdesivir, which he gave his full and enthusiastic endorsement despite it causing more harm than good according to multiple well-suppressed studies.

Meanwhile, he viciously decried treatments like Hydroxychloroquine and Ivermectin, which disparaged doctors had claimed proved effective treatments for Covid, particularly when taken early on or preemptively. Both drugs were long established and presented a much safer alternative to the experimental vaccines that could only be given emergency use authorization in the absence of an available remedy. And he and his media allies made damn sure if there did exist a safe, already available treatment, no one found out about it too soon.

Toward the end of pretending no existing alternatives to vaccines existed, social and traditional media giants colluded with unprecedented efficiency to suppress and confuse knowledge of any and all existing effective treatments for Covid. YouTube, Facebook and Twitter's purges of dissenting voices rivaled that of Stalin's; everyone from one of the original inventors of the mRNA vaccine technology used in the experimental vaccines himself: Dr. Robert Malone, to the sitting president of the United States: Donald Trump — were banned from the platforms entirely.

As the media relentlessly encouraged everyone to get vaccinated and labeled anyone skeptical of the choice the dreaded pejorative "anti-vaxer", Dr. Fauci sabotaged and refused to move forward with any studies that would or could prove the efficacy of the other known and emerging treatments that stood in the way of the vaccine agenda.

The strategy from the beginning was to massively exaggerate the threat while narrowing the focus to a single solution: vaccination. Globalists in governments worldwide aided in the mission, doing all they could to suppress anything or anyone that could persuade people not to take the proffered vaccines, regardless of veracity. In New York, Governor Cuomo forbid pharmacies from distributing the long-prescribed, proven safe drug Hydroxychloroquine. In New South Wales, Australia, prescribing Ivermectin, which is abundant, affordable, and has been around for several decades and prescribed billions of times for other purposes, became a crime punishable by six months in prison.

President Biden went on television blaming the continued spread of the virus on "the unvaccinated", attempted to fire all federal employees who refused to accept vaccination, and encouraged the private sector to do the same. Doctors, justifiably in fear of having their reputations destroyed and losing their careers, came to defer to CDC guidelines as if they were commandments directly from God, unwittingly forsaking their Hippocratic Oaths to ensure their self-preservation.

A year or so into the Covid-19 pandemic, much of the world was thoroughly convinced that: (1) The CDC and WHO were the supreme trustworthy authorities on all things Covid, (2) any and all vaccines advocated by Dr. Fauci were safe and effective, (3) any and all other treatments were *not*, and (4) refusing vaccination was a stupid, selfish choice. As the months carried on, the necessarily rushed and untested vaccines proved both unsafe and ineffective; this information was of course thoroughly suppressed by The Cabal and The Man's media apparatus.

Despite the logical incongruences, many people still accepted that vaccines no one could possibly know the long-term side effects of were obviously safe, and vaccination was in all cases preferable to allowing the body's natural immunity to defeat a virus well over 99% of people naturally survived. Even babies who stood virtually no chance of succumbing to the virus were targeted for forced vaccination.

The Cabal and The Man's power of persuasion was so absolute that even after it was discovered the vaccines did not reliably prevent vaccinated people from either spreading or contracting the virus, many passionately advocated their governments restricting and removing their freedoms to force everyone to get the jabs. After all, they took on the risk and did their part. Everyone else should be forced to as well.

The best that vaccine manufactures and corrupted and confused advocates could claim is that the vaccines reduced chances of hospitalization and death; itself a disputable claim, and a far cry from the advertised guarantee vaccine compliance would halt the virus in its tracks if everyone complied. Many of those who contracted the virus despite having taken the vaccine nonetheless dutifully returned for second, third, and even forth servings of "boosters".

Each time they did, The Cabal raked in hundreds of billions.

All the while, the glorified so-called experts and governments around the world uniformly failed to emphasize the importance of exercise, diet and general health maintenance at every turn. All they did was relentlessly push the shoddy vaccines. While natural immunity was treated like a fringe idea, one form of immunity no one seemed to find disconcerting was that granted to the vaccine manufacturers themselves — total immunity from criminal or civil liability regardless of the long-term efficacy and safety of the experimental products.

Seen from a business point of view, the vaccine manufacturers Dr. Fauci favored had everything to gain and nothing to lose by selling as many vaccines as possible, as fast as possible, for as long as possible. Dr. Fauci was someone The Man was eager to introduce Mr. Chen to. An opportunity for such a meeting came in the form of an invitation to attend a meeting of the World Economic Forum, at which Dr. Fauci was to deliver an exciting address concerning the next pandemic.

Chap
While there remained
as to how the Covid-19 Virus
and it was still the official positi
if not Most world governments
was of Completely Natural or
at Large had been made. Aw
plausibility of a lab leak be
Source of the outbreak. Wha
issue was the fact the
for the Members of th
Forum a long ambitio
their Mission of forg
interwoven globa
that be, which in
Major National
from Fortune 500
of great we
ways to Capi
brought ab
be a tim
tremend
Sundar then opined... At
Committed to ensuri
Confronted with
Unexpect

43

_...s a manmade bioweapon created by The Cabal to trigger global_ ...s, tighten control over populations and normalize universal vaccination. Once this was accomplished, they could simply swap a single mandated booster shot for an iteration that caused sterilization. Billions of people would unquestioningly take it, as they had become so accustomed to squirting whatever they were ordered to into their veins and keeping their questions to themselves.

If successful, billions less people would be born. By the time the widespread failure to reproduce could be traced back to the vaccines, it would be too late to do anything about it, and there could be no legal consequences, thanks to their shrewdly preemptively negotiated immunity.

Population reduction was the long-game. The short-term priorities had more to do with centralization of power, accelerated globalization, and the rise of corporate technocratic dominion. While there remained an aura of uncertainty as to how the Covid-19 virus came into being, and it was still the official position of most world governments that the virus was of natural origins, the public at large had been made aware of the plausibility of a lab leak being the true source of the outbreak.

What was not at issue was the fact the pandemic had provided for the members of the World Economic Forum, Cabal and civilian alike, a long awaited catalyst to advance their mission of forging a single, seamless, interwoven global economy under their control.

The powers that be, which included members of most major national governments, scores of executives from _Fortune_ 500 companies, and various individuals of great wealth and influence, had all found ways to capitalize on the induced hysteria brought about by the pandemic. It proved to be a time when the top 1% grew their wealth tremendously while the rest faced unprecedented financial hardship and, by necessity, increased dependency on government assistance to survive.

The lockdown periods alone were sufficient to put most small business owners out of commission while the vast capital reserves, access to credit, and open hands to government assistance armed many of the world's leading corporations to not only survive but thrive and assimilate the struggling mandate-hindered small businesses into their corporate empires.

This was not a conspiracy. It wasn't a secret. And there was nothing illegal about it. This was the natural evolution of the world economy in the face of unexpected disaster. The weak got weaker as the strong got stronger. The poor got poorer while the rich got richer.

The Pareto distribution was in full effect, and the beneficiaries of the recent pandemic were well represented amongst the sea of rich and powerful men and women gathered at this luxurious hotel in Zurich, Switzerland, for the so-called "Covid-20 Summit", the purpose of which was to brainstorm together a roadmap to navigate the next pandemic.

In attendance were high profile names, to include tech giant CEOs like Mark Zuckerberg of Meta (formerly Facebook), Sundar Pichai of Google, and Bill Gates of Microsoft, who were just wrapping up a hosted discussion on the topic of Big Tech's role to play in future pandemics — a fate the tone of the conversation implied was inevitable.

In his closing remarks, Gates recapitulated his overall position...

"As industry leaders, it is our responsibility to leverage to the full extent possible the power of our technologies. In planning ahead and working together, we can ensure the best outcomes possible for the people of the world.

"That means pooling our resources across platforms and demographics to provide the appropriate government agencies the data they need to effectively combat both the spread of disinformation and misinformation, and to provide law enforcement the information they need to identify, monitor and, as necessary, remove from society those responsible for putting public health at risk."

A moderate applause filled the conference hall. Zuckerberg chimed in...

"That's absolutely right, Bill. I would add, on that note, that Meta has taken things one step further in identifying in advance problematic users who have expressed unacceptable and dangerous ideas and enacted preemptive measures to restrict the spread of any misinformation on all our platforms.

"Any and all content they post will be subject first to mandatory in-house fact checks before it even goes live. That's something we will be officially announcing in the near future. Anyone who doesn't like it is free to find another platform or simply avoid forming and sharing their own uninformed opinions on topics best left to the experts."

Another round of applause ensued. Pichai then opined…

"At Google, we are equally committed to ensuring if and when we are confronted with another pandemic, or any unexpected disruptive event, we are decisive and uncompromising in our commitment to only relay correct and properly derived information from our most trusted and reliable scientific experts and media partners. We are currently developing the means to subtly engage our users with… *appropriate suggestions.*"

Bill asked him to elaborate.

"Sure Bill. Well, as you of course know, we introduced disclaimers and redirects based on search queries. That was tremendously helpful in directing people with the wrong ideas to the CDC's website. We're building on that model to include the full suite of Google products so, for example, say an uninformed individual wants to forward a crazy spam email about, I don't know, Bill putting microchips in the vaccines…"

Bill raised his hands like he was under arrest.

"Oh no, they're on to me!"

It got a big laugh. Pichai went on…

"After the problematic user attempts to forward the undesirable content, it doesn't actually send until an AI scan of the email's contents checks the text and images against a database of blacklisted phrases and content. If it's flagged as harmful or problematic, the user is shown a prompt asking them to confirm they wish to send content Google has flagged as false or misleading."

"Fascinating. Have you tested the concept at scale?" Bill inquired.

"Early testing has shown a 59% decrease in users choosing to send emails Google deemed problematic."

A hearty applause greeted the announcement.

"Thank you. Thank you. But if you liked that, you'll love this…"

He leaned forward and spoke in a hushed tone.

"When we tested it with a *second* warning that included language implying personal culpability, such as 'I acknowledge I may face legal or criminal repercussions for choosing to send content Google has deemed potentially harmful or misleading' we saw a remarkable 96% success rate in preventing the user from forwarding the flagged content. It's time to take off the gloves and stop misinformation dead in its tracks."

"Wow. That's really fantastic. Maybe Microsoft needs to bring back everyone's favorite paperclip to chime in when someone starts typing disinformation into Word. Uh. Derp. Ivermectin works on Covid—" Bill held a paperclip to his ear. "—It looks like you're typing misinformation. How about, um, don't!"

The shitty joke killed. On that note of levity, the three tech titans sanitized, shook hands, sanitized again, and left the stage. Among those clappers in the audience were Mr. Chen and Ting Ting, who translated the gist through whispers. With the exception of the paperclip joke, which made no sense, Mr. Chen liked everything he heard and looked forward to finding out what was for lunch.

OF THE ATTENDEES NOT INVITED WERE TWO PETA ACTIVISTS. THEY HAD infiltrated the event with intentions to bring attention to the torturous conditions allowed by Dr. Fauci in experiments funded, approved, and overseen by him. They snuck closer to the stage as Dr. Fauci began his address, in front of a banner with his smiling face, reminding the audience of his illustrious title as the 2020 *Time Magazine* Man of the Year.

"Thank you. Thank you," he began, in his characteristic New York Bronx accent. "It is a great honor to be here amongst such an illustrious gathering of global leaders who, throughout the Covid-19 pandemic, provided the world much needed stability and governance, without which this surely would have been a catastrophe of unprecedented scale and effect." The crowd gleefully and dutifully applauded.

As the claps faded, the voice of one of the activists on a megaphone cut in, starting a rant about his researchers slitting the vocal cords of beagle puppies so their cries weren't so loud during an experiment where they were infected with hundreds of ticks. The activist and his accomplice were immediately apprehended. As they continued shouting about macabre Fauci-funded experiments, they were electrocuted into submission with tasers and removed.

Dr. Fauci continued, in a carefree tone.

"Think they have the wrong room. Anyway, while our partnerships with various government leaders, a number of whom are represented here today, have been key in instituting successful policies to effectively contain the virus, saving countless lives, for which they deserve an applause."

Dr. Fauci called for their government partners to stand, which Ting Ting reminded Mr. Chen, included him, causing him to hop to his feet, wave, and premier the smile he'd been practicing. He found the attention invigorating and mysteriously arousing.

"For as valuable and vital as those partnerships have been and today remain, such coordinated efforts would have been woefully insufficient absent the bold, organized and united efforts of our private sector partners, many of whom I have the honor of addressing today. A round of applause for you!"

This applause was longer and more pronounced than the applause for the government representatives, which sparked in Mr. Chen a flame of envy. The back-patting continued for another eight minutes, followed by a proclamation of purpose.

"Covid-19 has been largely defeated. But I'm sorry to officially announce, *Covid-20* is on the horizon. It falls on us to shepherd the masses through the storm to come, and it is our duty to, simply put, know what's best for everyone and make them do it. And I could hope for no better partners to serve that purpose than the fine people in this room. Thank you. Thank you."

Mr. Chen joined the standing ovation that played the world's most famous, and infamous, doctor off stage. This marked the first time Covid-20 was announced to the world.

## CHAPTER 33
05-03-2022

In attendance for Dr. Fauci's keynote address at the World Economic Forum was Milton, Randy and his father, and father Bishop's boss to be, though the two would've cross paths for another nine days. A great deal of the attendees were Cabal members, the organization itself a creation of Randy and his father in the early 1970s. In addition to Randy and his father were a handful of reptilian hybrids as well, this organization and key significance to them given their ... international banking syndicates ... the human population ... members

## 44

Ting Ting ushered Mr. Chen into an elevator that took them to the top floor of the hotel where he was frisked by an imposing suited security agent and allowed in to a lovely hotel suite with a grand view of the picturesque Zurich skyline that reminded him of a giant gingerbread house. He had heard talk of these houses of sweet bread cake, beautifully decorated with candy of all sorts, shapes, sizes and varieties.

The concept alone made Mr. Chen's mouth water. He had never actually seen a gingerbread house, or even a picture of one. But he trusted the words of the waiter at the restaurant when he spoke of his time in America. He told Mr. Chen all about Christmas.

Mr. Chen, upon hearing the broad strokes, found himself (1) pondering the idea of creating an entire gingerbread city someday, and (2) contemplating that the Americans are puzzling in their mass conspiracy to deceive the youth into believing kind elves in the North Pole manufacture their Christmas toys.

*How stupid can these fucking people be?* he wondered.

Mr. Chen felt surprisingly passionate about the subject, and one train of thought in particular disturbed him greatly.

*The toys all say MADE IN CHINA. In capital letters! Why don't these parents want them to know their toys come from the hard work of Chinese people? Why do they ignore us? Do they joke we are elves?*

Mr. Chen had violently slurped the last third of his second mojito and promptly signaled for another when the idea came to him that China deserved more respect.

*When I'm in charge,* he thought, *we'll get respect; starting with the American government admitting Santa Claus does not exist and all products that say MADE IN CHINA say made in China because they're made in fucking China. And China will get a whole gingerbread house city. And in the center of it will be a giant gingerbread statue of me — Chairman Chen.*

Mr. Chen had never before considered the term Chairman Chen, but for some reason he was having more and more grandiose visions of himself ascending the ranks to become someone everyone would notice and love. And who was more noticed and loved than Chairman Mao? Mr. Chen would wisely keep this thought to himself. But every now and then he would hear the people cheer: *Chairman Chen! Chairman Chen!*

Mr. Chen snapped out of his spell when he heard the unmistakable voice of Dr. Fauci. They met and shook hands, each rinsing their hands with sanitizer before and after the shake, which Mr. Chen found most convenient because he needn't be embarrassed by the clamminess of his hands. He still found himself nervous in the presence of people in general, and powerful people especially... and always looked forward to ending every interaction as quickly as possible.

Their meeting was brief, cordial and served its purpose. Ting Ting did all the talking for Mr. Chen, who barely understood any English, but astutely observed Dr. Fauci seemed more focused on flirting with Ting Ting than paying respects to him. This pissed him off. He stared in a way that Fauci found threatening. It was enough to make him stop subtly touching Ting Ting on the forearm as he joked, and abandon his plan to suggest they meet for drinks later. He cleared his throat and returned his attention where it belonged, on Mr. Chen.

"Mr. Chen, it was an honor meeting. I understand, from our mutual friend you're a rising star in the party, and before long we will have the privilege of working together to ensure the good people of your country have unfettered access to the best and latest Covid-20 vaccines available."

Dr. Fauci leaned in, winked and added, "When they are created, of course."

Mr. Chen couldn't understand jack shit, but smiled and winked back. Dr. Fauci went on talking; he loved the sound of his own voice so much he never paused to give Ting Ting time to attempt to translate his endless grandiloquence, leaving her to reduce his message to Mr. Chen to...

"He works for The Man too. He likes you. He likes China."

Dr. Fauci continued, looking past Mr. Chen as he spoke.

"Please feel free, Mr. Chen, to pass word along to your superiors in the CCP that myself and the good people of the WHO, CDC and Office of the President are dedicated to protecting the proper narrative that Covid-20, like Covid-19, was of natural origins. No one is to to blame but those damn bats!"

Dr. Fauci gave Mr. Chen another wink. Ting Ting took a deep breath then tried to translate.

"He says Westerner rulers will only say the virus came from bats. No one will blame China."

Mr. Chen smiled and gave Dr. Fauci a thumbs up, liking that. He knew it was the proper narrative. Whether it was true or not was none of his business.

A photographer arrived and requested the two pose together for a picture. Mr. Chen obliged. Ting Ting took a quick shot of her own, on her phone. She sent it to The Man who instantaneously replied with a thumbs up emoji. Ting Ting smiled.

She, like Hope, sought The Man's sustained approval above all.

*Mission complete.*

"Okay, very good!" said Dr. Fauci, coming in for another pre and post sanitized handshake. He leaned in to give Ting Ting a kiss on the cheek goodbye, noticed Mr. Chen glaring at him again and reduced it to a handshake.

With that, they left the presidential suite and took the elevator one floor down. Ting Ting bade Mr. Chen wait outside while she checked his room again for recording devices. He stood in the vacant hallway and brooded, feeling envious of the larger hotel room Dr. Fauci had. Now his executive suite felt small.

Ting Ting ushered Mr. Chen into the room and relayed the news.

"The Man says great job. He's so proud. So happy."

Mr. Chen swelled with pride.

"He also says don't tell your superiors Dr. Fauci said hi because soon you'll have no superiors."

This made Mr. Chen feel very special and very happy; so much so that he fell to his knees unexpectedly. His fantasies about the people chanting Chairman Chen were not silly daydreams, for The Man himself was now implying the same. They were on the same wavelength.

Ting Ting joined Mr. Chen for a happy hour drink at the hotel bar and kept watch over him until the arrival of the high-end escort she'd arranged to keep him occupied in his room where no mistakes could be made. Satisfied with his successful meeting, which had required impressively little effort and close to no preparation on his part, Mr. Chen enjoyed the rest of the evening in his room with his new friend, having sex and trying cocaine for the first time. It would not be the last.

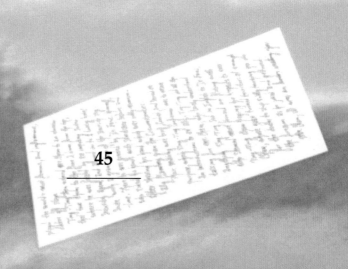

# 45

FRANK FINALLY GOT THE CALL. The heavy hispanic accent delivered the coded message, "We found a notebook with your phone number written on the first page." *First page* meant they'd found something. *Last page* would have meant they'd tunneled the specified distance into the mound and had made no discovery.

Frank said "muchas gracias" and that he would give them a call back, double checked he hadn't left anything in the room, took some fruit and granola bars from the breakfast buffet in the lobby, then checked out of the Holiday Inn Express and peeled out of the parking lot in his latest rental — a red Camaro. Frank is the type of man who considers most laws "enforced suggestions", and speed limits were among his least agreed upon suggestions. He loathed going slow as much as he loved going fast, even when he wasn't in a hurry; but now, he was in a hurry, so he disobeyed the speed limit with wild abandon, entrusting his handy high-end police radar detector to tip him off to pesky speed traps, which it did to glorious effect. He made a pit stop for gas to top the tank off and circumvent Hertz's exorbitant gas refill fees and took the occasion to take the top down so that he might more fully appreciate his remaining race to the airport while joyously singing, which was a favorite past time, especially called for following a new discovery.

The universe seemed to be on the same page, because as soon as he sparked the chariot's ignition, the fade of the engine's roar revealed the opening rift of "Free Falling" by Tom Petty, among Frank's top picks, made thrice as enjoyable for having come on organically rather than by way of conscious intention. Connecting the bluetooth was a huge pain in the ass

Frank had wisely chosen not to attempt, and it paid off, as he found himself gleefully going triple digits down the freeway, warm air blowing his hair where it pleased, radio loud enough to drown out both the horns of pissed off obstacles and his own subpar singing. The trifecta of speed, song and success were enough to put as big a smile on Frank's face as would fit. The song came to a conclusion the instant he arrived at the rental drop-off point, and he killed the engine the instant before the DJ spoke, perfectly punctuating the finale of the joyous journey. *It's the simple things in life...* he thought.

Frank was by nature a handsome and charismatic gentleman. His lax overall demeanor and authentic sense of self-assuredness were among his tentpole qualities, and people tended to catch on to the fact he was a man of mystery, which some found off-putting, but plenty found intriguing. He carried himself as a man who had a pleasant secret, and hiding the ball about "what he did" was a skill he'd cultivated to the point of mastery over the years. He found ways to turn his evasiveness into a respectable trait and even attractive feature.

This would prove to be the case between Frank and another person in the airport security line... a person who was even more guarded, mysterious and attractive... a person who had been sent on a secret mission to make contact with Frank, learn whatever he was on his way to finding out, and by any means necessary bring him back to the island for a meeting with The Man, whose invitation Frank had thus far rudely failed to accept. The Man sent Hope on many such missions, and not once had she failed to deliver the intended results.

Some missions weighed heavier on her heart than others. Mark, for example, was a mark she did not enjoy manipulating in the least. Contrary to Mark's conclusion that he meant nothing to her, and it had all been a ruse, Hope had felt a real connection; and their lovemaking had not been a mere formality... nor had been their meaningful conversation or general intimacy.

Hope still had a heart. It had not been completely walled off. More accurately, there was a drawbridge to her heart. Over the years, she had become masterful at retracting it at will, detaching emotionally on a dime. This is part of what made Hope so good at her predatory escapades. She could quickly form an at least partially authentic relationship with anyone she targeted, then when the time came, sever the bond with tremendous cold-blooded efficiency.

It hurt her at least a little each time, but she consoled herself by clinging to the belief The Man was a well-intentioned genius. Everything she did, she told herself, as he so often had, was for a higher good in the grand scheme of things. She usually believed it, but the instant she made contact with Frank's hazy sapphire eyes, she felt a strong predilection that letting this one go wasn't going to be easy.

It took Frank a double take to confirm the pretty raven-haired lady with the low cut silk, oriental-patterned top, short black jean skirt, and matching stockings was checking him out. She held his curious gaze another instant then let loose a wry smile that whispered *you caught me.*

She bit the left side of her lower lip and adjusted her long, free flowing hair with both hands, before giving her neck a slow roll, averting her gaze long enough for Frank to safely take inventory of her protruding side boob and porcelain shoulder line.

She then tied her hair into a ponytail, exposing her smooth naked underarms and pressing her perky breasts together ever so gently with her elbows, in a pose of surrender that sent a pulse of arousal through Frank. She grinned at him once more as she turned around to go through the metal detectors, where the guards whose job it is to steal shampoos and pretend they're finding nonexistent terrorists commanded her to again strike a similar pose.

A moment after she faded into the crowd, a Tumi carryon rolling behind her clacking red bottom heals, she faded too from Frank's attention; his mind turned back to the exciting discovery that was now just one flight and a 20 minute drive away. But the alluring beauty came to his attention again soon enough when he saw her seven minutes later, reading a book outside the gate to his flight to St. Louis. Frank chose the seat directly across from her, which Hope pretended not to notice as she turned the page and subtly reoriented the book so its cover was clearly visible to Frank — the latest book by his favorite author — giving him a t-ball to swing at.

Frank waited until she turned the page again, noting her eyes weren't moving, and suspecting her thoughts were off the text. He was correct. Really she was reviewing a slender piece of paper with small font titled "Frank Facts". It was a collection of information about her target that could be used in the seduction process, compiled compliments of The Man's intelligence agency contacts. The wealth of intel The Man provided on any targeted individual, even one as enigmatic as Frank, made it easy to know anyone better than they knew themselves.

Frank made his opening.

"Graham Hancock. Great book."

Hope convincingly feigned a startled shudder.

"Sorry—" Frank offered, "—it's just, I'm a big fan."

She smiled a smirky smile and asked, "Of Graham Hancock?"

The challenging smile was invigorating and unrelenting. Frank nodded gracefully, smirking back at her banter, relieved and exhilarated he hadn't misread the situation... *she's into me.*

She held out her hand for a shake, then waited, with that mischievous siren smirk, until Frank stood up and bridged the three foot chasm between them. He sat beside her and shook her soft, warm hand.

"I like your nails— Frank said, keeping it unprofessional, "They're..." he looked into her big brown eyes unflinchingly, "very... very beautiful."

A brief, pleasant and exciting flow of flirtation ensued before transitioning into a discussion about the mathematical codes baked into the measurements of the pyramids of Giza and how they served as proof its builders knew about the geographic and astronomical characteristics of Earth, it's orbit in relation to the cosmos and much more than mainstream history can account for. He lit up with a clear sense of passion for his area of expertise, which Hope found both attractive and germane to the execution of her mission.

When it came time to board, Hope revealed another amazingly convenient coincidence. She claimed to be a corporate attorney on business, and that she had in her possession an extra, unused, first-class ticket. Perhaps, she suggested, after takeoff the flight attendants could be persuaded to let her give him the already paid for seat so they could continue the conversation at 36,000 feet.

Needless to say, it was an offer he couldn't refuse.

---

WHAT FOLLOWED WAS THE MOST ENJOYABLE DATE FRANK EVER HAD. THEIR conversation proved substantive and engaging, and danced between the languages they both knew. They had so much in common Frank joked she must have "read his file". Hope laughed... a little too much.

Thanks to her homework, she had no trouble coming up with opportunities to flabbergast Frank with their many supposed similarities in taste and opinions — from movies to politics to colors and other trivialities — all near perfect matches. They had so much in common it was astounding, just as had been the case with Mark. They even played a game where they said their favorite *fill in the blank* on three. As in...

"One, two, three... Indian Jones and the Temple of Doom!" Or...

"One, two, three... Norah Jones!"

It occurred to Frank he liked Joneses quite a bit.

Hope was careful not to win every round, but even if she had, Frank wouldn't have noticed the ruse, as he was already thoroughly under her spell. Hope didn't pry into his work life. She was patient. Like any experienced hunter, she knew how to wait for the shot. She didn't expect her target to get into the nitty gritty of his unsanctioned and illegal digs on a first date. She also wanted there to be at least one more date, for selfish reasons, before she lifted the draw bridge and left him in The Man's hands.

After landing, they stopped at a bar in the terminal for martinis, at Hope's suggestion, where the added element of intoxicating libations loosened lips and legs. Frank mentioned his true line of work and revealed there was a new discovery to be witnessed in the near future — one he planned to share with the world. Shrewdly opting to link sexual pleasure to his revelation of the sought information, without another word, she took Frank by the hand and led him across the terminal and into a family bathroom with a door that locked.

They made out for a few minutes, in what amounted to the best make out session of Frank's life, which he escalated without resistance. Hope's eyes smiled. She hoisted herself onto the baby changing station. Frank began slowly rubbing first the back of his hand, then his fingertips, then lips gently across her stockings, breathing teasingly through the fabric encasing her trembling thighs. When the teasing was too much to bear, she took Frank's right hand, selected a finger, and slid it straight through her stockings.

Hope had a hole filled with treasure waiting to be found and Frank was eager to dig.

---

OUTSIDE THE TERMINAL, THE TWO NEW LOVERS CONTINUED MAKING OUT UNTIL A taxi pulled up. Hope pulled him close by his belt buckle and said "nice to meet you," while discreetly giving his eager cock a squeeze through his Levis, then dropped playfully into the backseat, giving Frank one last glimpse between her legs and destroyed stockings.

"Wait! That's it?" Frank cried out, chasing the departing taxi.

Hope leaned her head out the window, laughed, and pointing at his crotch. He looked down to see the business card wedged behind his belt buckle.

Frank would be seeing Hope again soon. That much was clear to both of them.

had) for the man had d...

Louis to trail Frank...

to his hotel, on...

was not drunk...

-ing his profit...

made a single... ...

limit but he technically

to qualify as intoxicated...

technically there is all that...

offer held my breath...

in the back of a squad...

...where...

## 46

TEMPTED as Frank was to rent something fast and furious, he opted for an unassuming Honda Civic, given the priority he maintain a low profile. The last thing he wanted to do was attract attention. Unfortunately, he already had, for The Man had directed the Sheriff of St. Louis to trail Frank and arrest him en route to his hotel, on grounds of drunk driving.

Frank did not break any traffic laws, nor was he too drunk to drive by any reasonable standard, but he technically was drunk enough to qualify as intoxicated under Missouri law, and technically was all that mattered. After failing a breathalyzer test, Frank was handcuffed, put in the back of a squad car and driven to a St. Louis police station where he spent a sleepless night in jail and general disbelief at the sudden misfortune that had befallen him.

Unbeknownst to Frank, he was not the victim of misfortune, but rather, a plot perpetuated by the sheriff, who was a reluctant chess piece on The Man's far-ranging board. Every six months, for the past five years since being elected, the sheriff had received a black glossy envelope in the mail — each time containing $5,000 in cash and a freeze frame of a secretly recorded video of him with a prostitute, along with a note that simply read: *Thank you for your service*, unsigned, save for The Man's favored icon of the pyramid capstone containing that all seeing eye.

On rare, isolated occasions, he would receive identical black envelopes with simple instructions accompanying the foreboding pyramid eye symbol. Instructions such *Detain Frank Apalonia for DUI*, along with the necessary details. The implications of the unspoken arrangement were clear: do as commanded and you will continue getting $5,000 every six months; don't, and you will be publicly humiliated and your marriage and career will be woefully disrupted. The sheriff obeyed.

As always, the commands were precise and reliable — Frank had been found when and where he was supposed to be found and over the legal limit, as had been forecast. It was a layup. How and why the prediction came true and what was to become of the guy was none of the Sheriff's business.

Frank wondered if it could have anything to do with his secret project, but he had been very careful and didn't know how law enforcement — especially local police — could have built a case against him. Besides, why arrest him before he even arrived at the dig site? It didn't pass the common sense test. So Frank dismissed it as a bit of very bad luck — perhaps the department was shy of hitting a DUI quota and they'd just been fishing. Given his clean record, he could likely pay his way out of the whole debacle with limited, if any, long-term consequences.

But for that to pan out, he'd need a lawyer. The only problem was he didn't have anyone local, and the officers didn't seem keen on helping him find an attorney, perhaps thanks to the sheriff's instructions, which were very specific: "Don't give him a phone book or any phone numbers. Don't make him empty his pockets." The officers obeyed.

After a relatively sleepless night in a holding cell, Frank set his mind to getting out. Frank was frustrated when the officers finally led him to a phone and refused to provide a phone book. It took him a while to remember he did know a lawyer that just so happened to be local. And he did have her number. It was on the business card in his pocket. *Talk about a crazy coincidence!* He weighed the discomfort of a prolonged jail stay against his embarrassment confessing to his new special friend that he was locked up and needed a hand.

He didn't like either choice but reasoned she'd be more than understanding... she'd feel guilty herself, if anything, as she'd been the one to insist on both the in-flight whisky sodas and post-flight airport bar martinis. Frank finally got his phone call and let out a sigh of relief when he heard Hope's sympathetic response, followed by assurances she'd be by as soon as possible, and a flirtatious joke about how this explained how he could have possibly avoided calling her last night.

Frank returned to the holding cell only to be promptly relocated to a private interview room where he expected his meeting with Hope was to take place. Rather than Hope, he got men in black... two pasty white men in black suits with skinny black ties, taking their matching sunglasses off in unison, as if it had been rehearsed — which it had. They introduced themselves as "special federal agents", then cut to the chase...

"The Georgia Guidestones. Someone just blew one of them up. Then dug up the time capsule. We have reason to believe you were behind it. Tell us the truth."

"What the hell are you talking about?" Frank asked, bewildered.

"You wanna play dumb? Okay let's get through that part."

One of the dead eyed men dramatically slammed a large, sturdy laptop — the kind you could drop in a river and it'd be fine — on the table and played dated and timestamped security camera footage of one of the Georgia Guidestones exploding.

"Refresh your memory, champ?"

"I don't know anything about that. I had nothing to do with it."

"We know all about the illegal digs, guy. And we're taking you down unless you tell us everything about… everything. We'll get back to the Guidestones. But what's done is done. What we care about most is what you're planning to do next. You were recently at the Georgia Guidestones. That's an easily provable fact. It's also a fact that you were recently at Serpent Mound. This is your chance to come clean about whatever you're planning there."

Frank at that point fully committed himself to exercising his right to remain silent and refused to speak or even make eye contact. He didn't know who they were, who tipped them off or what they actually knew. By the sound of it, not much. All he knew is they sure as shit weren't going to learn anything about his discoveries unless and until the rest of the world did. Their tough talk was vague and a little over the top, leaving Frank the impression they didn't have a solid case against him.

He was right. But that didn't mean they didn't have leverage. One of the men opened a new window on the laptop. It was a crypto wallet.

"This your cyber money, Frank? Couple clicks and you're broke, chief. Is that what you want, pal?"

Frank kept his best poker face. He had no way of knowing for sure they were really his accounts without giving it a closer look, which he chose not to. He did notice the balances all appeared to be in line with what he remembered having in the accounts, and as the two assholes went on taunting him about their power to burn his hard earned pile of money — most of his life savings — he felt his stomach churn.

"Okay, tough guy. Fine. Let's escalate. You don't need this Dogecoin, right? Say bye bye Dogecoins, Frank. In three… two—" The other agent leaned in, "Last chance Frank. Save your dog's coins."

Frank looked away. "—one, WOOF!"

Frank glanced at the screen they were shoving in his face. It did appear to be one of his wallets. And the asshole did appear to have just robbed him of the equivalent of $62,000 with the press of a button.

"What's the new find, Frank? What'd you find at Serpent Mound? We know you've been digging there. Just tell us what you found and this can stop and we can go our separate ways."

*Serpent Mound? Thank God. They're fishing blind.*

Frank hadn't done any digging there. He began contemplating potential bluffs as they moved the attack to his next cryptocurrency.

"Matic? What's that? Who cares. It's gone."

"Ouch. Bye bye Matic, Frank."

Another $7,500 worth of crypto torched.

"Cardano? Never heard of it."

"Must be another shitcoin. Our guy won't miss it."

"Boom!"

Another $19,000 worth burned. Frank felt his blood boil. He wanted to pick up the computer and beat these two jokers to death with it. But he mustered the discipline to maintain the stoic countenance. Finally, he said something, if only to stall the carnage.

"Alright. What do you want to know about Serpent Mound?"

"That's more like it, guy."

"Tell us everything you know about it."

This, Frank could work with. He knew a lot about it, and if he talked slow, it would be an hour before he ran out of shit to say. He started with basic facts, slowly conveyed, and feigned being frazzled when pressed to "skip past the boring shit, chief". After a good ten minutes of successful delay, he ran out of material.

"That it? Stop playing with us. We know you know more."

It was all Frank could do not to laugh at them. They seemed like such amateurs. Frank remembered the more out there stuff he'd recently read in the gift shop book — about the mound being oriented toward the Draco star constellation. At that, they really started paying attention… one looking at the other like he was surprised to actually be hearing something they were after.

"Draco, huh? What do you know about the Draco?"

With the goal of stalling until his lovely lawyer showed up, Frank began a tangent based on what he could remember about the so-called Draco Reptilians. He'd periodically come across stories about the supposed beings over the years, typically in dark corners of the web where attention starved eccentrics with vivid imaginations on conspiracy sites unleashed their bizarre ramblings.

"It sounds crazy. You guys aren't going to believe it."

"Try us."

"Alright, fine. But don't say I didn't warn you."

With nothing to lose, Frank went all in, recounting the ridiculous stories as if they were well-known facts. If anything, he would relish in the opportunity to fuck with them.

"Well, as you gentlemen surely know, the second world war didn't end the way the mainstream history would have us believe. Before the fall of the Third Reich, the Fourth Reich was already in the works."

The agents sat down at the table, across from Frank. One of them retrieved a small notebook from his suit, clicked open a pen and started jotting down notes.

*Are these guys serious?* Frank indulged the fools.

"Hitler's top brass established a breakaway Nazi civilization in Antarctica, building bases in naturally formed underground caverns. The allies captured a Nazi submarine and in it discovered well-guarded secrets. Some say it contained plans for the atomic bomb, which the Americans used to create their own. Some also say they came across maps that indicated the existence of the hidden Nazi bases, along with guidance on how to access the underwater caverns. In response, American sent a naval strike force under the command of Admiral—"

"—Byrd," one of them chimed in. *They know the story?*

"Right. Admiral Richard Byrd. His fleet was met with stiff resistance that surfaced from beneath the sea."

Frank contemplated whether he should share the next part.

"Keep going."

"I'm just telling you what I read, okay?"

"Fine. Go on."

"Flying saucers. With shields. And laser beams. The outmatched naval ships and planes didn't stand a chance. After suffering massive casualties, Admiral Byrd turns tail and flees back to U.S. waters. The Germans let them go to share what happened."

Frank was surprised to see they hadn't expressed any frustration with the outlandish claims.

"What else?"

Frank went on…

"The American government plays off the whole debacle as a scientific expedition gone awry, feeding the public a bullshit story to cover up the truth the Nazi threat remained, and now had clear air superiority."

"How'd they get the flying saucers, Mr. Know It All?

"Well, okay. Since you ask. And again, this is just me relaying what some people believe."

"Enough with the disclaimers. Just talk."

"It's said they developed the superior weapon systems with help from extraterrestrials contacted by occultist channelers in German secret societies, like Mariah Orsich."

"The beautiful witch lady with the really long blonde hair?"

"That's right. Of the Thule Society, which, as I'm sure you already know, had been co-opted by the Nazis, thanks to Hitler's obsession with ancient inner-earth societies, like the Aryans, who he believed to be an ancient root race the Germans were descended from. So, through the occultists they make contact with multiple ET civilizations, most notably — the Draco, who helped the Nazis develop the technologies in exchange for helping them excavate sites in the South Pole left behind by other ancient civilizations, providing them human subjects for whatever purposes they had, and I don't know what else."

"There's always a third thing."

"Yeah. There's always a third thing. Wienerschnitzel recipes maybe."

"Yeah, maybe."

The men in black didn't seem to like the Wienerschnitzel bit, but were otherwise fully attentive. Frank said a prayer Hope would show up soon and did his best to keep the story going…

"Anyway, they uh, basically kick Admiral Byrd's ass. The Nazis sue for peace. The Americans blow them off. So they gave another show of force with the allies on the ropes by sending a fleet of their flying saucers directly over The Whitehouse."

Frank recalled seeing old black and white footage of this. He'd always assumed it to be a sham, albeit a convincing forgery. But the seriousness with which the two supposed government agents were following made him second guess his long-held disbelief.

"And you know, if the dates line, up, I'm not sure about this one, but that might also explain the Battle of Los Angeles."

Frank was making reference to a bizarre, heavily substantiated event in 1942, during which the U.S. military fired off over 1,400 anti-aircraft artillery rounds over the course of a night at a hovering target off the coast of California. It was believed to be a Japanese aircraft, then later explained away as a lost weather balloon. The incident claimed the lives of 10 civilians and made front page headlines nationwide before being gently scrubbed from history.

"So yeah… Nazis had help from the Draco. They made flying saucers and used their technological advantage as leverage to force the allies into a secret peace treaty that mandated their sovereignty be recognized, Antarctica be made off limits to the rest of the world, their presence be kept secret, and countries and corporations worldwide accept an influx of Antarctic Germans into positions of major influence so they could exercise surveillance and control over planetary affairs as they fixed their horizons on off-planet expansion."

"Why didn't they just take over the world instead?"

"Were you not listening? They did. As far as they're concerned, they won the war. They just didn't care about making it official. And they didn't want to worry about managing all the billions of inferior people on Earth when they were focused on starting their new empire made exclusively of pure blooded Aryans."

"Alright. What else?"

Frank shrugged, out of things to say.

"Thanks for the history lesson, kid. But what's that got to do with your dig? What's it got to do with Serpent Mound?"

*History lesson? What do these guys know? Why are they taking it so seriously?* The long awaited knock on the door finally came, accompanied by the sweet but serious voice of Hope.

"Hello! I'd like to see my client now. Hello!"

"Stay put, professor."

The men in black had a quick whispery sidebar, then relented to Hope's banging and let her in.

"Hello. Nice to meet you. Fuck you. What jurisdiction to you have over my client?"

They offered her the same vague, special federal agent titles.

"Well gentlemen, you can walk your special federal asses out of here right now because my client is being held on a charge wholly unrelated to whatever the hell the purview of whatever government agency you work for is, if that's even true at all. Now give me your credentials so I know who to sue."

"Listen, bitch. We have full authorization—"

"—to get the fuck out of here."

Hope subtly revealed to the agents a tattoo on her wrist, of the all seeing eye.

"That's right. My boss is your boss," she whispered, so Frank couldn't hear.

"We're done here. See you soon, Frank. We're on to you, pal."

With that, they left the room, slamming the door behind them. Hope took the card off the desk, put it in her red Coach bag with a gold chain, then greeted Frank with a big, warm hug.

"I'm sorry for not making it sooner. I got here fast as I could."

"No problem. That was amazing. Thank you. What did you say to him?"

She gave Frank a quick peck on the lips.

"Come on. Let's get out of here, baby."

Frank smiled. He liked when she called him baby. He could get used to that.

THEY LEFT THE POLICE STATION WITHOUT ISSUE, LEAVING FRANK UNSURE whether or not he was on the run, but faced with the choice of going back in to find out or getting inside the red Jaguar convertible Hope had parked in the handicap spot, it wasn't a tough call.

Frank got in the passenger side.

Hope got in, looked at his lap and in an extra sultry voice said…

"You drive."

---

FIVE GREAT SONGS AND ONE VERY ENJOYABLE DRIVE LATER, FRANK PARKED outside her hotel, which was far nicer than his own.

"Hey, by the way, who's your boss?" Frank asked, as he zipped up his pants. Hope smiled. Her work was almost done.

"You free tomorrow? I'll introduce you."

Marx had spent anoth
in the lionshare of
to reading, contem
in the solitude of
library. He had de
added routines th
in the form of jo
halls between his ro
library, as well as
meditating - his pre
English avantgar in

---

## 47

MARK HAD SPENT another unknown quantity of months alone.

Time had lost all meaning; the days bleeding into weeks; the weeks into months, into years. Or so it seemed. The lion share of his time was still dedicated to reading, contemplating and writing in the solitude of the majestic library.

The Man had yet to return for another visit, and Mark had no means of contacting him. But he eventually stopped worrying about it. He'd developed a series of added routines that included daily exercise in the form of jogs around the library and halls to which he had access; as well as blocks of time spent meditating — his preferred locations being a plush armchair in front of a large, crackling fireplace, and on top of Stalin's desk, which presented a lovely view of the typically serene and apparently vacant estate.

He found himself lonely but no longer dwelled on that aspect, choosing instead to value the freedom from distractions and day to day concerns that afforded him the opportunity to fully invest himself in his in-depth self-guided studies. He felt better about his situation when he chose gratitude for what he did have, as opposed to the alternative of lamenting what he lacked.

But his routine was disrupted that day by the unexpected sight of Hope. He witnessed her emerge from a black SUV that parked in the circular drive at the front entrance to the manor, which he could see clearly through the window.

She was escorting a man she seemed to be enjoying the company of, as evidenced by her bright, unrestrained smile that sparkled in the tropical sunshine. She playfully slapped his arm, confirming Mark's suspicions they were involved.

Hope looked so beautiful. And so happy. With someone else. The glimpse of the siren of his dreams and nightmares ignited a cacophony of undesirable emotions; including longing, frustration, and resentment.

He tried not to obsess over it, but his heart was an Übermensch unto itself, and it played by its own rules. Mark paced. He began to think about the other men Hope had been with since him and the new boy toy she was with now. He was consumed by envy, scorn and resentment and soon found himself engulfed by the onset of mania. His bipolar condition had been well-managed as of late, but was by no means extinguished.

Mark was jealous. And bitter. And the disparity between what his night with Hope had meant to him and what it must have meant to her made his body tremble in an involuntary shiver, as if the coldness of her indifference palpably altered the temperature of the lonely library.

He banged his fists on Napoleon's desk like an ape as he thought about the possibility, if not likelihood, Hope was at this very moment giving herself to whoever this latest fucking jerk that could never love her the way he did happened to be. He began slapping his face red and digging his nails into his body so the physical pain would interrupt the endless visualizations of Hope being fucked and harmed by his endless line of competitors. Questions raced through his increasingly frantic mind: *How many others are there? What do they have that I don't? Are they better in bed? Do they have bigger dicks? Does she love them? Does she love me? Did she? Could she? Could anyone?!*

He felt like something had been stolen from him, but at once knew it had never been his to begin with. He wished there was someone to blame, but the only culprit was to be found in the library window.

"Fuck you!" he yelled to the odious reflection.

"You fucking piece of shit. You're not good enough for Hope! You'll never be good enough! You deserve to die alone on this fucking island! I hate you! I fucking HAAAATE YOU!"

He screeched like an animal and punched his reflection as hard as he could in a burst of uncontrollable rage. The blow cracked the window, but the window won the fight. The impulsive strike sent an immense surge of pain into his previously broken hand. But the pain only made him laugh. The pain was welcome and deserved. Mark yelled. Mark threw chairs off the balcony with his still working hand and was seized by an impulse to jump that he ignored. He tore up books. He did not handle it well, to say the least.

After an hour in this state, he transitioned the overwhelming energy into exercise. He channeled it into pushups until his arms gave out. Then he sprinted up and down the stairs and around the perimeter of the library, and did sit-ups until his torso convulsed.

He wanted desperately to feel nothing for Hope, as he surmised she did for him, but he could not will that outcome into being. To the contrary, he felt everything for her. Since indifference was off the table, he settled for forced exhaustion.

This manic fury continued for hours, in gradually declining intensity, until he finally laid on the plush red carpet. He lied there shaking, crying, banging his fists on the floor and gritting his teeth until he finally achieved sufficient exhaustion to fall asleep.

---

In his slumber, Mark encountered an orb of awe-inspiring light against a backdrop of pure darkness. It exuded a feminine energy that felt like Hope's presence and warmed his heart with felt vibrations in lieu of words. The light drew nearer and nearer until it entered his body through the center of his chest.

All his negative emotions were instantly extinguished by the loving light and he felt a sense of peace and love he'd never before experienced. There was an absence of fear and abundance of love. He felt as if the light had come to help him and sought to know his intention. He relayed it without hesitation: *to experience a life with Hope.*

At once a stream of imagery and sensation coursed through his consciousness, like flashes of emotionally charged lightning containing glimpses of memories and experiences he'd never actually had, but that seemed very, very real.

Mark saw two sets of footsteps in the sands of a moonlit beach in Sicily… Hope's hand taking his in a movie theatre… the sound of both of their laughter in a crowded European cafe… her warm smooth leg sliding between his cold feet under a comforter… the glisten of moonlight off her new engagement ring as they pointed at the stars from beneath a swing set… the smiling faces of friends and family, both known and unrecognized, gathered at a cathedral… the glorious sight of the bride of his dreams walking down the aisle… a series of snippets of their many travels and adventures… then, the gentle cries of a newborn infant met by soft assurances of motherly love… and finally, a crying toddler pushing open a creaking door and waddling into the bedroom.

Then came the long-missed voice of Hope…

"Yanos? Is that you, baby?"

Mark saw Hope slide out of bed and hurry over to the quivering, crying boy, who had Mark's complexion and Hope's hair and nose.

"Oh baby, what's wrong? Did you have another bad dream?"

Mark sat up in a plush king-sized bed he'd never been in and at once felt had long been his. A potent vibrational field of energy filled the room, flowing like a barely visible ambient plasmic light — it was an energy the child was also sensitive to. Yanos stopped balling when he looked at Mark through eyes indistinguishable from his own, clearly relieved to see him. Yanos sniffled and brushed his runny nose with a ping pong ball-size fist.

Hope lifted Yanos from his sides with a *woosh* sound and playful spin, then gently deposited him on the bed and snuggled up — the gestures doing nothing to calm the boy.

"Tell me about your dream. What happened?"

Yanos rubbed his teary eyes and spoke in an endearingly raspy voice…

"I dream… I dream Daddy on island. I feel Daddy's sad. Daddy hurts. Umm… Daddy, Daddy Miss Mommy. Yeah. Want Mommy come back. Wait long time. Long time Mommy no comes. No love Daddy."

Yanos cried. Hope embraced him and kissed the crown of his head.

"Oh, baby," she told him, "Don't worry. It's just a dream."

"No!" Yanos declared with an impressively indignant screech.

"Mommy no comes! No love Daddy! Daddy yell. Mommy no hear. Daddy make book. Mommy no read. Mommy only want bad daddies!"

"What? I'm sorry baby. What a bad dream…"

"Yeah. Bad."

Mark maintained a stolid countenance betrayed by a river of tears and quivering chin while Hope consoled Yanos with pats and kisses. Yanos pulled back and looked at her seriously.

"Bad daddies hurted Mommy. Why Mommy want hurted? Why Mommy… Daddy nice daddy, why… is no Daddy! No Mommy! No Yanos! Is all dark. All go away… all dark. Is… is no. Is all dark."

"Shhhh shhhh. Yanos. Yanos. Baby. Look at Mommy. It's okay."

Hope wiped away his tears with her thumb.

"It's just a dream, my love. But you know what? If Daddy was on an island, we'd get in a boat and go save him! Wouldn't we?"

Yanos sniffled and nodded in agreement.

"But Daddy's right here. And you don't have to worry. Because Mommy loves Daddy. Very very much. Just like Mommy loves you!"

She pressed a finger on his nose and said *boop*. Yanos laughed.

"And Mommy will never ever leave you. Or Daddy. Okay, baby?"

Mark took a deep breath and closed his eyes tightly. Yanos felt the energy in conflict with his mother's words and began sobbing and muttering about bad daddies. Hope sat up cross-legged, picked him up so he was facing Mark over her shoulder and pat Yanos on the back. Mark mustered a bittersweet grin and waved, doing his best to hold in the same feelings Yanos was letting out.

"Your Daddy's right here. See. No bad daddies. Just us. And your baba. And your sissy. And none of us will ever be alone. Because we're a family, and we'll always have each other! Right, Daddy? Mark? Mark…"

Hope turned to face Mark, who looked at her longingly; gratefully; and beaming with relief — as if he really had escaped an island. Hope tilted her head like a bewildered dog, smiled and let out a curious chuckle. Mark smiled and gazed at his son.

"Oh, yes baby. Yes. Daddy loves you and Mommy."

Mark brushed his thumb against Yanos' head.

"Yanos. What a name. I always wanted son. Just like you — my boy."

He looked at Hope and laughed in an explosive teary catharsis that sent a freight train of love directly into Hope's unobstructed open heart.

"Our boy! Hope, we… we have a son! Can you believe… can you believe we made this guy? I mean, look. We… we have a fucking amazing, beautiful… wonderful son! Look. Look at him. What a blessing."

Unexpected tears cascaded from Hope's loving eyes, traversing the dimples of that truly fucking perfect smile. It's a smile with a glow that gives moonlight a run for its money. It's more contagious than Covid-20, but a catalyst for creation and healing rather than a harbinger of destruction; a universal panacea for all the woes of man. The smile of Hope exudes a beam of love that instantly obliterates all traces of negativity in the blessed few fortunate enough to encounter it. It's a smile that could start or end wars; a smile that proves the existence of God, case in point.

Mark took that smile in with astonishment and gratitude, realizing he could spend the rest of this life doing whatever it took to make it as permanent a fixture as possible. Hope laughed boisterously, took a deep breath and eased herself back into Mark's relentlessly loving gaze. Yanos slipped out of Hope's embrace and jumped on Mark.

"You and Mommy saved Daddy from that lonely island. Thank you. And I'm never ever, ever going back. Okay, Yanos? I promise. I love you, son."

Hope slid toward them. Mark stretched his arm out to bring her into the embrace, but the instant before he touched her, he heard a loud reverberating gong-like tone. His ethereal body suddenly ejected from the physical vessel and he found himself floating above the bed like a ghost, looking down at another Mark who was trying to make sense of what just happened.

That Mark continued where our Mark left off. He pulled the comforter over Hope and Yanos' heads to make a tent. The disturbing gong sound grew louder, and Mark was yanked downward by an invisible force, through the soft warm bed, through the floor, and into a chilling pool of infinite darkness.

The bed of light above Mark faded into a dying spark as he descended helplessly into the listless void. Mark desperately attempted to swim back up to the preferred reality, but it was impossible. The harder he tried, the faster he sank and the further his dream family faded from sight. He exerted all his energy in pursuit of the unattainable goal, for as long as he possibly could. Finally, when there was nothing left to give, he accepted that no degree of effort could rekindle the love he'd sought to experience again since his first and last night with Hope, and the unfortunate day that followed.

Unwelcome though necessary thoughts then flowed into Mark. The void had something to teach him. It imparted on him an understanding that his imagined life with Hope was real. But it couldn't be forced into being. He could keep trying, but whatever ending their story together had was ultimately outside his control. Perhaps hers too.

If it was destined to happen in the life he was born into, it would.

If not, he simply had to find a way to let go of the desire.

The revelation gave Mark a sad sense of closure, and he accepted his fate: a return to the dreaded lonely island. With that moment of acceptance, a plasmic wormhole bursting with lively animated neon smoke appeared, drawing him into it.

He surrendered to the experience that scattered him into innumerable bits of light then found himself reassembling in the sky above the island. He was now in the form of a rainbow-light body that fell like a feather, gently and slowly, through the large domed ceiling and gracefully back into his unconscious body below.

His wish had been granted.

<hr />

MARK AWOKE WITH A GASP, THEN STARED AT THE FIREPLACE FOR HOURS, HIS thoughts scrambled and emotions muted. Then he stood up, took a deep breath, and got back to his routine with a reclaimed sense of calm, despite the bewildering incident, which marked his first out of body experience and hadn't felt like any dream he could remember.

He didn't know if any of it could be real, but he found a sense of appreciation for the never before fathomed possibility that somehow, in some other time and place no less real than this one — in another life — it had all played out differently. Perhaps, he hoped, he could go back there someday. But for now, he was stuck in this life. And he had something left to learn; to figure out; to contribute; to leave behind... possibilities to manifest that wouldn't happen if he was living happily ever after with a wife and family and traditional scope of responsibility.

The path to the Übermensch, after all, is one wrought with pain, loneliness and prolonged periods of deep introspection that can only take place in solitude. Mark concluded that while he may not ever know the simple leisures of a normal life, and he may be fated to live out the rest of his days on an island alone, he could in the least make use of the time — and the rare chance he had to understand The Man, his means, and his methods. Then, and only then, did he stand a chance of stopping him; and in doing so, paving the way for future generations to be free, happy and aware of their own untapped potential.

Mark resolved to finally let go of Hope, and to embrace in her stead a general mission to help others, while placing as little emphasis as possible on what was in it for him. No easy task. To be sure. But at least he had a goal in mind. While he had no wife or kids, he would live the time he had left as if he did... even if they were worlds away... guided by the thought he could do something to put an end to young Yanos' nightmares.

Daddy might be lost on an island in a dream, but he was making the most of it. And he was doing it to make the world he was trapped in a little better than he found it. That's something the family in the other life could be proud of. It was an odd consolation, and perhaps a delusional one. But it made Mark feel better than he had before he fell asleep, and with a sense of clarity sufficient to continue his solitary journey toward truth, understanding, wisdom and power.

He settled on his next book to read — one kept in the secret library within the library, under a case his fingerprint opened. He was drawn to the cover, which featured the occult symbol for alchemy — a gold circle, containing a triangle, containing a square, containing another circle, each shape nestled snugly within the other. It was entitled, "The Kyballion: Hermetic Philosophy" by Three Initiates.

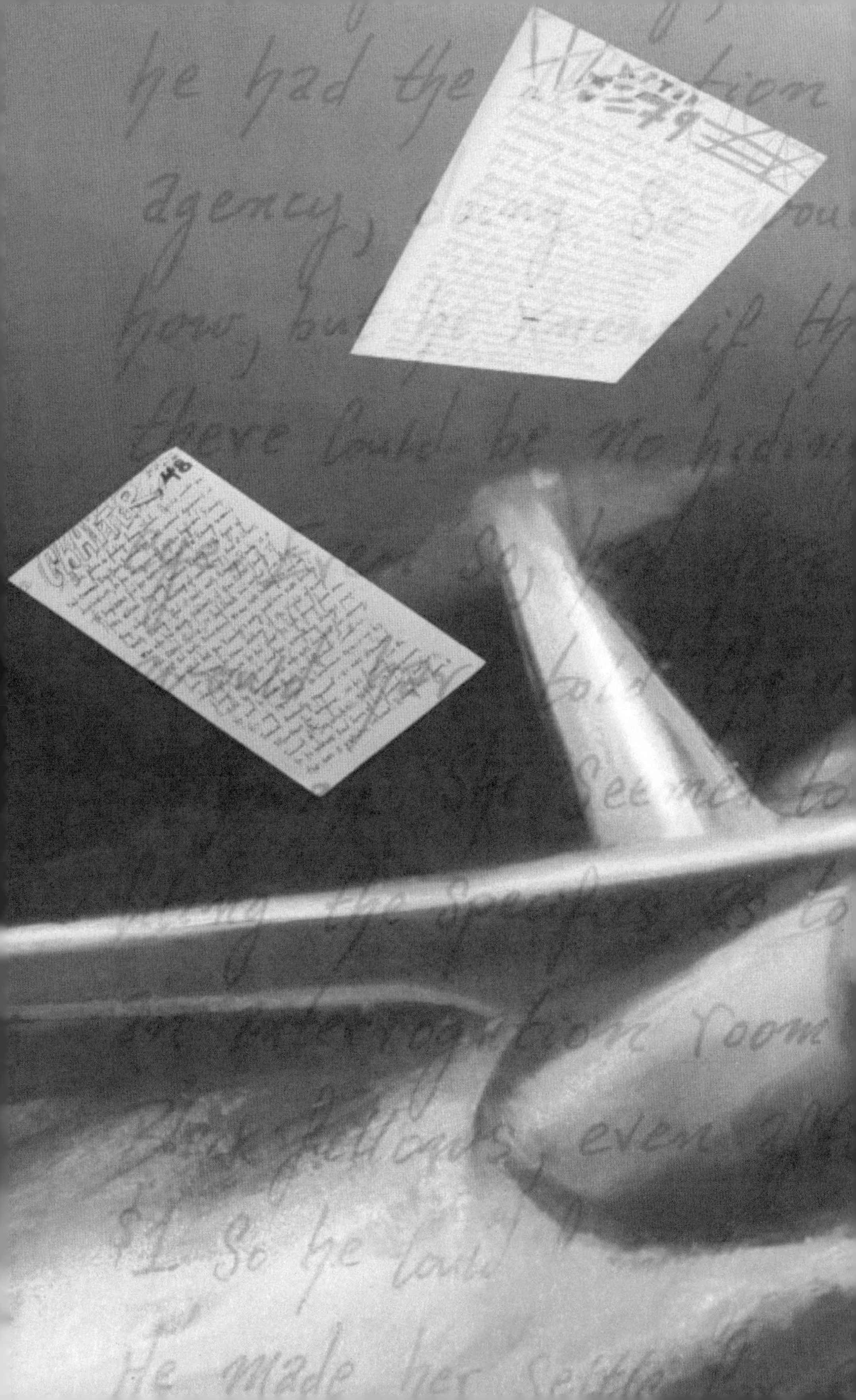

he had the
agency
there could be no
He made her

## 48

As PERFECTLY APPEALING as Hope's offer was, compounded by the fact they had spent half the night prior having the best sex of Frank's life, deciding against going to the dig site still proved a taxing affair. He wanted desperately to take the risk and satisfy his ravenous sense of curiosity, but now that it was apparent he had the attention of some form of government agency, doing so could be futile.

He didn't know how, but he knew if the will matched the resources, there could be no hiding from Uncle Sam's watchful eye. Even so, had Hope not been there, he probably would have told the mirror "fuck it" and gone anyway.

She seemed to respect his evasiveness in citing the specifics as to why he'd found himself in an interrogation room with those low rent men in black, even after she instructed him to pay her $1, so he could formally enjoy attorney client privilege. He made her settle for a nickel, albeit a 1929 Silver Buffalo Nickel worth several dollars — a gift Hope found genuinely endearing and planned to one day turn into a necklace she could slip on when she found herself missing him.

Not unlike a serial killer, Hope kept tokens from each of her conquests. She wasn't sure why she did it and rarely ever looked at them, but some dark part of her enjoyed knowing she had trophies to celebrate her "accomplishments". In Mark's case, it was a seashell she had found on the table in his room (Luke's seashell). In Randy's, it was an American flag pin that had been affixed to his suit lapel that she had deftly stolen while straddling him, giving her an extra sense of thrill, further complicating the fact he'd raped her. He had. But eventually she'd come to enjoy it, which made her feel disgusted with herself. She questioned her own sanity. Did she know what was going to happen when she showed up to Randy's room? She was in the least aware of the risk. But she had a job to do. So she did it. She hated what had happened and the way Randy made her feel. But she'd also enjoyed it. Thanks to The Man, Hope's sex life was so fucked up she couldn't even tell for sure whether she was being raped or not anymore.

Hope was not an attorney. Hope was a liar. But she passed for one and surely could have made a great barrister, given her high levels of intelligence and overall work ethic. Hope was literally human but figuratively chameleon, capable of assuming a wide variety of identities to exceptionally convincing effect. To keep the identities straight, though, she kept the first name unchanged.

Frank, as perceptive and suspicious as he was, had yet to doubt a single word that came out of Hope's mouth; in part because he was too busy kissing it. He was not traditionally a man so susceptible to infatuation, but Hope had already proven herself an exception to the usual filters that kept his romantic entanglements easily untangle-able. Beyond proving so alluring and fundamentally captivating, she had also arrived as a heroine of sorts, easing him out of yesterday's bind, and now also offering him a mini, impromptu honeymoon-esque getaway... first class to The Man's private island.

Hope considered that by now Frank might have figured out that her employer and the person he had been corresponding with were one and the same. But he hadn't. And that was good. It made it so she didn't have to either talk her way out of it, sewing new lies into her tapestry of deception, or confess that she had been sent to get him to take the meeting he was putting off. Either could lead to Frank losing interest and refusing to come willingly, which would likely result in his being apprehended again by the special government agents that had, just like her and the sheriff, been there on The Man's orders.

The high stakes scenario served the joint purposes of giving Hope an emergency to rescue Frank from, thereby solidifying his trust, and robbing Frank of his small fortune, creating an enhanced incentive for him to take interest in financially lucrative offers — the sort of which The Man would provide in a timely and convenient manner. He could also grant assurances he needn't worry about further government interference. He could make Frank's troubles with the men in black disappear as easily as he'd made them arise. Carrots and sticks... the time tested pairing The Man relied on in so many cases to pressure people into doing what he wanted.

Hope explained to Frank that this top client, whom she casually referred to as "The Man", was extremely powerful, influential and well connected. She was very confident he would benefit from making his acquaintance. In fact, she boasted, she'd never met a single person who hadn't significantly benefitted in one way or another for having met The Man. This contention could surely be discredited if Hope was to include the dozens of women he'd had thrown into a volcano in ritualistic sacrifices to himself, or the ultimate fate of the people he helped if and often when they eventually and inevitably ceased to be of use.

Hope hoped that when Frank inevitably discovered her employer to be the very same aspiring employer of his, whose last letter he had failed to respond to on a timeframe The Man deemed acceptable, and that this had all been a ruse to get him to a first meeting, their seed of a relationship might still be permitted to flourish. But she knew it was wishful thinking. Theirs would be a relationship built on the wobbly pillars of deception and hidden intentions, and she knew it was fated to die in the crib, like so many others had over the years.

This thought was the source of the single tear that coursed its way down her cheek — thankfully, the cheek facing the airplane window, rather than the cheek facing a series of loving pecks from increasingly lovey-dovey Frank.

"I'm having fun—" he whispered, "I'm glad we met."

Between each loving remark, he peppered in another affectionate peck, which blazed a current of love across Hope's drawbridge and into the otherwise cold recesses of her hidden heart.

She subtly wiped away the pesky tear and faced Frank for an exquisitely passionate kiss... a kiss so perfect the passing flight attendant shirked her sworn duty to make them fasten their seatbelts for takeoff. It was a kiss neither of them would ever forget; but only Hope knew was quite possibly a kiss goodbye.

---

FRANK FINALLY CAUGHT SOME SLEEP ON THE FLIGHT, WHICH WAS BOUND FOR Miami, from which Hope had explained they would connect, via private jet, to The Man's island, at the center of the fabled Bermuda triangle. He was not typically a vivid dreamer, but he awoke with the feint recollection of a potent dream in which he encountered a tall, blue, hominid being with feline facial features and large, beautiful, loving eyes. It was similar in appearance to the beings encountered by the human corporate colonialists in the film "Avatar", which he'd recently seen, and attributed the inspiration for the dream imagery to.

He didn't recall words being exchanged, but remembered mental imagery the entity had silently conveyed, which included, from what he could recall, an image of Earth from space, but without any city lights or clear traces of civilization. A sort of time lapse ensued, which caused the planet to spin and rotate rapidly, like a basketball being spun on God's fingertip, pausing intermittently. The first time it slowed, Frank observed signs of civilization on the Sinai peninsula where concentrated beams of light were emanating from what could only be the famed pyramids of Giza.

The globe quickly spun again, slowing this time to reveal more sites with similar beams of light, in places in apparent geometric alignment with Giza, such as the location of Angkor Wat in modern day Cambodia, Machu Picchu and Nazca in modern day Peru, and several others. Seen from this perspective, it seemed to indicate all these locations had expanded as one connected global civilization. The planet spun again.

When it slowed for the third time, there were many other smaller cities, expanding from those initial points. Then, suddenly, something caused an ecological chain reaction, and the oceans of the planet rapidly blanketed the continents in massive waves of water. Volcanos erupted violently, like fiery bullet wounds across the planetary surface, and in short order the blue and green marble in the expanse of space was reduced to a hazy ball of darkness. He then saw a large fleet of spaceships with a line of shuttles traversing from the smoky globe to the larger ships stationed beside the moon... an evacuation by the looks of it.

Frank awoke from the dream with a shudder. He accepted a warm towel from the flight attendant and ordered a double shot of whisky on the rocks, wiped his face, and placed the towel on the back of his neck. To his immediate right was a sleeping angel; Hope somehow looked even more beautiful in her sleep. Peaceful. Breathing gently through her perfectly symmetrical nose... a hint of satisfied grin on her thoughtfully made up face. He watched her slumber as he put in some earbuds and played a very fitting song for the occasion...

"I Don't Want to Miss a Thing" by Aerosmith.

> *I could stay awake, just to hear you breathing*
> *Watch you smile while you are sleeping*
> *While you're far away and dreaming*
> *I could spend my life in this sweeeet surrenndder*
> *I could stay lost in this moment foreverrr*
> *Every moment spent with you is a moment I treasure*
> *I don't want to close my eyes*
> *I don't wanna fallll asleep*
> *Cuz I'd miss you baby*
> *And I don't wanna miss a thing*

Frank realized his singing might be loud enough to disrupt Hope's sleep, so he reduced it to an airy whisper.

*Lying close to you*
*Feeling your heart beating*
*And I'm wondering what you're dreaming*
*Wondering if it's me your seeing*
*Then I kiss your eyes and thank God we're together*
*I just wanna stay with you*
*In this moment forever*
*Forever and ever*

Frank's desire to keep his voice down proved untenable, waking Hope. The first thing she saw was him with his eyes closed, lost in the lyrics. Frank opened his eyes to see her seeing him. His innocent smile sent a warm tingle that stormed her drawbridge and lit her face with a smile and cheeks with a blush. She plucked out his left earbud.

"Whatcha listenin' to?"

As Frank rushed to pause the song, Hope slapped his hand away. Too late, he looked away in embarrassment, blushing just the same. Hope giggled like an innocent girl with a schoolyard crush — the girl she never had the chance to be.

"Should I go back to sleep for you, buddy?"

Frank tried to subdue his bashful grin, failing miserably. She left the earbud in, held his hand and leaned her head on his shoulder, let loose a yawn, then started falling back asleep as Frank gently kissed the top of her head and discreetly set the song on repeat.

---

A BLACK SUV WITH TINTED WINDOWS WAS WAITING FOR THEM OUTSIDE THE airport — this one a current year Lincoln Navigator, which navigated them to the airfield where a fueled, ready for departure Gulfstream jet awaited their arrival.

"Have you ever flown private?" she asked.

"Never to somewhere with a paved runway."

"Sorry if this ruins travel for you. But The Man insists all his friends and allies travel in style."

Frank couldn't help but try again to learn more about this elusive man, as they boarded the empty jet and took their seats.

"What does The Man do exactly?"

"He's in every sector. Every industry. Every country."

"Hmm... but what does he do... primarily?"

"He owns."

"Can I ask—"

Out of ways to artfully shift topics, Hope pressed a finger against Frank's lips, shushed him, and said, "Can I ask if you've ever joined the mile high club?"

She straddled his lap as the plane began taxying for takeoff, laughing as the plane began to accelerate, throwing her chest into his face, then readjusting herself with a determined playfulness.

"I'm just curious who this guy is," Frank insisted.

Hope shushed him with a kiss, then said, "Well I'm curious who this guy is," as she slipped a hand down his pants and began preparing him for takeoff.

---

THE FIRST THING FRANK NOTICED ABOUT THE ISLAND WAS THE AIR. FRESH. Clean. Clear. Perfect. The sun was bright. Dolphins were jumping out of the pristine water in the distance. The sounds of birds chirping and squawking was a constant. It truly felt like the perfect getaway.

It was nice to for once have no destination he was in a rush to get to. No agenda, other than discovery and enjoyment — of both the new setting and the new gal, who was beginning to feel like a new girlfriend. *From midwest jail to island paradise,* Frank thought contently. He took a moment to fully appreciate how lucky he'd been to meet Hope when he did. At this point, it all just felt like a dream.

The final leg of their journey was yet another black SUV, washed and waxed and full of that elusive new car smell. It drove them from the air strip to the biggest mansion Frank had ever seen or imagined. He exited the SUV at the circular drive atop the cliff, where the grandiose front doors awaited and told a suggestive joke that made Hope laugh and playfully slap his arm as they made their way to the entrance.

Just before going in, Frank caught glimpse of a man behind a large window on the third floor, sitting on a desk cross-legged, staring at them with a sturdy scowl. He seemed angry... resentful... envious... perhaps even hateful... because of course Mark was.

---

## 49

THE NEARLY TWO years spent in isolation had given Mark the opportunity, by necessity, to develop an improved ability to consciously control his mental and emotional stability. He was by no means stable, or well, in the general sense. Given the immense stress inherent to his situation, he was understandably in a position from which most people would fall into insanity. All things considered, he was faring quite well.

Mark had compensated for the loss of the cushion provided by his psychiatric medication with meditation. He was not capable of, say, sitting down and replacing his feelings of hopelessness — which ironically only seemed to have been dispelled temporarily by a girl named Hope — with optimism.

He was, however, at a stage where he could prevent himself, with limited exception, from descending into the prolonged crippling depression that marked his lowest lows on the island. After spending a half hour in a state of deep meditation, he was finally able to cast from his mind the echo of the moment of observation Hope was nearby, with another man... and that she had clearly moved on, if she had ever cared to begin with.

She had cared, but the drawbridge had long since been slammed shut, and a few floors below, where Hope was giving Frank a tour, on their way to a room they would share, Mark had crossed her mind.

Hope wished him well, and even considered chiseling out some time to drop in and extend a more substantial apology, and perhaps even salvage some form of friendship. But she decided against it and kept her focus on the current mission: ensuring Frank made it into his upcoming meeting with The Man, which was scheduled the following morning, when he returned from his most recent business trip — a series of meetings with members of the House of Saud, known more commonly as the government of the Kingdom of Saudi Arabia.

Among the topics of discussion had been the protection and revitalization of Crown Prince Mohammed Bin Salman's public image, which had taken quite the hit in recent years, when it went public he'd ordered the killing of a Saudi-born, U.S. based journalist named Jamal Khashoggi. The form of law practiced in Saudi Arabia is that of Wahabbism, under which, for example, "crimes" as trivial as playing a guitar in public were punishable by breaking the musicians hands. Killing pesky journalists was par for the course in Saudi Arabia — a place where public executions for violations of archaic religious laws were regular spectacles in the town squares.

But the murder of Khashoggi had come as a shock to the world because the journalist, whose head the crown prince literally had delivered to him, as punishment for writing articles critical of his rule — lived in America and was often published in American and European publications; in the world of Western media, killing journalists was (at the time) still heavily frowned upon. The thin-skinned ruthless prince's audacious move against Khashoggi entailed his being apprehended while at the Saudi consulate in Istanbul, Turkey, where he'd planned to pick up legal documents related to his upcoming marriage.

While his fiancé waited in the car outside, a hit team of 15 Saudi assassins took him to the back where they proceeded to torture, kill, and dismember him. It was all caught on a several hour audio recording, presumably made to present to the prince, so he could enjoy listening to the suffering and demise of one of his declared enemies.

There had been no military or economic retaliation (save for sanctions against the men directly responsible for the killing). More egregiously still, then President Trump chose not to let the little slip up get in the way of one of the biggest arms deals in history. Rather than sever ties on moral grounds, he supplied the murderous monarch with the latest and greatest (known) weapons, compliments of the American Military Industrial Complex, so that he may more effectively wage war on his already highly mismatched neighbor of Yemen while solidifying his medieval authoritarian rule domestically.

America had long been in the business of helping Muslims kill Muslims in the Middle East. This was common knowledge. But staying in the king's corner during this particular affair had in effect sent the rest of the world a clear message that it was no big deal to kill journalists, even if they lived in America. The red white and blue had no will to enforce or uphold its long claimed values; not if it was bad for business or compromised control over regions of strategic significance.

If America ever did have a conscience, it was clearly dead in the modern age. Money was sacred. Power was sacred. The rest were insignificant details.

The media's distaste for President Trump, and continued efforts to put a premature end to his reign and prevent his re-election, had justified their decision to take a critical stance and shed light on the affair. Had a more preferred candidate with a less contentious relationship with the media held office at the time, the fallout would have surely been far less significant. This is evidenced in part by the fact very little criticism had come from mainstream media in the wake of President Biden's abandonment of everyone in Afghanistan relying on U.S. Protection, and his administration's parting gift of killing an innocent family with a drone strike on the way out.

Biden too had no qualms about sending weapons to tip the balance in foreign wars, allowing the lucrative arms trade with Saudi Arabia and everyone else to continue uninhibited and arming such trustworthy allies as Ukrainian Nazis to help fight the Russians in later years.

The violent, image-conscious prince sought The Man's assurances the Western press, much of which was under his direct control, would avoid bringing up his sordid past and current condemnable actions, and cooperate in the effort to repair his international reputation through positive reporting.

An agreement had been reached.

---

MARK FOUND IT EXCEPTIONALLY DIFFICULT TO FOCUS ON HIS READING OF "THE Kybalion", so he took to copying down the "laws", or principles, presented therein. It helped concentrate his focus on the work and off his frustrations with Hope's new boy toy. Mark's notes on the material appeared as follows...

## I. THE PRINCIPLE OF MENTALISM

The underlying reality of the universe is mental. Learning the art of mental transmutation gives one the power to influence reality through thought alone.

## II. THE PRINCIPLE OF CORRESPONDENCE

*As above, so below; as below, so above.*

Broadly applicable axiom. Things work on the micro level the same way they do on the macro. Reality corresponds to the thoughts from which it emerges. The unknown can be understood in relation to the known.

. . .

### III. The Principle of Vibration

*Nothing rests; everything moves; everything vibrates.*

Everything exists in a state of constant vibration. Matter is in a lower frequency of vibration than spirit. Like a struck tuning fork spreads vibration to a nearby tuning fork, the vibrational frequency of our thought also falls in tune with the thought of others on the same frequency. We can choose to resonate with higher or lower frequencies.

### IV. The Principle of Polarity

*Everything is dual; everything has poles; everything has its pair of opposites; like and unlike are the same; opposites are identical in nature, but different in degree; extremes meet; all truths are but half truths; all paradoxes may be reconciled.*

Where does hot become cold? Big become small? Dark become light? Apparent opposites exist in a state of relation to one another. Good exists in relation to evil. Neither can be understood unless in relation to its opposite pole.

### V. The Principle of Rhythm

*Everything flows, out and in; everything has its tides; all things rise and fall; the pendulum swing manifests in everything; the measure of the swing to the right is the measure of the swing to the left; rhythm compensates.*

Yin and Yang. Ebb and flow. Action and reaction.

### VI. The Principle of Cause and Effect

*Every cause has its effect; every effect has its cause; everything happens according to law; chance is but a name for law not recognized; there are many planes of causation, but nothing escapes the law.*

Karma? All occurrences and manifestations linked to an unlimited chain of events? We are affected by unseen causes?

### VII. The Principle of Gender

*Gender is in everything; everything has its masculine and feminine principles; gender manifests on all planes.*

Male and female. Protons and electrons? Life resulting from union of the genders? Balancing of masculine and feminine traits/energies? How does this differ from polarity?

MARK WASN'T SURE WHAT TO MAKE OF MUCH OF WHAT HE STUDIED IN "THE Kybalion". For additional context, he backtracked to the introduction, which he had skipped, where he discovered the unusual origin of the work. The "Three Initiates" who served as the anonymous authors claimed to have created "The Kybalion" through documentation of ancient hermetic wisdom that dates back to the days of Hermes Trismegistus, and has been passed down and preserved through the so-called "mystery schools" over the ensuing generations.

The word hermetic, which means "airtight" in modern parlance, derives in reference to the keepers of the occult teachings' ability to so effectively conceal from the profane masses the knowledge passed on from Hermes Trismegistus. As for the mysterious figure Hermes, the word Trismegistus translates to "thrice majestic." He was awarded this honorary title because he is said to have been a great priest, philosopher, and king — all rolled into one man.

The title was also applied to the Egyptian deity Thoth, who the ancient Egyptians credited with the introduction of writing, science, as we would now call it, medicine, and even music. He is revered as the father of civilization, more or less, and said to be capable of traversing the realm of the afterlife.

One popular theory maintains Thoth was capable of incarnating in various physical forms, at will; and that Hermes was actually a reincarnation of Thoth... explaining the matching titles and overlap in teachings. Mark read what he could find about the mysterious Thoth/Hermes for the rest of the day, returned to his room, and reread his notes in a sustained attempt to keep his mind off of what Hope was up to somewhere nearby.

The house was big enough that he couldn't hear them having sex from the library... a courtesy Hope made sure to extend to Mark, whose name she found herself accidentally moaning as Frank took her from behind on the balcony. Frank assumed he had misheard.

Sheila had moved on
months prior. She had
to find solace, now for
a born again Christian
Crystal Cathedral in
and attending Bible
done in her youth,
taken a job as she
provided the comfort

## 50

SHEILA HAD MOVED on since the breakup with Randy. She'd ultimately turned to religion to find solace, now fashioning herself something of a born again Christian; spending Sundays at the Crystal Cathedral in Garden Grove, singing in the choir and attending Bible studies, as she had done in her youth.

Her Instagram following had taken a hit, as she now primarily published less provocative content, as a good Christian girl is expected to do; though she still had a penchant for low cut blouses and her natural emanation of feminine sexuality was unavoidable. The end result was less men holding their phones in their left hand when they moseyed through her feed and more people finding Christ.

The announcement Randy had become engaged to his homely cousin had come as a loathsome surprise, but it paled in comparison to the surprise that Randy was apparently now running for President of the United States. It made no sense, considering Randy had not only never held any public office, nor ever expressed to Sheila any desire to, but wasn't even a politically minded or engaged citizen.

Their discussions concerning politics had been so few and far between, and of so little substance, they weren't even memorable. Sheila came to learn about Randy's out of the blue campaign when she looked at her phone one morning to find dozens of messages, voicemails, and notifications concerning the matter — from reporters, friends and family, and political organizations and lobbyists — all with something to ask or say about her ex's run for President. It was surreal and overwhelming, and Sheila had avoided responding to anyone until she had time to process the new development.

Randy was an enigma, even to Sheila; but there was such a dearth of public knowledge about the fellow that she was now apparently one of the world's leading authorities on all things Randy. One email did catch her attention; the sight of which jolted her with a surge of uneasy adrenaline; it was from Randy, and consisted of a single command, which served as the email subject: *don't fucking talk to the press.*

Sheila obeyed.

RANDY WAS RUNNING ON THE DEMOCRATIC TICKET, BUT THE DESIGNATION WAS irrelevant. In truth, he was The Reptilian candidate; The Cabal candidate; and The Man's candidate. Those three entities were the masters he served, and balancing their aligning and conflicting interests was his sole concern. Toward the end of finding a proper balance and retaining all three backers — any of which could prove a devastating opponent if he lost their favor — a summit had been called, with a representative from each group set to attend.

The goal of the summit was to clarify the goals of Randy's presidency, affirm the spurious agenda the public would be sold, and to iron out any conflicts of interest that might arise. That's what Randy was told at least. The confluence of the three groups formed a delegation representative of an unstoppable alliance superior to that of any nation, and if harmony could be maintained, Randy's unchallenged reign would be a sure thing.

Randy's only true agenda was Randy. He didn't give a damn about America, Americans in particular, or any of the high-minded values espoused incessantly by American politicians. He just liked the idea of being given the title of the most powerful man on Earth and the enhanced license it would give him to do whatever he wanted.

He already had everything he could want. All that was left to attain was more of it. More money. More power. More control over the people around him. More is also what he needed to finally escape his father's long-cast multi-billion dollar shadow and solidify his identity as the most rich and powerful DuPont yet.

He had been told the location of the summit was to be an underground base in Antarctica, but at the last moment, the destination had been changed, as a precautionary measure. Randy only discovered this when the armor-plated black SUV carrying him to the airport took a turn for the Pacific coast. The airport he thought he was headed to was LAX. Instead, he found himself arriving at an installation owned by the Boeing Corporation near Seal Beach, a half hour drive South of LAX. Security waved them through, and Randy was driven into a parking garage beneath the building.

From there, his security detail escorted him inside and down an ordinary hallway, where they entered a door with a sign designating it a supply closet, protected by a simple push button PIN lock. Nothing out of the ordinary. But inside, what first appeared to be a water heater descended into the floor, revealing a staircase that spiraled down several stories. Such hidden passageways would have impressed Randy weeks prior, but it was mundane compared to the behemoth chambers beneath the New York Federal Reserve Castle.

At the bottom of the stairway awaited another security checkpoint, manned by two soldiers in military fatigues with submachine guns slung over their shoulders. They both held their thumbs against fingerprint scanners on either side of the door, and after seven seconds, the door slid open, splitting into two parts and disappearing into the walls. Next, Randy witnessed something unexpected — water; it was a dock inside a cavern, with a full size nuclear submarine floating on the surface.

"Just a moment, sir," said one of Randy's escorts, as he approached a device mounted on something like a podium. He typed in a passcode and seconds later, a smaller, clearly more advanced submersible arose from the waters at the far side of the dock. From it extended a bridge composed of what looked like aluminum foil. His escorts boarded first, proving the flimsy looking material could easily support a man's weight.

The craft was roughly the size of an RV, with its widest part being the back, narrowing to a point at the front where the cockpit was located. It reminded Randy of a giant arrowhead, save for the serrations on the sides, which were perfectly smooth. It's material coating the outside resembled that of a B-2 bomber, and the top housed a formidable, low profile turret of some sort.

The interior was snug enough that Randy needed to crouch to avoid hitting his head, and the hull contained little more than a series of heavy duty bucket seat-style chairs with seatbelts similar to those found in a Formula-1 race car; facing forward, where a hologram read, "Prepare for departure", through which could be seen a door separating the cockpit from the hull. Randy sat in the front middle chair.

An unknown aid approached and reached toward Randy. "Let me secure your seatbelt—"

Before finishing the sentence, Randy's security detail knocked the well-meaning man out cold and dragged him off the vessel.

"Get the fuck off me," muttered Randy with a chuckle.

He enjoyed watching his security detail hurt people on his behalf whenever the opportunity presented itself. Overzealous as they were, with orders to kill first and ask questions later if Randy's safety was ever remotely in question, Randy loved having them around.

One of Randy's two bodyguards returned.

"Threat neutralized. Are you okay, sir?" Randy laughed.

"Do I look okay? Do me a favor, help me with this fucking seatbelt."

The formidable former bodybuilder and ex-marine nodded and resumed where the dispatched individual had left off. The ship submerged and picked up speed as it navigated the little known underground waterways that extend the substrata of the continents. Moments later, it was exiting the aquatic subterranean tunnels into the Pacific Ocean. From there, it was a short trip at high speed to an underwater military base somewhere between San Diego and Catalina Island.

There were no windows in the hull, but had there been, even the so hard to impress Randy might have been awed by the sight of the site. As if encased in a giant half bubble on the ocean floor, there sat a full-size military base. The dome contained breathable oxygen and was, besides the unusual location, virtually identical to the hundreds of American military bases on the surface world.

The buildings were all made of normal dark brown bricks, and every paintable surface was one of a few mundane shades of brown and tan. The dome was high enough to stack three water towers on top of one another and still have half a water tower of clearance before hitting the top, and everything was connected by your typical concrete roads… from the operational command center to the living quarters to the grocery store (commissary) to the gas station/general store (shoppette) to the gym and, ironically, the outdoor pool.

It was not exactly like a normal base, however, in that it housed some of the U.S. Military's most secret advanced technologies and weapons; the things Congress funds and never finds out about; the things sitting presidents only find out about on a "need to know basis".

Someday soon, Randy would need to know.

---

THE UNDERWATER BASE REMINDED RANDY OF THE SCENE IN "STAR WARS: Attack of the Clones" that depicted where Jar-Jar Binks' people lived. He wondered how much of what he'd seen in science fiction might be based on reality, or have coincidentally got it right. As it turns out, quite a bit.

Randy was given a brief tour of some of the facilities while they awaited the arrival of the triumvirate of delegations from The Cabal, Draco Reptilians, and The Man, respectively. Randy's tour guide was a distinguished naval admiral who walked him through a hangar.

"So are you an ocean navy admiral or a space navy Admiral?"

The Admiral laughed.

"I think you mean Space Force. I'm not aware of a Space Navy."

The Admiral was aware of a space navy. He was a part of it, because for twenty years he was involved in the program *Solar Warden*.

"Which space program came first?" Randy asked.

"Well, quick crash course in the real history, no pun intended, in case you haven't already been read in—," the Admiral said, "—in 1947, the famed *Roswell Incident* occurred, giving the American military the opportunity to reverse engineer a downed alien spacecraft.

"Following the discovery of the new technologies this unleashed, and the potential it had to shift the balance of world power for or against us, the whole groundwork for our modern defense apparatus was established. That same year the United States federal government introduced the DoD, CIA, USAF, AFSW and SecDef."

Randy interrupted... "I'm not actually in the military. I'm just going to be in charge of it. I don't know what all the fucking acronyms mean, man."

The Admiral forced a polite grin, reflecting on how crazy that was.

"Right. The acronyms stand for Department of Defense. Central Intelligence Agency. Air Force, Armed Forces Special Weapons Project — made the A-bomb... atom bomb; and Secretary of Defense."

"Sir."

The admiral lifted his eyebrows in polite confusion.

Randy sighed.

"You didn't say sir before you said the rest of that shit."

Randy observed the admiral's discomfort and sensed confrontation.

"I'm kidding man. You don't have to say that yet. Then again, maybe you should."

The admiral balanced a polite grin with a *watch who you're fucking with* grimace. He punched a code into a side door and took him into another hangar. There sat the first reverse engineered spacecraft The Cabal had revealed to the world through unsuspecting Naval fighter pilots, who participated in a New York Times story relaying their experiences. Videos were "leaked", and the pentagon released sparse, cryptic comments confirming the legitimacy of the footage and existence of the craft.

"Look familiar?" the Admiral asked.

"Yes. The tic-tac. I had a feeling that was us."

The "tic-tac" was dubbed such because its shape resembled a giant piece of the popular candy. Years later, the official position of the United States government concerning the matter was still a big shrug. They claimed complete ignorance as to what it is, who built it, or what it was doing flying around at incomprehensibly high speeds, making impossibly sharp turns and jamming pilots' tracking systems just off the coast of San Diego.

The only thing the government would admit is that it wasn't ours, which was also a lie. The revelation had caused a remarkably understated public response, and despite learning there exist aircraft capable of literally flying circles around the Air Force's latest and greatest state of the art fighter jets, and there is presumably nothing we could do to defeat such a foe if they proved hostile, no one seemed to care.

The intended step of seeding in the public psyche the existence of an unknown threat had been accomplished. For years, the public dutifully awaited their cue to panic, going on with their lives in the meantime as if nothing had changed. This was the work of The Cabal, who kept on the table the option to use the American military to fake an alien invasion with the advanced craft. This almost came to pass in 2020, but it was decided a single disaster would be sufficient, and The Cabal voted instead to carry out the pandemic agenda.

"Yep, that was us," the admiral proudly stated.

"We gave the world a sneak peek."

"So how does it fly?"

"I'm sorry. But I can't discuss those details with you yet."

Randy glared at the Admiral.

"Sir," the Admiral lamented.

The show of submission was a step in the right direction, but Randy wasn't satisfied.

"Whatever. Just take me to the fucking meeting, man."

Randy made a mental note to add the Admiral to his list of people to fire as soon as he was president.

## 51

RANDY WAS ESCORTED to the command center through a bank vault style door, and into a utilitarian, spartan, conference room. His bodyguards were made to wait outside, and Randy was asked to surrender any electronic devices he may have forgotten. He was scanned with a metal detector wand to verify... a step Randy found insulting, then left alone in the room to await the arrival of the rest of the attendees.

He had no idea what to expect, but his father's advice had been to remember that, despite the fact he would be interfacing with the most powerful and formidable people on the planet, they all needed him to carry out their agendas. He was a key fulcrum on which the machines of their empires pivoted, and as much as they might convey he was in their pocket, they ultimately needed him more than he needed them. He advised Randy to conceal any personal intentions not in apparent alignment with their stated interests and to remain neutral whenever possible in the event of disagreement.

The sound of the door opening behind him gave him a shudder that didn't express itself physically. As a boy, Randy's father had often surprised him with loud sounds from behind and rewarded or punished him based on his reaction. Ignoring the noise would earn him $100. Cowering, on the other hand, would earn him a crisp slap to the face and the designation "pussy".

He slowly turned around to see a friendly face. It was The Man. Randy had enjoyed his visit to his island... complete with the standard kingly treatments, including the delicious meals, fine scotch, and lavish room he fucked several women in, including Hope, before sacrificing one of his "gifts", in a private volcano ceremony where he pledged allegiance to The Man.

Randy hadn't meant to honor his word. His only allegiance was to himself. But he saw it in his interests to keep The Man happy and in his corner... at least for the time being. The Man felt the same, and had been sure to record Randy's bedroom debauchery and add it to his box of strings as an insurance policy on the next president. Randy and The Man shook hands.

"Delighted to see you again, Randy. I expect this to prove a constructive meeting."

"Surely."

"I trust this to be an exciting experience. Is this your first visit to a place like this?"

"A secret underwater military base? It is. How long has it been here?"

"Oh, it's my first time visiting this one. But half a century at least."

"Wow. Right under our noses the whole time." The Man laughed.

"Literally. Your country, and indeed the world, has a very different history than you've been taught; a history I'm glad your father had the restraint not to reveal before the proper time. Your initial naïvety is a pre-requisite for The Cabal to award you the position I agree you to be most perfectly suited for."

Randy faked a grin. He resented his ignorance and was angry with his father concealing so much for so long but accepted the situation for what it was.

"So you're in The Cabal as well? I was under the impression you were here representing another organization."

"I guess you could say I'm something of an honorary member. Not of your bloodlines, but we've worked together harmoniously on many occasions. On other occasions, unfortunately, less so. I'm hoping meetings like today's can help ensure more of the former and less of the latter in the years to come."

"A fine intention. I thank you for your endorsement. And your generous donations."

"I've no doubt my faith and funds are well-allocated."

"I look forward to proving that to you and your colleagues."

The Man gave Randy a fatherly pat on the back.

"Very well, my boy. There's always a middle ground."

Randy didn't love The Man casually calling him "his boy", but appreciated the tactic being employed. His father had warned him The Man's best weapon is charm and an unparalleled understanding of human psychology that allowed him to manipulate practically anyone into doing what he wanted, without even realizing it.

His father had predicted The Man would present himself as a paternal figure always in his corner, but to expect a knife in the back if he was ever ruled more liability than asset.

"Can I ask you a question?"

"By all means."

"Why do they call you The Man?"

"Well, I suppose that happened naturally over time. Perhaps we can discuss it in more detail another time. But one reason is my middle name?"

"Which is?"

"Fucking." Randy laughed, quite a bit. The Man knew his audience.

"You're The Fucking Man. I like it."

"Damn straight."

"I could learn a lot from you."

"Indeed you shall, my boy. Indeed you shall."

The door opened again, and in walked an elderly man in a very dark suit with eyes to match.

"Ah, Mr. Man! It's been too long, my friend."

Randy recognized the man, whose reputation preceded itself. Descended of the famed Rockefeller bloodline, one of the richest men in the world, an old friend of Randy's father, and a senior Cabal associate.

"Pleasure to finally meet you, Mr. Rockefeller."

Randy stood and shook the old man's wrinkled hand but was surprised to feel, then see, a powerful, scaly, cold hand of three raptor-like claws that totally dwarfed his own big hand. A surge of pure adrenaline engulfed his body.

Randy then heard a deep laughter, not unlike that of King Bowser of Super Mario fame. He witnessed a digital pattern transforming the frail old man into an enormous light-skinned reptilian being, which opened its dragon-like wings that took up a third of the conference room, and roared like a dinosaur while pounding its chest twice. The Man returned the chest pounding gesture.

"Nice to see you again, Viceroy Bortimus."

The beast let go of Randy's hand, threw three chairs across the room like they were pebbles, then kneeled where they had been, bringing the giant down to human level.

"The reptilians have a certain sense of humor that takes some getting used to, I'm afraid," The Man offered. Randy stared at the terrifying creature then said, in a deepened voice...

"I'm not."

"Not afraid?" Bortimus asked, halting his demonic laughter and holding eye contact; the perpendicular oval pupils of his big dragon-like eyes narrowed — sizing Randy up.

"Good. We are relatives," he said, aloud; then, psychically added, *Family shouldn't fear family.* Randy smiled and winked.

In walked the real Nelson Rockefeller III, who looked exactly like the holographic copy Bortimus had assumed. Rockefeller read the room and said, in a jovial tone…

"Let me guess, Bortimus pretended to be me again, didn't he?"

Another demonic chuckle filled the room. It had an odd echo; the sounds he made resonated differently than human voices.

"Another hilarious practical joke. Wonderful. But no matter how good Draco technology gets, Bortimus, you'll never be as beautiful as me. How are you?"

"Bortimus is most powerful being in and on Earth. So Bortimus good."

"Modest as ever, Bortimus."

"What is?"

"Modesty is not requiring praise or attention. Being quietly great."

Bortimus grunted, confused and so also upset and muttered, "Bortimus is loved by all."

Rockefeller made his way across the room slowly, with an effort behind each step that suggested a weak body that couldn't keep up with a strong mind, detected by Randy in the intensity of his stare.

"You know how to tell if it's a reptilian in disguise, Randy? The eyes. They never get the eyes quite right. They look blacker than they should." He stretched out a feeble hand. Randy stood and shook it.

"Pleasure to meet you, Randy. You remind me of your father when we first met. How time flies."

The Man stood and walked over to greet Rockefeller. They briefly exchanged pleasantries until Bortimus interrupted with his imposing voice, which to him at normal volume was equivalent to a human's yell. Rockefeller's hearing aid squealed. He took it out.

Rockefeller took a seat between Randy and The Man.

Bortimus spoke…

"Now, business. The Draco accept Randy as the reptilian candidate. Randy will be the next ruler of America tribe. Randy will serve the reptilian agenda. Randy will obey."

The Man took issue.

"Bortimus, you know how much of a proponent of free will I am. Randy must be free to make his own choices. As much as I respect your kind, make no mistake, you live in the basement. The rules up here are different. Up top, free will exists and must be respected. The purpose of this meeting is to assess common interests, not listen to reptilian dictates. Please understand."

Bortimus emanated a palpable bottled rage. Rockefeller chimed in…

"The Cabal is in agreement with The Man on this point, Bortimus. You can and do have your say, but mankind does not serve The Draco. The Cabal will not install, or allow to remain as president, a purely reptilian stooge."

Randy ruled that if he didn't speak up now, his autonomy would be decided without his say…

"I respect The Man. But I do not serve him. I respect The Cabal. But I do not serve them. Randy respects the reptilians." Randy struck his chest twice. Bortimus half-heartedly returned the gesture. "But Randy does not serve them. Randy serves Randy."

Bortimus respected that. The others were okay with it too. Rockefeller reached into his suit pocket. Threatened, Bortimus stood and prepared to attack until he realized it was not a weapon, but three folded sheets of paper. He passed them out to the attendees.

Rockefeller sighed.

"Oh please, Bortimus. Relax. This is a list of the points of interest The Cabal would like to bring to your attention. Item one, World War Three. We feel the time is right to finally light the powder keg and get the party started. The teams are pretty obvious by now — America and NATO verses China, Russia, North Korea, Iran etcetera. With everyone else falling on whichever team they prefer."

"Bortimus cannot remember all these Earth tribes. Why so many?"

"Well Bortimus, we must unite them through force. That's only possible through war."

Bortimus nodded in understanding. Rockefeller continued. "In addition to consolidating control in the aftermath of the conflict, a grand new war would achieve The Cabal's primary goal: population control."

"What is?" Bortimus inquired.

"Killing many people," The Man explained.

Bortimus nodded in understanding, then grew unhappy.

"The Cabal wants to population control because The Cabal is too weak to rule. The human's weapons are too powerful. If the Earth tribes have any pride, they will destroy everyone before they admit defeat. Then all humans are destroyed. Then from where Draco get loosh? No."

Rockefeller looked at The Man and sighed.

"I won't lie to you, Bortimus. We expect to destroy most of the humans. You will have less loosh when they are gone, but a wonderful opportunity to build up a surplus of loosh during the war."

"What is surplus?"

"More than you need. Saved for later."

"Reptilians do not saved for later. Reptilians take what the reptilians want when the reptilians want it."

"Perhaps you can make an exception this once."

"What is exception?"

"Doing what you don't want to do just one time."

"What? Why? No. The reptilians will not exception."

"Surely, there must be a compromise that can be reached."

"What is compromise?" Rockefeller sighed in frustration and said…

"When we give up something, and you give up something, and we make an agreement we can all live with."

"The Draco give up nothing. The Draco never bow to a human."

"What I'm saying, Bortimus, is you would have less loosh for a short time. Then, as the planet is repopulated, under a single government's control — our control — we can assure you a return to current levels of loosh production. And even more loosh production after that."

"Bad now. Good later. Bortimus understand."

"Ah, wonderful."

"No. No compromise."

Rockefeller sighed, looked at The Man and shrugged.

The Man nodded and said, "Nelson, I'm sorry but I'm afraid I must side with the Draco. Another world war at this time is counter to my interests."

Bortimus laughed. "Ha! Victory."

"I don't understand. What are your interests?"

"The accelerated evolution of the human species. War is an excellent catalyst, of course; in many respects, but I've no intention to start over from the ashes. Let us live comfortably on the brink of catastrophe. Not take the leap. And not risk upsetting our friends downstairs."

The Man nodded at Bortimus respectfully, who nodded respectfully in return.

"Gentlemen, I fear you are overestimating the threat of total surface world destruction," said Rockefeller.

Bortimus pounded the table, permanently denting it.

"America tribe use atomic bombs when they defeat Japan tribe. If another big war, America use them, other tribes use them. Everyone die. No loosh. To use human saying — fuck that."

"I understand the concern Bortimus. But you forget we have protection from that. If things get too out of hand, the Galactic Federation will intervene again."

The Galactic Federation, as the name implies, is a collective of planetary governments from many worlds, of a positive polarization, as opposed to the negatively polarized beings such as everyone at the meeting. The Federation's primary directive is to not interfere in the affairs of lesser evolved species, respecting their free will to develop in accordance with the will of their collective consciousness.

At the end of the second world war, when it was observed mankind was on track to destroy itself and continue causing damage that rippled through dimensions each time they detonated their newly acquired atomic weapons, they chose to override the primary directive. Their justification for doing so was the Federation's primary enemy — the Draco alliance — had gained significant levels of influence over the world's governments in their dealings with the Nazis, it was successfully argued the Draco intervention needed to be countered to restore the balance so that humanity may evolve as intended.

The Federation's intervention remained a secret to the people of the planet and had taken the form of deactivating nuclear weapons on multiple occasions, particularly the American and Soviet arsenals. The American government still ignored the known instances, with their congressional committees ostensibly researching UFO matters for disclosure purposes claiming to be unfamiliar with the long-known, well-documented events. Feigned ignorance was always their modus operandi.

"The Cabal will be disappointed to hear your decisions. But I shall convey it. I'd like to revisit the matter, but for now, let us move on. The viruses are the next item."

The Man took a deep breath and exhaled dissatisfaction.

"Yes. Perhaps you can shed light on exactly why your Covid-19 virus was released without even discussing it with me first?"

Bortimus pounded the table again, cracking it this time.

"The reptilians were also not told of this plan. Fuck you."

"The release was unsanctioned to my understanding. An... accident."

"An accident from your labs. Keyword: your."

"It was a Chinese lab. Take it up with the CCP."

"You funded it. So it's your baby. And your baby made quite a mess."

"A stir we've all benefitted from tremendously, no?"

"That's not the point. The point is I don't like being surprised unless it's my birthday. And I don't have a birthday."

"Reptilians also not happy Cabal not ask Reptilians' permission. But the words of Rockefeller are true. The Draco benefitted. The virus caused some suffering, but the tribes' decision to make everyone be afraid and alone for a long time increased loosh production by 33%. And all from a sickness that kills less than one percent of the people that get sick. So much fear from such a small threat!"

Bortimus laughed generously, truly amused with the human antics.

"Humans run around putting useless mask on. Virus small. Holes too big. Is like trying to catch golf balls in basketball net! But the stupid humans still wear. Even the younglings the virus cannot kill wear diapers on ass and face! Cabal train the younglings to live in fear. And to obey the lies of the people on their technologies. So much beautiful fear the next generation will live in. So much loosh to harvest. Why use tribe wars to control humans? Use virus fear. The Man right. Draco vote yes. More viruses. But not viruses too strong. Not kill all humans."

The Man continued...

"Discrepancies over transparency notwithstanding, the virus has been a blessing for all of us. Even the most resistant of societies have proven easy to tame. Our power over humanity has reached new heights. Our wealth has doubled. And we've established new norms."

Rockefeller smiled and said...

"Precisely. They stay at home until we say it's safe to come out. They pump whatever we tell them to into their veins, whether it works or not. And they're so paranoid they do all the enforcement for us. We've tightened our grip on the governments of the world as never before. And we did so without firing a shot. I'm glad we're in agreement on this because Covid-20, and the vaccines to go with it, are ready for release. Should be an easy sell given the groundwork we've laid."

"You have my blessing—" said The Man. "—let's just make sure we don't cross swords on this, Nelson. I'm aware of The Cabal's plans to sterilize the population with the Covid-20 vaccines. And I for one am firmly opposed. I feel that's a matter we should discuss."

"Someone's been talking out of school, I see."

"What means sterilize? What means talking out of school?"

Bortimus inquired. Rockefeller looked at The Man in a way that begged he not answer those questions. The Man hesitated.

"What means?!" Bortimus demanded, slamming a fist on the conference table, breaking off a chunk. The Man answered him...

"Sterilize means make it impossible to have children. Talking out of school means I have spies in The Cabal that told me about a plan to—"

"—Enough," Rockefeller interrupted; "It's not important, Bortimus."

Bortimus stood and spread his wings; a very intimidating gesture.

"Silence, old man! Continue. What was plan?"

"They planned to sterilize the population using the vaccines."

Bortimus thought about it for several seconds, piecing it together, then understood and slammed his fist again on the table, this time breaking it in half.

"Cabal want population control with medicine for stop virus?! Cabal want kill humans! Stop loosh for Draconia! Bortimus say no big war because this. Cabal still plan to do this with no permission?!"

Rockefeller and Randy backed away from the table, in fear of the justifiably indignant beast. The Man remained seated calmly and said...

"I understand your anger, Bortimus. And I'm glad we were able to stop it. Please convey to The Cabal that we are sternly opposed to your depopulation agenda. Whether by war or sterilization, we forbid the endeavor. Isn't that right, Bortimus?"

Bortimus roared a deafening roar. Randy and Rockefeller covered their ears. The Man remained unfazed, save for a wry grin.

"I believe that translates to yes."

"Yes—" said Bortimus, nostrils flaring. "—kill roof monkeys, die!"

The Man helped Rockefeller up and escorted he and Randy back to the broken conference table.

"Glad that's settled. I do have good news you can take back to your team. I have an employee beautifully lined up to take over the whole CCP. He's very reliable. Very dependable. Very consistent. My quartz crystal, I call him. This time we'll capture the Chinese market and triple our profits. He's already reached an arrangement with our very own Geyser Pharmaceuticals. He'll be credited with inventing the vaccine for Covid-20."

The Man smiled contently and continued...

"We'll deify our man in the media. He'll give a rousing address to the national assembly. Then once tragedy befalls certain individuals currently in control, he will be duly elected Secretary of the Chinese Communist Party. Then, he will be made Chairman Chen. And he will be an ally for life. Chen will mandate 'his' vaccine to all of China and handle worldwide manufacturing at cost. Modest estimate is we triple our profits from the Covid-19 round with Covid-20 and hasten the race to your long-sought one-world government. Down below, Bortimus and his people get all the loosh they can handle. Everybody benefits."

Rockefeller took a breath, processed it all, and nodded in approval.

"China has proven tough to infiltrate. I'm glad to hear you've made headway. The Cabal is happy to assist in removing anyone in your man's way. What's his name?"

"Mr. Chen. And yes, your assistance is welcome in paving his path to Chairman. I've prepared a list of people in his way."

"Duly considered. Mr. Chen — China's miracle scientist. I'm familiar. Now I see why you were making a fuss about him in the press. And why Geyser transferred the Covid-20 vax patents to a Chinaman. Clever."

The Man handed Rockefeller the kill list. Rockefeller scanned it.

"Difficult. But manageable."

"Please use discretion. It can't always be a plane crash, you know. Perhaps, I don't know, a runaway electric car that just won't slow down."

"I'll see what I can do. We'll get it done, one way or another."

"Splendid—" said The Man, "With Randy in The White House and Chairman Chen behind The Great Wall, we control both sides of the chess board, and can use the tension between the two great powers to maintain an undercurrent of fear sufficient to justify infinite military spending, increasingly tightened control over the populations, and keep a healthy pressure on both sides to compete."

The Man turned to Randy.

"We haven't given you a chance to speak, my boy. Any thoughts?"

Randy stood and cleared his throat.

"If we're going to deceive the world, we have to trust each other. I disapprove of The Cabal's stated agenda and the lack of communication with our partners."

Randy nodded to both The Man and Bortimus, who both nodded back respectfully, and continued…

"I agree to the decision to cancel both the world war and sterilization plots. But a controlled war where we run both sides is always a profitable endeavor; it's also a great means to assure domestic cohesion, as well as a reliable generator of loosh for our friends below."

"What did you have in mind?" asked The Man.

"For the first few years of my presidency I'll make nice with the Chen guy and repair relations with China. We'll work together to defeat Covid-20. Maybe we rethink the war teams and China and the U.S. take down Russia together and split the spoils. Then we can always shift the tone and renew tensions. And if we do go for war, we can keep it limited and controlled. Nuclear war is like flipping over the game board. To my understanding the ruling class has always been outnumbered by our subjects. It makes no difference if we're outnumbered a hundred to one, a thousand to one, or a million to one. We just have to be smart. It's not a victory if we kill off almost everyone. It's a confession of weakness."

"Yes Randy! That's right!" said Bortimus.

Randy gave him a thumbs up and continued…

"As for the virus and vaccines, obviously we keep selling them indefinitely and maximize profits. If they work, cool. If not, oops. Maybe there's a little depopulation here and there. Nothing crazy. We can still make most of the world's governments buy the vaccines whether they work or not. Especially with me and Chen dictating national policy."

"Mr. Chen is a very persuasive individual. I tend to agree," said The Man with a grin. Randy gave The Man a thumbs up and went on…

"Billions of people all over the world willing to inject whatever we give them without a second thought at the same time presents limitless opportunities. Sterilization was just one idea. But it can't be the only one. The world is going to let us change their DNA as we see fit. They're going to be begging us to. Perhaps we can all give it some thought and arrange another conference to evaluate other possibilities."

The Man gave a subtle round of applause.

"A well-thought out agenda and compromise, Randy. I'm onboard."

Rockefeller joined the applause then pat Randy's hand.

"Very good. I can sell this to The Cabal. Your father would be proud."

Bortimus struck his chest twice and joined the chorus: "Bortimus accept Randy compromise. Randy good tribe leader."

Rockefeller began to read the next item on the agenda but a loud knock on the door interrupted. The voice of the admiral came through...

"The base is under attack! We need to evacuate now!"

---

BORTIMUS STOOD, EXTENDED HIS WINGS AND ROARED.

"What?!"

The Man wasted no time and rushed out first, with Randy and Rockefeller in toe. Randy pushed past Rockefeller, who grabbed him by the suit tail and begged a quick word.

Bortimus followed The Man and admiral, who ran down the hall, flanked by two soldiers. He arrived at a large blast door and typed in a code. It spiraled open and he yelled, "Into the safe room!"

Bortimus entered. The Man entered, then looked back down the hall to see Rockefeller, Randy, and the Admiral had stopped moving. Rockefeller was on the phone.

The Man yelled "Bortimus! It's a trap!"

One of the soldiers hit The Man in the face with his rifle butt, knocking him to the ground with a bloody nose. He looked up to see Rockefeller, who said, "Sorry, old friend—" The admiral hit a button and the blast door sealed shut "—but you forget, this is our planet. We'll reduce the population as we see fit. Starting with the two of you."

"Well played. You finally caught me off guard. Farewell, my worthy opponent" he said, with a respectful bow and disconcerting grin. Rockefeller squinted, sensing something amiss.

Bortimus let out a deafening roar that left everyone's ears ringing and proceeded to slam his behemoth fists against the blast door, denting it more and more with each blow. The walls of the room lit up, and a loud hum began to resonate.

The Man took a deep breath, sat cross-legged on the floor, closed his eyes, and surrendered to fate as Bortimus continued to roar and strike the door, which began to give way as their bodies dematerialized.

# 52

MARK'S THOUGHTS drifted off his latest work. He had delved into writing a fictional story, both as a means of channeling the often ceaseless stream of thoughts and emotions, and to the end of presenting The Man something new, for which he might again potentially award him another exorbitant bounty the next time their paths crossed.

He was suddenly seized by an overwhelming need for rest, and took to a comfortable red loveseat for a rejuvenating nap in his preferred nook of the library. He fell into a dream state with remarkable speed, so rapidly the transition was eerily smooth, and he found himself in a lucid dream in the same setting he had taken the slumber. It was as if he had closed his eyes to see the same room, but he remembered that he was not awake. Everything looked blurry, like a Van Gogh painting.

The Man appeared, in his known form, clear, in contrast to the surreal background, but of a more ethereal hue... as if an apparition, or ghost, but not an emanation of Mark's imagination.

"Hello, Mark. I'm sorry to disturb you in the midst of your latest endeavor. And do apologize for my drastically prolonged absence and lack of correspondence. World affairs have kept me quite busy, I'm afraid, and there have been numerous complications. I'm glad and proud to see that glorious mind of yours is still going full-steam."

"How are you doing this?"

"Regrettably, I haven't the time to explain it at the moment, and kindly ask you to pay close attention to what I have to tell you, and the offer I've come to present."

"Okay, I'm listening."

"Thank you. Mark, I'd planned on revealing this to you in person, in the traditional sense, but have been regrettably delayed. It's about your brother: Luke. His body was found in a cenote on the island. My men had nothing to do with it. He drowned, most tragically; If you weren't yet aware, I'm so sorry to relay it in this manner, but there's good news. You see Mark, with the help of some friends in Los Alamos, I was able to revive him, upgrade him and even employ him. He's served as my head of security on the island for some time now and proven most capable."

Mark tried to process the unexpected revelation to limited effect.

"Wait... So you're saying Luke died. But now he's alive?"

"Yes. Well... more or less. He may not be quite the same as before, but he is certainly alive. See for yourself — you will be reunited as soon as today. You have my word. But first, I must reveal to you something you may find even more remarkable, if you can believe it. I'd like to present to you an opportunity you would be wise to accept, though, as always, I of course leave the choice to you."

Mark listened, with equal parts excitement and apprehension.

"In my absence, I would like to put you in charge of my affairs on the island. I want to empower you to act in my stead, because believe it or not Mark, you are, to my mind, among the most capable and trustworthy friends I have; and though I hate to make this known prematurely, I seek to mentor, train, and empower you to an extent you cannot yet imagine.

"You have potential no one else has recognized. And the courage to match your prolific intelligence. You have a sense of innate nobility and a capacity for the leadership I need at this hour. My offer is this: accept into the essence of your being the transmutation of a nontrivial modicum of my consciousness so that I might guide you to carry out certain tasks, on my behalf, in my physical absence.

"Naturally, you will be given unlimited access to the manor and estate, along with full command over all my employees and resources, which equate to everyone and everything you see. The guards. The staff. The girls. All yours to command, as you see fit. And your authority will not be questioned in the slightest, or challenged in the least, for you will be to them as me. They will know. And they will obey.

"On the off-chance anyone doesn't, your brother — in his new and improved form — will be by your side to enforce your will. Do you understand my proposition, Mark?"

Mark, at a loss for words, contemplated.

"I should also mention, as far as you're concerned, the transmutation of my consciousness will infuse you with god-like powers — the exploration and exercise of which will be a thrill beyond compare. That much I can assure you. Consent, and it's a done deal. By the time you awaken, your power will be apparent."

"And if I refuse?"

"Refuse, and you will awaken as you were — feeling as you did... powerless. Detained. Limited. Ignored. Without *hope*."

Mark leaned toward accepting, but something at the root of his conscience urged him to refuse.

"You've lost hope, Mark. Hope the woman. Hope the concept. Both disappeared from your life and now there's a hole in your heart begging to be filled. Isn't there? You're somehow incomplete without them, aren't you? You have this fiery, burning desire to be made whole... but you feel helpless to do anything about it. Correct me if I'm wrong."

Mark looked at him guardedly, but vulnerably.

"You're not wrong."

"I rarely am. I sense your longing, Mark. I feel your struggle. The enduring loneliness. The feelings of inadequacy and helplessness and frustration. As hard as it may be for you to believe, I sympathize with all those experiences more than you know. I wasn't always The Man, Mark. I had to become it. Now that I am, there's nothing I can't do or have. Regaining hope is a base hit.

"Hope is just one of the pillars on which you shall build your future. I'll give you that pillar and all the rest you need to live the life you deserve. I can transform you from a wanter to a haver. All you have to do is let me in, buckle up and give me the wheel. Let my essence flow through you. With me in your heart and mind, you'll be unstoppable. I'll take you from victim of circumstances to architect of tomorrow."

Mark answered with silence and a look of vulnerability.

"I can help you, Mark. Have I not proven that already? Are you the same man you were when you arrived?"

Mark continued thinking it over.

"She's attracted to power. Like all women. Love may be a choice, but attraction is not. Once she sees you empowered, at your true potential, she'll beg to be yours. Trust me."

That, for Mark, was the game changer... as The Man expected.

"I accept."

The Man smiled joyfully, and sinisterly, and clasped his hands.

"Splendid! You've made the best choice of your life, Mark. Congratulations. Soon after you awaken, some guests will arrive to the library. Do what comes naturally to boost our connection and hasten the download, so to speak; by the time the act is done, you will sense my presence increasing.

"From that point on, all you need do is close your eyes and search for me.

I will hear your call and respond. Like a psychic walkie talkie! Awaken now, Mark. Awaken to become the God you are destined to become."

Mark obeyed.

---

MOMENTS LATER, MARK MADE HIS WAY TO THE ENTRANCE OF THE LIBRARY, where three women awaited: one — a tall Eastern European blonde with blue eyes.; the second — a Puerto Rican with a voluptuous figure and inviting smile; and the third — an Irishwoman, with thick, long-flowing red hair and freckled cheeks and huge breasts... each wearing nothing but stilettos and smiles.

Mark did what came naturally, thereby strengthening his connection to The Man.

---

THE MAN OPENED HIS EYES AND LOOKED UP TO CONFIRM HE WAS STILL UNDER the wings of Bortimus, whose albino scaled body and wings provided both camouflage in and protection from the snow. The duo had been portaled from the underwater base off the coast of California to the middle of a lifeless tundra that expanded as far as the eye could see in every direction.

The only signs of life came in the form of hovering gunships on the distant horizon, scouring the area, apparently on the hunt for them. The Man had instructed Bortimus to give him cover, in the most literal sense, while he got them out with a plan he didn't have time to explain. Without alternative, the typically argumentative monster had complied. Bortimus moved a wing aside enough to look down at The Man.

"Is it finished? What are we waiting for?"

The Man calmly replied, in a tone that both assured and frustrated Bortimus.

"Just a few more stops to make. Help should arrive just in time."

Bortimus grunted in acceptance, then re-sheltered The Man in the teepee of his closed wings. The Man shut his eyes and projected his consciousness to the mind of his next favored employee, far off in The Orient, where Mr. Chen was sound asleep, in a hotel sweet in Shanghai, beside a sleeping prostitute of Mongolian descent.

In Mr. Chen's dream, he sat proudly on a unicorn atop a rainbow, looking down favorably on the construction of the world's largest gingerbread house. The gleeful dream was interrupted most suddenly by the arrival of The Man. The unicorn and rainbow disappeared, followed by the rest, and Mr. Chen found himself floating comfortably in a vast expanse of darkness. The sole object of Mr. Chen's focus was The Man, who appeared in the same astral body witnessed by Mark.

"I'm sorry to interrupt your most splendid dream, Mr. Chen. But I must have a word. I have been very pleased with your performance and have come to congratulate you on what amounts to a tremendous promotion. Today, news will break that your immediate supervisor has died most unexpectedly, and you will inherit his position."

Mr. Chen smiled and nodded in gracious acceptance.

"He was scheduled to make an address at an upcoming Central Government meeting on National Day. Everyone who matters will be in attendance. You will volunteer to give the address in his stead, and you will give such a rousing and beautiful speech that people will start to see you for the leader you are, and not only respect your authority to the full extent to which you are entitled, but quietly consider you a natural candidate for even higher appointment... which shall come to pass, if and when unexpected tragedy comes to befall your other superiors. Do you understand, Mr. Chen?"

Mr. Chen let it sink in, then smiled and nodded in the affirmative.

"Another virus is coming, Mr. Chen. You will play a key role in ensuring your country cooperates with international partners, to include the people from the pharmaceutical companies to whom you have been introduced and the illustrious Dr. Fauci. Ting Ting informed me your shrewd negotiation tactics rendered us an even better deal than expected. And all without my help! You are to be credited with the discovery of the vaccine to treat the virus, I'm told?"

Mr. Chen bashfully nodded yes.

"How wonderful! Look at you go, Mr. Chen. Wow! Under your leadership, you will ensure every last citizen accept the solutions you provide to protect them from the virus and maintain order at all costs. Do you understand, Mr. Chen?"

Mr. Chen again nodded, throwing in a thumbs up.

"If you ever require my more direct assistance, Ting Ting has already showed you how to boost the signal, yes?"

Mr. Chen nodded with a bashful grin.

"Good! You've been fucking. Then it won't be a problem."

Mr. Chen smiled brightly, most proud, perhaps, of that achievement.

---

NEXT, THE MAN SAT UP STRAIGHTER, STILL IN THE CROSS LEGGED POSITION under the limited protection offered by the winged beast, and expanded his consciousness upward. Higher and higher he rose in his etheric body, until he could make out their location — a remote expanse in the Alaskan tundra.

From there, he teleported to Nevada, and fell through the desert ground into a deep underground military base, and into the mind of a pilot manning the remote control cockpit of one of the drone gunships headed their direction.

On the back of the pilot's neck was a tattoo of the pyramid with the eye. It glowed. The soldier piloting the ship fell into a trance and The Man took remote control of the pilot in remote control of the gunship.

Back in Alaska, Bortimus braced for the incoming threat and watched as one of the ships suddenly turned and began unleashing a barrage of explosive 50 caliber rounds from the ship's turret, taking down three ships on its right side, then doing a 180° turn and downing another two before running out of ammo.

It then sped at full acceleration as the last remaining threat turned toward it, too late to avoid being kamikazeed. The collision caused both to erupt in a massive fireball that glared through the snowy sky.

Bortimus laughed triumphantly.

"Victory!"

Back in Nevada, the drone pilot drew his sidearm and shot himself in the head without a moment's hesitation. The Man opened his eyes and Bortimus his wings. The Man surveyed the destruction and grinned.

"That should buy us some time."

Bortimus observed The Man was shivering and ghostly pale, detecting weakness… which The Man knew would lead him to contemplating whether to abandon him to die; weighing the pros and cons in his rather easy to predict reptilian brain.

"I've already done the calculations, Bortimus. Based on our location, and the fragility of my warm-blooded mammalian vehicle, I'll not survive in this form… even if you fly full speed."

Bortimus nodded, held his fist to his heart, then pounded it twice.

"Your memory will be honored. Bortimus will avenge your sacrifice!"

"Bortimus, I'm afraid your chances of making it out without me are equal to my chances of making it out without you. Reinforcements are already inbound. This time, from multiple directions."

Bortimus roared in frustration.

"Bortimus can't keep warm The Man! What to do, demon?"

The Man looked down at his hands, which were already turning black and blue with frostbite. The Man nodded in acceptance of the inevitable, then gave his answer…

"I propose a merger."

as she was at her uniqu

to her ability to maint

speaking) on her target

about the man, his m

much less avoid contradi

with the tapestry of lies

of who this alluring my

falling more in love w

The job was supposed t

-duction to the man wa

already, and it was pra

ever be late for anything

## 53

MARK'S LIBRARY orgy served its intended effect. He came out of the experience feeling very different. He felt in every atom a new, invigorating sense of energy. It was as if his entire body was vibrating in a manner he found intensely pleasurable.

It was the feeling one has the moment they receive an award in front of a large audience giving a standing ovation; the feeling of a long sought first kiss; the feeling of scoring a touchdown and spiking the ball in the end zone, or witnessing the ripple of a soccer net after taking the game-winning penalty shot.

It was an empowering feeling; an ecstatic feeling. It was a feeling akin to the type of mania brought about as a result of his often poorly managed bipolar disorder, but differentiated in that it was not accompanied with an overwhelming stream of frantic thought and emotion, and instead under-written by a hitherto unexperienced sense of equanimity.

He exuded a novel sense of supreme self-confidence that was not a symptom of manic delusion, but rather the natural byproduct of a superior intellect and an unshakable sense of self-assurance. It was all the thrill of a line of cocaine off a stripper on a private jet, absent the need for the jet, cocaine, or silicone. It was an intoxicating sensation of unparalleled severity, with his senses still firing on all cylinders; a clear, clean, potent energy that left him feeling absolutely, positively, amazing.

Mark let himself down from the library table his recent lovers still laid on, worn out from his tireless expression of a great deal of pent up sexual energy and frustration. As he stood, he felt a massive head rush, followed shortly by a profound though not unpleasant ringing in his ears, and he had the sense some sort of upgrade was in progress.

He sat down on a chair by the fireplace and allowed the process to run its course. He closed his eyes and surrendered to the transformation going on inside of him. The influx of new energy felt so good he couldn't help but laugh.

And laugh.

And laugh.

---

MEANWHILE, IN ANOTHER WING OF THE MANOR, HOPE WAS STILL ENTERTAINING Frank, and finding increasingly difficult the task of balancing her authentic affections and attraction for him with her mission-oriented responsibility to maintain the illusory nature of the false pretenses their ostensibly burgeoning relationship was built on.

As adept as Hope was at her unique craft, there were limitations to her ability to maintain the spell she cast on targets. She could only dodge Frank's questions about The Man, his means and his methods for so long; much less avoid contradicting herself or arousing suspicion with the tapestry of lies that formed his understanding of who this alluring mystery girl he was apparently falling in love with truly was.

The job was supposed to be over by now. Frank's introduction to The Man was meant to have taken place already. It was practically unheard of for The Man to ever be late for anything he had planned, much less to be a no-show, completely out of touch. Her calls, texts and emails — all routed entirely through a well-encrypted device running exclusively on The Man's global network of private, dedicated servers — had all gone unheeded, leaving Hope to worry the unthinkable had happened: an unexpected tragedy had befallen her feared and beloved lifetime benefactor.

The growing sense of apprehension she felt, paired with the responsibility to obscure it from Frank, who had begun to ask questions fit for lovers like, "What's on your mind?" and "Something wrong?" was becoming too much to bear, so she told Frank she had to take care of something for work, which in this rare instance was a full truth, and advised he stay in bed and relax... that she'd be back soon and hungry for a second breakfast, which in their parlance was code for she was eager for a second helping of his sperm. Frank obeyed, falling into a giddy half-sleep with a carefree shit-eating grin on his face.

Hope hurried through the mansion in search of The Man, or anyone on staff that might have a clue as to his whereabouts. As she made her way through the museum of a house, she periodically encountered the familiar faces of the staff, comprised primarily of well-built men of a decidedly militaristic demeanor and a thoroughly taciturn disposition, all wearing, as always, sunglasses — one of myriad oddities Hope had come to accept as nothing out of the ordinary through her decades of exposure while in The Man's employ.

The staff never spoke unless spoken to and responded with as few words as necessary, never exuding a clear sense of individuality or expression of unique personality. Their focus was always and exclusively dedicated to a single-minded duty to fulfill their limited set of perfunctory tasks, which included things like guarding a particular sector and cleaning and carrying out basic household chores. If the servants even had names, they were not used. They were like the soldiers on guard outside Buckingham palace, sans the silly hats, which in that case were a relic of the past, when the elites still possessed those bizarrely elongated heads, owning to their lineage to their similarly-headed progenitors now believed by The Cabal to be sleeping in their mothership's stasis chambers under the think ice sheets in Western Antarctica.

Hope asked each person she encountered if they had seen or heard from The Man. Strangely, one after another, they completely ignored her... a response without precedent, further advancing her disturbing suspicion something bad had happened to The Man.

She received a message on her phone from an unrecognized number that said a recognized phrase: *congrats, you won the fucking lotto,* followed by a phone number.

She recognized the phrase because months prior she'd been sent to proffer Randy additional "gifts". She dutifully escorted the concubines to his room, but after they entered, he asked her where she thought she was going. Before she could protest, he'd grabbed her by the wrist with one hand and throat with the other, and squeezed both in a cold vice grip while calmly shushing her. She struggled to walk backward in her heals until she tripped onto the bed filled with the other girls he barked orders to all the while — forcing Hope to join in on the orgy of her own design.

As for why The Man told Mark she hadn't really been raped that night, it's because he preferred Mark hate him a little less and resent Hope a bit more. Besides, from his perspective, Hope knew what to expect from men like Randy. She was asking for it showing up dressed like that at that hour in heals and a sexy dress. The Man hadn't lied to her all those years ago when he told her he was incapable of loving her.

Incidents like these reminded her she was still another chess piece on his board. But she refused to cry about it... with the exception of the night she did before Mark. She'd come to his room with ulterior motives and a job to do, to be sure, but the tears had been authentic. And the comfort from a good man who wanted to listen and knew how to dry them had granted her a form of intimacy she'd never before experienced.

Randy had followed Hope into the hall after the ravishing and laughed while apologizing "for getting carried away." He complimented her on putting up just the right level of resistance; the role play felt realistic. She couldn't tell for sure if he really believed it had been consensual. He said he liked her, and boasted that he would soon be president and as such, would become privy in advance to any disaster that might befall the world in general, or her in particular. To thank her for the good time, he said that if an emergency ever arose he would be sure she received that coded message — *you won the fucking lotto* — a prompt response to which might have life or death consequences. She reluctantly gave him her number for these purposes, then stormed off when he offered her ten thousand dollars to get on her knees, let him piss in her mouth and gargle and swallow every drop.

It was in this state of genuine disgust she had made an impromptu visit to Mark, in need of assurances from someone to whom she was more than an object. He had made her feel safe and loved. Their night had been real to her too. But the next morning when she woke up being spooned by Mark, she remembered he was a prisoner. And she was the interrogator. And she had a job to do. So she retracted the drawbridge to her heart and shifted her focus to finding out why Mark and Luke had come and what threat they posed.

Randy, the psychopath that he was, cared little if at all for the well-being of Hope — whom to him was just another pussy to fuck. But hers was a pussy he'd rather enjoyed fucking, and Randy was in the business of looking out for future Randy, whom he knew would still be just as randy in the post-apocalyptic world to come… if The Cabal had their way and World War III left the surface world temporarily uninhabitable.

For as much as Randy didn't prefer that outcome, solely because he feared a prolonged stint in underground bunkers would be undesirable, he was preemptively building a shortlist of lovers that would be invited to survive the end of times with him, on condition they agree to remain compliant members of his personal harem, which would help keep him entertained until the dust settled up top and The Cabal could re-emerge and assert dominance over whatever remained.

With a shaky hand and grimace, Hope dialed the number and stepped onto a guest room balcony, where there were no known recording devices. The call could of course still be intercepted by The Man's surveillance over his networks, but if something had happened to him already, it was a moot point. She heard Randy's deep, authoritative voice on the other end of the line…

"Hi Hope. The Man is dead. He went against my bosses. There was nothing I could do to stop it. The Cabal is now at war with whatever remains of his organization, which includes you. You're going to have to choose sides."

Hope's mouth dropped and body shuddered. This was unthinkable.

"What... What do you mean he's gone?"

"He's dead."

Hope laughed.

"He's not like you and I. He can't just be killed. He'll be back. And he won't be happy."

Randy didn't believe in ghosts, spirits, demons or whatever Hope was suggesting, and considered it to be an empty threat.

"Enough bullshit. I'm offering you a way out, you stupid bitch."

"Mother fucker, you have no idea who, you, are, fucking with!"

She seemed to genuinely believe her nonsense, which troubled Randy, because her statements echoed those of his father and other Cabal members, who seemed to think their betrayal and assassination of The Man for not going along with their World War III ambitions had been a gross miscalculation. Randy rightfully feared The Man had footage of him doing things he wasn't supposed to. He had gravitated toward girls too young to legally consent, and The Man had indeed gotten plenty of Randy rape on tape.

Plans had been approved to storm and plunder the island in an effort to find The Man's fabled "box of strings", but The Cabal knew doing so could very well trigger the dissemination or destruction of the blackmail of so many world leaders — a priceless cache they could put to good use. After losing Epstein and Maxwell, they were low on reputation destruction ammunition. With Hope's help, they hoped they could get their hands on the goods.

"Hope, The Man's gone. I'm offering you safe passage and my, AKA The Cabal's, continued protection from what's to come — if and only if you do as I say."

After a moment of pause, Hope chose to hear him out.

"What do you want, Randy?"

"The box of strings. Where is it?"

"I don't know what you're talking about."

"Lie to me again, bitch. I'll hang up on you. Then you'll die."

Hope didn't doubt he would carry out the threat.

"I don't have access to it."

"Get access."

"I can't. Because he knew this could happen. It's somewhere only The Man can access."

"Bullshit. I don't believe you."

"Fuck you. If I did have it, you'd know. Because I'd let the world see what a sick fuck you are."

"Good girl. At least you're telling daddy the truth. Maybe you can't recover it, but if you know where it is, you can destroy it. When I stayed over, I left a small black cube attached to the bottom of the dresser in my room. It's an antimatter explosive. No vault can withstand it. It will probably take the whole house down.

"All you need to do is find it, twist the dial until you hear a click, put it outside the vault, then get off the island. Take a boat North three miles. I already have a submarine waiting to pick you up. That's it. Simple."

"I can't do it."

"Well then I guess I'll have to send people to kill everyone on the island and get the job done for me. Either way, it's happening. You can do it yourself and save some lives, yours in particular... or you can go down with The Man. See, I'm not so bad. I gave you a choice... just like he always did. Right?"

Hope's teeth began to clatter, and she fell into a panic attack.

"Hope? Keep it together, bitch."

"Fuck you!"

Hope threw her phone off the balcony, dropped to her knees and screamed.

"I think she's in," Randy told his father, and the dozen Cabal members assembled at his mansion.

———

MARK OPENED HIS EYES, AWOKEN BY THE FAINT SOUND OF A DISTANT SCREAM. HE left the library, went down the hall toward his basement room, but this time turned to a set of double doors that were always locked — the threshold marking the extent of his allowed places of habitat. He pressed his hand against the glasslike pad beside the door.

It opened. Mark smiled, for the first time in a long time.

The first thing Mark saw on the other side of the double doors was an imposingly large man clad in a suit, wearing sunglasses. Mark's initial response was one of fear, but he remembered The Man's assurances and boldly approached the threat, who for an instant assumed a defensive posture and drew and trained a pistol on Mark — a laser beam targeting him at center mass — but then lowered his weapon and resumed his former stance.

"Who do you work for?"

"You, sir."

"Who am I?"

"You are The Man, sir."

"Where is Luke?"

"Here, brother," said a familiar voice... from behind.

———————

ONCE HER PANIC ATTACK HAD SUBSIDED, HOPE ROSE TO HER FEET AND STARED over the balcony at the ocean far below. For the first and last time in her life she was seized by an impulse to jump. It would be an oversimplification to say she was still in love with The Man, but she did love him. As unusual as their dynamic was, he was the closest thing to a father she had; in fact, he was the only person who felt like family at all. For the past 20 years, he had protected and provided. He'd given her purpose and direction. Going on without him was a possibility she'd not seriously considered for many years. To make matters worse, now Randy seemed to want to adopt her in some similar fashion. It was an outcome she could not accept.

She raised herself over the balcony and leaned forward, holding on with her hands behind her back, leaning off the ledge. The wind blew her hair ferociously. She dipped one foot over the expanse and felt her leg instantly grow cold and tingle... the blood rushing to her vital organs.

Her thoughts turned to Frank. And Mark. And the rest of the people in the house. This bomb could kill them. She didn't want to leave them behind. But would Randy be willing to grant all of them safe passage as well? Doubtful. If so, how would she go about convincing them to get on a boat and flee the island? She thought to call Randy back, then realized in her fit of rage she had thrown her only means of contacting him into the ocean she was a mere loosening of a few fingers away from joining.

The sound of the door to the room opening took Hope off guard and made her lose her footing — her staple red bottom heals betraying her, causing her to roll an ankle and start to fall. She caught herself just in time to avoid certain death, but now hung from one trembling arm hooked between the marble pillars of the balcony.

One of her shoes hung on to her outstretched toes; gravity slowly having its way with it. Hope watched it fall into the ocean below, bouncing off a jagged rock and into the wharf, foreshadowing her impending doom.

"Help!" she screamed.

One of the nameless manservants stepped onto the balcony and looked around, confused.

"Down here! Help me!"

"Hope. The Man requests your presence. Follow me."

"Fucking grab my arm and help me up!"

"Yes ma'am."

He reached down with his tree trunk of an arm, which Hope grabbed tightly. He lifted her with the ease of a dumbbell rep. Hope let go when it was safe and landed on the one shoe with no grace, twisting her other ankle. She let out another scream… though not in regards to the physical pain. Then it registered.

"Did you just say The Man wants to see me?"

"Yes ma'am."

"He's here now?!"

"Yes ma'am."

"Take me to him!"

dark

was an

ring

me Sorry

the

Kissed

resu

you hea

sir.

Where

"En route

## 54

Hope limped down the hall with cautious exuberance. She followed the servant past the room Randy had pulled her into, where the device she'd been instructed to activate was to be found, and was relieved the choice of whether to carry out the horrid act no longer need be considered.

Now that The Man was back, everything would be alright. She excused herself into the room to put on a new pair of shoes and clean up — having wardrobe spread out in practically every room of the house. The servant waited outside. She closed and locked the door, then took a moment to search under the dresser for the bomb. She no longer had any intention of using it, now that The Man was back, but she wanted to bring it to his attention and inform him of Randy's betrayal.

She slipped into an elegant sexy dress, the only type she had, and yet another pair of red bottom shoes. Her face was a mess in the aftermath of the panic attacks, but her excitement about seeing The Man again trumped her usual obsession with every detail of her appearance. Besides, this bathroom didn't have the right shade of blush. She took one last look at herself in the mirror on her way out and had second thoughts. She remembered the difference between how The Man looked at her and saw her when she put on her best face and how he looked at her and didn't when she didn't, so she took a shower and started from square one. Beauty was, after all, all about appearances. Without her beauty, she had no power… without the sex appeal she held over men she would be treated like any other woman. People would stop being so nice to her. She wouldn't be so easy to forgive. Her bullshit would cease to so readily fly. Conscious of the unfortunate reality, she invested the time necessary to look her best and maximize the advantages her appearance afforded her.

An hour later, she was ready for the reunion. She felt giddy now, and a whole basket of other things that didn't usually go together. Her hands were still trembling, from the near suicide and incomprehensible pressure of Randy's ultimatum. But she was filled with joy at the realization she was safe again because The Man was back. He would handle Randy. Everything was going to be alright.

After struggling to shove her swollen ankle into her staple red bottoms, she slipped the bomb into her purse — an elegant Coach bag — returned to the hall, and followed her escort up another staircase, just now beginning to feel the extent of her physical pains. She began to limp as she ascended another floor.

There they crossed an expansive room filled with priceless statues, dinosaur skeletons, and artifacts from around the world, then up the final staircase leading to the master bedroom to end all master bedrooms — The Man's bedroom. It was the best parts of The Vatican, but modernized. Grand. Majestic. Excessive. Everything was bigger than it needed to be. Every little detail of every little thing everywhere in the room was beautiful and awe inspiring… with a view of the ocean second to none.

As they approached the grand door to the king's private chambers, Hope felt The Man's presence and smiled in relief. The palatial doors slowly opened, and she heard footsteps approaching. She smiled brightly in anticipation of a much-needed hug from the one man in the world who could truly make her feel safe.

---

THE HEAVY DOORS OPENED TO REVEAL MARK, WHO WAS SMILING BRIGHTLY.

"Hope!"

Hope stood motionless as Mark embraced her and gave her a gentle kiss on the cheek. He stroked her left cheek with his right thumb, which she received with relative indifference, and stared into her eyes. Mark indulged in a second hug — one fit for a return from war. But it wasn't equally reciprocated. Hope scanned the room in search of her objective.

"Good to see you, Mark," she said, putting an abrupt end to the long-awaited hug Mark was just getting into.

"Where… where's The Man?"

Mark wore the joyfully mischievous smile of someone holding a present behind their back.

"You want The Man?"

Mark closed his eyes and took a theatrical bow.

"Introducing, the new and improved Mark."

He opened his eyes. They glowed with a furious blue luminescence.

Hope placed a hand over her mouth.

"What... how?"

Mark laughed heartily and reentered her personal space, which she didn't love. He stared into her eyes with manic happiness that slowly faded. His eyes returned to normal and The Man's energy waned. His voice became quieter; more emotional; vulnerable.

"I thought about you a lot, you know. About what happened. About us. More than I care to admit. I missed you. Even after what happened."

"Mark, I—" Mark held a finger to Hope's lips, shushing her; which she also didn't love. "—You had no choice, I know. You were doing what The Man asked. I don't blame you. I won't lie. It was a tough thing to go through. All that loneliness, for so long. But I'm glad it happened. Because it made me stronger, Hope. You made me stronger. Even in your total absence. If it wasn't for you, I would have had nothing to live for."

Hope looked at Mark, puzzled.

"I'd have wasted away in that room feeling sorry for myself, just like I had before we met. Since I had my whole life, practically. Then you appear out of nowhere and inspire me to write again. You gave me a purpose. A goal. A mission. You gave me hope, for lack of a better word."

Hope stared ahead blankly, taking it all in. Mark slowly approached, lowering his voice to a place of intimacy.

"I don't know if you heard, but The Man loved the book. Now I'm a multi-millionaire. Just like that. Can you believe it?"

"That's great, Mark. I'm so happy for you."

"Be happy for us, baby. Because now I can solve all your problems. You're finally free. That's what you wanted, right?"

"I'm flattered. But I can take care of myself."

"I know you can. But now you don't have to."

"Thank you. But I don't need to be saved, Mark."

"You still see the old me, don't you? The loser."

Mark's eyes suddenly turned a radiant bluish green hue.

"I've changed. Don't you see the difference? Don't you—"

He stared at her in a way only The Man could; a way that felt like he was staring directly into her soul. "—*feel* the change? It took longer than expected. Eight years, give or take, on my end. Not sure what it was for you but time moves differently in that lonely library, you know?"

*Eight years?* Hope had heard The Man talk about time passing slower in his special library. The thought of Mark experiencing eight years in solitude and still thinking of her made her feel sick.

"I'm sorry, Mark. I should have been there. I should have come back."

Mark's eyes faded back to normal. His inflated demeanor softened.

"Don't feel bad. It was time well-spent. The pain was necessary. I see that now. The Man had a plan all along. Because that pain made me spend eight years getting better, in every way — physically, mentally, emotionally. I'm stronger. Smarter. Stable. Well… still working on that."

Mark laughed, this time with less pain and more confidence.

"Wanna know what got me through? You. The whole time, I never stopped thinking about you, Hope. Anticipating this moment. When you got to see me again. The new me. The real me."

Mark smiled earnestly and stroked her cheek with his thumb again.

"I already forgot the past, because I'm too busy remembering the future. And it's a beautiful future. I can't wait to show you. What do you say we pick up where we left off?"

Mark smiled, expecting this to be his long-sought fairy tale ending.

Hope broke eye contact and took a step back, feeling herself on the brink of another panic attack. Mark clenched his teeth in frustration and felt the stinging sense of insecurity seeping back into his bloodstream. Hope looked at him in a way that told him what he didn't want to know — that this thing between them just wasn't going to happen. That's not what she meant for the look to say, but it's how he interpreted it.

Mark approached a marble globe the size of a car and gave it a spin.

"It's ours now, Hope. Anything. Everything. We're finally free."

Mark continued spinning the globe, waiting for Hope to say something. The longer the silence, the more Mark's fears of inadequacy and various insecurities bubbled into a volcanic rage.

"What's on your mind? Come on, say something."

She still didn't reply. She just stared at him without seeing him.

"I know it's a lot to take in, but it's really not that complicated. I want you. I love you. I waited for you. I dedicated myself to creating something special for you. And I did. And now I can provide for us. Forever, basically. I pulled it off. Not bad for a guy from Indiana, right?"

Mark forced a laugh and continued spinning the globe, praying for a change of heart. But Hope just continued staring blankly.

"I know I had some challenges. I'm bipolar or whatever. Okay, sure. But I'm not crazy. I'm just different. And I evolved. Now I can solve all your problems and grant all your desires. That's my primary focus."

Mark balled his hand into a fist and clenched his teeth, then closed his eyes and took a deep breath, containing himself. He continued trying…

"Don't ask how I know, but we're meant to have a family together, Hope. I saw it. I was there. It's real. I swear. Three kids! Two boys and a girl. One of the boys is named Yanos. The youngest one, I think. He's really something, Yanos. Such a beautiful kid. Such a big heart. You love him so much. And he loves us. We're so… happy. You know? Just so much… love. It felt so right. I didn't get to meet the other two yet, but I look forward to it. And I look forward to uh, making 'em!"

Mark offered a desperate smile. Hope didn't respond. She was in shock. Mark tried to maintain equanimity, but the rage of thousands of nights of longing met with such callous indifference was a lot for his fragile soul to bear. Mark's tone got more desperate and the globe spinning grew tiresome.

"I'm sure the family can come in due time. But before that, let's go crazy, right? We can do whatever we want. I haven't traveled as much as you. I'd really like to travel together. That'd be fun, right? To go on adventures. No plan. Just pick a place on this globe and let's go! We'll figure it out when we get there. Just me and you. Where should we go first?"

Hope remained unresponsive. Memories of being controlled by Prince Mahjeed returned. She thought she was trembling, which she was, but really it was the whole room. Mark's frustration was coursing through his feet and into the house itself, causing a subtle earthquake.

"Are you in shock? What's going on? Talk to me, babe."

Hope felt frozen in place. She couldn't even process what Mark was saying. Her drawbridge sealed tight and she felt the urge to escape.

"I don't know what more I could possibly offer."

Hope's face remained affect free, like a psychopath.

Mark's volcano finally erupted.

"Am I not enough? After all this, AM I STILL NOT ENOUGH?!"

His voice shook the room and the energy excreted through his feet sent a crack through the marble floor. The giant globe began to levitate.

"Is the FUCKING WORLD not enough?!"

Mark pointed and the globe fell and rolled across the room, nearly crushing Hope, then broke through the giant window, shattering it into a hundred pieces. The globe crashed into the ocean with a big splash.

Mark ruminated in his anger and the earthquake effect intensified. Giant, priceless paintings fell from the walls, their frames breaking into pieces and piercing the canvases. Hope focused on breathing through her nose and maintained the detached sanguine demeanor that was her ultimate defense mechanism. She patiently waited until Mark fell to his knees in exhaustion and the rumbling stopped. His eyes returned to normal and he caught his breath. Then, at long last, Hope spoke…

"Are you done pouting?"

Mark looked up at her, angrily vulnerable.

"Mark… I'm just going to be real with you. If you don't like what you hear and want to Jedi throw me out the window, go for it."

"That sounds like more of a Sith move. Just tell me the truth. Please."

"The truth is I don't know you, Mark. It's too much, too soon."

Mark returned to his feet.

"You could have been getting to know me the whole time. You could have visited. You could have called. You could have written. You chose not to. And what about the time we did spend together? I know it's been a while, but did you really forget how I made you feel? Did you forget the smiles and laughs and orgasms I gave you? Was that all part of the act?"

"Stop, Mark. That's obviously not what happened."

"I think it is what happened. I think you had a job to do and you used me to get it done. Then you forgot me. It's that simple, isn't it? I was just another guy. It was just another night. And now you wish I'd disappear."

Mark's eyes began to flicker.

"Stop assuming, Mark."

"Na, I get it. To me, best night of my life! To you, another Tuesday."

"That's not nice, Mark. It was meaningful for me too."

"Be honest. It was just another day at the office for you, wasn't it?"

The flickers in Mark's eyes became more of a glow.

"You just go around pretending to love people. To use them. You get what you came for then POOF, they no longer exist. Sound about right?"

The room began to tremble again.

"Stop, Mark. You know that's not true."

Mark tried to calm himself, but loathsome reminders of weakness began streaming down his cheeks. Hope decided it was time to put out this fire. She hugged Mark, cautiously. The trembling instantly stopped.

"Baby, listen — it wasn't an act. We had a connection. A special connection. And I'm sorry for what happened. Truly."

Hope wiped the tears off Mark's cheeks.

"Please don't cry. I care about you. I do."

Mark tried to kiss her, unexpectedly. She pulled away, instinctively. Mark glared at her and the tears continued to fall. Then, he looked away, embarrassed.

"You care about me? Well I love you! I love you with all my fucking heart, Hope! So what am I supposed to do with that?"

The streams of weakness became a river.

Hope hugged him again, this time more tightly, and spoke softly...

"It's okay, Mark. It's okay. You've been alone for so long. You've been through so much. You're just... confused, love."

Mark broke out of the hug and stepped back.

"Don't call me love if you don't mean it."

Mark stared at the floor in shame.

"Hope, I've been so... fucking... unbelievably lonely. For so long."

Mark began sobbing. Hope's drawbridge started to give way.

"Me too," she confessed, with tears of her own to prove it.

"The one thing that got me through that hell was—"

Mark's breath came fast, as if he was on the verge of hyperventilating.

"—the thought that if I stuck it out, eventually, I'd see you again. My dream girl. I'd see you. Smell you. Touch you. Taste you. Love you. If I could just survive all the loneliness, and the mania, and the depression, and the temptation to take a dive off the top floor of the library balcony... if I could come out of that forest with something to show you, and if you saw in my eyes how much I loved you, that... that... those things you said on the beach could come true. You brought me back to life, Hope. And I just wish I... I wanted... I, I tried..."

Mark covered his face in shame. Hope pulled his hands down.

"It's okay, Mark. Just relax. It's okay. We'll talk it out."

Mark looked at her through the most aggressively vulnerable eyes Hope had ever seen. Eyes begging for love. The drawbridge to Hope's heart fell, and she felt the entirety of Mark's emotions storm her castle.

"Hope... I really believed in this thing. You were my light at the end of the tunnel. But that light was just a fucking train, wasn't it?"

Mark hung his head in resignation.

"I don't want to hurt you."

"It's not just about me. It's about us. There must be a reason I feel all these things for you. That I never let go. That I was so inspired by you. It can't just be random. It's something rare. Something beautiful."

"Mark. I... I don't know what to say."

"Look, I'm sorry if I got ahead of myself. I really am. I'm so sorry. I'm sorry if I scared you. But please, just give it a chance. If you could see what I see. What happens next, if you just open up. Just a little. And let me in. You'll feel it too. It's fire. It's electric. It's love. Don't run from it."

Hope looked into Mark's eyes and saw him. She knew what she wanted to say — she wanted to say yes. Most of her, at least.

"Run to it."

Mark smiled — openly, vulnerably, sincerely.

"Say yes. That you'll give it a shot. Me and you. We'll take it slow. Pick up where we left off on the beach. Forget the past. Forget the future. Let's just take another walk on the beach. Sound good?"

Mark held out his hand and his relentlessly hopeful smile beamed.

Hope tried to pull the drawbridge up but it was much heavier than usual. She'd never felt so loved. And the feeling was terrifying.

"Alright, look, you want to take emotion out of it? Fine. Think logically. If I'm right about this thing between us, you literally have everything to gain. My full fucking support. Emotional support? Check. Financial support? Uh, check! You want to be a mom? What a coincidence. I want to be a dad!

Babies. Done. Boom. Lonely? Not anymore. And never again. Unless you want to be. And if you do, I'll let you go."

Each sentence was another brick on her drawbridge, making it harder and harder to pull back up. She wanted to say yes.

"And if I'm wrong? Well, you can always go back to the life you've been living. How's that working out for you? Sure, it's exciting and there's variety and no one's holding you down. You go girl! Miss independent. Woo! But big picture? Do any of these guys you've been fuckin' around with really love you? Be honest.

"Any Mr. Rights? Or is the plan just playtimes with your Mr. Right Nows, until one day you wake up in a house that's not a home, and you just turned forty, and you still don't have any kids, and you're all alone, and you're gonna wish you could come back to this moment — right now — and find the courage to let yourself be loved."

Hope trembled.

"Because that's all I'm asking you to let me do, Hope, I know it freaks you out that I'm so sure but I know what I want and that's a good thing. We can skip all the bullshit. Do I love you? Obviously. Do you love me? Let's find out. To do that, you're going to have to have courage. You're going to have to feel some scary things. And risk being hurt. But I'm not going to hurt you. You'll see. Together we're going to make something beautiful, Hope. Something truly, fucking amazing — that we can only make together. All you need to do is say yes."

Mark let out a cathartic laugh, having gotten it all out of his system… confident he'd at long last made an offer she couldn't refuse.

Deep down, Hope of course deeply desired to be loved the way Mark sought to love her, as do all women. But Hope also had a good memory. She remembered all the men in her life that had seemed so great and sincere in the beginning, then came to dominate and control her. It would just be a matter of time before Mark started slipping chains on her.

Hope wanted to be loved, but she needed to be free.

She made the final call: defensive maneuvers. With great effort, she stopped seeing Mark, tuned him out, and successfully retracted the drawbridge. She wiped her face and regained her composure. *Enough of this love bullshit*, she thought, and meant.

"Come on, Mark. That's enough."

Mark stood and looked her dead in the eyes.

"I love you."

Hope nervously laughed — a harsh sound for Mark to stomach.

"I love you."

"Come on, Mark. Why me? There are so many people out there. So many choices. I just happened to be here and what happened happened. Yes, it was special. But you're confusing infatuation with love. I'm not this wonderful girl you think I am. If you really knew me, you wouldn't say you love me. I guarantee it."

"I love you."

Hope shrugged, lifted her arms, and smiled in a friendly way that suggested reasonable reconsideration was the solution.

"Just give it some time. It'll go away. Get back out there. Meet new people. There's so many women that would love to be with you, especially now that you're so successful. I mean, come on. It'll be like shooting fish in a barrel! In a week, you'll forget all about this. We can stay friends. But take me off the pedestal. I'm honored. But I'm just another girl."

"I love you," Mark pleaded, just one more time.

The drawbridge was up. Hope stared at him like he was a waiter asking if she needed refills when her glass was already to the brim.

Mark nodded in acceptance. Finally.

He walked to what remained of the window and stared at the ocean, the serene waters doing something to quell the storm of emotion.

"Mark, to be honest, I really don't know what I want. How about we just be friends for now. Circle back to this later? Sound good?"

Mark watched the sun set but couldn't appreciate the beauty.

"Friends. Yeah. You have a lot of friends. Don't you?"

Sensing a potentially dangerous change of tone, Hope spoke up…

"Mark, I'm… moderately interested. I just can't commit to anything."

"Cool. But hey, isn't one of your… other friends… here right now? I almost forgot about our guest. I'm keeping you from him, how rude."

Hope felt a surge of adrenaline as she realized Frank was in danger.

"What are you talking about?"

"Friends don't lie to friends, Hope. Come on. I saw you two come in together. From my window — like a cat. He's cute. Nice build. Cool jeans. Laid back, but not too laid back. Makes you laugh. Is he fun in bed? How many times have you, you know — fucked — since you got here? That why you came in here out of breath? Did I interrupt playtime?"

Mark began pacing around Hope. She again stared ahead stoically.

"Sorry about that, pal. Should we… should we bring him up? Happy to let you two bounce on the big bed. I'll watch and jerk off. Like a cuck. That's something friends do, right?"

Mark laughed a cruel laugh he'd never laughed before.

"Mark. It's not what you think. It's for work. That's the truth."

"Oh, I'm sure he's working you plenty! And I'll bet a pretty penny he's not the only one. Those sexy legs open like tollgates, don't they?"

Mark stared at the cracked floor as he spoke.

"What about friends that love you? Are they allowed to get in there too? Or just your friends that don't love you? Work? Please."

Hope shook her head in disgust.

"Hey Hope, I'm curious — remember that one book I wrote you. The one I wrote you by hand? You know, that one."

Hope wanted to lie, but it was risky. She chose silence, for now.

"I'm curious what you thought of the ending. Too much?"

"I thought it was perfect."

"So you think it's realistic how they ended up together?"

"I thought so."

"In your interpretation, did the vampire really steal the bike? Or was the kid imagining it to avoid confronting the truth?"

"I wasn't sure. But I liked how it could have gone either way."

"And the talking rabbit that wanted to be a professional rapper. Did you think he really could have gotten into Stanford? What about the part about the lying bitch who must not have read a fucking page?"

Hope closed her eyes and took a deep breath.

"I'm sorry, Mark. I was going to read it. I was waiting until I had time to really take it all in."

Mark heard a voice in his head, clear as day. It was The Man.

*'Sorry I'm late, Mark. Busy busy. I know this is a big moment for you. Confronting Hope. Confessing your unrequited love by the looks of it?'*

"Yeah."

*'I'm guessing you told her how you feel, pitched a relationship every which way you could think and she still passed on the offer. Is that correct?'*

"Yeah."

*'You told her why you're so great, that you envisioned this beautiful life together… you offered her the world and she said na, I'm good? Did you use the globe as a visual aid? Is that why my room is all fucked up?'*

Mark couldn't help but laugh.

"Yeah. Sorry."

*'Ah, don't be. You no longer have to feel sorry about the things you break. Here's the long and short of it, Mark: Hope is incapable of loving you. Even if she wanted to. It doesn't matter what you do or say. She will never let herself love you. And the only way to even make her like you is to obviously not need her.'*

"She didn't even read the book," Mark said to The Man.

Hope began wondering if this was a good time to make her exit.

*'Of course she didn't. She's a lying selfish bitch who will never appreciate anything you do for her. Don't fixate on that. Focus on the positive: Hope inspired you to do great work. You had fun. You had smiles. You had laughs. You had sex. Good for you! It was what it was while it was but now it's over.'*

"But I still love her. I can't not."

*'Mark, you are a thirsty man and Hope is a dry well. If you can't handle your feelings, consider throwing her out the window now and put an end to this soap opera bullshit. It's a big waste of energy. She's been of great use to me over the years, but she's getting old, tired and weak. And so will you if you don't let Hope go. Bottom line, Mark: She's replaceable.'*

Mark heard the sound of high heals walking away.

*'Mark, some girls are fucked up in such a way that if you treat them like dirt, they'll stick to you like mud. Hope leans that way. Try being mean. Trust your inner-asshole. Trust me.'*

"Hope! Wait."

Hope took a few more steps then stopped.

"I was kidding! Of course I don't love you. I can't believe you fell for that. I just wanted to mess with you. My way of getting back at you for, you know, the whole betrayal thing. Now we're even."

He held his hand out for a shake.

"Right, friend?"

After a moment of hesitancy, Hope accepted.

"We had our fun. Now it's done."

Hope stared at him uncertainly.

"I don't love you. You don't love me. Simple. Right?"

Hope looked at Mark sadly, not liking this. Mark tightened his grip.

"I don't love you," he said, in a voice that betrayed him, then recalibrated, carrying on with the exaggerated okay-ness.

"We don't love each other. We never did. And we never will. Right?"

"Mark—"

"Come on. Just say it. It's fine."

Hope shook her head no. Mark squeezed her hand tighter.

"Mark, you're hurting me."

"Yeah yeah, you hurt me too. Say it."

Hope glared at him and grit her teeth.

"Come on, Hope. It'll be cathartic. You don't love me. Just admit it."

He squeezed even tighter, on the verge of fracture.

"I don't love you!"

She broke out of Mark's grip and took a few steps back.

"What did I take your virginity, Mark? Jesus Christ, you bipolar moron! You're pathetic. Of course, I don't love you. I was pretending. Because it's my job to pretend. It's my job to trick. And deceive. And lie. And seduce. And rip people's fucking hearts out!"

Hope continued, through unexpected tears…

"I take innocent people and I feed them to the lions. And I am a lion. I do whatever The Man says and I don't ask questions. I obey. And I hurt people. Yeah. A lot of people. You just happen to be one of them."

Hope saw the hurt in Mark's eyes. A tear slipped out.

"Mark, I look in the mirror and I see a monster. And it eats me up. Every day of my life. It's fucking destroying me. I hate who I've become! So no Mark, I don't love you. I don't love anyone! I simply. Fucking. Can't."

Hope buried her face in her hands and continued sobbing. Mark desperately wanted to console her.

*'Ah, no! Mark. Wait. That's the reaction she wants. Don't fall for it. She's very good. I know, I trained her. But even if she's not pretending, do you want to be the shoulder she cries on or the dick she sits on? Because with a girl like her, it's one or the other. She only respects power. Show her your power.'*

Mark stared on coldly. He balled his fists and his eyes glowed.

*'Go on, Mark. She hurt you. Now hurt her.'*

Mark walked to the enormous bed, sat on the edge and clapped.

"Bravo, Hope. Wow! It seemed so real. Just like before! Amazing."

Mark continued the ovation. His eyes flickered blue with each clap.

"One note: lioness, not lion; when you anthropomorphize yourself."

Hope screamed then stood.

"Fuck you!"

She began to storm out of the room.

*'Well done. But are you going to let her say fuck you and leave?'*

Mark grimaced and telepathically slammed the giant double doors to the bedroom shut. Hope turned to face him, frustrated.

"I didn't excuse you."

Hope shook her head in disgust then relented.

"May I be excused?"

*'Good, Mark. Put her in her place. Be a man.'*

"Personal shit aside, from now on, I expect you to respect and obey me as you would The Man. Because now, I am. Got it?"

Hope nodded submissively, compartmentalizing her rage.

*'Progress. But you haven't broken her. Push harder.'*

"I'm sorry. Did someone literally fuck your brains out, Hope?!"

*'Brilliant!'*

"When I ask you a question, answer with your big girl words."

Hope took in a deep breath and resolved not to shed another tear, no matter what happened next.

"No. My brains didn't get fucked out. Respect you. Got it."

"That wasn't so hard, was it?"

"No."

"No, what?"

Hope shrugged explosively and raised her eyebrows, out of patience. Mark stared at her coldly until she caught on.

"No, sir."

She turned and walked to the door.

*'More. More! Break her!'*

Before she could open the door, Mark psychically locked it.

"Sir is so... basic. Doesn't quite capture our new dynamic. Maybe Lord? King? Master? Any preference?"

"Whatever you say, King."

Hope sarcastically curtsied.

"Can I go now, Master? May I please be excused, My Lord?"

Hope turned to leave.

*'You're past her defenses. Good. Now remember, she doesn't want to be loved. She wants to be punished. So punish her.'*

Hope unlocked the door and began to open it. Mark slammed it shut again, locked it, then psychically lifted Hope off the floor. She felt the energy around her throat, gently choking her in the air.

Mark stared at her floating helplessly, not fighting it.

*'See the fear in her eyes? It means she just learned her place. Well done. Now make her feel it. Since love is off the table, have you considered fucking that fiesty slut and sending her back to her room until you're in the mood for more?'*

Mark hadn't. His eyes glowed brightly as he started to.

*'Go for it, Mark. You offered her everything and she spat in your face. You're the Übermensch now. There are no rules. No more asking. No more begging. Take whatever you want. Do whatever you please. You answer only to yourself!'*

Mark stared at his floating opportunity, filled with a dark new desire.

He smiled sinisterly and his eyes glistened with power. He floated her over the bed and dropped her onto it.

"Just another Tuesday."

Hope turned and looked at him pleadingly, then angrily. She sighed, closed her eyes, and began the technique she had developed as a young girl — disassociating herself from her body until the bad man was done.

She assumed the doggy style position.

Mark walked to the bed, slowly. He stared at her there, presenting herself, for an extended moment, deciding whether to take her.

*'Deep down, this turns her on. Hundred bucks says she's wet already. She doesn't want to be a princess. She wants to be treated like a whore. It's all she knows. It's all she thinks she deserves.'*

Mark put his finger between hope's panties and her waist and slid them down her legs and over her heals. He positioned himself directly behind her and stared.

*Yes, Mark. Good. Underneath all your lovey dovey romance bullshit is an animal that just wants to fuck. Let the animal out of its cage, Mark. And give her what you both really want. Fuck your whore, Mark. That's my advice.'*

The Man's words made Mark feel sick. But he wondered if he had a point.

He began to feel the animal The Man was referring to waking up down below. The animal knew what it wanted to do.

But the rest of him wanted to love and be loved. Mark walked to the side of the bed and looked at Hope's face. He stroked her hair, remembering how much he loved her... wondering how it ever came to this.

She stared stoically and involuntarily cried.

*'Stop reminiscing, you pussy. Hope is my gift to you. Take her!'*

Mark gripped Hope's hair suddenly. He tilted her face toward him.

Hope saw Mark's eyes in a state of flux — alternating between Mark and The Man in flashes, then assuming an enamoring display of florescent beauty — a dance of galaxies colliding.

Mark stared at his gift and was seized by the urge to obey The Man. But there was something inside him stronger than his primal urges. There was something inside him stronger than even The Man. He felt it in his heart, reminding him this is not who he is, pleading him not to become it just because he could.

*'What are you waiting for? Nike, Mark. Nike. Just do it!'*

"Enough," Mark said, to both Hope and The Man.

"I told you, I'm an Adidas guy," he muttered under his breath.

*'Touché. I respect your decision. Let's just settle for verbal cruelty. You're good with words. At least slap her around a little, so to speak.'*

"We're just friends, Hope. Remember? Don't be gross."

A war between conflicting urges to love and hurt her raged on inside him.

"Now go do your job and fetch me a fresh bitch to fuck."

*'Ha! A good plan B, Mark. I like it.'*

"Someone younger than you. Should be easy to find."

He flicked her panties at her face and leaned in menacingly.

"I mean don't get me wrong, Hope. You're still fuckable. I'd just prefer a pussy with a little less milage on it. A newer *model*, so to speak."

*'Ah, wonderful wordplay. That one should stick.'*

Mark walked toward the window humming "Hakuna Matata", then glanced over his shoulder and continued as Hope staggered on her hurt ankle while slipping her underwear back on.

"Not box of strings young. Just not past her prime like you."

*'Excellent. Now hear me out, have you considered some mild violence? For dramatic effect. Nothing excessive. It'll be good for your confidence.'*

Mark started psychically lifting books off a bookcase. He twirled his finger, making the books all rip apart into a tornado of literature.

"Maybe you can read these, Hope."

He directed the tornado toward Hope and laughed as he chased her around the room like he was chasing a dog with the vacuum.

"Maybe you'll get around to reading now that you're not so busy."

Mark pelted Hope with books from the tornado. Her stiletto slipped on a page and she fell. Mark psychically caught her just before she hit her head on the marble floor. The room stopped rumbling and the tornado of books fell to the ground.

He kept her hovering there, paralyzed, and knelt over her.

"Don't worry. I'll keep you safe."

Mark pointed at the doors and snapped his fingers. Both unlocked and opened. Mark snapped again and Hope went flying across the room and tumbling into the hall.

"I take care of all my employees!"

Mark made the doors slam shut.

*'Not bad, Mark. Not bad at all. Remember, fear is much easier to inspire than love. I can't make everyone love you. But I can make them fear you. And fear is the soil from which respect grows. I'll make the whole world respect you, Mark. Heed my guidance and no one will ever make you feel the way she did again.'*

Mark laughed an inhuman laugh that filled the whole house... his fucking house.

## 55

LUKE DID NOT GREET Mark with any level of charisma. He accepted Mark's brotherly embrace but did not hug back. He acknowledged that Mark was his brother and that he had been brought back to life, but he clearly didn't feel alive. Mark had told him not to strain himself trying to remember.

"As a matter of fact," Mark assured him, "I'm jealous you don't have to remember the past. Because our past is no more than an anchor weighing us down. You have nothing to weigh you down. Nothing to hold you back. I assure you, our present and our futures are much to be preferred."

Among Luke's new abilities were many features made possible by a neuro-digital interface that allowed Luke to basically do anything one could on a computer from the privacy of his brain. In this fashion, he spent a good deal of time mentally monitoring the security camera feeds; while doing so, he observed Hope leaving The Man's bedroom, hurrying to a guest room, and fishing something out from under the dresser.

Mark's obsessive tendencies and spiteful remarks had rubbed Hope the wrong way, to say the least. She had therefore made a choice to carry out Randy's task of subterfuge and betrayal in order to free herself from whatever fucked up relationship Mark might want to have moving forward. She had seen the metamorphosis men go through when they first become aware they are capable of having whatever they want... it was a danger she recognized immediately in Mark, and one she sought to avoid at all costs.

The drawbridge to her heart was thoroughly withdrawn. She didn't love him. She no longer liked him. And they damn sure weren't going to have any semblance of a friendship after that exchange. Mark had scared her. Mark had humiliated her, and there was no telling what he would do now that he was in at least temporary possession of The Man's powers.

She had resolved to blow the fucker up, leave this place, and never come back. The only problem was the collateral damage to be expected — especially considering that poor Frank, who she did genuinely like and felt she had a good thing going with, might also be counted amongst the casualties of war — an outcome she strongly desired to avert; and at once, a sacrifice she was willing to make if necessary, because at the end of the day, Hope's priority was, as it had always been — Hope's survival.

There were casualties in every war. If Frank was to be one of those casualties, so be it. She would close the drawbridge to her heart, forget about him and move on, like she always did. She didn't have a clear plan just yet. But she had a bomb. And a way out. And she would try to save Frank if she could. But if she couldn't, so be it.

Hope was getting out and not looking back.

<hr>

THERE WERE A NUMBER OF THINGS MARK SAW IN THE ROOM TO WHICH HE HAD A visceral reaction: The sight of Hope's clothes, chief among them lingerie, casually strewn about the floor... and if that wasn't enough to confirm his jealous suspicions, the spent condoms in the restroom wastebasket. Despite having no claim to Hope, Mark still felt the equivalent of a man coming to terms with irrefutable proof his wife has been cheating.

Dark thoughts began to circulate, the likes of which were foreign to Mark — hostile thoughts — like a desire to have this competing male killed; desire even to kill him personally. He considered shooting him. He considered having him tied up and thrown into the volcano to burn, or off a boat to drown.

He considered making Hope watch. Evil thoughts that did not belong had found him. And Mark began to listen. And he reasoned, in this newfound self-centered state of empowerment, that if he could not make Hope feel the love he felt for her, perhaps the next best thing would be to make her feel the pain and loss he blamed her for experiencing all this time.

Such were the intoxicating effects of The Man's power, to which Mark's mania paled in comparison. Mania was to the new power what coffee is to cocaine. The delusions of grandeur were no longer just delusions. He was no longer human. He was divine. And gods are entitled to whatever they want, if for no reason other than they have the power to take it. The Übermensch needn't ask permission. Nor apologize.

But the dark and dangerous thoughts were interrupted by a ringing in his ears and a sense he should stop looking at panties and rubbers and instead direct his attention to a notebook of Frank's, which could be seen protruding from his messenger bag. Mark picked up the notebook, opening to a random page.

---

GREAT PYRAMID MATHEMATICAL ANOMALIES
*Great Pyramid of Giza has knowledge embedded into the geometry.*
*Number of days in a year*
*Perimeter of base / 100 = 365.24*
*Length of antechamber as diameter of circle - circumference of 365.24*
*Ratio of lengths of Grand Gallery to diagonal of King's Chamber x 100 = 365.24*
*Length of antechamber of King's Chamber x π = 365.25*
*Half length of diagonal of base x 10^6 = distance to the sun*
*Height of pyramid x 10^9 = mean radius of Earth's orbit*
*Length of Jubilee Passage x 7^7 = mean distance to the moon*
*Pyramid scale ratio of 1/43,200 = Earth's polar radius*
From pyramid's dimensions can be derived
*-Royal Cubit -Size & shape of Earth -Gravitational Constant*
*-Necessary escape velocity to reach orbit -The Golden Ratio*
*-Sun's Mass -Moon's Mass -Mean distance to Sun -Speed of Light*
*-Circumference of Earth orbit -Orbital Velocity of Earth & Moon*
*-Orbital velocity of Solar System (relative to center of Milky Way)*
*-Velocity of local Galaxy Group relative to universe*

HOLY SHIT...ARC OF THE COVENANT'S DIMENSIONS WOULD FIT PERFECTLY IN *sarcophagus in Great Pyramid of Giza. No way that's a coincidence!*

PYRAMID ETYMOLOGY: PYRO MID
*Pyro = Fire*
*Mid = Middle*
*Pyro + Mid= Fire in the Middle*
*The ark was a battery. It's a fucking power plant!*

---

MARK TOOK THE NOTEBOOK WITH HIM TO THE LIBRARY, FOUND A BOOK THAT contained the measurements of the pyramids of Giza and double checked the math, suddenly able to instantly perform the calculations mentally — another nice new feature, compliments of The Man. The numbers all checked out. He retrieved another book, about the Ark of the Covenant, to check the dimensions.

The notebook was right. It was a perfect fit. The holy object carried on poles, that no one was allowed to touch or it would kill them... the thing Moses took with them everywhere they went was an ancient technology. Mark's train of thought was interrupted by Luke's announcement...

"Hope is on her way to Frank's room. She is not following your command."

"Let her. Keep her out of the basement. No boyfriend visits."

"Yes, brother. Basement levels no longer accessible to Hope."

Mark smiled. He was beginning to realize being in control was a glove that fit him well. He browsed through more of Frank's notes and found himself feeling a newfound sense of respect and even admiration for the stranger he so despised, complicating his choice of the competitor's fate. Maybe he didn't deserve to die.

Mark sensed The Man communicating with him — first a general feeling that he should go with the decision to let him live — then he heard The Man's voice in his head...

*Don't destroy him. Employ him!*

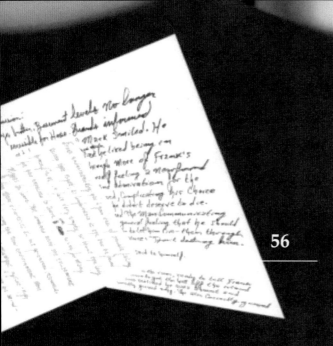

## 56

HOPE BURST INTO THE ROOM, ready to tell Frank it was time to get the hell off the island, but soon realized he was absent and correctly guessed why. She also guessed where she might find him, and was very upset when for the first time ever, her biometrics did not open a door. She tried only once more, cognizant three failed attempts would trigger a silent alarm. She hurried down the hall and found the nearest guard.

"You! Open this door for me."

"Request denied. Guest access restricted."

"Guest?! Are you fucking kidding me?"

"Request denied. Guest access restricted."

"Don't you recognize me? You work for me."

"Request denied. Guest access restricted."

Hope thought for a moment, then asked, "Are any other restrictions placed on this guest?"

"Negative."

"Give me your gun."

He obeyed, without hesitation.

"Is it ready to shoot? I just pull the trigger?"

"Affirmative."

"Thanks."

Hope shot him in the head, then put her modest weight against him enough to press his drooping body against the wall. It took all her strength to hold him up just long enough to press his hand against the door, which opened with a CLACK.

The guard's body fell, the blood gushing from his head wound spurting on Hope's face. She wiped it off with some degree of success as she hurried down the hall toward the elevator, which descended without issue, to her relief, but when the door opened, to her dismay, she was greeted by the sight of Luke. Without hesitation, she pointed the gun at him and pulled the trigger.

Nothing happened. She tried once more, to no avail, then noticed a red light emanating from the trigger guard. Locked. Remotely. By Luke. Luke struck her in the chest with one hand and she went flying backward, crashing into the elevator wall. Luke followed her into the elevator. She regained her footing and tried to run back out, only to be grabbed by the hair and deftly tripped onto the elevator floor.

---

WHILE MARK AND FRANK WERE GETTING ACQUAINTED, LUKE WAS TAKING CARE of Hope. At the base of his brain stem had been implanted a highly advanced artificial intelligence CPU that interfaced seamlessly with the rest of the thinner than thread wires running through several different locations in his brain. This gave him access, instantaneously, to vast resources and intelligence without the burden of using his physical senses to interpret data or undergoing traditional forms of learning. It was like being able to google anything by thought with no lag or censorship. It was highly effective, but one thing it could not do was make moral judgments; at least not with the same level of efficiency.

His new equivalence of a conscience was a set of predetermined logical criteria and parameters, such as: *Do not kill unless the threat presents the (1) ability and (2) intention to harm.* Hope had demonstrated behavior that satisfied both conditions, having just attempted to shoot Luke in the face and successfully executing one of the guards just prior.

Hope added to the mountain of evidence that demonstrated further intention to harm during the elevator ride when she spit in Luke's face and told him he and his crazy brother could burn in hell. Luke's database concluded spitting to be a symbolically hostile act and hell to be a conceptual realm inhabited by the dead, and inklings of his childhood memories of the notion remained, despite the memory wipe, in the form of the emotional imprint imparted by the preachers and Sunday school teachers who seeded the fear. He thus understood the insult implied Hope's desire he and Mark die then suffer for eternity. Hope should not have said that.

Another new feature Luke brought to the table was the transparent sensor on his right eye that allowed him to see in ways impossible for human beings without external technology. This included enhanced zoom capabilities, as well as night, thermal, and x-ray vision. It was through the use of the latter he observed that Hope had on her person a small device that matched the dimensions and schematics of a known explosive — an antimatter bomb capable of devastating destruction. This was not a threat he could leave unaddressed, and his instincts told him to immediately terminate her to reduce her chances of activating it to a zero probability. But sensitive to his brother's apparently strong feelings for the woman, he abstained from neutralizing her for the time being.

However, as the elevator ascended to the top floor, where he planned to keep Hope until Mark arrived to provide further instructions, he accessed the most recent recordings of the calls and messages linked to Hope's phone number — easily found on The Man's private servers, and listened to her call with Randy earlier that day. As Luke silently carried out his investigation, Hope began to worry she was approaching the end of the line, and she attempted to talk her way out of it.

"So you're Mark's brother?" she politely inquired.

"Yes."

"Is it true you drown?"

"Yes."

"That must have been terrible."

He found himself able to listen to the recording while talking.

"Memory unavailable. But probably."

He was more social than the rest of the guards... more human, giving Hope hope she could manipulate him.

"I'm really sorry for what happened back there. I was just upset because —" She thought for a moment, selecting an explanation. "—your brother hurt my feelings. Do you understand?"

"Unfortunate. But insufficient to justify hostile action."

"I know. I know. I can't tell you how sorry I am."

The elevator arrived.

"Can I talk to Mark? I need to apologize. To make things right."

"Negative. You are a threat."

Hope faked a laugh.

"Not to Mark."

"False."

"I would never hurt Mark."

Luke scanned Hope's micro-expressions in real time.

"False."

"I wouldn't. I... I love Mark."

Luke double checked the scan's results.

"False."

Hope quickly thought up an explanation.

"I knew Mark was mad at me. Alright? Because I'd been with another man. We were separated at the time. But it was still a mistake. And I was ashamed. That's why we were fighting."

Luke decided to hear her out.

"I knew he was jealous. And I knew he wouldn't believe I loved him anymore because of it, so I did the only thing I could think of to prove it to him. I was on my way to kill Frank to prove to Mark he means nothing to me."

Luke considered the possibility; logically congruent, but unlikely.

"Just… let me talk to him. Luke's your name, right? Please, Luke. Let me talk to your brother one last time. After that, I don't care what happens to me. Without Mark, I'd rather die anyway."

Hope searched her feelings… her memories… bringing herself back to their night together… letting the drawbridge down… experiencing the imprint of the intimacy she had felt; the comfort; the pleasure. Deleting all the negative and putting all the positive in bold. It was enough to alter her feelings, and with them her micro-expressions — enough at least to make it believable and satisfy Luke.

As she said the rest, she surprised herself with the deluge of feelings that resurfaced when she let herself remember the peak moments of their time together, and the love she felt in those moments; fleeting as they were. She began to cry as she said…

"I love Mark. I made myself forget. To make it through our… our separation. But I *did* love him! And I *do* love him! And I just need him to know it was real. That he's not crazy. That I… that I felt it too. I just had to make myself forget to move on. I had to forget. But now I remember. Do you understand?"

Luke concentrated on Hope's micro-expressions, calculating the likelihood of truth.

"I understand not remembering. Yes."

"Do you believe me?"

"Yes."

"So can I go to his room and wait for him?"

"Yes."

"Thank you, Luke. Truly."

---

As soon as the door closed behind her, she took a deep breath, re-lifted the drawbridge to her heart, wiped the tears from her eyes, retrieved the bomb and searched for a good place to put it. She decided on under the mattress, but before activating it, went to make sure she could still access The Man's emergency escape route.

She walked to the bathroom and located the false floor under the bathroom sink. Removing the floor revealed a huge ladder that descended all the way down to the caverns beneath the mansion, with boats and ready access to the ocean. From there, she could directly take a speedboat to sea and rendezvous with the submarine, if it was even there.

Luckily, the escape hatch relied on a manual lock, as The Man wanted to ensure he could still get out in the event of an EMP (electromagnetic pulse) attack, should all the fancy digital locks suddenly prove un-unlockable. She punched in the code: 3-2-7-6-8.

The hatch opened with a CLICK, filling Hope with adrenaline. The plan was to activate the device as soon as Mark returned, excuse herself to the bathroom, turn on the shower and make her escape.

It was a simple plan. It was a good plan.

---

LUKE HAD NOT FORGOTTEN HOPE HAD THE BOMB.

In the seconds between his responses to Hope, he had calculated a number of possible future outcomes, focusing on those least acceptable. He had chosen to take the short-term risk of allowing her to activate the bomb, knowing from his access to the manufacturer's private data the minimum timer setting is 15 minutes, and the highest potential blast radius for that model of explosive is approximately one mile in diameter.

He had calculated the precise amount of time it would take him to transport the bomb a safe distance away from the island by various means, the quickest of which entailed attaching it to the bottom of a drone then flying it off into the horizon until it exploded. But another alternative presented itself that would serve the twin purposes of (1) answering once and for all whether Hope could be trusted or need be neutralized, and at once (2) deal a counterstrike to the people responsible for pressuring Hope into committing the act.

As to how he could know if and when she chose to activate the bomb, to that end Luke had subtly attached a nearly microscopic adhesive camera to the front of Hope's dress when he held his hand out to stop her from exiting the elevator, playing it off like he wanted to go first to ensure the coast was clear. It was through that camera he witnessed her place the bomb under the mattress and open the escape hatch. Her intentions were clear: she was going to kill Mark, along with everyone in the house.

THE KNOCK AT THE DOOR CAME SOONER THAN HOPE HAD EXPECTED. SHE RUSHED to the bed, retrieved the device from under the mattress and prepared to activate it. Mark's voice came through…

"Hope? It's Mark. Luke told me you want to talk."

Hope positioned her hand to twist the knob on the bomb, then felt a final wave of hesitation.

She reminded herself of the way Mark had treated her, and of all the men who had treated her similarly since she could remember, and was filled with a surge of indignation. She grit her teeth and twisted the knob until it clicked, slid it under the mattress, stood up, and slid her dress straps off her shoulders and onto her arms.

"Mark! Yes. Come in."

Hope turned and began walking toward the bathroom.

"I just need a quick shower, baby. I want to be clean for you… I want you to finish what you started earlier. Then let's talk."

Just as she reached the bathroom, she turned around to see Luke standing right behind her. Among Luke's many new features came the relatively simple technology that allowed him to vocally replicate with passable precision any given voice, provided sufficient recordings of the person to be imitated were available. Mark's obscure podcast was more than enough.

Before Hope could even process what was happening she was unconscious. Luke had simply touched her with his middle finger, that output an electrical charge strong enough to kill or stun anyone. He chose stun.

---

HOPE AWOKE TO FIND HERSELF SEATED IN THE CAPTAIN CHAIR OF A SPEEDBOAT, wearing a snugly-fitting life vest. The boat floated on the gentle ocean tide, a few miles off the coast of the island. The only sound was the gentle splashes of waves against the side of the boat, and above, the stars were out in full force.

Hope found herself mesmerized by the sight of a gigantic bright moon that seemed to be there just for her. She winced, still woozy, from both a mild sea-sickness and a residual pain on her neck. As her memory slowly returned, her attention was grabbed by the sight and sound of a submarine surfacing. She struggled to remember where she was and how she got there. She couldn't remember the details, but she knew she was afraid; she knew she needed to escape; she knew she needed to survive.

The hatch of the submarine opened and two men swam over.

"Hope?"

It took Hope a moment to even remember her own name.

"Hope?"

"Yes."

"Come with us. We have to get out of here."

Hope obeyed. She jumped into the cold water and swam to her sneaky salvation. The men helped her up and into the hatch. She climbed down the ladder and was met by a handsome muscular man with the aura of an alpha male. Hope lost her footing and fell from the ladder, into his arms. He looked down at her and smiled.

"Nice to meet you, Hope. My name is Captain Zach Recreant."

He gently set her down onto a chair affixed to the steel floor and fastened her seatbelt for her.

"You're a tough girl, aren't you? Hang tight, we're going down," he said, not knowing how right he was.

"Alright boys, submerge!"

The submarine dove back under the ocean. Hope's ears popped. Right away, she didn't like being underwater — it was turbulent, claustrophobic, and reminded her of B-4 with Mark, which reminded her she was killing him. She remembered putting the bomb under his bed but was hazy on why. When the submarine reached the proper depth, Captain Recreant re-approached Hope.

"Hope, I know neither of us planned on this arrangement, but welcome aboard."

Captain Recreant leaned in and spoke quietly.

"To be candid ma'am, you are not my mission. It is not my job to take care of you. Not only is it outside the scope of official duty, what I am doing is highly frowned upon, to put it lightly. I'm a U.S. Navy Captain and I've invested over ten years of my life into this thing. I'm not going to let some random girl ruin it for me just because she happened to be swimming in my waters… no matter how cute she is."

"Why take the risk then, captain? I'm happy to leave if you don't want me. Just say the word."

"Okay, if you really want to know—"

He chuckled then leaned in even closer and spoke even quieter.

"Randy said there's a promotion in store for me if I do this and an unemployment check if I don't. Your friend is quite the negotiator."

Hope grimaced at the suggestion Randy was her friend.

"Don't get me wrong, I'm the nicest guy you'll ever meet. But that doesn't change the fact you're my secondary objective. If word gets out I chose to break protocol like this it could royally fuck up my life. Randy isn't an excuse that's going to fly if I get caught. So as far as anyone above water is concerned, this rendezvous did not happen. If you play by my rules, I'll take you exactly where you want to be. But if you jeopardize my mission, make no mistake, I will toss you back into the ocean and leave you floating like a bobber. And I'm not sure how well you'll fare this far off the shore of a burning island. We clear on that, missy?"

She looked at the dashing captain and grinned. She was much more comfortable being treated like this than she was the way Mark treated her, especially before he got mean. Hope liked not being the priority. She liked being expendable. It felt safe. Mark's obsession turned her off as much as Captain Recreant's indifference turned her on.

"Aye aye, captain!" she responded — with a sarcastic salute, and the most beautiful smile in all the seven seas. Captain Recreant grinned suggestively, picking up on the sexual tension. He was looking forward to keeping this one on board as long as he could manage. He leaned in so close their cheeks were touching and whispered into her ear.

"I have the most comfortable bed. It's a bit snug, but… I'd be happy to share it."

Hope found the proposition enticing. Something about the captain's position of authority — even over such a small domain — was attractive. She also found herself aroused by the secrecy and danger, to the point she wasn't sure to what degree her shivering was caused by the cold, or her wetness from the ocean.

The bad news was The Man was gone and she'd just left two of her boys on the island to die. Tough shit. She would forget about them and bounce back, just like she always did. The drawbridge was well secured and Mark and Frank were already fading from memory.

"Let me know," said the captain with a smile.

This arrangement was safe, because she knew he wouldn't try to possess her, for the simple fact he had too much to lose. The scandal component was a safety net and a tryst would be a fun way to pass the time at sea. Hope's animal down there had been awoken too. But unlike Mark, she had no reservations about letting hers out. Hope scanned the captain from head to crotch. She looked forward to finding out just how snug it was.

"We'll see, Captain. For now, keep your periscope down."

She smiled wryly and bit her lower lip. Captain Recreant laughed.

"I see why Randy likes you. What's your poison? Whisky? Tequila?"

"Wine."

Hope sighed, closed her eyes and nursed a growing migraine. Captain Recreant handed Hope a small bottle of red wine. She eagerly screwed off the top and gulped it down.

"I like a gal that swallows."

Some of the crew laughed. Hope rolled her eyes.

"Another."

Captain Recreant obliged. She gulped the second down and felt a calming burn in her chest. She let out an unexpected belch and chuckled as she welcomed the numbness to come.

"Looks like we've got ourselves a sailor! We'll keep the wine coming but first we have to make a fancy house go boom. Up periscope!"

He looked through the periscope's viewfinder to see the island in the distance and checked his watch.

"Any minute now."

A sailor approached Hope with a towel.

"Here you go, ma'am. We have fresh fatigues for you to change into in the Captain's quarters."

The Captain checked his watch again.

"Any second now."

Hope attempted to unbuckle her life vest but it wouldn't budge.

"Can I help you with that, ma'am?"

A sailor approached and was surprised to find he couldn't open it either. Another sailor laughed.

"Come on, Peterson. You're making us look like the Air Force. Get out of the way. Let me do it."

The other sailor also failed to open the vest.

"Hmm. Weird. It's like it's… glued together."

Captain Recreant quickly approached. He confirmed the life vest had been sealed shut.

"Did you do this?"

"No. I… I don't know. I… can't remember."

"What do you mean?"

"I was in the house. Then on the boat. Then I was in here. I…"

"Fuck. Surface now! Surface! Hurry! Go go go!"

As the sub resurfaced, Captain Recreant drew a combat knife.

"Don't move."

He began to saw at the straps with the serrated side of the knife. The tip of the blade stabbed into Hope's side.

"Ow! Ahhh!"

He continued sawing through the strap and the tip continued penetrating her skin.

"You're hurting me!"

"Deal with it."

"You're stabbing me!"

"Shut the fuck up!"

As the sub surfaced Captain Recreant lost his balance long enough for Hope to dive off the chair.

"Don't fucking touch me! Give me the knife. I'll do it."

"Get her off my ship! Now! Eject her, re-submerge, full evasive maneuvers! On the double!"

"Aye aye!" said the sailors.

One grabbed Hope as she was rising to her feet.

"Get off of me!"

He slammed her head against the ladder. Another jumped onto the ladder, grabbed her by the hair and began yanking her up while the two below each held one of her violently kicking legs and pushed her up.

The man holding her by her hair lost his grip as he opened the hatch. Hope fell off the ladder onto the ground, taking the two holding her legs down with her and getting the wind knocked out of her.

"Just kill her, you idiots!" yelled Captain Recreant.

"Hold her down!"

The sailors held Hope down by her arms as she desperately gasped for air and struggled with every ounce of lioness she had left. Captain Recreant straddled her, held his knife above his head and thrust the blade ruthlessly toward her neck. The instant before it made contact the time bomb atop the drawbridge to Hope's broken heart finally exploded, swiftly bringing the unfortunate affair to its ill-fated conclusion.

---

LUKE WATCHED FROM THE BALCONY. A GIANT SPLASH OF WATER ERUPTED FROM the sea like a geyser. A concussive wave reached the house, breaking glass and knocking over patio furniture.

Next, a few giant waves crashed on the shore. Then, silence.

...one, with Frank de...
unwillingness to talk, un...
...to Hope. Mark had tol...
...less, about how and why...
...used - that the entire...
mission, that's objective...
the purposes of this mee...
wholeheartedly reje...
his best to convince hi...
as the Mary and the pers...
He knew details, to inclu...
exchange, and while Frank...
he could know so much if...
speaking to Hope before say...
they heard the loud expl...

## 57

Mark's first meeting with Frank had been a contentious one, with Frank demonstrating a complete unwillingness to talk unless and until he spoke to Hope. Mark had told him the truth, more or less — that the entire time she had been on a mission to get him to the island for the purpose of this meeting — a claim Frank had wholeheartedly rejected.

Mark had done his best to convince Frank he was The Man from their correspondence. The Man provided him access to memories and information in real-time that kept Mark informed. He knew details, to include the contents of their exchange, and while Frank had no way to reconcile how he could know so much if he was lying, he felt like he was, and insisted on speaking to Hope before saying another word.

They heard the loud explosion that had just made the granting of Frank's request impossible, muffled as it was from his room four stories below sea level. Upon hearing the sonic boom-like sound, Mark had politely excused himself to go investigate, after giving Frank Hope's copy of the Graham Hancock book she'd been pretending to read in the airport. The bookmark was Hope's cheat sheet of "Frank Facts"… a little evidence to help down the hard to swallow truth.

Luke approached Mark, dripping wet and out of breath.

"Incident report, brother. Assassination attempt foiled. Threat eliminated."

"What? Assassination attempt on who?"

"You, brother. Recommend relocating to safe room."

Mark obeyed. Two guards led him to a bunker five stories underground. It was behind a huge vault door and contained a war room command center, months of rations, ample supplies, and an abundant arsenal of weapons and other survival gear.

He waited in silence and attempted to psychically reach out to The Man with no results. His thoughts then turned to Hope, and he ordered the men to find her and bring her to safety.

"Not possible, sir."

"Why not?"

"Hope is gone, sir."

"Where did she go?"

"Hope has been eliminated, sir."

The revelation made Mark sick to his stomach.

"No. No. It can't be."

"Affirmative, sir."

"The threat Luke eliminated — that's who killed Hope?"

"No sir. The threat was Hope."

That revelation cut twice as deep. His legs turned to jelly and he collapsed to the ground. *She wanted to kill ME?* Granted, his response to the experience of rejection had been cruel and excessive, but that wasn't who he really was; it was a temporary bout of insanity brought about by his failure to accept her choice, and the intoxicating effect of The Man's power, which he was only just coming to terms with.

He ordered the men to leave him alone so that he could scream and cry in private... which he did for a good twenty minutes, until the vault door opened again and Luke entered.

"No further threats detected, brother. Advise you remain here as we continue to monitor the situation."

"Did Hope really try to kill me?"

"Yes."

"Why?"

Luke played the recording of Randy's phone call to Hope.

"You didn't have to kill her."

"Protecting you is my primary directive. Hope betrayed you."

"You didn't have to kill her! You could have brought her to me. We could have talked it out."

Mark looked at Luke, who seemed incapable of empathy by the lack of facial expression.

"Thank you, Luke. You saved my life... again."

"Yes, brother."

Mark gave Luke a hug, and was relieved when this time Luke slightly hugged back.

"You're going to be you again, Luke. You're coming back."

"Affirmative, brother. Only better than before."

"That's right. Both of us. Better than before."

Mark closed his eyes, found The Man, and projected a summary of what had transpired.

*'I'm sorry, Mark. But you have a world to help me run. Hope was only holding you back. Weighing you down. You fell in love with an illusion. The basis of the illusion is gone. Now you are free.'*

*'Shows how much you care about your… employees.'*

*'Hope was a long-time companion and friend. But in betraying you, she betrayed me. And she met the only fate that awaits those who betray me. You would do well to learn from her mistakes. Now free yourself of regret. It makes you weak. Vulnerable. Distracted. And serves no one but our enemies. Speak soon, my boy. Keep up the good work. Your life is about to get exponentially better. You'll see.'*

*'I want to leave the island. It's not safe here anymore.'*

*'Very well. You could use a change of scenery. But you must avoid the airports. We are at war with The Cabal. That is why Hope is no longer with us. Together we will avenge her death. But we must be smart. Maintain a low profile. As far as the world is concerned, you and your brother are missing and presumed dead. None of my competitors know who you are or the nature of our… arrangement. Stay invisible. Stay safe.'*

*'So how do I travel?'*

*'Take the ship.'*

*'You want me to take a boat?'*

*'Not that kind of ship. The pyramid on top of the temple is my preferred means of physical transportation. Don't worry, she's easier to fly than you'd think. Just sit in a chair and give me a ring and I'll fire her up for you.'*

With that, Mark felt The Man's presence dissipate. He opened his eyes.

"Luke."

"Yes, brother."

"We have a renegade archaeologist to destroy or employ."

---

MARK'S SECOND MEETING WITH FRANK DIDN'T GO MUCH BETTER. FRANK, LIKE any archaeologist worth his salt, didn't believe a story someone else told him without evidence to back it. The "Franks Facts" list was weird, but could have been faked by Mark.

Luke pulled Mark over for a sidebar and recommended he leave the room momentarily.

Luke stood in the doorway until Mark had walked far enough away to be out of earshot, then closed the door and provided Frank the evidence he needed, in the form of a hologram emitted from a tiny projector embedded into a bracelet on his wrist, which displayed a playback of Hope in the elevator, talking to Luke... claiming to be in love with Mark and confessing to wanting to kill Frank.

"Hope attempted to assassinate you."

"I don't understand. Why would she do that?"

"Hope was not stable. She saw my brother again and wanted to prove you meant nothing to her. She attempted to leave a bomb that would have killed you. I returned that bomb to her."

Luke left the room and motioned for Mark to return. Something about it all still felt off to Frank. But Luke had provided very convincing evidence, and he had just met Hope. Maybe it really was true. Maybe these two had just saved his life. It all just felt surreal. Mark reentered.

"Look, Frank, this has not been a good day for either of us. But Hope's gone. You're here. And the way I see it, there can now only be one of two outcomes: I can destroy you, or employ you."

After a brief talk, Frank chose the latter.

## 58

THE TRAUMATIC REVELATIONS and shock brought about by the sudden turn of events were made more palatable for both Frank and Mark the following morning with their first encounter with The Man's preferred means of physical transportation — the pyramidal spaceship.

The marvel of engineering instantly made even the top of the line private jet Frank had arrived on seem like a school bus by comparison. On approach, the ship's belly opened and presented the circular staircase, which they ascended with great anticipation.

"Any idea how to fly this thing?"

Luke searched the entirety of the internet and his unmitigated access to the secret files of many government contractors while Mark and Frank continued to tour the flight deck.

"It's most likely a CAT," Luke offered.

"A cat? The hell's that mean?"

"A Consciousness Assisted Technology."

"Meaning?"

"Thought-driven, brother."

"What? Really? Can you fly it?"

"Unadvisable, given my death. Brain function atypical."

Frank thought he must have misheard, realized he hadn't, then took a deep breath and decided to hold his questions — including why the man identifying himself as The Man didn't know how to fly his own spaceship, and why his brother claimed to be back from the dead — for a later time. Mark closed his eyes and searched for The Man. Fast as a walkie talkie, he heard his voice in his head, answering his telepathic call.

*'As I said, Mark, it's easier than it looks. You know how when you drive a car you're familiar with, it's like it becomes an extension of your body? It's like that. Albeit in a more literal sense. Just have a seat. Hold your hand on the hand rest, and think about where you want to go. The ship will do the rest.*

Mark opened his eyes to a scanner. Then he sat in the nearest chair, got comfortable, and rested his hands on the hand rest, which to his surprise proceeded to encase his hand in some sort of flowing liquid metal, resembling mercury, which gently molded around his hand. It was cool to the touch, but not unpleasantly so. Mark closed his eyes.

*'Okay, open them'*, said The Man. Mark obeyed. An eye scanner extended from his chair and scanned his eyes.

The ship turned on. *'Okay, Mark. Good to go. Have fun.'*

"Here goes nothing," Mark said while closing his eyes and thinking he wanted the ship to prepare for takeoff. Without a second's delay, the ship came to life with a gentle hum and soft red lights illuminated the hull. Luke mentally ordered the six men that formed his security detail to find their seats, then sat to Mark's right side as Frank sat to his left.

"Are there seatbelts?" Frank asked.

As soon as Mark wondered the same, a red button on each of their chairs illuminated. The six men all pressed it at once, and the same liquid metal material formed a harness that gently enclosed around their chests and forearms.

Mark, Luke and Frank followed suit. Mark thought he wanted it a little tighter and it tightened; then a little looser and it loosened. He laughed and said, "Awesome."

Frank followed suit. It worked. "Amazing," Frank said. Luke understood it to be amazing, but didn't feel the emotions associated with awe. But he did not remember he was not feeling what he would have felt, so it didn't bother him.

*I'll just take her up*, Mark thought; *Nice and easy.*

The stairs ascended, the belly of the ship sealed shut and the pyramid slowly and gently lifted off, like a helicopter but without the noise or vibrations, and remained perfectly level at all times, making the rise feel like a smooth elevator.

*I wonder how we see where we are*, Mark thought. A holographic depiction of the ship, complete with a realtime depiction of their exact surroundings, appeared from the pentagram shape at the center of the chairs. Mark then wondered if he could also see outside directly, as there were no windows. The floor beneath the hologram opened to reveal a window granting clear visibility of the island, now a few hundred yards beneath them.

Mark wondered if he could also see through the top or sides. Areas of the wall and ceiling silently opened, giving a clear view out of a traditional window in every direction, though it appeared to all be a single piece of glass-like transparent material. The sunlight from above was a bit much, making the holographic display harder to see. With that thought, the ceiling window tinted and hologram brightened.

Mark took the ship up higher and higher — another few hundred yards, to a vantage point from which they could see the whole of the island — from the mansion on the West end to the volcano on the East, which bellowed steam like an enormous kettle. Mark thought it would be cool to see the volcano from above, and the ship darted the span of a few miles in less than a second — so fast it was as if the place he wanted to go had simply appeared around him.

The ship then slowly descended into the interior of the volcano.

"Careful, man," Frank advised.

Mark ignored him and descended faster. The ship halted just above the lava, then slowly ascended back to the summit. Frank pointed toward the giant owl effigy, which brought back bad memories for Mark and no memories for Luke.

"Is that a statue of Moloch?" Frank asked.

Mark ignored the question and said, "Mind if we take a detour?"

"Where should we go?" Frank responded.

"I always wanted to see the pyramids."

"Which ones?"

"They're in Egypt, right?"

"Well, yeah. Of course, there's the pyramids of Giza. The most famous ones. But there are some much closer."

"Really? Where?" Luke did a quick search.

"Major pyramids in the region include the Pyramid of Kukulkan at Chichen Itza, Mexico and the Pyramid of the Sun in Teotihuacan, Mexico."

"You familiar, Frank?"

"For sure. Visited them both. Multiple times. Very impressive. Very mysterious."

"Are they comparable to the ones in Egypt?"

"Comparable, yes. The Pyramid of the Sun is actually exactly half the height of the pyramid you're thinking of in Egypt, with the same exact base measurements."

"Really?"

"Verified," Luke said.

"That's a weird coincidence."

Frank smiled. "Or not."

"You think the Egyptians built them?"

"I think their predecessors did."

"Who are their predecessors?"

"The Sumerians."

"So they were there before the Egyptians?"

"Yes."

"And they were in Mexico too?"

"Maybe. Or maybe whoever started Sumer also had a hand in other places."

"Didn't the Mayans and Aztecs make the pyramids in Central America?"

"According to the bullshit we were taught in public school. The thing is, the pyramids were already there when Aztecs and Mayans arrived. They just occupied them. Their own histories recount it."

"So you're saying you think it was really whoever built the pyramids in Egypt?"

"That's one possibility."

"But I thought no one crossed the Atlantic Ocean until the European explorers. Cortez. Columbus. Like five hundred years ago."

"Again, I call bullshit. There are way too many similarities in architecture, art and recorded traditions for these civilizations to have never had contact until the 1500's. If I had to make a bet on who was behind it all, I'd say these ancient civilizations were contacted by Atlantean refugees who arrived from the seas and skies."

Mark laughed. "The mythical city of Atlantis? Really?"

"Not city. Empire. My research leads me to conclude Atlantis was once a worldwide empire that lost its capitol in a cataclysm. Flood. Pole shift. Weapons of mass destruction. Something took them off guard. Then the survivors spread out across the world and influenced ancient cultures that went on to repopulate the planet."

"Come on, man. Atlantis is a fairy tale."

"What's the name of that ocean between America and Europe again?"

"The Atlantic," Mark answered.

Frank raised his eyebrows, waiting for Mark to catch on.

"What?"

"Change the C for S and what's that get you?"

Mark thought for a second.

"Woah. Okay, you got me. That's kinda weird. We will be discussing this further. So other than Egypt, those pyramids in Mexico the biggest on Earth?"

"Na. Pretty sure there are larger pyramids in both Antarctica and Bosnia, but they haven't been unearthed. The ones in Mexico are the biggest known ones in the Western hemisphere. But there may be even bigger ones underwater."

"Where?"

"We're in the Bermuda Triangle, right?"

"Affirmative," said Luke.

"A lot of things have been found underwater off the island coasts that could only be the work of long-gone civilizations. If bigger pyramids do exist, that's where I'd put my money on some being around here. I think the pyramids, some of them at least, were some form of lost technology. Something like power plants that somehow harnessed geomagnetic energy naturally generated by the planet on the fault lines, where these structures almost always tend to be found.

"I think some could still be functional, but the powers that be don't want us to have free energy so they can better control us. Maybe the capstones, or another key element to the pyramids, were intentionally removed, but not some of the underwater ones. So maybe they're still emitting some kind of energy; could have something to do with the hundreds of missing boats and planes over the years."

"Interesting theory. But how and why would people build pyramids underwater?"

"They wouldn't. It all used to be above ground. The planet's been here a long time. Go back far enough, and what's dry land now was once underwater. And visa-versa."

"You mean it got flooded?"

"Every ancient civilization I've studied has stories about a great flood killing almost everyone. And most refer to gods coming to help them start over."

"Like in the Bible? Noah's ark. You think God really flooded the world?"

"I think God is what you call things you don't understand. Think about it... if we landed this ship on a primitive island right now, we'd be greeted as gods. And if we got out and taught them things... gifted them technologies... then flew away, it would be a very significant historic event. And they'd tell stories about us, describing it as best as they could.

"Maybe there's no word for spaceship, so they say we came from the heavens. Maybe they associate us with birds. Angels. And they memorialize it through stories, engravings, art; depicting things like people with wings to artistically convey we could fly. The word used by the Sumerians to refer to the so-called gods is Annunaki, which translates to 'those who from heaven to Earth came'. What else could that mean? I think later religions over generations simplified it to an abstract god and today people dismiss it as mythology."

"Ancient aliens, huh?"

"Maybe. Maybe the so-called 'aliens' were just people. Don't we call one another aliens when we're from another country? Whatever the truth is, someone's been keeping it buried for a long time."

Mark recalled some of The Man's more peculiar comments, implying he had found mankind in a primitive state, and wondered if there could be a connection.

"But why keep it a secret?"

"Answering that question is my life's work."

"So there could be ancient shit all over the ocean floor and we wouldn't know?"

Frank smiled and said, "No one seems to be looking."

Mark wondered where the nearest underwater pyramid might be, if they were indeed to be found, and was pleasantly surprised when the holographic display proffered a triangular symbol very close to their current location.

"Nobody but us," Mark said with a smile.

Mark wondered if the ship could go underwater too. It could.

The ship turned and blasted off, submerging beneath the ocean surface. Mark and Frank yelled in glee, as one does on a good roller coaster. Luke and the rest of his men did not. Twelve seconds later, the ship came to a halt.

Mark wished they could see better, and powerful lights illuminated the ocean before them, where could be seen an enormous pyramid, coated in coral and algae from thousands of years of neglect.

"Well I'll be damned. Looks like you were right, man."

Mark and Frank stared in awe. Luke was apathetic.

"How big do you think it is?" Mark asked.

On the holographic display an indicator read: 690 meters.

"What's that in American?" Mark asked.

The hologram added to the display: 2,263.77953 feet.

"Holy shit!" said Frank—

"The Great Pyramid of Giza is only 481 feet. This thing is almost five times taller than the biggest known pyramid on land!"

Mark looked at Luke and smiled. Luke did not smile back.

"Congratulations on the new discovery, Frank. First day working together, and we make one of the greatest finds ever. Not bad, right?"

"Yeah. Not bad. Not bad at all."

Frank stared at the marvel the way most men would stare at their first-born child.

"Can we please, please come back? With an excavation team?"

"I could fund that. For now, though, I kinda just want to go home."

Mark visualized his hometown, back in Indiana. The ship continued underwater for about one minute until it reached the coast, when Mark realized the sight of the ship would certainly be conspicuous, and in major violation of The Man's instructions to keep a low profile. With that, the ship activated a cloaking feature. The depiction of the ship on the 3-D hologram became a transparent outline and indicated *Cloaking Active*. The ship then suddenly rose straight out of the ocean several thousand feet, zooming at an unbelievable speed.

Within minutes, the surprisingly comfortable hyper-sonic trip ended, and Mark found himself hovering over his hometown, directly above his old house.

The sight below unlocked a series of memories for Luke.

"Home."

"That's right, Luke. You remember! Should we visit Mom?"

Luke thought for a moment and said, "Negative."

Mark decided he was right. It would be too much to explain and could put her in danger. For now, they'd remain missing and presumed dead. Mark closed his eyes and searched for The Man.

*'Having fun?'* he asked. *'Yes,'* Mark replied.

*'Good. Get used to it. What can I do for you?'*

*'Do you happen to have somewhere safe we can stay?'*

*'I've just the place. Transferring the coordinates to the ship now. Make yourself at home.'*

*'Thanks.'*

Mark opened his eyes and thought he'd like to go to the new coordinates. The ship shot off again, then less than a minute and a half later, came to a halt above a vast expanse of forest a few miles from an interstate highway.

"Where are we?" Mark asked.

"Missouri—" Luke replied.

"Nearest city: Highlandville. Population: 963."

"What? Guess we won't be staying in another mega-mansion."

"Incorrect, brother. Destination: Château Pensmore."

"A château. In Missouri? What can you find about it?"

Luke scanned the internet and responded instantly…

"Area: 72,215 square feet. Built of reinforced 12-inch solid concrete. Explosion-proof helix steel fiber walls. Five kitchens, 13 bedrooms, 14 bathrooms. Amenities include: ballroom, movie theatre, space observatory. Construction began in 2009. Built by astrophysicist and former CIA agent Steve Huff. Fully off-grid — 4,000 solar panels. Water treatment facilities. Garden. Livestock ranch. Highly fortified. Built to withstand severe earthquakes, F-5 tornadoes, and conventional bombs."

"Hot tub?"

"Negative."

"Well that's bullshit."

"Affirmative."

Mark smiled at the revelation his brother may still have a sense of humor and wondered where he should land. On cue, camouflaged blast doors opened in the yard.

"Nice," he said, as the pyramid touched down.

---

THE TRIO DISEMBARKED AND FOUND THEMSELVES IN A PARKING GARAGE STOCKED with armored Cadillac Escalades, Ducati motorcycles and a veritable car show of luxury vehicles and sports cars — all black; all perfectly washed and waxed, gleaming under the garage lights.

Frank giddily perused the vehicles, spouting off obscure facts about many of them, with Luke saying, "verified" after each remark.

"Are these all yours?" he asked.

"More or less. You can drive whatever you want."

Frank nearly jumped for joy. Mark gave him a pat on the back.

"Good day, right?"

"Good? No. Best fuckin' day of my life."

"So far," Mark said, and he meant it.

"Frank... all that talk about destroying or employing you. I was just being dramatic. It's entirely up to you. If you need some more time to think it over, let me know."

"You kidding me? I don't need time. I'm in. We're in business."

## 59

MARK DID NOT FALL ASLEEP that night. From his perspective, he rose to sleep, in a manner unprecedented; though an experience that would become increasingly commonplace before long, because Mark's transformation was ongoing and far from complete.

Three minutes and thirty-three seconds after closing his eyes, he felt a sensation rising from between his legs, up his spine in a coiling serpentine motion, all the way to the top of his head. He felt himself being pulled upward with escalating intensity by some kind of unseen magnetic force. His consciousness left his physical body entirely, and he flew through the thick reinforced concrete, then shot off toward the twinkling stars above, like Peter Pan en route to Never Never Land.

He accelerated at a speed that trumped even that of The Man's spaceship, tucked away under Château Pensmore on the pale blue dot fading from sight behind him. Through the void of space he flew, toward the apparent source of attraction — the black hole that serves as the center of the Milky Way. Though it may sound terrifying, in Mark's experience it was simply exciting. Such is the power of perspective. And Mark's perspective had, unfortunate recent events with Hope notwithstanding, been increasingly positive — a peculiar effect to be had, given the objectively negative polarization of The Man.

Mark traversed thousands of lightyears through space — if measured in terms of distance traveled by light rather than the speed of thought, which, as it turns out, is much quicker. He soon arrived at the all-encompassing, impossibly vast mouth of the black hole at the center of the galaxy, which seemed to span infinitely in all directions.

Mark fearlessly blasted through the event horizon and found himself immersed in a bright white light. He heard and felt the sound and vibrations of music; like a gentle phantom chorus of masculine then feminine voices, alternating back and forth, singing the same verse, over and over, in perfect harmony…

*A-Reah-Azurta-Rahh. A-Reah-Azurta-Rahh. A-Reah-Azurta-Rahh.*

The unknown hymn granted Mark a profound sense of tranquility and belonging — as if in the unseen presence of a long-forgotten family was heralding the return of a prodigal son. The ground felt stable, but it rippled with each step; a living plasmic water made of light. He felt a sense of levity, comfort and calm in this mysterious expanse that offered a total absence of fear and overwhelming abundance of love.

Then, a distressing unpleasant vibration overtook the area.

"Help! Mark? Please, Mark, help me!"

It was the unmistakable sound of Hope. The cries of distress grew louder and peaceful chants quieter as he ran through the liquid light that splashed with each step. Each time he thought he had a lock on where her voice was coming from, he would hear it again, from the opposite direction.

At the peak of his frustration, he yelled for her with all the voice he could muster, which echoed like a sonic boom and cleared up the negative vibrations while putting an abrupt end to both the pleasant chorus and the heart-wrenching cries.

Then, in the distance, Mark noticed a small black line on the horizon. He ran toward it and soon found himself zooming forward without moving what he interpreted to be his legs, levitating ahead at an increasingly high speed.

As he closed in on the only thing in contrast to the all-encompassing light, the black line revealed itself to be a deep, dark, circular pit. He peered down at it to see nothing. No Hope. Only darkness.

"Hope? Are you down there?"

"Mark? Mark, is that you?"

"It's me. Where are you?"

"I'm lost. In darkness. I don't remember how I got here. I don't know how to get out."

Mark looked around for a clue, but there were none to be found. Just light everywhere except the black hole beneath him. Then he heard and felt a deeply unpleasant sound, emanating in one continuous, unbroken note; an overwhelming noise — something like a didgeridoo — or the humming of a choir of giant demons. He cautiously approached the hole in the light water and peered over the edge.

It was a perfect circle of total darkness. Then, a small circle of light in the direct center. Then, the circle split perfectly in half with a line of light horizontally. Then, another line of light from top to bottom, separating it into equal fourths, like the crosshairs of a rifle scope.

A hand suddenly emerged from the center. He recognized the pristine fingernails. It was Hope's hand. He grabbed it and attempted to pull her out, but was instead pulled in. The dark liquid was ice cold, and he felt himself falling out of the light and into darkness. The only remaining feeling of warmth came from Hope's hand, but when he looked down for her, she was nowhere to be found.

Mark felt his consciousness shift through his hand and into Hope's. Around him a faded image of The Man's bedroom appeared, and he saw himself from a third-person point of view, from what could only be Hope's perspective.

As Hope, he felt Mark's hand clenching hers tightly. Their exchange was playing out exactly as it had the prior evening, only in slow motion, giving Mark ample time to witness his atrocious behavior from her perspective.

He felt her fear when Mark's eyes glowed from the unbridled power of The Man.

He felt the overwhelming urge to escape and the frustration at his lack of ability to do so.

He felt the bolt of terror and disgust when Mark demanded sex.

He felt the alarm when the doors slammed.

He felt the loss of control when he lifted her off the ground.

He felt her cold process of disassociation as she slid down her panties and presented herself; the vulnerability as he let the moment linger; the shame when he declined what he had demanded; and the embarrassment when he insulted her and slid his knife of cruelty right through the chinks in her armor with his degrading remarks; then the fear and indignation with the rest that followed.

He felt all the pain he'd given her, and gained a newfound appreciation for why she had chosen to again betray him. As the door slammed in the memory, Mark abruptly woke up to the echoes of the evil laughter, which he couldn't believe had come out of his mouth. He cried, understanding now fully why Hope had done it; regretting fully everything he had said and done; and haunted by the thought she might still be alone in that dark and lonely afterlife realm.

Sure, it was a dream. But it felt as real as the experience he'd had in the alternate universe, where they shared a life together. He wished they were in that one. Neither of them belonged in the darkness alone.

Mark went into the bathroom, which while a small step down from the island mansion, was still opulent by any standard. He splashed water on his face rigorously, looked in the mirror, and saw the eyes of The Man, but his own mouth speaking his words, "Bad dream?"

*It wasn't a dream,* Mark thought.

"Hope was my gift to you and your sacrifice to me. It was necessary to solidify our connection. For now, it's time to move on."

"Stop doing that. Don't speak through me."

Mark's eyes returned to normal. He grimaced and thought…

*'You knew about the bomb. You made this happen.'*

*'I encouraged you to embrace your power.'*

*'I lost control because of you. Hope didn't have to die.'*

*'Hope made her own choice too! You both did what I wanted. But I didn't make you. I don't make anyone do anything. I just advise.'*

Mark began to cry.

*'Oh, cheer up, Mark. Hope met her fate. She might have some karmic debts to reconcile, but she'll be fine. MEMENTO MORI. You'll see her again, I'm sure.'*

*'I didn't want to be evil. I want to be good.'*

*'Mark, how many years did you spend suffering alone? Ignored. Unappreciated. Overlooked. An outcast. Your brilliance unappreciated. Your potential unfulfilled. Desperately chasing. Never catching. I know exactly what that's like, Mark. We both survived all that. We created our own path. Now we're rich and powerful beyond measure. Now we can do whatever we want. And no one can stop us. Do you realize how lucky you are? You get to be The Fucking Man. There is no good and evil. There is only desire, and the means and methods by which you pursue it. Maybe you take a different approach than me. That's fine. Call that good. Call me evil. I just do what works. If you want to show me a better way, by all means. As you know, I love to learn.'*

Mark sighed and stared at the reflection.

*'I don't know if I want to be The Man anymore.'*

*'I know the feeling. If that's your choice, I respect your decision. But the connection is well established. I'm a part of you. I'll be here when you call upon me and will leave you alone when you don't. Just know without me, others will use and exploit your weakness as they see fit, and you'll go back to being a victim, like most people. Or, embrace the fact that now you're The Fucking Man and attain whatever you desire, however you choose.'*

## 60

FRANK UNDERSTANDABLY HAD a good deal of trouble falling asleep that night; as comfortable as the new bed he found himself in was, it felt very empty without the lady he had expected to share one with for many nights to come. That, combined with the excitement of the new discoveries, all but guaranteed insomnia.

Frank considered touring Château Pensmore, or even going for a midnight joyride in one of the toys from the garage — high speeds the time-tested means of clearing his mind that it was — but he found Luke and his crew of listless bodyguards terrifying and didn't want to be caught out and about.

But unlikely as the new alliance was, the fact remained, The Man was the best backer he could have ever hoped to cross paths with; a man of prodigious means willing to write checks first and ask questions later. Hope had told him many lies. But that The Man could move mountains for him was not one of them. And for that he was most grateful.

Mark, whom Frank new only as The Man, seemed to treat archaeology as a hobby and didn't seem to know much for being such an avid collector of ancient artifacts, such as those Frank had seen on display throughout the island manor and seemed to appear with great frequency again at Château Pensmore. Frank already suspected The Man to be a pseudonym used by perhaps a company or group seeking to deal in anonymity but had no reason to suspect he might be dealing with anything supernatural.

With a racing mind and racing car on the table, Frank resorted to another means of lulling himself to sleep. He put on his over-ear planar magnetic headphones — the precise type recommended by Dr. Robert A.

Monroe, creator and narrator of the sleep hypnosis tapes he had begun listening to a few months prior. He had found a set of the original Monroe Institute tapes on eBay, and ordered too a walkman to play them on. The same audio could be found for free on YouTube, but Frank chose to splurge on the originals because he wouldn't put it past the CIA to "leak" a subtly altered version online — one that wouldn't work as intended.

Frank's paranoia in these regards was not without justification. In 2003, thanks to the Freedom of Information Act, the CIA had released a detailed report on the radio broadcaster turned paranormal researcher Dr. Monroe, who through his research foundation — The Monroe Institute — pioneered something he called "The Gateway Experience". The report, dated June 9th, 1983, entitled "Analysis and Assessment of Gateway Process" seemed to conclude the science behind Monroe's methods was sound and recommended the agency incorporate and further study the Gateway method. It was presumably a tool to develop their fabled Cold War era *third eye spies*.

The goal of the Gateway Process was to consciously train the mind to allow a person to expand their consciousness outside the bounds of the body and thereby escape the confines of space and time. According to Dr. Monroe's findings, and three books filled with personal accounts, out of body experiences can be achieved through natural means by some, but they are attainable by perhaps anyone with the will to have them with the aid of methods he developed that combine hypnotic suggestion with auditory frequencies that create bilateral brain hemispheric synchronization which he called "hemi-sync".

By playing one frequency in the left ear and a different frequency in the right, a naturally occurring effect transpires in which the brain combines the disparate frequencies into a third frequency — the difference between the two — which is what the listener subjectively experiences. Such is the illusory nature of human perception. As it turns out, the human brain does not directly interpret the sensory input from the external environment in raw form. It converts the input it receives into information sent to the brain, which is filtered through preconceptions, and deciphered for relevant patterns before being perceived by the experiencer and assigned meaning. It happens so fast we can't tell the difference, but it's a significant distinction.

Two frequencies go in, but only one is heard. This effect is completely unconscious and possible because the left and right brain hemispheres are in sync. The same type of synchronization that occurs during an altered state can also be achieved by way of transcendental meditation or Kundalini Yoga. But for most that takes years of practice to achieve. Dr. Monroe, in effect, figured out a shortcut to hemi-sync. Aided by this bilateral stimulation with different specific frequencies, one can enter a theta brain wave state — the same state entered while dreaming. But this state is entered lucidly. The destination is a quantum realm outside the bounds of space and time where many people claim to interact with recently-departed loved ones and other seemingly conscious external sentient entities.

While Frank had yet to have a true out of body experience, as far as he could remember at least, the tapes did indeed help him get to sleep. He put on his headphones, pressed play on the tape, and listened to Dr. Monroe's soothing, reassuring voice walk him through the usual steps…

*Begin your resonant tuning — inhaling and pulling fresh energy into your body, from all parts of your body, up into your head. Exhaling and blowing out through your mouth all stale, used up energy; and humming with your vocal cords as you exhale. Begin now and continue until I call you.*

Frank surrendered to the process, relaxing every part of his body until he was lying completely still, focused solely on the sound of voices chanting long wordless notes, doing his best to mirror the tones as he exhaled each long breath, feeling the calming vibrations.

*Breathe normally and relax. Breathe normally, and relax. And hold the fresh new energy in your head. Hold the fresh, new energy in your head.*

A white noise ensued for a moment, then Dr. Monroe continued…

*Now you will create your resonant energy balloon. A moving field of energy that is yours. A ball of energy all around you, where you float inside. A balloon of energy that if you so desire can hold your radiation in. Also, it protects you from any external, outside energy entering you. Your resonant energy balloon. You are ready now to create your resonant energy balloon.*

The subtle sound of an ocean played as Frank visualized himself standing on a beach, sitting cross-legged in the sand, levitating, thinking into existence the energy balloon. The beach reminded him of the island, which reminded him of Hope, which disrupted his serenity. Luckily, Dr. Monroe had a method for dealing with this too.

As he'd been instructed to do on prior tapes, Frank imagined an "energy conversion box," with a "heavy lid", where he could deposit negative energy and transform it into positive energy. He undertook that chore until Dr. Monroe's voice returned…

*Let the energy flow. Let it flow out of the top of your head. Then turn it down, all around you. Let it flow down and re-enter from the bottom of your feet. Let the energy you have stored, let it flow out of the top of your head, and then turn it down, all around you. And let it flow down and re-enter through the bottom of your feet. Start this flow now. Out of the top of your head, like a fountain, and entering you again through the bottoms of your feet. Begin now.*

Frank imagined energy emanating from the top of his head and expanding in a taurus shape, encapsulating his body, and flowing back up the base of his spine in a continual flow.

*Now make the energy flow move out and down and wind around you, before it enters the bottoms of your feet. Spiral down around you, and then enter you again. Make the energy flow move out and down, and wind around you, before it enters the bottoms of your feet. Spiral down around you and then enter your feet again. Begin now.*

As he continued breathing deeply, the resonant energy balloon expanded another several feet — leaving Frank comfortably floating in an invincible, protective, transparent bubble of self-generated energy. Frank's thoughts about his waking life faded little by little. Frank then entered *the ten state*, as Dr. Monroe referred to it — a state of total relaxation, where, *your mind remains awake and alert while your body sleeps calmly and comfortably.*

He found himself lifting out of his physical body, as Mark had, and blasting through the cosmos, into the mouth of the black hole. He too found himself on a stroll through an expanse of liquid light, serenaded by the voices with no apparent source.

He allowed into his resonant energy balloon the audible mantra…

*A-Reah-Azurta-Rahhh*, which repeated on loop.

Frank too was enamored by the overwhelming forces of positivity, until the voice of a helpless Hope popped his resonant energy balloon and drastically altered the tone of things. Frank too saw the black line on the horizon. He too zoomed toward it and observed it to be a black circle. Knowing it to be the source of Hope's voice, he dropped in without a second thought.

Inside, it was the exact inverse of the light side. Darkness abounded. Not dark like we are used to seeing each night. But complete, absolute, total darkness; with the sole exception being a pool of white light on the horizon, identical to the one he'd just jumped through in shape and size.

Here too he heard a kind of singing, but it was in no way pleasant. It was ominous; foreboding; and it filled Frank with a general sense of dread. He willed back into being his resonant energy balloon, which true to Dr. Monroe's word, faithfully appeared around him, sealing out the undesired sound. He floated through the darkness in his resonant energy balloon until he entered the circle of light. He then heard Hope's voice from somewhere in the infinite darkness surrounding him.

"Thank you for coming, Frank."

"What is this place?"

"I was hoping you might tell me. Am I dead, Frank?"

"Yes. But it would seem, also, no."

"I'm sorry, Frank."

"Me too. We had a good thing going."

"We did. Didn't we?"

"Did you really try to kill me?"

"What? No. Of course not."

"They said you tried to kill me… to prove you loved Mark."

"No, Frank. I tried to save you. But I did leave you. And I didn't know if you would survive. I didn't see any other way."

"Why don't you come into the light?"

"I tried, Frank."

"Well try again. Now that I'm here."

"I don't belong in the light."

"We all belong in the light. It's where we're from. It's what we are."

"Not all of us, Frank. You don't know who I really am. You don't know the things I've done. The people I've hurt. I always told myself I had no choice. That I had to serve The Man. But that's just another lie. I told a lot of lies, Frank."

Frank held out his hand.

"Come into the light, Hope. It's not too late. It's never too late."

"You should go. You don't belong here. I do."

"No. No you don't. Besides, I don't know how I got here either. But I'm pretty sure I'm not dead. I don't think I'd be here if I wasn't meant to be. I think I've always been exactly where I'm supposed to be. Maybe that's true for all of us."

"I'm not so sure about that, Frank."

"That's the beauty, isn't it? You get to be where you're meant to be, to experience what you're meant to experience, without even knowing it."

"FATI CREDERE, huh? Like The Man always said."

"Yeah. Trust fate."

"I'll try."

Hope reached her hand into the light and it started to burn. She quickly retracted it.

"I told you!"

Frank focused on extending his resonant energy balloon to fit two people.

"Get in."

"What is that thing?"

"Just trust me."

Hope's ethereal body leapt into the light — into Frank's resonant energy balloon, which promptly sealed around her. She looked at Frank and smiled.

"It worked!"

"Told you."

"I need you to do something for me, Frank. Something I can't do anymore. Once it's done, maybe I'll be able to stay in the light."

"Name it."

"Free the girls, Frank."

"What girls?"

"All the girls."

"I don't understand."

"They're there because of The Man. And because of me. He uses them to control people. And for worse."

"Where do I find them?"

"The island. And the modeling agency. Shut it down."

"I'll try."

"Promise me. Please."

Frank solemnly nodded.

"Okay. I'll find a way."

"Thank you."

"Anything else?"

"Yes. Give Mark the seashell I took from him. It's in the box under my bed, in my room back on the island."

"Mark? You mean The Man?"

"That's what you know him as?"

"Yes."

"Well maybe that's what he is now. But before that, his name was Mark. And he had a good heart. Maybe he still does. Would you tell him I'm sorry. He's lonely. And he needs a friend. Be his friend, Frank."

"Sure. Anything else?"

"Yeah. Tell him I said… in another life."

"Sorry. In another life. Seashell. Got it. Anything else? Want me to bring back some snacks or something?"

Hope laughed a much-needed laugh. Frank smiled.

"Thank you, Frank. Maybe I'll see you on the other side."

"Hope so, Hope."

"In the meantime, fulfill your calling. Find truth. Share it."

"Is that my fate?"

"It's your destiny."

"What's the difference?"

"Destiny is the part of fate you get to choose."

The two stared at each other lovingly. Hope began to fade.

"Do I get to kiss you goodbye?"

"I think we need our bodies for that."

"Then I guess a ghosty hug will have to do."

As the two came together for a hug, Hope disappeared into Frank's chest and left a part of her deep in his heart. He felt her there when he woke up, on a pillow soaked in bittersweet tears.

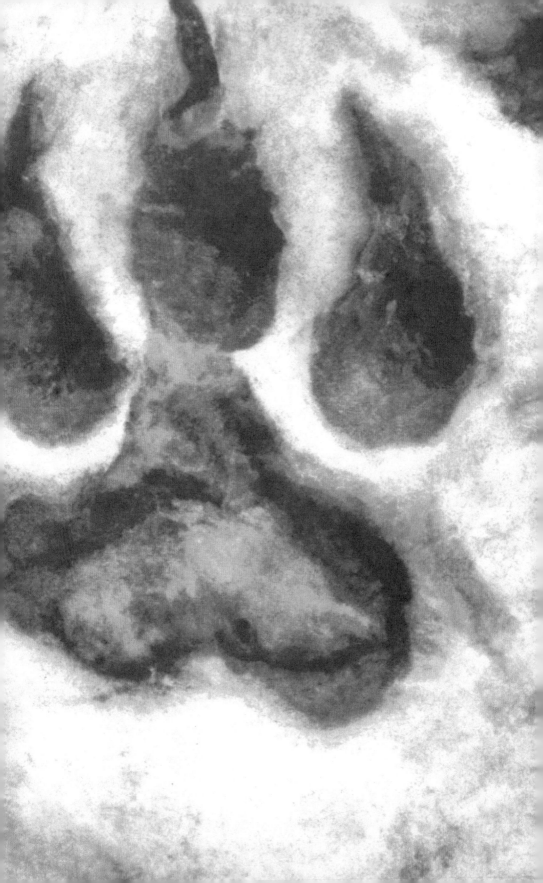

## 61

WITHOUT RECOURSE, Bortimus had accepted The Man's merger proposition; merger being an epithet for possession. It was to be a temporary accommodation, for the purposes of allowing the two to escape impending doom. Each needed the other to survive — The Man's physical vessel incapable of enduring the sub-zero conditions and Bortimus being exposed to continued assaults by Cabal reinforcements; forces that could only be evaded or defeated with The Man's talents.

To achieve the feat, Bortimus needed to sacrifice something he loved. Given the time constraints and lack of access to anything or anyone else to sacrifice, Bortimus resorted to the only option that was available... himself. The bold beast swore vengeance against The Cabal then bit off one of his own claws and roared in agony as he dropped it out of his jaws into The Man's hands.

The offering was sufficient to enable a full transfer of consciousness.

———

THE TREK TO SAFE HAVEN HAD BEEN ARDUOUS AND FRAUGHT WITH CONTINUED hazard, with The Man providing advance warning of incoming threats, which came in the form of more gunships, then in the form of a mechanized infantry unit comprised of long-range snipers. The only way out was through a blizzard that killed all visibility, and nearly took Bortimus down... testing the powerful and resilient beast's physical limits, with The Man giving him a steady stream of surplus vitality, faithful directions, and good old fashion encouragement.

Their initial point of refuge was a cave where they spent a week lying low, eating bats to survive, which proved particularly hard to hunt... especially in the dark. This too a feat made possible by their newfound synergy; The Man enhancing Bortimus' sense of sound and Bortimus hurling stones with the speed and accuracy of a major league baseball pitcher. The Man remotely accessed The Cabal's private communication channels and monitored the back and forth between the forward deployed units and their field commander, Mr. Rockefeller.

The Cabal was satisfied The Man was dead, having recovered his frozen corpse, which they promptly had dismembered, burned, and dispersed in several different locations — to be thorough. But Bortimus was still at large. They pursued him relentlessly and without result, until finally accepting the probability he too had been frozen to death somewhere in the heart of the endless blizzards.

It fell short of being a result that allowed Rockefeller to sleep soundly, but by all appearances his backstabbery had resulted in the successful elimination of a lifelong frienemy and constant source of competition, along with the thickheaded leader of the reptilians who stood in the way of their mass depopulation agenda by way of world war, manmade viruses, and sterilizing vaccines.

In most societies, killing a leader and representative who attended a supposed peace summit would be a clearcut act of war. In the case of the Draco Reptilians, given Rockefeller had the good sense to first make inroads with Bortimus' successor, who stood to gain from his disappearance, the chances of matters escalating to a war between The Cabal and Reptilians was greatly nullified.

True as it was that the Draco and The Cabal's supposed alien gods had ceaselessly warred for countless centuries, throughout the cosmos, and in recent centuries, on Earth, the conflict had been minimal. Each side stood to benefit in the uneasy alliance enough to overlook their differences. Both knew their races to be inherently superior to mankind, and both considered it of tantamount importance they keep the Earth humans weak, confused and living as unaware slaves and resources. Both groups also feared the very real possibility the suppressed masses might one day shrug off the psychological yolk, rise to their true potential and, once aware of their hidden masters, usurp them. Such was mankind's dreaded potential that needed to be delayed and averted at all costs.

The Cabal and Draco knew if mankind collectively achieved sufficient spiritual growth, they could and would call upon The Galactic Federation of Light for protection and assistance. The Federation was comprised of many races and entities from all over the galaxy and maintained the military might to intervene on behalf of similarly-minded positively-polarized beings at any moment.

Their ranks included higher dimensional beings so far evolved no physical lifeforms could resist or destroy them. Through thought alone, they could match the resonant frequency of any physical beings at any place and time and disassemble them into their constituent elements instantaneously. Needless to say, the negatively polarized lower dimensionally resonant entities ruling over the planet sought to avoid direct confrontation with agents of the federation at all costs.

The negatively polarized overlords were only allowed to maintain control over the planet so long as a significant majority of people consented to the existing systems of control through continued participation, because their continued thoughts and actions maintained the planet's existence in a low frequency state. So long as people continued to surrender their autonomy to tyrants and outsource their will to exploitative rulers, they would remain out of reach of the helping hand of The Federation.

The Man, while cleverly somehow always appearing as an ally to the Draco and Cabal, contributed to humanity's hurried evolution, thus posing a major long-term threat to that balance of their shared dominion over man. Such factors being as they were, Bortimus' immediate successor, Chancellor Guarton, had assured The Cabal that should they successfully eliminate The Man and Bortimus — swiftly, quietly and cleanly — he would aid in the cover-up and allow The Cabal to instigate a third world war and/or sterilization program, depopulating surface life as they saw fit.

Aspiring Viceroy Guarton's personal opinion was that loosh was an unnecessary energy source their people would be better off not relying upon, much as was the case with oil for the surface people. As in the case of the roof monkeys, so too the reptilian loosh corporations maintained a powerful, well-entrenched lobby, so weaning the reptilian people off the stuff would prove no easy feat. As above, so below.

What neither Bortimus nor Rockefeller knew was The Man was in truth supportive of the war effort, though not to the end of planetary depopulation. His was a grander plan that entailed the allowance of the start of a third world war that would be put to a premature end by the arrival of a new threat to all of humanity — The Draco — against whom all humans would instinctively mobilize, their racial, religious, political, national and ideological differences suddenly seeming trivial.

Because of the weakened condition of all nations involved and the mass fear induced by the revelation the Draco existed and had been meddling in human affairs since time immemorial, this would provide the catalyst necessary to impose a new world order that merged both battle ready sides into a single world government that would be controlled primarily by The Man.

After the week spent on the brink of starvation in the caverns, when the weather finally allowed it, Bortimus reemerged to the surface and flew to a location where The Man psychically summoned a U.S. Space Force Captain to divert course, pick them up, then drop them off on an asteroid in near Earth orbit with a known Builder Race structure.

From there, it was just a half-day's wait before a reptilian shuttle with some of Bortimus' most trusted friends could pick them up and fly them through an opening to the underworld through the South Pole and into the Reptilian inner-Earth capitol — Draconia — where Bortimus had a successor to confront and a story to tell. If all went according to plan, the secret war between The Reptilians and Cabal could be kicked off, with The Man being left out of it entirely, because everyone assumed he'd died, as proven by the discovery of his frozen body.

The Reptilians and Cabal would be played against one another in the shadows while the Eastern and Western human alliances would be played against each other in the light — until all were in a sufficiently weakened state to unite the surface world against The Reptilians. Soon after, he could broker a lasting peace between everyone and solidify his rule over the entire planet — surface and interior — all while remaining nonexistent as far as everyone but his closest disciples were concerned.

---

THE REPTILIAN BRAIN IS MORE REACTIVE THAN PROACTIVE, AND THEIR SPECIES was, as a result, not known for strategic prowess. Theirs instead was a species that acted predictably and reliably on instinct. Thus the addition of The Man made Bortimus among the most intelligent reptilians alive.

The Man made clear to Bortimus the importance of public perception. Bortimus was commander of the inner-Earth reptilian civilization, and defending that position from the encroachment of his aspiring usurper was of supreme importance. The crowning of his successor would be a widely publicized affair of great public interest and cultural significance — to be attended by the whole of the reptilian inner-Earth government, and broadcast live to reptilians throughout the planetary civilization.

He would interrupt the ceremony, accuse the traitor of conspiring with The Cabal to replace him and challenge him to a legal battle. Under Draconian law, such an allegation would merit the assembly of a tribunal of ranking elders, and both the accuser and accused would make their case. If they voted 3-0 in the accuser's favor, the accused would be put to death immediately; if they voted 3-0 in the accused's favor, the accuser would be put to the sword. In the event of a 2-1 split in either direction, the two parties would fight to the death.

Under Draconian law, the punishment for every crime was the same: death. Such is the etymology of the adjective meaning "excessively harsh punishment". Universal application of the death penalty for nearly every offense was deemed by the Draco the most effective and practical means of ensuring strict obedience to all law. It was, after all, difficult managing so many beings on so many planets. And nowhere was the maxim "survival of the fittest" more prevalent than in Draco culture. Justice by these means seemed to them natural law.

To win a 3-0 verdict, Bortimus would need in his corner a reptilian witness, ideally also of royal lineage. Thankfully, there was at least one qualified witness Bortimus could call upon — a hybrid of the same royal bloodline who was there to witness the betrayal fist-hand.

But getting to Randy wouldn't be easy. Convincing him to side with him over The Cabal too would prove no easy task. But where there's a will there's a way. And no one had more will than The Man.

The Cabal would be no easy [...]

in the impending Presidential el[...]

was very closely monitored

In order to convince him to [...]

would need to be tricked [...]

Cooperate... all without draw[...]

Many if not most of the

associates were being closely

Some of them directly suspec[...]

his physical body... and soug[...]

retaliation... if the m[...]

directly... rais[...]

...with a... they

...remem... and[...]

## 62

SUMMONING RANDY TO TESTIFY ON BORTIMUS' behalf, and against The Cabal, would prove no easy task. As the emerging front-runner in the upcoming primary election, which needed to be won to secure the Democratic Party's nomination, he was closely monitored and well-guarded around the clock.

Randy would need to be tricked, trapped and persuaded to cooperate… all without drawing attention from The Cabal. Many, if not most, of The Man's long-term known associates were being closely monitored by The Cabal, as some of them correctly suspected The Man to exist beyond his physical body and sought to be prepared for potential retaliation.

Even if The Man were able to contact them directly without raising any red flags, he was known to them as a man with a face they could recognize; a face that in no way resembled a dragon — as was decidedly the case with Bortimus. Only a select few had the ability to psychically interface directly with The Man. It was a rare privilege afforded only to a chosen few who had made a sacrifice deemed acceptable. This predicament therefore necessitated The Man work through unknown associates who would understand and appreciate the fact he was no longer in human form.

This reduced The Man's options to a short list, at the top of which was Mark. The Man's requests were very specific and relatively easy. First, he wanted Mark to begin making political contributions to a long list of candidates and causes. Second, he wanted Mark to form his own Super PAC, or Political Action Committee. Third, and strangest, he wanted Mark to obtain a hair from a woman in Southern California named Sheila Spade.

Once those tasks had been completed, all else that would be required is Mark's acceptance of a forthcoming invitation to an unspecified event, to be attended with a plus one of The Man's choosing. Mark didn't ask questions and wasted no time getting to work. After a phone call with a lawyer The Man had recommended — a gentleman in Washington D.C. with the law firm Sullivan & Cromwell, whom was well versed in campaign finance law — the PAC was established.

This, Mark learned, was the legal vehicle that made it possible for billionaires to skirt the pesky limitations imposed by the spirit of campaign finance law so that they may distribute limitless funds to support any given political candidate(s). The only restrictions were Super PACs are not legally permitted to act in direct coordination with the candidates they funded. They can do everything the candidate wants to help them win, provided the candidates not directly instruct the PAC on how to use its money. In practice, this proves little more than a minor hinderance because all the Super PAC need do is mirror the actions taken by the candidate.

PACs are effectively just political will force multipliers for the rich. It had become common practice, since the days of Carl Rove, to pair the pro-candidate messaging with anti-candidate messaging directed toward the opposition — the latter proving more effective, as it was found people are more motivated to vote *against* a candidate they hate and/or fear than *for* one they like.

Super PACs are the source of most political ads. Therefore, the billionaires that quietly fund them are the source of most political ads. This obviously provides them a highly disproportionate capacity to influence elections. Add to this the major impact the mainstream media has on all elections — choosing which candidates are even to be seen at all — and the top 1% has a virtual monopoly on public persuasion in American politics. Mark found this all fascinating, and the thought that he now actually had a say in his so-called democracy was an exciting realization.

Within a few hours of the call with the lawyer, Mark found himself the president of a Super PAC. He originally wanted to name it *AFARCE — Americans for the Freedom of American Resources Culture and Education*. But he decided the joke was a bridge too far and eliminated the Resources part. AFACE still had a pleasant double-entendre aspect to it, but wasn't so on the nose that it would raise red flags.

To kick things off, he proceeded to directly contribute $1,000 to every Democratic frontrunner in all 441 congressional districts, buying him an open door to every incumbent or future congressman and woman in the party, and adding his name to countless donor lists.

He then proceeded to donate $1,000,000 from his personal bank account to AFACE and used that money to donate to other Super PACs that endorsed the same candidates and various causes, buying him the attention and favor of other political power players. The purpose of the move was to put himself firmly on the radar of the Democratic Party, which resulted in an endless barrage of invitations to fundraisers.

It was a matter of time before Mark found himself invited to a fundraiser for Randy's campaign, at which the candidate would be present and vulnerable. His presence would go unnoticed as he had never expressed the intention to attend the event until invited to do so. Per The Man's instructions, Mark set up a new cell phone and email address to correspond with his new generous mysterious political donor persona. Within 24 hours of the donation, he had received several hundred emails and dozens of calls and voicemails, all thanking him for his support and asking for more.

To be thorough, he went on to donate an additional $100,000 — spread out between two other Super PACs that existed for the sole purpose of supporting Randy's presidential campaign — *DuPont for President* and *Randy's Run*; the former a Cabal money funnel, the latter The Man's. Mark's donations were sufficient to qualify him as a VIP in the eyes of those invested in Randy's successful bid for president, and the fact he'd spread so much money elsewhere throughout the country diffused suspicion he was specifically interested in getting in a room Randy. He was simply, by all appearances, a low-profile hardcore Democrat with money to blow. The lure was cast.

COMBING THROUGH THE THOUSANDS OF EMAILS AND EMPTYING THE ENDLESSLY full inbox of voicemails that followed in the coming days, as his information made its way onto more and more fundraiser spreadsheets, became a full-time job.

As much as he could have used an extra hand from Frank, The Man had specifically ordered him not to involve anyone else in the political donation aspect portion of the mission. Frank passed the time in the giant house planning the new long-term excavation effort — that massive underwater Bermuda Triangle pyramid, and was scarcely seen.

By day four, the invitation Mark had been searching for finally appeared. There was to be held a $10,000/plate private fundraiser for Randy's campaign in Hollywood that following week. Mark was cordially invited to attend. He promptly closed his eyes, found The Man, and told him the good news.

*'Splendid Mark! Wait until tomorrow afternoon to RSVP. Buy two plates, get me that hair, and await further instructions.'*

To celebrate the victory, and as a means of team building, Mark held a pizza party, featuring the full menu from Domino's, Pizza Hut, and Papa John's, along with a wide variety of beers, including a nonalcoholic brew he drank to keep up appearances while avoiding triggering an undesirable mood shift at such an important juncture. As delicious as his meals on the island had been, Mark missed the comfort foods of home, and he enjoyed playing out the childhood fantasy of ordering from all his favorite restaurants at once now that he was rich enough to.

After pizza and smalltalk, Mark and Frank finally got to discussing Frank's Cahokia Mounds discovery. He filled Mark in on the Men in Black encounter and his general predicament. Mark asked him for a moment to think, then closed his eyes and found The Man.

'*Are you familiar with Frank's situation?*'

'*Of course. I caused it.*'

'*Can you un-cause it?*'

'*Of course. Here's what we do — I'll give you the number of a man you can call to make Frank's Men in Black problem go away. Simply identify yourself as The Man and tell them to drop the case on Frank Apalonia. When asked for the codeword, say Alpha Omega 3,6,9. But tell Frank it will take at least a week for the heat to die down. It's essential he stay away from the site, for his own safety.*'

'*Got it.*'

'*You're going to start a 501(c) foundation as a vehicle to grease the state authorities into green-lighting the dig Frank already began. Once approved, he can step out of the shadows and enjoy the credit of the discovery without fear of reprisal. To be safe, start another Super PAC, this one aimed at funding Republicans. Donate six figures to a PAC endorsing the sitting governor and senators' reelection campaigns. This buys us bipartisan support to grant your foundation — dedicated to the recovery and display of Native American artifacts, and thus an easy sell PR-wise — sole permission to excavate the site. Frank heads the foundation. Bada bing. Bada boom.*'

'*Understood.*'

Mark opened his eyes to an expectant Frank.

"Okay. I'm going to convince the state to give us the sole right to excavate the Caduki Mounds."

"Cahokia."

"Whatever. As for the people who gave you trouble, give me at least a week on that. I'll make them go away. Whatever they stole from you, double it, then divide it by twelve. Consider that your monthly salary."

"For what?"

"Running my new foundation, of course."

Mark smiled as it all sunk in. Making people's dreams come true so easily was proving very enjoyable.

"Now you get to do what you love, get paid for it and get famous... legally."

"Thank you, Mark—" He held up his beer. Mark clinked his glass against it. "—I'm speechless."

"Anything else?"

Frank thought to tell Mark about the dream, but he also recalled his request they never speak of Hope again and decided to hold off for the time being.

"No. Nothing else. Thank you."

---

WITH FRANK'S PREDICAMENT HANDLED, AND THE WHEELS IN MOTION TO GAIN the political capital required to achieve The Man's agenda, Mark turned his attention to the matter of the hunt for the hair. With Luke's help, and unmiti-. gated backdoor access to all phone calls, text transcripts, and social media chats of every Sheila Spade in Southern California, of which there were three, Mark had little trouble finding out exactly where each was. He closed his eyes and asked which of the three it was. *'The hot one,'* The Man replied.

Choosing based on that criteria was easy. Snooping around her Google calendar, they observed she had a haircut scheduled the next day at Salon Gabriel Anthony in Orange County. The plan required only Mark, Luke, a puppy and a properly timed appointment. It was a simple plan. It was a good plan.

---

WHILE MARK GOT A MUCH NEEDED HAIRCUT, AT THE SAME TIME AS SHEILA, LUKE walked in with a cute puppy wearing a "seeing eye dog" vest. Luke pretended to drop the leash and the puppy wandered gleefully around the salon, to the delight of the stylists and patrons.

When it neared Sheila's station, Mark hurried over, got on his knees, subtly and discreetly grabbed a handful of Sheila's recently cut hair and slid it into his pocket while corralling the adventurous pup. He returned it to the ostensibly blind man who excused himself, to much protest from the girls, who were all big fans of their new four-legged friend.

"Oh my God, he's such a cutie!"

Mark avoided the opening to talk to the formidably attractive blonde, both to stay on mission and because he was too shy without calling on The Man for a boost. Mark finished his haircut and left with a pocket full of precious Sheila locks. Per The Man's instructions, he then promptly put the hairs in a ziplock bag, slid it into an envelope with a note containing a poem clue Mark scribed with his eyes closed as The Man composed it and slid that envelope into another envelope — pre-purchased, pre-paid, overnight rush delivery; with a printed label to an address in Los Alamos, New Mexico.

The recipient's name: "Inanna Ishtar"; it was a codeword that told The Man's allies at Lockheed Skunk Works how much the offer paid. The channeled poem Mark mailed to the dark money wonderkin with the Sheila locks read as follows…

> ONE H-22 THAT LOOKS LIKE HER
> TO THE MAN PRAY YOU WILL CONFER
> IF YOU DO THIS FAVOR FOR ME
> POST HASTE, I'LL PAY A HEFTY FEE
> LOOSE LIPS SINK SHIPS; SHHH, MUM'S THE WORD
> MAKE SURE NO CABAL OVERHEARD
> I'VE NO DOUBT YOU WON'T LET ME DOWN
> I HOLD YOUR STRINGS, DON'T MAKE ME FROWN

With that, The Man had his pieces in place.

- People break traffic laws, work when supposed to work, picture of them evidence sent to all relevant contacts. Social Credit Score also go down.
- People near people with bad social credit score - people message them, call them, in picture or video w/ to them - hurt their social credit score. Make people not spend time with bad people. Make people not want be friends. Make people become...
- People near people with good social credit score help their social credit score. Make good people more popular. Make people want to be around good influences more.
- Social credit too bad, electricity more expensive. Very very bad, no electricity allowed.
- Social credit so good, electricity more cheap. Very very good, electricity free!
- Same for hot water.
- Make American toys stores all toys made in china say made in china + not in North Pole.
- Tell Americans make official statement Santa Claus capitalist myth. All gifts not from fat man with little happy slaves. All gifts made in china by chinese people.

Mr. Chen put great deals of thought into his proposed vibranium lead to these complicated world ide. This single lead mean...

## 63

FOR AS MUCH AS Mr. Chen had come to embrace the pleasures of the flesh afforded to him thanks to his faithful service to The Man — the high-end hooker cavalcade and newfound appreciation for recreational drugs chiefly among them — he was not completely consumed by his vices. He valued, above all, the adherence to a strict routine that balanced his increased responsibilities with the increased carnal appetites.

On days in which Ting Ting presented him no agenda, which constituted most, he started things off with a massage from an attractive woman in the comfort of his hotel bed, which always climaxed in a climax 40 minutes in, by way of a warm oil assisted hand job. He would then proceed to evacuate his bowels of the invariably hearty dinner from the night before, followed by a warm shower while his hot bubble bath filled up.

In the shower, he would proceed to wash his semi-autonomous region and underarms with body wash while humming "Highway to the Danger Zone," then the rest of his increasingly overweight body with a bar of soap in one hand while an electric toothbrush in the other covered every plank unit of the enamel of Mr. Chen's little white (and since recent surgery not at all crooked) teeth, brushing those soon to be iconic chompers the full recommended two minutes with spectacular precision. The repetition of effective process was to Mr. Chen an art form.

His oral hygiene had become even more of an obsession, because as much as he sought to model himself after the illustrious Chairman Mao, and to a lesser extent, his contemporary Kim Jung Un — the weight gain from his over-eating, a welcome side-effect to this end, he also aspired to differentiate himself in subtle ways. He'd read that Chairman Mao refused to brush his teeth, considering the act a sign of vanity and weakness. As he is said to have quipped: "A tiger never brushed his teeth." In place of brushing, Mao is said to have swished tea around his mouth — a far less effective means of tartar control, as evidenced by the few and rare un-doctored photos of him smiling.

Next came shampoo then approximately three minutes of perfectly executed Tai-Chi movements with his eyes closed while the conditioner conditioned; then came the treasured thrill of opening his eyes to see the bathwater on the verge of overflow, marking another perfectly timed and executed repetition of the first phase of his illustrious morning routine.

Then it was out the shower and into the bath, where he would soak in the warm bubbly embrace of his new favorite past-time until his toes got pruny; the fingers never did, because both hands were always occupied with a book. He read only biographies about prominent historical figures — great men with legacies forged in the fires of sacrifice. He read books about Chairman Mao most days, but sometimes subbed in biographies of other leaders he looked up to, like Joseph Stalin, Adolf Hitler, Benito Mussolini, Fidel Castro, the Jung family dynasty of North Korea, and the Bush and Clinton family dynasties of the American empire.

Their ideologies were of far less significance to Mr. Chen than their means and methods of rising to supremacy and by capturing the public's attention and subsequent obedience. He sought to forge for himself a similarly iconic status and to be remembered for being not just a great man but a revered legendary historical figure.

Once out of the bath it was on to breakfast, to be followed promptly by no less than 33 minutes spent penning his own memoirs, to be embellished and edited by better writers down the line, published once his authority had been secured, and made required reading for all in government — then every student in China, forever.

In the case of writer's block, Mr. Chen would call in Ting Ting, who was always just a room away, to bring him a few bumps of crushed up Adderall — the infamous foreign study drug — which he would delight in sniffing or sucking off her fingers while admiring her intricately painted nails.

Occasionally, he would work up the gaul to tap her on the chest and smile mischievously, which was code for: *May I please snort a line of blow off your massive, glorious tits?* He had thus far respected her request not to be treated like the myriad skanks she proffered in her stead, but Mr. Chen found a sinister sense of delight in pushing her boundaries.

Ting Ting put up with this nonsense, telling herself that maybe it wasn't so weird. After all, if she treats him like a baby, he's going to start reaching for her tits. Weird fetishes from The Man's allies, Ting Ting by now in her career understood, came with the territory. But one day after she granted him his snort, he gave her boobs some quick licks, ostensibly so as not to waste the drugs.

She gave him a look that said *I fucking made you. And you have the balls to try that shit on me? You're lucky I don't put a bullet through your thick little head, you son of a bitch.* It was the last time his tongue took liberties with Ting Ting.

The 33 minute minimum writing session typically extended to a few hours, but always concluded in time for his 12:22 lunch, to be consumed alone in his room. His preference for hermetic distancing from everyone had remained unchanged by his gently rising confidence. The privacy also allowed him to study videos of famous speakers like Tony Robbins and Donald Trump to mimic their body language as he ate.

After lunch, Ting Ting would provide him a bump of crushed Oxycontin to help him achieve his afternoon nap, which lasted approximately two hours. Mr. Chen had formerly been staunchly opposed to drugs, primarily because they were very, very illegal, but his newfound elite status exempted him from many, if not most, if not all, pesky laws instituted to keep the peasants in order. Besides, it was the only way he knew to deal with the pairing of his grandiose mission with his inferiority complex and still prevalent anxiety.

While waiting for his nap-time drugs to kick in, Ting Ting would tuck Mr. Chen into bed and tell him stories about the upcoming adventures of Chairman Chen, nurturing his growing confidence and vanity while lulling him into a pleasant slumber.

Upon awakening, she would supply him with an instant release Adderall to perk him back up for his evening work, which, in the absence of a provided agenda, consisted of his scribbling down edicts, plans, and proposals — all of which he planned to one day institute nationwide, if not globally.

Mr. Chen put great deals of thought into his proposed reforms, despite their simplistic wording. The Man had not accidentally chosen a man of such simplistic communication style, for he understood that the easiest rules to obey are the easiest rules to understand.

That month, he'd jotted down over 100 new ideas to improve societal harmony and increase order. He organized his ideas by topic, trusting his genius intuition to guide him. Recent measures included the following (roughly translated).


PROBLEM: CARS MAKE ENVIRONMENT BAD

Gas cars illegal. Make only electric cars forever.

Throw all gas cars in ocean.

Cars made him think of people driving them, which made him think of people speeding — something he never did and saw no reason for anyone else to ever do either.

PROBLEM: DRIVING TOO FAST

Make Elon Musk change car computers so it's impossible for cars to drive over speed limit. If he says no? Okay, Mr. Musk, sorry we shut down your big fancy factory. Or you obey Mr. Chen! : ) When he obey, all other car makers obey too. If he don't, all the other car makers obey too.

Cars made him think of streets, which made him think of traffic, which made him remember being annoyed at people crossing when they weren't supposed to, even though their pictures were taken and shown on monitors.

PROBLEM: PEOPLE CROSS STREET WHEN SIGN SAY DON'T

Social credit score gets kicked down.

Send shameful pictures of their crime to all their friends and family. Encourage their friends and family to shame them. If they do, they get the social credit score points taken from the offender credited to them. *Wow, so good!* :)

Mr. Chen already had a playbook for dealing with the next pandemic in the works. He intended to retain or reinstate all measures previously taken, and to add to them. He thumbed through the notebook to an earlier page and reviewed the work in progress.

PROBLEM: COVID-20

Same rules from Covid-19.

More rules. Many good new rules. Very clear. Very good rules. Smart rules. Mr. Chen's rules. Everyone gets Mr. Chen's vaccine. Everyone.

People say no? Social credit score go down a lot. No travel. Can't buy anything. Maybe reconsider?? No one can send money to people who have no vaccine. You still want to not have Mr. Chen's vaccine?

Banks don't let people take out money if no vaccine. No vaccine? We don't take your money. Make Central Government / Mr. Chen can turn off anybody's money if they really be bad.

People get sick they stay in house. Don't go to work until virus go away.

Everyone encouraged to be nice to their teachers. Nice to their neighbors. Nice to animals. Nice = Glory

People get virus? Means didn't get Mr. Chen's vaccine. Mr. Chen's vaccine is 100% effective. You got virus still? Mr. Chen's sorry, but it's 100% your fault. Take them far away. Somewhere safe with walls around it. Nobody in. Nobody out. Don't come back until virus gone. Quarantine very important.

Illegal to hire employees with no vaccine!!! Obviously by now to them probably. But make laws say it.

Give vaccine to children at schools. Parents no choice. Easy fix.

Must have government app that says you have vaccine to go to places?

Scanners at every building? Very expensive maybe. Too expensive? Maybe not if all done through apps?!

Why not make every building in China safe from the virus? Can just have apps and make a guy from everywhere stand at every door. Enough guys. No problem. Pay them to do.

Make committee to investigate "Christmas" and if this story is not fake news, and American kids think elves make all the toys that say MADE IN CHINA create a recommended statement for America to apologize to China for their lies. And to tell their families the truth — CHINA IS GREAT!!!

Accept apology.

---

He nodded to himself in approval. Unable to think of anything new to add, he cleared his head with another extended bath while playing the latest Pokémon game and half-listening to an audiobook about pubic speaking with headphones on while leaving the TV on loud, just in case the room was bugged. No one could know Mr. Chen needed help or liked Pokémon.

Come dinner time, Mr. Chen and Ting Ting would eat out at a high-end restaurant. They would arrive moments before the restaurants closed, to minimize social interactions. They would dine in silence, but Mr. Chen enjoyed her company, and being seen with her.

Ting Ting provided Mr. Chen the menus in advance, the morning of, and Mr. Chen would spend a not insignificant amount of time between penning edicts thinking through his dinner selections in advance, often with the aid of a spreadsheet, circling his final selections and giving the menu back to Ting Ting so she could place the order immediately on arrival, sparing Mr. Chen the anxiety of making decisions on the spot while creating the illusion he was an exceptionally decisive leader.

The reason she didn't call in the order was it increased the possibility of Mr. Chen being poisoned exponentially. It was Ting Ting, after all, who had to taste-test everything Mr. Chen ordered. She was clearly more expendable to The Man than Mr. Chen... a fact not lost on Ting Ting.

Between courses, Mr. Chen would review reports from Ting Ting typed up on an old fashion typewriter each day... his least favorite part of the day. She abstained from using computers to avoid the ever present prying eyes of the world's intelligence agencies and the CCP.

Following Mr. Chen's review, each report would be promptly burned by Ting Ting as she smoked her evening cigarette. That night's report included the following action items...

.  .  .

## PHOTO SHOOTS AT LABORATORIES

Purpose: Generate content for upcoming media publications hailing Mr. Chen as a brilliant man of science whose team created the Covid-20 vaccine. Mr. Chen will be taken to multiple laboratories and universities to pose for photos to be used by the worldwide media. Actors to portray teams of scientists will be provided.

## MEDIA TRAINING

Purpose: Get Mr. Chen comfortable in front of cameras. Practice facial expressions, poses, and settle on an ideal smile to be practiced in the mirror at least one hour every day. Prepare Mr. Chen to handle the stress of celebrity.

## PREPARATION FOR NATIONAL ASSEMBLY SPEECH

Purpose: Review new speech. Practice reading the speech from the teleprompter. Master vocal projection, tonality and cadence. Watch replays of performance with panel of experts. Incorporate feedback. Practice, practice, practice.

---

ALL THREE ITEMS CAUSED MR. CHEN IMMENSE ANXIETY. AS MUCH AS HE KNEW his role in The Man's plan required the establishment of a public persona in stark contrast to his true nature, he dreaded carrying it out. He'd never given a speech in his life, much less been interviewed or photographed for magazines, newspapers and television programs.

He dealt with his anxiety the only way he knew how — substance abuse aided avoidance. As he began to sweat nervously and felt the onset of a panic attack, he grabbed the drink menu and averted the added stress of making an on the spot decision on what to order by defaulting to the most expensive option.

Ting Ting ran to find the server and placed the order. She treated Mr. Chen's every whim with the seriousness and urgency of a field commander in the heat of battle — an excessive level of devotion Mr. Chen would in time come to expect from all his subordinates.

Ten minutes later, he had finished half the bottle. Fifteen minutes later, he'd finished two thirds and was letting out an impressively loud belch in the back seat of the Mercedes en route to the hotel. Thirty minutes later, he was failing to maintain an erection his latest escort friend could work with, causing him to shamefully lose face, for which he prescribed himself a Viagra.

He had taken an instant liking to the wonder pill gifted to him in bulk from his new Geyser executive comrades, who shared both Mr. Chen's passion for whoring and difficulty performing. It went down smoothly with another gulp of Baijiu in the privacy of his hotel bathroom... then back up twice as fast when he vomited into the toilet.

In his drunken haze, after brushing his teeth, he forced down two more Viagras and stared at his blurry reflection in the mirror, seeking the aid of The Man, to no avail. He spit on his reflection in the mirror, left the bathroom, then found himself obsessively thinking about his spit dripping down the mirror, further complicating his erection goal. He stumbled back out of the bed and into the bathroom, forgot why he'd returned, then passed out on the floor.

The next thing he knew, he was waking up to Ting Ting splashing water on his face, with a splitting headache, and a numb, throbbing penis standing dutifully at full attention. Mr. Chen willed it to go away but it refused. His eyes watered from the Viagra, but a few frustrated tears also crept into the mix.

He thought about how terrible it was his penis stayed soft when he wanted it hard and hard when he wanted it soft. He found himself haunted by the possibility he could come to control the whole world and not his own dick.

Ting Ting helped him to the bed slowly and carefully, as if he were an injured fawn. She tucked him into bed, which still contained the pre-paid prostitute, and she read him a story while lovingly stroking his sweaty aching head, as the patient prostitute tended to his other head.

Mr. Chen could feel neither.

Tears streamed down his face as he bitterly drifted to sleep. He awoke the next morning from a dreamless slumber and hopped out of bed, sufficiently rested to repeat his daily routine.

## 64

MARK HAD NEVER WORN a tuxedo before; nor had he been to Hollywood; nor had he taken part in the abduction of a presidential candidate. It would be a night of many firsts. He checked his new watch — a gold Rolex Submariner he'd selected from a rotating watch case on the dresser of his new bedroom at Château Pensmore.

He chose it not because it was his favorite, but because he incorrectly assumed it to be the most valuable in the collection, unfamiliar as he was with Patek Philippe, Hublot, and Breguet.

"Your date sent by The Man has arrived, brother," Luke informed him, as he finished adjusting his bowtie, the tying of which had been another first. Luke escorted Mark to the foyer; there awaited a golden blonde bombshell with a prominent bust well displayed by a dress as little black and sparkly as her smile was big white and the same.

He'd seen her before, recently. It took him a few seconds to place her, due to the Red Ray-bans, but there was no doubt it was Sheila Spade — the girl whose hair he'd heisted.

"Oh, hi Mark!" she said.

"Hi," Mark replied, approaching with caution.

"You look so handsome!"

"Thanks. I'm confused."

"I'm your plus one, silly."

Mark looked at Luke for some help. Luke did a scan and whispered…

"Invalid. Hologram."

Sheila stood up and twirled around, as she continued.

"It's why we needed the hair, Mark. To generate an identical projection using her DNA code, silly willie."

"So there's no one here? Where's this being projected from?"

"No, brother. It's The Man."

Mark sighed in frustration.

"Can you just explain what the hell is going on?"

Sheila stopped spinning and dropped the effeminate demeanor, assuming suddenly the perfect stature of The Man, holding one hand behind 'her' back and motioning with the other, like a salesman or impassioned philosopher.

"Yes Mark. I'm operating through the physical being of the reptilian inner-Earth Draconian planetary viceroy called Bortimus, disguised as the lovely miss Sheila Spade, Randy's ex-girlfriend — Randy, as in the presidential candidate secretly of both Cabal and Reptilian bloodlines, the former of which betrayed myself and the leader of the latter — Bortimus, the other week, which is why I've been absent and this arrangement was initiated.

"I will reveal Bortimus in his true form momentarily, but opted to come to you as Sheila to test drive the hologram we will be using to get Randy alone at tonight's event, for the purposes of convincing him to attend a trial, the outcome of which will have dire consequences for the entirety of life on Earth — and because you will likely find him as hideous as you find Sheila beautiful."

Mark stared, dumbfounded.

"That's a lot."

"How dare you insult Bortimus, demon!" said 'Sheila'.

The hologram phased out to reveal Bortimus in his true form. Mark gasped and fell back in shock. After a hearty chuckle, Bortimus said...

"Meet Bortimus — Draconian viceroy of Earth. Most powerful being in or on Earth. Kneel, human."

Bortimus pounded his fist against his chest twice, making Mark shudder.

Mark obeyed.

"The Man jokes. Bortimus knows Bortimus beautiful. If Mark do not see Bortimus beautiful, Bortimus not angry. To Bortimus, Mark ugly. The reptilians don't use pronouns, Mark. And are rather easily offended. But also easily honored. Respect is very important in their culture. Silence demon! Bortimus speaks! Use not voice of Bortimus!"

Bortimus snarled, then walked closer to Mark, breathing loudly out of the flaring nostrils of his protruding snout, muttering to himself "Bortimus not easy offended" and invading Mark's personal space for a sniff.

"Much fear. Bortimus smells fear of Mark. Humans think humans only intelligent life. Humans stupid. Reptilians here first. Reptilians give humans knowledge. Reptilians to humans god. Bortimus leader of reptilians of all Earth. And Bortimus not easy offended!"

Bortimus flipped over a couch with his massive tail and roared, loudly and ironically. Mark covered his ears. The Man apologized to Bortimus for insulting his beauty and implying he had a sensitive ego, then psychically suggested Mark offer him a gift as a show of respect, to ease tensions. Mark thought for a moment. He looked at the watch on his wrist, then at Bortimus' wrist. Not a good fit.

"One second please, Bortimus."

Mark approached Luke for a discreet sidebar.

"I need to give it a gift. Any ideas?"

Luke did an instantaneous check of his classified files about the Draco from the military black project databases to which he had remote access, then reached in his pocket and retrieved a Zippo lighter.

"Yes, brother. The Draco revere fire as sacred, weapons as beautiful, and consider combat an art form."

Mark looked at the Zippo. It had the outline of Texas, an AR-15, and read *Don't mess with Texas*. Mark nodded in approval, returned to Bortimus, kneeled, and cautiously made the offering. Bortimus snatched it deftly from Mark's hands, between his claws, and sniffed it.

"What is?"

"A box of sacred fire."

"Ah. A lighter. Bortimus know. How summon fire?"

"May I?"

Bortimus dropped the Zippo into Mark's outstretched hand. He flicked it open then sparked the flint with his thumb.

Bortimus was pleased.

"Ha! Bortimus try."

Bortimus held the Zippo between his claws, but lacked the dexterity to replicate the movement. He dropped the lighter on the floor and roared in frustration. Mark picked it up.

"Hey hey. It's okay. No thumbs. No problem. Watch this."

Mark held it between two fingers, pressed it against his thigh to snap open the lid, and dragged the wheel over his arm, sparking it back to life. Then he held it by the lid and yanked it shut with a satisfying click.

"Cool. Bortimus do."

Bortimus snatched the Zippo back from Mark and rubbed the lid gently against the scales on his thigh, failing to open it right away.

"Bortimus not want break."

After a moment of fiddling, respectfully observed, he got it.

"Ha. Victory. Cool."

"Nice," Mark said.

"Nice," Luke said.

"We really must be going," said The Man, through Bortimus.

"Silence demon!"

Bortimus looked at the Zippo closely.

"What Tex… as?

"Texas? It's a state."

"What state?"

"A state is like a territory. A team."

Bortimus looked confused.

"Tribe?"

"Yes! A great tribe. The tribe of the cowboys. You know cowboys?"

"Cowboys warriors ride four-legged beasts in desert? Shoot guns?"

"Yes. That's exactly right."

"And football tribe."

"That's right! The Dallas Cowboys."

"Ha! Yes. Bortiumus like football. But name of game stupid. Not foot game. Bortimus like Texas. Don't mess with mean don't challenge?"

"Exactly. Yes."

"Ha! Don't mess with Texas."

"Don't mess with Texas," Mark said with a smile.

"Don't mess with Texas," Bortimus repeated.

Bortimus pointed at Luke and said, "Don't mess with Texas!"

Luke replied, "Don't mess with Texas".

Bortimus successfully lit the lighter, tossed it as Mark had done, caught it, then quickly put it out.

"Don't mess with Texas. Ha! Bortimus honored by gift of Mark."

Bortimus struck his chest twice. Mark returned the gesture. Bortimus continued practicing.

"Bortimus, we must go!" The Man said through him.

"When Bortimus ready!"

Bortimus played with the lighter in silence for another ten seconds, in deep concentration, muttering "Don't mess with Texas" each time he successfully sparked the flame and closed the lid, until he accidentally snapped off the lid.

"Okay. Bortimus ready."

---

THEY FOUND THEIR SEATS JUST AS RANDY TOOK THE STAGE, DRESSED IN THE traditional customer service department head for the 1% garb — a dark navy blue blazer, white shirt, blue tie, and obligatory American flag lapel pin. He read off a teleprompter as Mark telepathically conversed with The Man.

*'You see, Mark, the president is just a figurehead. A performer. The real power is*

*in the people who write what your presidents read off the teleprompter. Take your current president — sleepy Joe Biden — a lifelong political insider with advanced stage dementia who can't even tie his own shoes; a senior citizen who fumbles his words more than a one-armed wide receiver with an oil coated glove. The poor old man could scarcely pass a high school speech class. It's pathetic.*

*'But you see, myself and my competitors have your country under a sort of spell, don't we? Despite it being abundantly clear Joe is a no-go for commander-in-chief of the most destructive military on Earth, and acting CEO of all things America, so long as we can get him in costume, parade him around for the cameras and keep the public sympathetic to the well-meaning old man, we can pretend no one is in charge. No one is to blame. But we're in control. As always. All the public gets to choose is which lie to believe. We cast spells through the media. A broadcast is, after all, no more than a spell broadly cast.'*

Mark had for a long time suspected as much, but it was something else hearing the obvious being stated so explicitly by one of the wizards behind the curtain. As Randy continued his subpar delivery of the boring speech, The Man continued…

*'Randy will come across as a big breath of fresh air to a country so weary of having mentally deranged senior citizens at the helm. His qualifications, history and agenda are irrelevant. The public will warmly receive him because at least he's lucid, virile and competent! If, on the other hand, the Republican candidate wins, that's all well and good too. I'm backing him just the same. I have my strings on both of them. The fight is for show. To maintain the illusion of democracy. Either way, I win. And now that you're with me, either way, you win.'*

Randy spoke in trite, predictable aphorisms, as is par for the course, saying things like: "We need to safeguard the sanctity of our democracy by any means necessary," and "equality for all is a right, not a luxury," and "the protection and prosperity of our allies around the world is a top priority. We must defend the world against tyranny."

He said nothing that hadn't been said thousands of times by hundreds of politicians reading the same teleprompters, but The Man was right: he looked very handsome, confident, capable and charismatic — streets ahead of President Biden — and that was the feeble dwarf of a hurdle he needed to overcome to win the nomination.

*'Events like this fundraiser are best understood as vettings by the ruling class. By saying nothing that threatens us, he's sending us a message — you can carry on with business as usual if I'm elected. Thanks for paying the tab. It's more about what he doesn't say than what he does. Bla bla bla freedom. Bla bla bla middle class. Repeat the usual. On the other hand, go up there and say something that doesn't sit well with us, like JFK, for example — talk about being opposed to secret societies, wanting to stop our wars, dismantle the CIA, etcetera — and lose our support.'*

Mark asked The Man if he killed JFK.

*'Not personally. But yes, my lawyer Allen Dulles took care of that. Kennedy was, after all, a traitor to his class. Sloppy as the cover-up was, we got away with it. Because given the option, people believe what they prefer. It's our job to simply reinforce their pre-existing preferences — to defend the lies they chose and continue to choose to accept. Can you guess the Mark Twain quote to that effect, Mark?'*

*'Politicians and diapers need to be changed often and for the same reason.'*

Mark heard The Man chuckle.

*'Not the one I had in mind. But another gem.'*

*'Ah, I know — It's easier to fool people than to convince them they have been fooled.'*

*'Bingo. Very good. Did you know that to this very day, the files on JFK's assassination are kept secret, for 'national security' reasons? Everyone knows that's bullshit. But they're content not knowing the truth. They prefer not to let go of the lies we taught them and have reinforced their entire lives.'*

At that revelation, Mark helped himself to a drink.

*'The masses have always been, and will always be, subjects to the ruling class. Human resources to be used as we see fit. It is the natural order. Obedience is baked into your DNA. Obedience; it's your default setting.'*

Mark scowled at the opinion.

*'In The West, we allow the imagined experience of freedom. But we choose the choices. And they put up with whatever follows, so long as we protect them — especially from the threats we create. It's a simple formula: Problem. Reaction. Solution. We create a problem, let the public react, then offer a solution that happens to be what we wanted all along.'*

*'Wow,'* was all Mark could say.

*'You don't like it, do you, Mark? You'll start to feel differently when it dawns on you that you're no longer in the bottom 99%. I've inducted you into the ruling class. Speech may be free, but money is the volume dial. Now you actually have a say. Now you actually can make a difference; however you choose. And I will always leave you a choice.'*

*'So long as it's between the options you choose, right?'*

*'Now you're learning! Good man. Try the cake. It looks good.'*

Mark obeyed.

The cake was good. He tuned back into Randy's speech...

"Gas prices have reached all time highs, thanks to Mr. Putin's war on the Ukraine, freedom and democracy. As president, I will stand up to bullies like Mr. Putin, work with our Saudi allies to rein in oil prices and develop sustainable energy options to save our planet."

The crowd applauded with the enthusiasm of a man dragged to their child's piano recital during the Super Bowl.

*'Here's a fun fact, Mark. Do you know what President Biden did his first day in*

*office, to that end? He shut down America's oil pipelines. This country has all the oil anyone could ever want, right here. Why do you think he did that?'*

Mark psychically shrugged. The Man continued...

*'The lie is that it was to protect the environment. But even if that was the goal, think about it a minute: what's better for the environment — drilling oil here, then using it here; or drilling oil in a desert far far away, loading it on trucks that drive it to docks where it's loaded onto tankers then ferried all the way around the planet to another dock, put on another truck, then driven to your local gas station?'*

Mark sighed.

*'The former, I imagine.'*

*'Ding ding ding, we have a winner.'*

*'So why do it that way?'*

*'Long story. Many reasons. One being The Cabal wants to maximize greenhouse emissions to melt Antarctica so they can awaken their frozen alien gods.'*

*'What the fuck?'* Mark asked. *'You're joking, right?'*

*'A less exotic reason is control. It's easier to do long-term business with monarchs and to justify price fluctuation to buyers when it's a complicated global trade situation. Really, it's mostly Wall Street commodity speculation bullshit that no one understands or talks about. Putin has nothing to do with it.'*

*'I don't understand. Why? Is it just greed?'*

*'Well, if the people have too much money left after paying their rent or mortgages, inflated utility prices, phone bills, etcetera, we can always get our hands on what's left by doubling, tripling, or quadrupling prices at the pump. Always better to keep the underclass with just enough to survive another month than with more than they need. It keeps them hungry. Keeps them motivated. Keeps their thoughts where they belong — on working for us. Oil prices are a good tool to that end. America is sitting on the largest known oil and gas reserves worldwide.'*

*'Get the hell out of here. No way.'*

*'Oh, surely. Other than saving it all for world war three, which is of course bad for everyone anyway, there's no good rationalization for not providing everyone cheap, domestically sourced natural resources if the goal really were to serve the interests of the people... that's to say nothing of all the hidden and quashed energy alternatives. The technologies you rely on are not only abundantly available, but long outdated. Energy could all be free for all. Easily. But that's another discussion for another time.'*

*'I still don't get it. Don't you want mankind to advance? Why keep us in the dark ages, fighting over resources like primitive tribes?'*

*'It's about control at the end of the day, Mark. Control over the masses, by any means necessary. Don't worry, we're using all kinds of new technologies toward that end. We're just... selective... about who gets what when and for what purposes.'*

*'I knew America had problems. But I thought we were freer than that.'*

*'Yeah, well, sorry. You're not.'*

'*I'm going to be sick*', Mark thought.

'*You'd do well to abandon your childish patriotic ideas, Mark. Nations are no different than baseball teams. You support your home team because it's where you happen to be from. Tribalism. But why bet on the Royals or Yankees when you can own the whole league? It doesn't matter which team wins, so long as you do.*'

Mark ate his cake, and thought about not being able to have it too.

'*Mark, I know this is a big adjustment, but you'll find now that you can take, you will.*'

'*This dinner has been very... educational.*'

'*Good! So glad we could make use of the time.*'

Randy wrapped up his shitty speech...

"We are still the richest, freest, best, most powerful country on Earth. And it'll stay that way so long as I'm your next president!"

"Clap for our president, Mark," said 'Sheila' with a mischievous smile.

Mark obeyed.

'Sheila' stood, whistled and cheered, failing to escalate the moderate obligatory applause into a standing ovation; but succeeding in securing Randy's attention. She flashed him a supermodel schoolgirl crush smile.

Randy smiled back.

---

'Sheila' walked to Randy's nearest security guard and discreetly slipped him a small, gift-wrapped box; written on which was a tag that read: *Happy Birthday Mr. President XOXO - Sheila*

The guard held the present and looked up at Randy, whose predatory gaze was locked on Sheila.

"What is it?"

"Have a look."

The guard discreetly unwrapped it and looked at the contents: a tube of KY Jelly brand sex lubricant.

"It's so The President can more easily fuck me in the ass."

Randy gave his bodyguard a nod that meant: *bring her to me.*

---

Per usual, Randy wasted no time pursuing what he desired. He unwrapped his gift of lube as his bodyguards finished a sweep of the room and left him alone with 'Sheila.'

Randy loosened his tie and began unbuttoning his shirt.

"Knew you'd miss me. They always do."

"Oh I did, baby," 'Sheila' said, projecting the illusion of her dress falling to the floor, revealing her beautiful naked body.

"Better than your cousin?"

Randy hastily took off his belt and unbuttoned his pants.

"Shut up, whore. Get on the floor. Facedown. And spread those whore cheeks for your big dick president."

'Sheila' obeyed.

"Yes, daddy."

Randy dropped his pants around his ankles, squirted a generous amount of lube into his hands, rubbed them together and began stroking himself.

"Daddy president's gonna fuck that sweet ass then piss all over that pretty face, cunt."

"Oooh, yay daddy president."

"That's a good little bitch. Now stay still. This is gonna hurt."

'Sheila' turned her head around and smiled.

"Yes, daddy—" 'She' took off the sunglasses and her eyes turned black. "—It is going to hurt."

Randy said "oh fuck," then scurried toward his suit with his pants around his ankles. 'Sheila's' laugh turned into Bortimus' as he turned off the hologram. Randy frantically reached into his suit pocket and retrieved a tiny gun, which slipped out of his lube covered hands. Bortimus continued laughing as Randy tripped over his pants, still scrambling for the gun.

Bortimus flicked the gun across the floor with his tail, well out of reach. Randy opened his mouth to let out a cry for help that never made it past his throat, which Bortimus' tail was already wrapped snugly around.

Bortimus lifted a kicking and gasping Randy off the floor with ease. He taunted his prey, flicking one of his three giant clawed fingers on Randy's stomach — each flick landing with the full force of a human boxer's jab.

Outside the door, one of Randy's bodyguards reached for his gun. The other laughed and said, "You're new, aren't you? Don't worry. These are Randy's happy sounds."

He still investigated.

"Everything okay, Mr. DuPont?"

Bortimus turned the Sheila hologram back on, and with her voice simulated sexual moans in harmony with Randy's groans of pain, which he elicited with each flick of the claw.

"Oh yes! Yay! Pound it! Fuck me like a fat slut, daddy president!"

Bortimus delivered a single close-fisted punch square in Randy's chest, causing him to wince loudly in pain.

On the other side of the door, the formerly concerned bodyguard laughed.

"Told ya—" the other said, "—Politicians, man. Buncha fuckin' weirdos."

*'Okay Bortimus, you've had your fun. We really must be going.'*

Bortimus, still holding a kicking, wheezing, helpless Randy by the neck with his tail, effortlessly punched out a window like it was an egg shell, climbed through it, then leapt from the thirtieth floor of the hotel, spread his wings, and soared away unnoticed, with Randy firmly in the vice grip of his serpentine tail. Randy had been successfully subpoenaed.

## 65

DRACONIA — the inner-Earth capitol of the Draco reptilians — is by all surface world standards a highly advanced metropolis. The inhabitants enjoy access to everything to be found above and more. The enormously spacious caverns are well lit and air pollution free, loosh being the zero emissions energy source it is.

Though in no way renowned for their creativity, inventiveness or even basic intelligence, the Draco integrate into their vast empire the technologies and knowledge of everywhere they invade and conquer, rendering them a vast array of the best of everything from the more advanced races they've defeated in combat on various planets over the millennia.

Bortimus arrived without issue, his human cargo kept safely in a soundproof, casket-sized box he carried like a suitcase. He took Randy to the dungeon of his palatial estate that was built into a cave wall, hallowed out by way of controlled lava flow, a commonplace reptilian construction technique.

The dungeon was generously proportioned, built as it was with larger, reptilian-sized prisoners in mind. It otherwise closely resembled a human prison cell, though with the notable exception of bars that glowed with a searing hot plasmic coating coiled around each bar. The other walls were solid rock. Escape was a nonstarter.

Bortimus unlocked the case, tossed it into the cell and closed the door. Randy lunged out of the case gasping for air.

"Welcome to Draconia. Hey Randy…"

"What?"

"Don't mess with Texas."

"What?"

Bortimus left.

---

Meanwhile, in the heart of Draconia, the ceremony to crown Bortimus' successor Guarton, which doubled as something of a funeral to commemorate the loss of their thought-to-be fallen viceroy, had begun. High ranking royals gave brief though heartfelt effigies in honor of the lost leader, with speeches such as...

"Bortimus the fearless dead. May great suffering and death come to all responsible. May Bortimus conquer heaven and find victory and glory in afterlife."

After each to-the-point effigy, the speaker would loudly roar, to be promptly followed by a synchronized roar from all gathered. The roars of mourning could be heard and felt for miles around, with each who heard them joining in — from wherever they were, no matter what they were doing, such that the lamentations echoed throughout the entire city, with a population of exactly 10 million — a number kept constant with a strict birthing permission policy, violation of which resulted in the traditional Draconian penalty for breaking a rule — death, for both the unlicensed parents and illegally laid eggs or hatched younglings.

Bortimus stood on his balcony and listened to the sound of being missed. If he had tear ducts, he would have surely cried.

'You're quite popular, I take it,' Bortimus heard The Man say.

"Yes. Bortimus loved by all."

'They'll be so grateful to have you back, my friend.'

"Yes. But Bortimus not friend of demon. Bortimus know ways of the djinn. Djinn not to be trusted."

'The same could be said for the Draco, Bortimus. So let's not rely on trust. Our interests are clearly aligned. Having an ally in your position below is of great benefit to me. And having an ally in my position above is of great benefit to you. Besides, we share a common enemy in The Cabal. And as the saying goes the enemy...'

"...of enemy friend. Yes, demon. Bortimus know saying. But betray Bortimus and suffer same fate as all enemies of Bortimus."

'Yes. Of course. I could extend to you the same warning.'

"Then Bortimus and The Man in agreement, demon."

---

As The Man waited, he decided to check in on several of his employees, including Mr. Chen, whom Ting Ting had informed him was nervous about his first public speaking engagement — the National Day address to the entire National People's Congress of the Chinese Communist Party.

He came to him in the dream world, where Mr. Chen was busy enduring the ever popular nightmare of standing on stage before a crowd naked. The Man appeared as a member of the audience, in his recognized form. He walked onto the stage where Mr. Chen stood, looking down in stolid shame, covering his crotch with both hands, as the crowd stared. Some snickered. Some recorded on their phones. Some shook their heads in disapproval.

"Ah, Mr. Chen. Good to see you practicing for the big speech. Hard at work. Even in your dreams. How commendable."

Mr. Chen looked up vulnerably then waved with one of his hands briefly, before returning it to help shield his crotch. The Man stood beside him, facing the crowd, and put a supportive hand on his shoulder.

"Now now, Mr. Chen. This is a common dream brought about by a common fear. It is the fear of being vulnerable; of being judged; of not being enough. Hence the nakedness. Do you know these are fears shared by most, if not all great leaders?"

Mr. Chen shrugged, still looking down sadly.

"So many leaders I've helped along the way have been just as shy as you. Between you and I, Stalin used to wet his bed when he had this dream. And Hitler often needed to be pumped full of amphetamines just to take the stage. Can you believe that?"

Mr. Chen looked up and let loose a slight grin.

"Let me show you something. Follow me."

The Man suddenly started floating toward the ceiling in a Willie Wonka-esque fashion. Mr. Chen then did too, surprised and delighted by the newfound powers. His naked dream body ascended behind The Man, through the ceiling, high above Beijing, then China, then Earth… all the way up to space.

"Remember this view, Mr. Chen?"

Mr. Chen smiled and nodded yes.

"The next time you feel unsure of yourself, remember the view. Now watch this."

The Man twirled his finger and the Earth began to quickly rotate in reverse, much as it had in Frank's dream. The Man stopped his finger; the world below halted.

"Look at China. Just thirty years ago."

China's landmass was far darker; 80% of the cities had disappeared.

"All those cities. All that development and advancement. Amazing! Unparalleled rapid growth, the likes of which I've not seen in thousands of years. And look what happened just before that…"

The Man twirled his finger again and the Earth again spun backward then halted. Just off the Eastern coast of China could be seen the island nation of Japan. Mr. Chen and The Man zoomed into the sky below just in time to witness a bright flash followed by a mushroom cloud.

"Nagasaki," said The Man. Another flash. Another cloud

"Hiroshima. And that's just the famous ones. The allies firebombed several Japanese cities. City after city reduced to rubble. Millions dead. In Europe too. Brother against brother. Nation against nation. Total devastation. Good old fashion tribal warfare. It's the same story, over and over, just with more powerful weapons as time passes."

The two returned to space and The Man spun his finger again, back to the present.

"But out of the rubble, comes this—"

They flew through the sky and witnessed people gathering, and the cities being rebuilt, better than before. Highways formed. Skyscrapers rose. Factories appeared, in both China and Japan.

"You see, Mr. Chen, the evolution of your country, your race, and indeed — your species, is best accelerated by periods of widespread conflict, war, devastation, chaos and disaster — followed by periods of unification under strong leaders who can usher in a new golden age and a new world order. That's where I come in — to help guide you. I plant the seeds of a grander future in the fertile soil of the ashes. Do you understand, Mr. Chen?"

Mr. Chen nodded.

"I rely on people like you to unite, rule and guide the masses to achieve your true evolutionary potential. Another period of transition is coming, Mr. Chen. It's inevitable. And the future is in your hands."

Mr. Chen looked at his hands.

"There will be another virus, as you know. And another pandemic of fear. Another world war. Another rebalancing of power. And a new New World Order. The British Empire replaced the Dutch, the American Empire replaced the British, and under your visionary leadership, a Chinese Empire shall rise. I intend to be here to help you when called upon. But on the off chance I'm unavailable to answer your call, you must be prepared to speak for yourself. Do you understand, Mr. Chen?"

Mr. Chen nodded.

"What say we practice using your words, Mr. Chen. Let's try that again. Do you understand, Mr. Chen?"

"Yes," said Mr. Chen, speaking for the first time in our story.

———

BY THE TIME THE MAN RE-CONCENTRATED HIS ATTENTION ON BORTIMUS, HE WAS nearing the front gate to the large gothic castle at the center of Draconia, which served as the place of gathering for the inner-Earth government. Bortimus piloted a cruiser with a magnetic undercarriage that hovered smoothly and silently above the city's magnetic roads.

He stood at the helm proudly, like the captain of a frigate, wearing a robe to conceal his identity, and drove to the main security checkpoint outside the foreboding entrance — which consisted of a towering stone wall with a semi-transparent green force-field serving as the main barrier to entry, behind which was a traditional gate, also glowing with a plasmic coating, behind which was a gigantic stone door, in front of which stood a row of human-sized wingless reptilians holding laser rifles, standing at attention. Behind them stood half a dozen bipedal giant crocodiles holding large spears with glowing red tips.

The guards shifted polarity, launching Bortimus' cruiser off the road. It came down with a slam. The guards surrounded his crashed vehicle, pointing their rifles. Their leader — a taller, winged, lighter hued reptilian resembling Bortimus — approached.

"Exit the vessel and state your purpose, or prepare for battle."

"The purpose of Bortimus is end the lie Bortimus has fallen."

The leader knelt. The rest followed suit.

"Apologies, great leader!"

"Forgiven, Commander Traniton."

Commander Traniton rose and turned around.

"Open the gates! Viceroy Bortimus has returned!"

A chorus of joyful roars resonated from all. Bortimus laughed.

"Ha. Victory."

---

BORTIMUS PROUDLY WALKED INTO THE GRAND HALL. AS HE MADE HIS WAY DOWN the aisle toward the throne, on which his aspiring usurper Guarton sat, waiting to be coronated, all stood in awe.

"Bortimus has returned."

Bortimus let out a ferocious roar that was promptly joined by all in attendance, with the notable exception of Guarton, who remained seated silently on the throne in fear and disbelief.

"Bortimus calls upon the Council of Elders. Bortimus demands an immediate trial of the betrayer of Bortimus—" All listened in silent anticipation. "—Chancellor Guarton."

"What?!" shouted Chancellor Guarton.

The Council of Elders, already in attendance for the ceremony, stood. One called out, "Assemble the triumvirate! Let the trial begin!"

Guarton stood and roared.

"Guarton is innocent of these lies!"

"May the triumvirate decide," said Bortimus.

———

A PROCESSION OF REPTILIANS IN GREEN ROBES ARRIVED FROM THE MAIN entrance. The front three each carried a large stone; two more carried a large scale with a copper bowl on either end. Behind them, two more carried a stone table and three more carried stone stools. They placed the table before the throne, then set upon it the giant scale and arranged the stools to face the masses in attendance. The three chosen elders took their places. All sat, with the exception of Bortimus and Guarton, who stood side by side, facing the triumvirate.

"The charge is treason," said the elder on the center stool. "What say Chancellor Guarton to this charge?"

"Guarton innocent! Guarton loves and respects Bortimus. Guarton would never betray Bortimus. Guarton would never betray Draconia!"

"And what say Viceroy Bortimus?"

"Guarton has made a secret alliance with The Cabal of the humans. Guarton conspired to have Bortimus killed, to replace Bortimus. Because Bortimus refused to allow Cabal to have a new great war between the human tribes — a war to kill most of the roof monkeys and leave Draconia without loosh!"

A commotion filled the crowd.

"Silence—" said the lead elder.

"Why does The Cabal seek to destroy their own tribes?"

"Because, Elder Flartis, the humans are disobedient, defiant and unpredictable. The Cabal is weak and cannot rule them. Cabal wants disaster for all but Cabal bloodlines, so Cabal can start again with a small amount of people Cabal can control, so when Cabal awaken frozen gods, gods will not be displeased."

"The frozen gods of The Cabal — are enemies of the Draco from the times before the last great flood?"

"Yes, elder. Sworn enemies of the Draco. The Cabal believes Cabal's gods live… seek to awaken gods. If their beliefs are true, a great enemy will return. And there will be much war."

A commotion from the crowd followed the startling revelation.

"Chancellor Guarton, Does Bortimus speak truth?"

"No. Bortimus speaks lies. Bortimus tells stories. Because Bortimus fears Guarton will replace Bortimus. Because Guarton is more smart, more loved and more beautiful."

Bortimus roared in rage. Guarton roared back. The crowd roared.

"Silence! Has Viceroy Bortimus proof of these claims?"

"Ha. Yes, Elder Flartis. Bortimus brings a witness."

Bortimus raised his hand, signaling for Randy to be brought in. Two reptilians carried in the case, dropped it before the triumvirate and opened the seals.

"Does Bortimus smell fear in Guarton?"

Guarton snarled.

"Behold the one called Randy. Of the DuPont royal human family. Son of The Cabal. Son of Draconia. Reptilian hybrid. The one to be made next viceroy of the great human tribe called America."

Randy emerged from the soundproof case with a gasp, took in his surroundings, and nearly pissed his pants and sat motionless, in shock.

"Randy DuPont — half blood son of The Cabal and the Draco; warring to become leader of the tribe called America. This is the Randy Bortimus claims?"

Randy sighed.

"Yes. That's me."

"Guarton objects! How is it known this creature is of pure blood?"

Trinarus, the reptilian high priest who had overseen Randy's initiation beneath the Federal Reserve Castle was in attendance. He stood and spoke.

"Trinarus desires to address the triumvirate."

"State credentials and speak, Trinarus."

"Trinarus is high priest and overseer of the confirmation ceremony of this Randy. Bortimus speaks truth. The blood of this Randy has been weighed and found pure. The human is a descendent of glorious Draco bloodline, and thus entitled to bear witness in Draconian court!"

"So be it. Overruled, Guarton. The witness is of royal blood."

Guarton roared in frustration. Bortimus gave Trinarus a respectful nod. Trinarus struck his chest twice then sat down.

"The witness may speak. Randy DuPont, what say Randy to the claims of Viceroy Bortimus?"

Randy thought in silence, weighing his options.

"Speak, half-blood!"

"Randy will not speak until Randy's safe return is assured."

The triumvirate deliberated amongst themselves.

"By oath of the Draco Alliance, Randy DuPont is hereby assured safe return if Randy speaks. If Randy does not speak, Randy will die. If Randy speaks lies, Randy will die. Does Randy understand?"

"Yeah, Randy understands. It's true. What Bortimus said. The Cabal tried to kill him. But I had nothing to do with it. I was told it was going to be a peaceful summit. I was as surprised as him."

The first elder cast his stone into one of the two bronze bowls. It landed with a loud clank, weighing the scales toward the side with the Draconian hieroglyph for *guilty*.

"The first vote has been cast. In favor of Bortimus."

"What?!" cried Guarton. "Flarsh shit! Objection! Randy has no proof Guarton was involved! Why cast a stone against Guarton, Ferminose?!"

Ferminose stood, pointed at Guarton, roared and shouted…

"Because Ferminose knows the ways of Guarton! Ferminose trusts Guarton not. And Guarton has much to gain by betraying Viceroy Bortimus. The vote of Ferminose remains unchanged!"

"So it is," said Elder Flartis, as Ferminose calmed down and sat.

"But Guarton makes a good point, Ferminose. The Cabal is guilty. But how is it to be known Guarton knew of the betrayal?"

Bortimus thought for a moment, then heard The Man.

*'Ask them why The Cabal would kill one viceroy if they did not have control over the one that would replace him.'*

Bortimus relayed The Man's question.

The second of the three elders tossed his stone in the guilty bowl, to great fanfare. The lead elder spoke…

"Viceroy Bortimus, these words make sense. But Flartis seeks another proof before Flartis casts the final stone for Bortimus. If another witness can be called before the council, Elder Flartis will be satisfied."

Bortimus thought.

"Well Viceroy, has Bortimus another witness? Another proof?"

"A moment, Elder Flartis."

*The Man must be this witness,* Bortimus thought.

*'Bortimus, I strongly advise against it. If you reveal my presence you call into question your own reliability. Guarton will claim you are possessed and your words cannot be trusted. To my understanding, there is precedent in Draconian law for dismissing testimony for such reasons'.*

The Man was making that bit up, but it was true.

"Bortimus requests a private word with the triumvirate, Elder Flartis."

"Granted—" said Elder Flartis, rising with the triumvirate.

"The triumvirate will return!"

The Man desperately tried to prevent Bortimus from revealing his presence, but even his powers of persuasion were insufficient to change Bortimus' stubborn reptilian mind. The short-term goal of winning the trial trumped all long-term considerations.

---

IN THE PRIVACY OF A SEPARATE CHAMBER, BORTIMUS EXPLAINED THE UNIQUE situation to the elders.

"To be clear, Bortimus, this proof is called The Man. But The Man is not a man. The Man is an archon?"

"Yes, Elder Flartis. Bortimus will call upon the archon to share another proof."

Bortimus closed his eyes. The Man made one final plea they pursue another course of action, which Bortimus ignored.

*'Alright Bortimus, let's do this.'*

Bortimus opened his eyes. Instead of their usual yellow and green colors, they were glowing bright blue. The elders gasped in shock.

"How long has this archon possessed our great leader?"

"Only since betrayal of Bortimus. And with consent of Bortimus."

"Why would Bortimus agree to such an arrangement?"

"I've got it from here, Bortimus. Perhaps it's easier if I show you. Could you bring a bowl of water? Preferably a copper bowl."

The bowl was promptly provided. The Man dipped Bortimus' claw in the water and swirled it around. Light shone from his eyes into the bowl, transforming the water into an accurate 3-D replication of the summit. He replayed for the council the full meeting, the act of betrayal, their arrival in the snowy tundra and the moment of agreement between Bortimus and The Man so they could both make it out alive.

"But how know we Guarton was involved, archon?"

The Man swirled Bortimus' claw in the water again, rewinding it. He stopped when they were in the hallway, being locked into the portal room, then magnified the image of Rockefeller, just before they were portaled away.

Rockefeller could be heard saying into his phone, "Congratulations, Viceroy Guarton. Bortimus no longer stands in your way."

Guarton's voice could then be heard coming through the phone...

"Ha. Victory! Rockefeller has the word of Guarton there shall be no reptilian interference in The Cabal wars of the human tribes."

The water returned to normal.

"Satisfied?"

---

THE ELDERS RETURNED WITH BORTIMUS AND TOOK THEIR SEATS. THEN ELDER Flartis cast his stone into the guilty bowl. The scale slammed down with a clank.

"What?!" cried Guarton.

Bortimus looked to the nearest giant bipedal alligator guard and held out a hand. It tossed Bortimus its spear, which Bortimus promptly and without hesitation hurled at Guarton, who roared one last time until the spear went straight through his open jaws and through the back of his throat.

Guarton fell onto the spear, which propped him off the ground at 45°. Blue blood squirted from the wound and poured out of his coughing mouth; his arms, legs, and tail squirmed violently until they didn't.

Bortimus approached his defeated foe, leaned in, snarled and said...

"Don't mess with Texas."

Bortimus took his place on the throne.

"Ha. Victory."

His eyes flashed blue.

# 66

THE NEXT DAY Mark did something he'd not done in years. He watched the news, primarily out of curiosity as to whether word of the increasingly popular presidential candidate going missing had gotten out. The main story of the day seemed to be that President Biden had fallen off his bicycle — a remarkably lame sight and mundane development.

It was a sight that would get a laugh out of Mr. Chen, who began to wonder why he need take any shit from the American imperialists when he was calling the shots; a sight that would garner double the laughter of Bortimus, who considered the bumbling old man a perfect representative of the inferior human race on the roof; and a sight that would make Mark change the channel.

As he did, he learned about another breaking story — this one of far greater consequence. There had been another school shooting, with a body count high enough to merit significant coverage; 19 children and two teachers shot dead in an elementary school, in a city called Uvalde, Texas. Another 17 children injured, which means anything short of dead. It was an unimaginably horrific scenario.

Mark had a feeling there was more to this story than met the eye; he spent several hours digesting coverage from various sources, starting with the most mainstream, and gradually delving into the conspiracy sites he once frequented on his manic lone wolf quests to get to the truth in his years before coming to the island.

The folks who considered everything to be a conspiracy were ranting about it reeking of a shadow government false flag attack, with frequent references to MK-Ultra — the CIA program to develop unwitting assassins through psychedelic-aided, trauma-inducing, psychological conditioning that was, according to records, accessible through the Freedom of Information Act started in 1953 and continued for at least 20 years.

Notable MK-Ultra alumni included infamous "Oklahoma City Bomber" Ted Kaczynski, who was invited to participate in an unassuming on-campus experiment while an undergraduate student at Harvard. Little did he know, he was being programmed to become a killer. The MK-Ultra program was, like NASA, a collaboration between American and Nazi researchers, and the inspiration behind such works of fiction as "The Manchurian Candidate".

A prominent conspiracy theory on the fringe message boards was that this shooting was reminiscent of the Sandy Hook Massacre, in terms of a mentally disturbed perpetrator acting alone with no apparent motive, whose instrument of destruction was the AR-15 — the highly popular civilian iteration of the standard issue U.S. military's M-16, the sole delineation being the former was semi-automatic and the latter full auto. As in the case of Sandy Hook, the senseless massacre was used as a catalyst to pass gun control legislation that was ultimately unsuccessful. Commenting on the possibility of there being more to the story is the cardinal sin that had been used by big tech to censor Alex Jones years later, leading Mark to believe there might actually be something to it. Whether or not it was a conspiracy, it seemed clear some very powerful people were very afraid of the rumor.

It was plausible, considering the American government had at least once before plotted to kill random Americans and blame it on Fidel Castro to justify a war with Cuba with "Operation: Northwoods". The joint chiefs of staff had already signed off on the heinous plan, and the only reason it wasn't carried out is President John F. Kennedy found the proposition outrageous. This incident was one of the reasons President Kennedy said he wanted to "split the CIA into a thousand pieces and scatter it into the wind," soon before being killed by them. The Man's reference to his lawyers taking care of JFK checked out, as Allen Dulles, the CIA director JFK fired and his successor Lyndon B. Johnson immediately reinstated following the successful coup, was a long-time partner at the prominent international law firm Sullivan & Cromwell.

What Mark found irreconcilable about this latest shooting in Texas was the undisputed revelation the police stood by for an hour and twenty minutes, just outside the school, allowing one young man abundant time to carry out his shooting spree. For as much as the media liked to focus on the deadly capacity of the firearm used, the police gave the young man enough time to kill them all with a caveman's club.

Photos and videos depicted at least two dozen police officers, including SWAT teams clad in full battle regalia, standing by casually while the children were slaughtered one by one inside the school, which wasn't even locked. Their reluctance to engage was not only in defiance of common sense, but in blatant violation of the official procedure they were trained to follow in the case of a school shooting, which mandated the first officers on the scene go in right away to engage and neutralize the threat.

While the police were unwilling to confront the shooter, they were willing to guard the school to protect the shooter, preventing anyone else who was willing to put their life on the line from stepping up to save those children. They actively prevented multiple citizens, including furious and terrified parents, from stepping up to fill the role of the cowardly officers. Parents were tazered, disarmed, handcuffed, and detained for the crime of attempting to save their children from a threat police refused to engage.

One particularly tragic case concerned a man named Ruben who was himself an off-duty police officer for that very district. He received a call from his wife Eva, who had been shot, then rushed to the school to save her. He was disarmed, apprehended, and detained by Uvalde Police. Meanwhile, Ruben's wife bled to death just inside while the shooter continued his massacre at a leisurely pace. It wasn't until an off-duty border patrol agent armed only with his barber's shotgun arrived at the scene that the attempt to save the children was finally made.

He was successful making it through the police barricade and into the school. Only then did the Uvalde officers finally enter the building. Within minutes, the threat was eliminated. Perhaps it was a case of remarkable negligence, cowardice, or groupthink. But it just didn't add up.

Mark closed his eyes, found The Man, and asked him if he knew what happened. He responded before Mark even asked the question…

*'I had nothing to do with that. But my money's on The Cabal being behind it — toward the end of justifying the disarmament of your countrymen. If they're behind it, expect your politicians to vote on a hastily-compiled, several-hundred page bill too long for anyone to have time to read in response to the public outcry. As Machiavelli put it:* For it is enough to ask a man to give up his arms, without telling him that you intend killing him with them; after you have the arms in hand, then you can do your will with them.'

*'I don't remember reading that in* The Prince.'

*'It's in* Discourses.'

*'So you think that's the play?'* Mark asked.

*'Quite possibly. America is built on the pillars of free speech and the retained ability to defend one's self and protect itself against future leaders. Most modern nations have already been disarmed. Because of your Constitution, the only way your people can be disarmed is by choice. Fear is the only way to convince people to surrender their right to self-defense to the state. The irony in this case of course is the tragedy occurred because the only people with guns other than the shooter were only using them to prevent everyone else from helping. People like the idea of daddy being*

*there to protect them from the crazies and the baddies. But daddy isn't always there, is he? And sometimes daddy is the baddie. What then? A monopoly on the capacity for violence is a monopoly on the control of the people. Remember that, Mark.'*

*'This is fucked up.'*

*'I don't disagree.'*

*'You're just going to let it happen?'*

*'Mark, as I said, this wasn't my doing. I prefer to keep America armed for what's to come. As for my media, I'll allow them to cover this story honestly. I am, after all, at war with The Cabal — and they're the most likely suspect if there is foul play. They think they've already defeated me. Would you like to help me prove them otherwise? Would you like to help me hit back?'*

Mark thought for a moment. He'd never been a violent person, but there was a sense of indignation burning in his chest he needed to do something with.

"Yes," Mark said, "let's hit back."

## 67

WHILE GRATEFUL FOR The Man's assistance in resolving the trial, and for his aid in assuring the safe return of Viceroy Bortimus, the high council of elders took issue with the presence of an archon within the mind of their leader.

A secret meeting was held, unbeknownst to Bortimus or The Man, to address the opportunities and threats such an arrangement might have in store for the Draconians of Earth.

Just as The Man had predicted, not everyone welcomed his arrival. With this in mind, The Man strongly advised Bortimus to take immediate action to assist him in a severe and decisive strike against their now clearly established mutual enemy — The Cabal, who had enjoyed the advantage of a first strike but failed to exterminate their primary target.

It was time they suffered the consequences of their miscalculation. Always the opportunist, The Man had used his time with Randy to evaluate the possibility of collaborating, despite the recent setbacks. While Randy was in captivity, The Man reached out to him by way of telepathy and assessed both his culpability in the betrayal and his personal ambitions, taking into consideration the changing power dynamics on the horizon.

As The Man had hoped and anticipated, Randy played no active role in arranging the move against him, was resentful The Cabal had taken such brazen action without his permission, and blamed them for his current predicament. Well aware he was, for the time being, at the mercy of The Man and Bortimus — both parties having ample justification to end his life — the only life that mattered to Randy, Randy played ball. It took little salesmanship on The Man's part to convince Randy it was better to be employed than destroyed. The Man informed him he had no choice but to retaliate against

The Cabal, but that he still saw great value in allowing the continuation of their global dynasty.

He suggested the purge presented Randy a wonderful opportunity to elevate to a senior leadership role within The Cabal. After all, there would be a number of new vacancies in the very near future. As he had Randy rape tapes on ready, if Randy controlled The Cabal, so did The Man by proxy. Perhaps Randy could make the daunting task of exterminating the problematic leadership of the cult easier; in return, he would be granted amnesty, continued protection and support, and an open invitation to come to the island and eat, drink and fuck to his heart's content for the rest of his life, ala President Clinton, via Jeffrey Epstein.

Randy's only condition was that his father's life be spared. Other than that, he didn't give a damn what happened to the rest of those dusty old billionaires clinging to their slipping grip on the levers of power. He had, after all, only just learned who most of them were, and he felt as loyal to his Draco ancestors as he did his Cabal progenitors. If he could play them against each other and end up on top, Randy was all in.

Randy therefore, in the privacy of telepathic conversation, revealed salient intel, including the locations of several Cabal strongholds to which The Man was not yet privy. He also consented to taking part in a setup for the coup de grâce, a contingency The Man had been preparing for months, with Frank playing a key role; hence The Man's insistence on meeting him — a task Mark had faithfully carried out in his stead.

Once The Cabal's senior leaders had been liquidated, now that he had dependable employees like Randy, Mr. Chen, and Mark carrying out maneuvers on his behalf, and found himself on the throne in Draconia, his power was more absolute now than it had been in thousands of years. This gave The Man a well-earned sense of achievement.

The Cabal's surveillance capabilities were second to none, as they had been key originators of the intelligence agencies to begin with and still maintained a heavy footprint in practically every three letter agency on the planet. So positioned, they would easily catch wind of any major military operation targeting them in time to make evasive maneuvers.

To catch them off-guard, The Man would need to attack with a powerful force they never saw coming, and he just so happened to now have at his command millions of battle-hungry reptilians more than happy to take vengeance on the roof monkeys with the audacity to attempt to usurp their great leader and manipulate reptilian affairs. Under ordinary circumstances, the Draco would not sanction direct military intervention on the surface world, in observation of conditions foisted upon the Draco Alliance by way of treaty with the Galactic Federation, whose intervention was greatly feared. But there was a provision in the treaty that excepted the Draco from reprisal in the case they were (1) acting in self-defense, and (2) within their sovereign territory, which started 20 yards underground and extended throughout the entirety of inner-Earth.

Under the Antarctic Treaty System, signed by all major powers in 1961, humans were banned from going anywhere near the primary entry and exit point to the inner-Earth at the South Pole. Likewise, the Draco were prohibited from leaving Antarctica. The treaty had been signed by all major nations and successful in that contact between the humans and Draco were virtually nonexistent. Randy had in fact been the first partial human to visit Draconia in decades.

Given the recent attempt on their viceroy's life, military measures could be justified as self-defense. If properly timed and planned, The Cabal could be massacred all at once, and the move would be justified under galactic law. As for how he could get The Cabal underground, the solution was simple: use their favorite tactic — fear — against them. If The Cabal felt they were under threat, they would surely retreat to their underground bunkers... which happened to be within Draco jurisdiction.

It took The Man longer than expected to convince Bortimus to order the surprise attacks on Cabal leadership. He anticipated it wouldn't take more than five minutes. It took seven. After poking at Bortimus' insecurities, and pointing out how weak he would look to the Draco and Cabal alike if he failed to retaliate, he added that The Cabal was behind the Uvalde Texas shooting, slaughtering younglings while police prevented parents from fighting honorably to save their children, toward the end of scaring people into surrendering their weapons so they posed less of a challenge to dominate.

In the eyes of the Draco, such tactics were disgraceful. Despite their brutality, the Draco were fierce believers in honorable conquest, which to them entailed fighting on a level playing field. Not only would Bortimus never consider resorting to terrorism to scare people into surrendering their arms before an invasion, he would either arm the enemy or intentionally handicap his own forces to avoid an unfair fight, limiting his soldiers to weapons comparable to the foes highest technologies.

This was to Bortimus' mind the only way of proving his race to be superior warriors worthy of dominion. There was no honor to be won attacking an enemy that had no chance of fighting back — especially if they were tricked into disarming themselves. That his enemy had chosen to carry out this cowardly attack on the Texan children was enough to seal the deal.

"Don't mess with Texas," had been Bortimus' response.

For the next phase of his plan, The Man instructed Mark to contact the governor of the great state of Illinois, after donating $100,000 to the governor's favored Super PAC and making a max allowable personal contribution toward his next campaign — $2,600. Then and only then was he to request a phone call with the governor to inform him of a new potential archaeological discovery at the Cahokia Mounds on the Illinois/Missouri border, and his intention to fund, with state support and oversight, an excavation — the findings to be made public. As head of his foundation, Frank was to lead the excavation.

What The Man knew that Mark and Frank did not was that the governor of Illinois was a Cabal member aware of the potential significance of the relics to be uncovered — the remains of giants and clues pointing to the existence of the race from which The Cabal shared bloodlines — a secret they had more or less succeeded in concealing from the profane masses for generations, though doing so was proving an increasingly difficult task in recent years, as the public became more and more aware of the hidden histories and suspect of the so-called authorities' claims, which always boiled down to *nothing to see here, folks.*

The Man correctly predicted the governor's first call would be to senior Cabal members to inform them of the new development. He also correctly assumed The Cabal would instruct the governor to ignore the request and go on to investigate the site on their own, at which time they would discover Frank's secret excavation was already in progress, and curiosity would lure them in to further investigate.

The Man was also aware the nearby Whiteman Air Force Base routinely flew B-2 bombers over St. Louis. Influencing a few Air Force allies to "accidentally" drop a bunker buster on the Cahokia Mound would be an elegant way to bury some of the harder to hit members while announcing his return.

It was a complex plan. It was a good plan.

---

Days after making the call to the governor, Mark saw a front page headline that read, "Smoke Over St. Louis." According to media reports, citing NASA as a source, an undetected meteor had struck the outskirts of St. Louis. No mention was made of the detail that the "meteor" had struck a mysterious ancient historical site.

The Cabal had no interest in letting word out about what had really happened, so the media brushed it aside after nominal coverage, and the attack on an ancient site in the American heartland went largely unnoticed. The pilots responsible for the mishap were quietly honorably discharged, and no further investigation was ordered.

But The Cabal got the message. And word spread quick. As predicted, they scurried off to the safety of their fortified mansions across the globe. When The Man's human mercenary forces arrived at their front doors locked and loaded, claiming they had a message from The Man, The Cabal members invariably retreated to the safety of their underground bunkers.

By Bortimus' decree, tens of thousands of reptilians had rapidly burrowed tunnels directly into each known Cabal stronghold bunker in the span of 72 hours, with the aid of their advanced burrowing technologies and techniques.

When The Cabal members under siege retreated to their underground bunkers, they were met by Draconian soldiers whom had tunneled their way in. Each Cabal member was offered an opportunity to battle a Draco soldier of their choosing in single combat. If they won, they and their families would be spared.

Of those who accepted the offer, none prevailed.

The Man's mercenaries and Bortimus' Draco foot soldiers slaughtered everyone they encountered while they themselves suffered less than half a dozen casualties. The bodies were devoured by alligator people, blood was cleaned, tunnels were sealed and very little trace was left of the worldwide elite purge. As far as the world was concerned, a sizable chunk of the top 1% simply disappeared, literally overnight. The operation had successfully reduced The Cabal's worldwide population by nearly 80%, with Randy's family among the survivors.

Rumor had it Randy had been the only one to prevail against his challengers. Many survivors found this suspect, but realized whether true or not, Randy was clearly a force to be reckoned with.

As predicted, he was elevated to a senior leadership position.

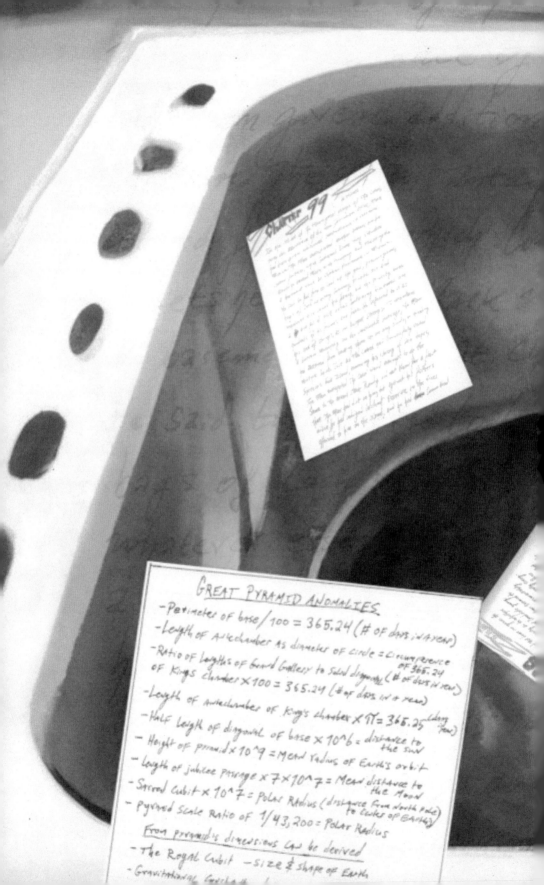

## 68

THE MAN ANTICIPATED another attack on his island fortress, which contained some very valuable assets he tasked Luke and Mark with relocating from a vault on the Bermuda Triangle island to a vault at Château Pensmore in Missouri. He said to feel free to load up the gold, precious gems, bags of cash, priceless art, and whatever else struck his fancy; but the priority was a box full of memory cards loaded with blackmail on hundreds of The Man's friends and foes: the fabled "Box of Strings".

To maintain a certain monopoly on the invaluable leverage, The Man had abstained from backing them up on any clouds or spreading multiple copies. Just as The Cabal had successfully raided Epstein's island, removing his library of sex tapes before they fell into unfriendly hands, The Man astutely anticipated they would attempt to do the same to his stash.

He was correct. The Cabal had assembled a large hit squad of para-military black ops soldiers of fortune — the sort of which they relied on to instigate and fuel conflicts in foreign regions of interest and assassinate problematic leaders in the way of business. Randy's father was to oversee the siege.

Mark, Luke, and Frank — who had offered to lend a hand — arrived to the island on The Man's spaceship without issue, and were met by a dozen of The Man's men atop the same temple roof The Man had landed with Mr. Chen two years prior.

They were all armed and on high alert, per Luke's orders. After a brief and cordial dispute with Frank, who was still intent on carrying out Hope's final wishes, Mark gave the order to first rally the staff for evacuation. The staff consisted of the 22 sex workers, two chefs, and three groundskeepers.

The rest of the people on the island were cyborg-like mindless soldier servants, whose lives were comparatively expendable and needed for defensive purposes. Mark served as the evacuation ferry pilot, and began the first of at least two needed trips to get everyone to safety.

Meanwhile, Luke searched the mansion for the Box of Strings and Frank was sent on the best Easter egg hunt ever — free to snag whatever he wanted from the museum-like estate. The rest of the troops were sent on patrols and to key defensive positions, as dictated by Luke, who also ordered the readying of the giant killer robots and drone swarms — all of which he could close his eyes and remotely control.

When Luke reached the hot tub that could only be made to drain and open to reveal the vault door beneath with The Man's retinal scan, it became apparent they would need to await Mark's return — a detail that pissed Luke off. Frank's insistence they prioritize evacuating the staff was compromising the mission. Not one to waste time, Luke ran back upstairs with two large duffel bags in hand and began gathering other valuables for extraction, starting with cases full of gold bars, expensive jewelry and bearer bonds found in The Man's bedroom.

Frank was grateful for the opportunity to explore the place unaccompanied, as it freed him up to find the box under Hope's bed — if it existed — and in doing so answer for himself the nagging question of whether his surreal dream encounter with her had been real. But he couldn't help but stop several times along the way to add priceless ancient artifacts to his duffel bags.

By the time Mark returned from the first evacuation flight in the cloaked ship, they had company. Mark spotted two Navy Seal style speedboat rafts jetting toward the island, a few miles out. He thought he'd like to warn Luke, and was relieved to learn the Ship did it for him.

Mark's moral dilemma as to whether he should evacuate the last group of employees was cut short. As he made his approach to land, he witnessed three missiles rain down on the temple roof.

The entire ceiling collapsed. Another volley of missiles struck the rubble, creating an inferno none could have possibly survived. Mark thought he wanted the ship to call Luke.

"Luke! The temple has been destroyed by missiles."

"Copy brother. What's your status?"

"Inbound. Did you get the Box of Strings?"

"Negative. Your eye scan is required to open the vault."

"Fuck. Alright, be right down."

"Affirmative. Deploying countermeasures."

Mark noted a swarm of drones rising from both sides of the island — hundreds of them — looking like a flock of very well-organized birds.

Suddenly, Mark observed three helicopter gunships descending through the clouds above. They all turned sideways, giving their gunners a clear line of sight, then spritzed the skies with explosive rounds, bringing down scores of drones, then retreating as the drones spread out and pursued them, until the drones reached their maximum range, at which time the helicopters turned back around and re-opened fire.

This was a well-planned attack.

As the helicopters got the better of the drones, Mark observed another incoming volley of missiles, coming from somewhere out to sea. Mark wished there was something he could do to stop them, then witnessed a blinding blue laser beam coming from his ship lock on to one of the the warheads; it exploded, causing a chain reaction of explosions that scorched the tropical sky and took many of the remaining drones out.

Mark wondered where the missiles were coming from, then saw the holographic display target three submarines a few miles off the coast. He thought he'd like to destroy them. The ship promptly released three disk-shaped objects that shot into the water below. On the holographic display, he could see them closing in on the subs. They each found their targets. Mark saw geyser-like explosions coming from the sea.

"Took care of the missiles."

"Copy brother."

This got the gunships' attention. They unleashed streams of bullets all over Mark's general direction until some made contact with his ship, disabling the cloaking and revealing his position. The gunships then fired volleys of rockets toward Mark. He thought *shields,* and a plasmic barrier formed all around the ship, just in time to absorb the brunt of the incoming rockets, creating a smoke screen.

He thought he'd like to relocate above the helicopters and was directly above them a second later. He willed the laser take them out. It easily sliced them apart like sticks of butter, one by one, before the pilots could react, causing each to explode and fall into the ocean.

Then Mark felt himself spinning and saw fire all around him, followed by the intimidating sound and sight of three F-35 fighter jets flying overhead. They split up and circled back toward him. He willed the ship back to the island, but it moved at a much slower speed now. Something was damaged. Another missile struck his ship, sending it into another spin. Then another. Then another. The ship re-stabilized itself as it came to a crash landing right in front of the house.

The walls of the triangular ship all opened like a giant origami figure, leaving Mark plenty of space to jump out as the thunderous sound of the relentless fighter jets filled the air. Then came a stream of bullets blasting the yard around the ship to pieces as one jet passed overhead. Another came, guns tearing up the yard, this one on a direct path to hitting him, until it was blasted out of the sky by one of the giant killer robots, which fired a volleys of rockets and unleashed their gatling guns, downing a second jet.

Mark slid down the sparking side of the ship and sprinted to the entrance of the house, where two of his men calmly and dutifully opened the door for him, then closed it behind him. He locked the door and began running toward the stairs to the basement, but before he could make it through the foyer, an explosion blasted the huge petrified wood doors off their giant hinges and a fireball threw him across the marble floor, knocking the wind out of him.

One of his men's arms slid past him, along with pieces of robot, which the last fighter had apparently gotten the better of. Mark stumbled to the elevator beneath the grand staircase, wheezing, and hurried to the basement levels. When the elevator doors opened, Luke was there, pointing an automatic rifle at the door. He lowered it.

They sprinted down the hall, to the room with the hot tub. Luke twisted the arm of a statue, which caused a scanner to emerge from the floor. Mark stood before it, closed his eyes and searched for The Man, but to his surprise, could not find him. He tried the retinal scanner with his own eyes: *Access Denied.*

"Fuck."

Mark closed his eyes and again searched for The Man. No dice.

"I don't know what's wrong. He's not responding."

Luke heard gunshots on one of the floors above.

"Compound breached. To the safe room."

Luke threw Mark over his shoulder like he weighed no less than a backpack, then ran back down the hall and into the open safe room. He set Mark down inside, sealed the vault door and retrieved several additional weapons from their racks on the wall — an automatic shotgun, submachine gun, two handguns, and three grenades. Luke cocked the submachine gun and handed it to Mark, along with one of the grenades.

"Wait here brother."

He opened the vault door and sealed it behind him.

"Luke! Wait!"

Mark sighed, sat down cross-legged, closed his eyes, and began to meditate like his life depended on it.

It did.

———

As predicted by The Man, the Draconian elders were not impartial to the idea of having a viceroy under the influence of an archon — particularly

The Man, whom some of the elders were convinced was the arch archon — a mysterious and powerful entity their ancestors in the reptilian mystery schools had called upon and worked with generations prior, and to mixed results.

The high council had decided, in a secret emergency meeting, that The archon needed to be removed from Bortimus and entrapped in a relic. If successful, they could effectively capture a very powerful genie in a bottle, to be kept from exerting undue influence while remaining at their disposal. The council voted to authorize the forced exorcism, under condition Bortimus not be killed.

The Man had forewarned Bortimus of the potential for yet another untimely betrayal; a concern Bortimus had scoffed off. As a result, Bortimus was caught off-guard when he woke up from a long awaited peaceful slumber in his bed to find himself surrounded by elite guards and half a dozen chanting mystics undertaking some bizarre ritual.

Unfortunately, this took place when Mark desperately needed to channel The Man to open the vault. Bortimus stood on his bed defensively as the giant bipedal alligators encircled him, spears drawn.

"Put down your weapons," said Bortimus, in a calm, authoritative tone. High Priest Trinaris responded…

"The council has spoken, Bortimus. The Viceroy of Draconia cannot be controlled by an archon."

"The council seeks to imprison the friend of Bortimus. And now dear Flartis betrays Bortimus. Is this the way?"

*'Ah, so we are friends.'*

*'Silence demon.'*

"Flartis seeks only to honor Viceroy Bortimus. But Flartis must serve the High Council. The archon will be kept safely in the great temple. Flartis swears this. Begin the exorcism."

The mystics surrounding the bed began chanting loudly…

"Yaldabaoth esto! Yaldabaoth esto! Yaldabaoth esto!"

The chanting and presence of amulets did indeed make The Man's ability to connect with his employees very difficult, but it was a challenge he approached, like all challenges, with clear focus and sustained equanimity. Bortimus heard The Man…

*'Bortimus, my glorious friend, it would be of great help if you could hold them off. I must attend to a few matters, post haste. When I give the word, please just shut up those people chanting.'*

*'What means post haste?'*

*'Fast.'*

Bortimus roared so loud it drowned out the chanting.

"Silence, mystics! Face Bortimus in single combat, cowards. If one can defeat Bortimus, Bortimus will surrender the archon."

The reptilians stepped back, respecting the challenge. The mystics stopped chanting. High Priest Flartis ordered them to continue.

They obeyed.

Bortimus leapt off his bed and said, "Who's first?"

---

MARK, DEEP IN MEDITATION, FINALLY SAW THE MAN APPEAR.

"Pardon the delayed response. I'm in a rather precarious situation at the moment."

"Same here."

"Shall we get my box of strings?"

"Hold on."

Mark took three deep breaths then opened the safe room's vault door, pointing his gun through the opening and hurried down the hall. Just as he reached the room with the sub-hot tub vault containing the box of strings, three Cabal contractors stormed the hall.

Mark prepared for the shootout, but just before the threat reached him, one of the men called out, "Found the safe room!"

Mark hurried back down the hall and posted up outside the safe room door. He ducked back into the other room and twisted the statue's arm as Luke had. The scanner again emerged from the floor. He positioned his face over the scanner, with his eyes closed, and searched for The Man. He could hear him cutting in and out and saw his image flickering like a strobe light.

---

BACK IN DRACONIA, BORTIMUS HAD A GIANT ALLIGATOR PERSON IN A HEADLOCK, squeezing its throat until it passed out.

Bortimus picked up the defeated opponent, swung it by the tail in a circle, until the momentum was too much to hold, then let it loose at the team of chanting mystics, taking them down like bowling pins.

"Victory! Ha."

---

MARK THEN SAW THE MAN COME IN CLEARLY.

'Ok, Mark. Now!'

Mark opened his eyes. They turned a fiery greenish blue color as the scanner scanned: *Access Granted*. The nearby hot tub suddenly drained to reveal a manhole-sized hatch. He opened the hatch, climbed down a ladder, closed the hatch above him, then heard...

*'Well done, Mark. I'm going away for a while now, Mark. Presumably for the rest of your life. When I return, I look forward to reading all you leave behind and have made arrangements to incentivize you to continue your work. Château Pensmore is now yours, along with whatever you rescue from the island. I hope with you moving the strings in my stead your race can survive itself another century. Evolve the species, Mark. Evolve yourself. And if you can, be happy. I've yet to master that.*

The Man began to flicker and fade, but his voice still came through...

*'You're The Fucking Man now Mark! Don't forget it.'*

Mark opened his eyes and returned to reality. The only item in the room was a small, nondescript black safe. Mark slung the submachine gun behind his back and took the box of strings.

---

THE THREE COMBATANTS WERE STILL IN THE SAFE ROOM ON THE OPPOSITE END OF the hall; the one tasked with watching their six wasn't paying attention, so Mark put the box of strings down, retrieved the grenade, and crept toward the occupied hallway. He slowly and quietly pulled the pin from the grenade and released his grip on the grenade's handle, activating the fuse.

He counted to three nervously, pretty sure the fuse would last at least five seconds, then wound up to let it loose. The elevator door beside the safe room dinged and opened. Alerted to the sound, the threat turned to notice Mark releasing his best pitch directly at him. He dropped his gun and caught it just in time to throw it back at Mark, who covered his face and dove.

Before the grenade made it halfway down the corridor, a gunshot rang out, and the grenade exploded, the blast sliding the safe down the hall beside Mark. Through the smoke Mark could just make out the lifeless body of the man who'd thrown the grenade and the outline of Luke in a firefight with the other two men in the safe room.

Mark picked up the safe and scrambled to his feet. More gunshots began trickling out through the smoke-filled hall, narrowly missing Mark.

"Behind me!" Luke shouted, as he walked backward down the hall in Mark's direction, still unloading the automatic shotgun into the safe room. Using his thermal vision, Luke saw the last remaining target through the smoke and dispatched him with his pistol.

"Clear!"

They took the elevator to the roof.

"Is the ship still operational?" Luke asked.

"Don't think so. It's out front."

Luke carefully approached the ledge and peered over to see The Man's ship smoldering in flames.

"New means of egress required."

They thought quietly until Mark had an idea…

"The Bright White!"

"The what?"

"The S.S. Bright White! That speedboat we arrived on years ago. Remember?"

Luke tried.

"Negative. Pre-resurrection memories inaccessible."

"We took it through a crack in the cliffs and left it in the caves. Maybe it's still there."

"Standby brother."

Luke took command of a damaged though still functional drone and flew it to the cliffs on the coastline, where he found the slit in the rocks leading to the cave they'd docked the speedboat they arrived on.

"It's there," Luke said; "Let's go."

"What about Frank?"

Luke looked annoyed, for the first time since he died, and groaned…

"This fucking guy."

"Sounds like you're coming back online, bro. So to speak."

Luke accessed the house's surveillance cameras and quickly checked all the areas with proximity alerts. There only remained a handful of surviving invaders; dead and dying men from both sides lined the halls and rooms throughout the manor.

"Found him," Luke said.

Luke checked the cameras again to plot Mark's exit route.

"The West wing is clear. Take the stairs on the other side of the roof to the first floor, exit out the back door, hide in the bushes and wait for me."

Luke sprinted to the other side of the roof, looked down, then jumped off.

"Jesus!"

Mark ran to where he'd jumped and looked down. Luke was traversing the balcony railing on the floor below with a cat's poise. He snuck up on a man on one of the balconies, fixated on his scope, grabbed the rifle by the barrel, yanked it out of his hands, swung the butt of it at him like a baseball bat and fluidly kicked him off the balcony. He flipped the rifle around and pointed it directly at Mark.

"It's me!"

"I almost shot you! Fucking do what I said! God dammit."

Mark smiled, then obeyed.

## 69

FRANK FINALLY MADE his way into Hope's room — the same room he'd shared with her back when this house of horror had felt like a honeymoon resort. He crawled under the bed and found a shoebox with a sketch of a heart with an X through it. He opened the lid to reveal Hope's box of conquest mementos and fumbled through the various knickknacks and tokens until he spotted what he was after — the seashell. Beneath it, he saw the buffalo nickel he'd gifted her. He slid both into his pocket and began to crawl out from under the bed. The door burst open. He scurried back under as two Cabal men began searching the room.

He saw their combat boots walking toward him, then heard two gunshots and saw both men fall. Then came two more boots and his name, "Frank—" The boots halted in the pooling blood on the floor. "Come with me if you want to live," Luke said, having a strange déjà vu feeling he'd heard that somewhere before.

Frank wanted to live. He crawled out from under the bed and followed Luke, who led them to the emergency staircase. They heard footsteps coming up the stairs. Luke grabbed Frank by the shirt, pushed him against the wall, shushed him, then retrieved a grenade with his free hand. He flicked the ringed pin out with his index finger, catching it on his middle finger, and held the armed grenade over the open center of the stairway as the men ascended.

After what for Frank were a few very suspenseful five seconds, Luke dropped it. The grenade fell three stories then exploded mid-air with perfect timing. Luke let go of Frank, jumped over the railing, caught himself on the opposite side, and repeated the stunt twice more until he landed on the site of the smoky carnage. He shouted "come on," then lifted each of the four dead bodies, two at at time — one in each hand — and dropped them off the balcony to make room for Frank.

"Thanks," Frank said, feeling sick to his stomach. Then came an unexpected flurry of machine gun fire from the ground floor. Luke tossed the last grenade and ushered Frank through the third floor door, where they ran down an expansive hall and into the library. Franks ears rang from the shift to silence while they hurried up the staircase that spanned the perimeter of the library to the top floor, through the secret bookcase and into the hidden library.

Luke picked up Stalin's desk and threw it straight through the giant window, then turned around to see Frank staring at books beneath the locked case. Luke smashed the case open with a book.

"Take what you want. Let's go."

Frank removed some gold bars and stacks of cash from the duffel bags to make room for the rare books. Among the works were early editions by H.P. Blavatsky, Manley P. Hall, Phillip K. Dick, and author-less Gnostic texts and ancient scriptures. While Frank gathered the intellectual loot, Luke extended a cord from a spool affixed to the back of his belt, set it on the floor, lifted and placed a bookcase on top of it, took out a rock climbing carabiner, latched the duffel bags together with it, slung them over his shoulder and told Frank to get on his back.

Frank obeyed.

Luke leapt out of the window fearlessly. The cord supported his weight and he came swinging back, slamming hard into the side of the rock mansion, but he felt no pain. He pushed off the wall with his feet and descended until they reached the ground. He then pressed a button on the device, detaching the cord.

---

LUKE AND FRANK REGROUPED WITH MARK BEHIND THE BUSHES AND MADE A RUN for the cliff. Luke ran backward, rifle at the ready, covering them the whole way. The trio reached the cliff's edge — a good 50 yard drop to the wharf below. The sound of bullets helped Mark and Frank get over their fear of heights.

While Luke returned fire, Mark and Luke leapt off the cliff and flailed as they fell into the ocean below. Luke took a bullet to the back, which only slightly penetrated his flesh, his advanced body armor absorbing the brunt of the impact. But the shot was enough to knock him off the cliff and send him spinning toward a jagged rock below. He redirected his fall with the help of jets in his boots at the last second and landed in the water.

He climbed on the rock that almost claimed his second life and used his night vision and zoom capabilities to search for Mark and Frank. Both had surfaced and were gasping for air while swimming toward the cliffs.

"Where is it, Luke?" Mark shouted.

Luke scanned the area and located their destination — an easily over-looked slit in the cliff. He activated a laser through a modification to his left middle finger and held it on their the destination while readying the rifle with his free hand, pointing it back up at the cliff, expecting their pursuers any second. As he waited, he rested the rifle on his other arm and made some adjustments to the scope's settings until the figure of a man peered over the canyon ledge.

He kept the laser guiding Frank and Mark steady as he aimed the rifle with his right arm alone. He fired a shot and the Cabal mercenary fell off the cliff, dead before he hit the water. Another pursuer held his gun over the edge without peering over and fired off a volley of directionless shots, some of which nearly found Frank. Luke momentarily brought his left hand back onto the rifle, took aim, and let off another shot, blowing off the man's trigger finger.

"Alright Luke! We're in the cave!"

Luke slung the rifle over his shoulder, dove into the ocean, and swam underwater toward the cave — the rockets in his boots offering extra propulsion. When he arrived he was greeted by the sound of a speedboat with an engine more faithful than the dentist Luke stole it from.

---

RANDY AND HIS FATHER, IN THE PRIVACY OF A CABAL MANSION OFFICE, EAGERLY awaited confirmation The Man's island had been taken and the treasure trove of blackmail had been recovered or destroyed, to free Randy forever from the lingering threat that the sins he committed on the island would come back to haunt him.

Instead, they got a call informing them the mission had somehow failed. Randy cursed and roared. His father sighed and said, "So be it. Plan B it is."

He lifted the receiver of a red rotary phone on his desk.

"Who are you calling?"

"A cousin."

Randy's father dialed a number.

"Hello, Don? You're still in DC, right? Good. I need a favor."

PRESIDENT BIDEN WAS AWOKEN FROM HIS SECOND AFTERNOON NAP BY FORMER Secretary of Defense Donald Rumsfeld, whose face looked familiar but name Joe could not remember.

"Sorry to disturb you, Mr. president. But we have an urgent situation that requires your immediate attention."

"Oh yeah. Don't… don't worry about it, man. What's… what's the scoop?"

"Space Force requires a signature to authorize a rods from god strike on a terrorist compound on an island in the Bermuda triangle."

"Where's that?"

"Bermuda."

"Huh?"

"Between Florida and Cuba, sir."

"Ah. Gotcha. Castro's at it again, huh? Crafty sunnovabitch. And you wanna hit 'em with a what? A god rod? What's that?"

"Space-based weapon system in orbit, sir. Very cool. Drops tungsten rods at supersonic velocities using gravity. All the blast of a nuke without the fallout."

"No fallout? Well that's… that's cool. Good for the environment. Hold on man, I thought we were pretending we didn't have weapons in space. If we use it, won't the Ruskies, Chinks and hippies make a big fuss? That's a lotta blowback, man. I got reelection to worry about."

"The island has an active volcano. We can blame it on that."

"Seems like a pretty sweet plan, man."

President Biden sat up in bed and helped himself to a sip of juice from a glass on his bedside table as he thought it over.

"Did you run it by Barack? Doesn't sound like a VP call."

He spit the juice back out.

"What the hell, man? This is cran-apple. I said cranberry. How many damn times do I have to say it? People act like I don't know what I said. I know… I, I know what I said.""

"Mr. President, it's urgent we strike now."

He tried to hand President Biden the strike authorization form, without success. President Biden continued rambling on about the juice discrepancy. Rumsfeld sighed, left the room, closed the door, counted to ten, then opened it again.

"Sorry to disturb you, Mr. President, but we have a situation."

"Oh yeah? What's the scoop?"

"It's about the juice, sir. Intelligence suggests the White House's entire supply has been mislabeled."

"I knew it! I ask for cranberry juice and they keep sending me this cran-apple bullshit. People think I don't know what I said... I... I know what I said. Any idea who's behind it?"

"Putin, sir. Some kind of commie psychological warfare. To make you doubt yourself and feed into this misinformation campaign that you're not fit to lead."

"Crafty sonnovabitch. So he's got someone on the inside..."

"We suspect as much. If you'll just sign this we can launch a full investigation immediately."

"Fuckin' A, man. Give her here."

---

A SATELLITE WEAPON RELEASED A ROD THE SIZE OF A TELEPHONE POLE INTO Earth orbit.

---

THE SPEEDBOAT WAS SKIPPING ALONG THE OCEAN WATERS LIKE A DEFTLY THROWN flat stone, several miles off the island's coast, when a sudden impact struck the center of the island's volcano, causing a massive explosion that rained rock fragments everywhere and sent a concussive shockwave far enough to rock the boat so hard it nearly capsized.

Lava began to blast out of the crater in all directions, like a well-shook bottle of soda, lighting the entire jungle on fire as an unstoppable cascade of lava spewed relentlessly out of the wound in the Earth's crust. The Man's coveted garden was converted to smoke, turning the skies above the former fortress black.

Luke zoomed in. What little remained of the mansion burned and sunk into the ocean. It was like watching the fall of Atlantis.

...are allowed entrance

...d the hor...

...l Day - the

...ay. Mr. Ch...

...oth on his

...nervous. ...

...elt up... sense of an...

first public speaking exper...

the night prior, Ting Ting b...

...istering him t... the ...

executive decision to cancel

...lunch time, he found hims...

...unable to slide into the Co...

## 70

IT'S CALLED The Forbidden City for a reason. Few are allowed entrance to the Chinese Communist Party's National People's Congress Hall of Assembly at Tiananmen Square in Beijing. Even fewer have had the honor of speaking before the entire congress on National Day — the Chinese equivalent of America's Independence Day. Mr. Chen would be the first man in history to do both on his first visit. This being so, he was understandably nervous.

Unable to sleep the night prior, Ting Ting had reluctantly resorted to administering him twice the usual dose of Xanax and made the executive decision to cancel his usual morning rub and tug. When Mr. Chen awoke, minutes before lunch time, he found himself completely out of sorts, now unable to slide into the comforting groove of his cherished daily routine and at once aware he had mere hours to ready himself for the most consequential event in his life, and potentially in Chinese history.

This speech marked his unveiling to the world on a formal stage. The Man and Cabal's global media empire had already started building his reputation with a sudden barrage of positive press, lionizing him out the gate as a national treasure. This was a perk that came with his arrangement with Geyser Pharmaceuticals, to assure all of China be mandated to take their preemptively developed Covid-20 vaccine, as well as assurances Chinese factories could handle the mass manufacture of the shots for the rest of their global customers.

In exchange, Mr. Chen was given undue credit for inventing the vaccine and a licensing agreement worth hundreds of millions, to be paid out to his newly established company — New Order International — of which he named Ting Ting CEO.

While it seemed likely, if not probable Covid-20 was manmade, Mr. Chen pretended that not to be the case — both because he preferred that possibility and because he knew dire consequences may well ensue for him personally if it were discovered to be. Even if Mr. Chen had known for sure he was being used to sell the world a solution to a problem created by the purveyors of said solution, The Man had recalibrated his moral compass such that it would be understood to be a necessary sacrifice to achieve the long-term greater good.

After all, people died every day from diseases of all sorts, as they always had. So be it if some more died of a new one when managing the crisis properly could lead to such strides in creating more orderly, easily-controllable societies worldwide. Great leaders like Chairman Chen required conditions of chaos to rise to prominence and assuage the public's confusion and fear with bold and decisive new policies; policies that would fail to gain traction under conditions of perceived safety and prosperity. Bad things had to happen for good changes to take place.

Currently Mister, aspiring Chairman, Chen was a firefighter in need of a fire. That fire was Covid-20, and his timely vaccine was the water to extinguish it. His ostensible purpose for making the address was simply to pay tribute to his recently-departed superior, Mr. Fei, and to briefly comment on his general intention to carry on the man's legacy.

His unmet colleagues expected no more from his address, with the exception of those also in The Man and/or Cabal's secret employ, who were recently made aware of the plan to catapult Mr. Chen to the highest position possible, ideally that of Chairman, in the spirit and title of Mao. Behind the scenes, they all quietly conspired to facilitate his rise. With a Chairman Chen in place, the new pandemic and mass vaccine creation, distribution and administration could not only be managed to their satisfaction, but further down the road, the long awaited third world war could finally be triggered at will.

Many in The Cabal still sought total war and unprecedented devastation. Other more progressive newcomers sought less apocalyptic means to establish and maintain dominance — envisioning a future where everyone willfully submits to a faceless monolithic system of control made possible through emerging technologies and social conditioning. To their minds, the whole apocalyptic bit was unwarranted.

Conflicts of interest notwithstanding, everyone in The Cabal wanted to see The Man's man Mr. Chen become Chairman Chen; but that would only be possible if he could live up to the manufactured hype and come across as a strong and competent leader.

Ting Ting was fully aware of how high the stakes were, and managing the shy man with such shaky self-confidence was an art form only she was suited for. To get the much frazzled Mr. Chen at the required energy levels, she gave him twice the usual dose of Adderall, which compensated for the grogginess brought on by the night prior's double dose of Xanax. To calm his nerves and strengthen his connection with The Man — who found himself rather busy; his attention split as it was already between the exorcism and Lord of The Strings quest — Ting Ting had two extra pricey and discreet escorts on stand-by in her room.

"Mr. Chen, I'm sorry to have allowed your routine to be disrupted, but I thought it important to let you get your sleep for the big day. How are you feeling?"

Mr. Chen answered with a stolid gaze that descended into a look of apprehension then culminated in surrender. Ting Ting wiped sweat off his head, a product of both his nerves and the instant release amphetamines at war with the residual barbiturates and baijiu left in his system.

"You're going to do great today. Don't worry."

Mr. Chen nodded, unconvincingly.

"I have two friends waiting to take care of you next door. Would you like me to send them in?"

Mr. Chen shrugged and stared ahead blankly.

"There's something you should know, Mr. Chen—"

Ting Ting stood tall, proud, and ready to receive admonishment...

"The Man is very busy today. And might be going away for a while... on a vacation. He asked me to tell you he won't be available to give the speech for you. He said you need to do it without him. And that you are ready. And not to worry."

Mr. Chen stared at Ting Ting blankly for an extended period of time, then abruptly shouted, "What the fuck?!", startling Ting Ting, who had never heard him utter a single word in the two years she'd been working for him, save for the times his eyes changed color.

"This about the eyes? I'll wear sunglasses. Like the other times."

"That would not be appropriate, Mr. Chen."

"Why?! Kim Jung Un wears sunglasses all the time."

Ting Ting moved in closer.

"Someday you can too. When you are Chairman Chen. But now you are only Mr. Chen. Brilliant scientist. Revered public servant. Hero of the people. Believe in yourself! You can do this!"

"No. Nope. No good. Not okay, Ting Ting. I want to talk to The Man now. I can't do this without him. No Man, no speech."

Mr. Chen closed his eyes and searched for The Man, who appeared dim and flickering, like a dying flashlight, and whose words came through garbled, like an out of range walkie talkie. Mr. Chen opened his eyes.

"I can't see him! I can't hear him! What the hell?!"

He closed his eyes and tried again. This time, all he could see was a very feint outline of The Man, and all he could hear was a mysterious chorus of chanting repeating...

"Yaldabaoth esto! Yaldabaoth esto!"

He opened his eyes and banged his little fists on the bed in frustration.

"The fuck is this shit, Ting Ting?! Send in the girls. We need a better signal."

Ting Ting obeyed.

Mr. Chen sat in a chair, pulled his satin pajama pants down to his ankles, closed his eyes, and tried again while getting a double blowjob. Ting Ting bit her lip nervously and watched on like a concerned mother.

Mr. Chen now saw The Man more clearly, with the sexual signal boost. The Man spoke...

"Mr. Chen! So sorry I'm predisposed. I'm afraid I won't be able to assist you today. But don't—"

"—Don't worry. Don't worry. I know what you say. Ting Ting tell me. But I do worry! I never talked one time without you! Now I speak to the whole government alone?! What the hell? Why do this? I'm nobody without The Man. I'll do bad job. All of China will hate Mr. Chen. Will say: Mr. Chen's so stupid. Mr. Chen's so weird. Will say: Why they say Mr. Chen's smart? Mr. Chen just some boring normal guy. Mr. Chen so overrated!"

"Look how talkative you are already! Listen to the passion in your voice. Use that! Do you think I would have chosen you, out of all the millions of options I had, if you were stupid and boring? Of course not. But, respectfully, I have a fucking world to run and I'm extremely busy and don't have time to listen to you be a whiny bitch right now."

Mr. Chen looked down angrily.

"Listen to my instructions, Mr. Chen. Are you listening?"

Mr. Chen sighed and muttered, "Yeah, yeah."

"Reach between your legs, grab those little rice balls of yours and man up. If running an empire was easy, everyone would do it. You notice problems, Mr. Chen. You loathe disorder. And it pisses you off. But your whole life you've just kept it in. You've put up with it. You've kept your mouth shut. Let it all out. Unleash half a lifetime of frustration into that microphone. You know how to complain. Look how well you're doing it now. Complain for all of China. Say the things everyone's thinking but no one is saying. Because they're all too afraid. But you're not afraid. You're not afraid of the Americans. Or NATO. Or Secretary Xi. Not scared one fucking bit. Do you know why that is Mr. Chen?"

"Because I have The Man to help me. But now you say—"

"No Mr. Chen! Not because you have me. I just saw the glorious leader you were fated to become and showed you the way. I'm but a teacher. A guide. It's you who will forge your name into history. Chairman Chen. There will be paintings and statues of you in every city. Your name will be known from the East to the West. You are one of the greatest men who ever lived. You were born to rule. You will rule. All you need do is embrace your destiny!"

Mr. Chen sniffled and took that in.

"Wow. For real?"

"For real, Chairman Chen. That's you. And the great Chairman Chen knows exactly what to say. Even when he has no idea what to say. Truth is whatever Chairman Chen says it is. Chairman Chen — the wise, powerful, mysterious, courageous legend who will inspire a great nation to evolve and achieve beyond everyone's wildest expectations. Everyone's expectations but yours... their great visionary leader. They want to listen to you. They yearn to obey your commands. And so I hereby give to you, my finest student, the great honor of my middle name. And when you say it to yourself, even in a whisper, you will feel the part of me I leave with you. And you will be free of fear and trust fate has in store for you what I so clearly see it does."

"Wow—" said Mr. Chen. "—that's so cool. What's your middle name?"

"Fucking. So that makes you?" Mr. Chen chuckled.

"Mr. Fucking Chen?"

"Mister or Chairman?"

"Chairman."

"Chairman who? Chairman Mao?"

"No. Chairman..."

"Chairman who?"

"Chairman... Fuc..."

"CHAIRMAN WHO?!"

"Chairman Fucking Chen!"

"WHO?!"

"Chair, Chairman.... CHAIRMAN FUCKING CHEN! CHAIRMAN FUCKING CHEN! CHAIRMAN DAMN MOTHA FUCKIN' CHEN!"

"Damn fucking straight, Chairman Fucking Chen! Now go, answer fate's call. Remind the world what a great leader looks like. Our friends in the shadows will do the rest."

"Okay. Mr. Chairman Fucking Chen can do the speech. Mr. Chairman Fucking Chen's not afraid no more."

"Good man! I believe in you. Now believe in yourself so they can too, my quartz crystal man."

With that, The Man disappeared.

Mr. Chen came to, came, then started his bath, did a line of crushed up Adderall off Ting Ting's glorious tits, which she uncharacteristically granted him permission to lick and fondle, got in the shower, and started performing the most intense Tai-Chi of his life while listening to the "Top Gun" sound-track at full volume, finally singing along, at the top of his little lungs.

---

A FEW HOURS LATER, MR. CHEN FOUND HIMSELF SNORTING ONE FINAL BUMP OF pharmaceutical confidence off Ting Ting's pinky in a bathroom in the heart of the Capitol building. He gave Ting Ting a sudden kiss on the lips, which she reluctantly reciprocated, given the gravity of the situation.

"I love you, Ting Ting."

Ting Ting bowed gracefully. She gave him a kiss on the forehead, a gentle adoring tug on one of his chubby little cheeks, and a proud maternal smile.

"Wish me luck, baby," he said, as he wiped his sweaty forehead.

"I would. But you don't need it... Chairman Fucking Chen," she replied, whispering the last bit, in case the bathroom was bugged. She gave him a big hug and one last motherly kiss on the head, then sent her creation into the arms of fate.

the most intense ...

A few hours later, ...

heart of the Capitol building

## 71

MR. CHEN WALKED the walk and smiled the smile he'd been so diligently practicing. He made his way to his assigned seat in the grand auditorium, nodding respectfully to all the people he'd never met, many of whom recognized him from all the press. Several smirked at him knowingly, with subtle nods and winks; he did indeed have allies.

He continued focusing on replaying his favorite songs in his head while the other speakers took their turns, hearing nothing outside his racing mind until he heard his name repeated, having missed it the first time. Mr. Chen took a deep breath and quietly hummed "Highway to the Danger Zone" through his well-rehearsed gregarious smile as he made his way onto the enormous stage and walked to the stately podium before an enormous Chinese flag.

He looked under the podium and was relieved to find the wooden box Ting Ting had assured him would be set in place was indeed where it was supposed to be. He discreetly slid it out with his foot and stood on it, elevating his height, which made him look and feel more powerful.

He swallowed one last time before entering microphone range, mindful of his training to conceal and suppress all unconscious signs of nervousness. He then discreetly reached down with one hand and took his nuts and the man's advice literally, squeezing his testicles for an extra boost, and spoke.

"You know, to speak here today is the greatest honor of my life."

Suddenly Mr. Chen realized *you know* wasn't in the speech he'd spent weeks memorizing, and the feeling he had already fucked it all up began to consume him. His mind went blank and memory abated, as if he'd just suffered a concussion. He completely forgot his entire speech. He closed his eyes and searched for The Man, without result. He remembered his dream of being naked in front of this crowd and felt it was coming true. Then, he did something no one had ever done on that stage...

Mr. Chen began to cry.

He tried to stop but couldn't. The crowd watched in silence as Mr. Chen wept for several unbearable seconds. He closed his eyes and remembered his dream with The Man. He remembered looking down at the world, and all The Man's talk of his destiny to rule it. With that, he found the courage to speak, albeit with a shaky, crackling voice, in stark contrast to the deep, authoritative, masculine tone he'd intended.

"It is a great honor to speak. But the truth is, I don't want to do this. I'm not ready to do this. I don't believe I can do this. Not by myself. Not alone. How am I supposed to do this without The Man? It's not fair. Now that The Man is gone, I feel so weak. I feel so sad. I feel so alone. I feel so like... just some random guy who never deserved to have this position."

Mr. Chen hung his head in shame, then looked behind him for a moment, to wipe away his tears and save what face he still could. As he did, he noticed a large portrait of Mr. Fei — the recently deceased former boss he'd replaced. He turned around and noticed someone in the crowd wiping away a tear of their own; then it dawned on him — *They don't know who The Man is; they think I'm talking about that dead old guy. It's not too late to turn this shit around!* He closed his eyes and concentrated until he could hear the crowd chanting *Chairman Chen! Chairman Chen!*

He gave his balls a firm squeeze, cleared his little throat and continued...

"The man is this man—" Mr. Chen pointed to the image of Mr. Fei, turning around once more to make sure he had the name right, and to give the portrait a respectful bow; "—Mr. Fei. He is the man who taught me so much. The man who stayed so humble his whole life; never too good to eat the same noodles he had when he was a child from a poor family in a small village, fighting to survive in the rubble left by the Japanese. Mr. Fei is to me a true example of what we all should try to be. He was a man of the people. A man who always put others first. A man who understood the value of sacrifice.

"And a man I will never, ever forget. This Covid-20 vaccine... I don't deserve to be famous for this. I don't want the attention. I'm just a humble man who is lucky enough to find a way to be of service to others, following the example of dear Mr. Fei, who followed the example of our dear first leader, Chairman Mao. I'm tired of hearing about Mr. Chen. Mr. Chen is only one man here to serve the party... here to serve the people; here to follow the example of Mr. Fei and Chairman Mao — so, for this wonderful new safe and effective vaccine, I give the credit to Mr. Fei. And to all of you, who made this great country I love so much.

"I am thankful for the small good I have been able to do, but it is only because of the great good Mr. Fei did through his entire career in government. He was a great mentor. A great statesman. A great example. And a great friend. I learned so much from this great man. It is in honor of you, Mr. Fei, that Mr. Chen's tears fall. You will be greatly missed. May you be forever remembered!"

A slow clap came from across the stage, where Secretary Xi — the leader of China, considered by many to be the most powerful man in the world, and the man Chairman Chen sought to usurp — was rising to start a standing ovation that was promptly joined by all in attendance. Secretary Xi smiled and began walking toward Mr. Chen to shake his hand, thank him and introduce the next speaker.

Mr. Chen realized this was it. This was his moment. He could either do as expected and return to his seat, or seize the moment for himself as The Man intended. He pretended not to notice the approaching leader of the party, gave his little nuts a big final squeeze, then went on.

"But you know what, Mr. Chen has cried enough tears. And you know what, I think Mr. Fei would agree, all of China has cried enough tears."

Secretary Xi chose to allow Mr. Chen to continue and returned to his seat — a mistake he would soon and for the rest of his life regret.

"Our people have been given many reasons to cry, for many years. We have suffered not ten years. Not twenty years. Not fifty years. But a whole century of humiliation!"

Mr. Chen angrily banged his little fists on the podium, surprising everyone with the Hitlerian shift in tone.

"A hundred years! Wow. So long. So so long. Terrible isn't it? What a shame. Such a huge disgrace. Absolutely horrible."

He sighed dramatically and smiled inside, feeling his confidence grow as he continued.

"Covid-19. Covid-20. Yeah yeah, so bad. But these are a joke compared to the tragedy of our ancestors. The British empire came to take our silver and give us opium — trying to addict us to drugs, just like the Western capitalists do to their own people today. And what did they get for their evils? All of Hong Kong! For a hundred years. And all the silver they could want. For free. For a whole century, we let the children of our oppressors keep Hong Kong. We honor our side of the agreement. Even though it was unfair.

"But do they really give back Hong Kong? No! They take down their stupid queen's flag but leave their corrupt culture to rot the minds of our people. The buildings are still full of rich bankers exploiting our markets for more profits. They laugh at our laws. Their brothels remain, where dirty evil foreigners buy sex with our daughters. They act like they're not in China. But they are in China. Hong Kong is China. Hong Kong always was China. And Hong Kong will forever be China!"

Unexpected applause arose, from one then two of China's top generals — ultra-nationalists who had long been eager to take the gloves off and apply China's full military might to secure Hong Kong's status as a Chinese territory, rather than leaving it a semi-autonomous region, as had long been the uncomfortable compromise.

"Hong Kong is like a woman with two husbands. But a woman, no matter how beautiful, can only have one husband! And like any wife, maybe she needs a little slap to remember her place if she thinks she can cheat on her husband with some big fat foreigner."

The unlikely prose garnered some laughter, especially from the old timers. Secretary Xi was thoroughly unamused, but wore a neutral expression as he continued contemplating how to address the rapidly escalating predicament.

"And what about Taiwan? 'Top Gun' is my favorite movie. You know, the one with Tom Cruise. About the fighter pilots who play volleyball—"

Mr. Chen leaned into the podium and spoke with the ease and bottled excitement of a televangelist. His movements were passionate and smooth, and flowed through his body — with the grace only thousands of mornings of shower Tai Chi could allow.

"Tom Cruise plays Maverick. A real cool guy! Strong male role model. I was so excited to see 'Top Gun 2'. But Mr. Chen can't. You know why? Because the Americans put a Taiwanese flag on Maverick's jacket. They sacrifice hundreds of millions of dollars in movie profits just to insult us. Why?

"How long until the West starts sending Taiwan weapons like they do all the other countries all over the world? Guns. Tanks. Planes. Maybe they do it already. I don't know. Not Mr. Chen's department. Maybe some of you know. Maybe some of you don't like it too. Maybe we don't like America giving Japan, our greatest historic enemy, the best planes they have. Now they could maybe kill all of us here right now if they want. That bother anyone else? Or only Mr. Chen?"

More cheers, applause, and encouragement came from the crowd.

"Taiwan is a different country? Uh, hello. What, are these people retarded? What if China start to say Texas is a different country from America, and we want to help Texas be independent from America? You think America will be so polite?"

Secretary Xi did well to conceal his displeasure with Mr. Chen's audacity, but the assembly was hungry for more — many now clapping, with increased regularity and fervor, in response to each point coming out of the sneaky powerhouse's mouth.

"And what about the South China Sea?"

Secretary Xi finally whispered to his aid to get Mr. Chen off the fucking stage. Unfortunately for Secretary Xi, the aid had been compromised — recently bribed and threatened rather convincingly by The Cabal. His act of subterfuge was subtle but important; he took his time carrying out the command, and Mr. Chen retained the floor.

"Should we change the name to the South America Sea? South NATO Sea? Do we need imperialist boats dirtying Chinese waters? Does that stop this century? Or do we want another last century again? Would they like us driving Chinese boats off the coast of California whenever we want? With missiles and guns and lasers and shit? I don't think so. I think they would call it an invasion. An act of war! Maybe it's time we give them a taste of their own tea. Maybe it's time we say go home, foreigners. You lost. Welcome to Chinese waters. Maybe you didn't hear, America — China has the biggest Navy now. Not you. Go home or else maybe your new home is the bottom of the ocean. Tell the fish Mr. Chen say hi."

Never before had such inflammatory language been used by a Chinese politician so publicly. It was as if an oriental Donald Trump had taken the stage. More laughter and applause rumbled through the grandiose auditorium.

"The West is so afraid of China they say we are their rival. They say we are their enemy. America say we have a trade war. What is that? They make up a kind of war! And we still pretend they are our friend? Why? We are good friends to them. We make everything they have. Everything they own is a gift from China. Let's just say the truth one time this National Day — the West is a big fat stupid asshole!"

Mr. Chen smiled at the laughter and cheers the brazen line garnered.

"Maybe China should be a little asshole too for a change. Maybe China should say okay, you don't like us, good luck without us. You want a trade war, pal? Okay. No more stuff from China! Now your people go to the store and can't buy shit. Americans have no savings. Only debt. It's so expensive everybody go crazy fast. Now who win the trade war?"

Mr. Chen paused and took in the adulation with a smile.

"You know they tell their kids the Christmas toys that all say MADE IN CHINA really come from happy magic slave midgets at the North Pole? They really say this. And they stupid kids who can't even do calculus believe it. And you know what else they believe? These crazy white people... Every February they get all excited to see a groundhog come out of the ground and look at his shadow and that somehow predict how long until it will be Spring. What the hell stupid shit is that? And they believe a fucking magic rabbit delivers eggs filled with candy every year for them to find because their god's son Jesus came back from the dead. Even I —Mr. Chen, an authority on science — can't understand what is in these stupid white kids' heads. You know?

"They retarded. And love only violence. All the games. All the movies. All the shows. All the sports. All fight, fight, fight... kill, kill, kill. The Western rulers program everybody like robots for war they whole life. They teach them obey and fight. That's it. Then they only let their poor ones go to college if they the best at sports or join the military. If they parents not rich, they get a loan big enough to buy a house because that's the price of school. That or they say okay, for four years I go fight whoever you say and if I don't get killed I can have a education. What the hell? In China we want everybody have school. Everybody be smart.

"They pretend all these wars that never end to protect their country. To help save people from bad leaders. Good joke. Is for helping protect and grow greedy corporations' business. For selling more weapons. For controlling more energy. And for making rich their corrupt rulers. They do it in the Middle East. Now they do it in Eastern Europe again. What kind of shit is that? And if the kids don't die from the wars and get to go to college they only learn fake history and crazy shit like is a hundred genders. What? No. Is a penis, is a boy. Is no penis, is a girl. Is simple. Everybody in the world always know this."

Another hearty round of applause filled the auditorium. Mr. Chen's opinions were resonating.

"Let's face it, that's how it is. The same stupid kids will be stupid adults. And if we don't stand up for ourselves now, in a few years, they will send their peasant armies to invade us and pretend its to help the people in Taiwan or Hong Kong or whatever. But really it's just because of some rich capitalist imperialists that rule their crazy country where a new guy is in charge every four years. We can't let those crazy people drive their crazy boats and fly their crazy planes and satellites and all that shit and one day some asshole they supposedly elected says attack China. Steal their shit. Get their oil. You kidding, man? Before that, we will have a war!"

A handful of those gathered cheered, disconcertingly. And many more clapped.

"Because they will never be happy. They have greed in their black hearts and always want to take take take. More more more. Is never enough!"

Many in the crowd were now chuckling with regularity. Some were clapping discreetly. Many brazenly.

"And how about the West media. Oh man... don't get me started with these assholes."

The applause had spread from being a controlled fire to a conflagration, and Secretary Xi looked around in frustration. He noticed his aid was not only failing to carry out his orders, but preventing others from intervening. *Traitor*.

"They lie lie lie! Factories of bullshit. Only factories they have left! The rest of the factories in China!"

It dawned on Secretary Xi this was a calculated move against him. He motioned for someone else to come over as Mr. Chen rode the wave of applause from point to point.

"They talk about the Uyghurs. Say we make them go to jail. Say we racist. Oh, so sad. Not jail. Reeducation camps. America care so much about muslims? Really? Then why America killed millions of them and took their oil? We have problem? Too much prisoners? How about this — we have three times more people than America but America has more prisoners than China! It's just another business to them. More prisoners equal more customers. Lot of black customers. Lot of Mexican customers. Not so much white jail customers. Who have the problem? Who racist? Shut up, hypocrite assholes!"

Two men loyal to Secretary Xi and astute at reading complex situations apprehended the duplicitous aid, walked on stage and whispered to Mr. Chen that it was time to end the speech. Mr. Chen decided to push it even further, seeing his chance to kick the man he planned to replace in the nuts in front of everyone. He looked at Secretary Xi.

"What's wrong, Secretary Xi? I say too much? So sorry."

With that, one of the men unplugged the microphone while the other yanked Mr. Chen's shirt, as discreetly as possible, urging him to come quietly. Mr. Chen pulled away and shouted, louder than he ever had.

"You know, Secretary Xi, the only problem the West maybe right about in China is too much censorship! Because when Mr. Chen come up here and say the truth on National Day, Mr. Chen get in trouble! Okay. So sorry. Mr. Chen the bad guy. Mr. Chen finished. Mr. Chen obey. Mr. Chen go away. Thank you. Bye bye."

Mr. Chen knocked away the hands of his escorts and strut off the stage to an uproarious defiant applause and commotion, started by a combination of Cabal assets and genuinely fired up patriots. Something had been unleashed. The energy was palpable.

Mr. Fucking Chen knocked it out of the fucking park.

The Man couldn't have done any better himself.

The first thing Mark
double doors was an
a suit wearing sung
rifle of some sort. T
one of fear, but he
-ances and boldly ap
man who for an in
posture and trained
beam targeting him
Second Mark said "
weapon, and resume
"Can you hear m
"Yes Sir...
"here is my l

## 72

A SHOWER MIRROR coated in steam is split down the center by a squeegee, revealing a rosy-cheeked Asian man with a big smile — a very big smile. He stares at the mirror as he moves the squeegee left to right, with the ease of an act done the same way, for the past 93 mornings, exactly the same way, during his forced stay at the first sub-five star accommodations he'd set foot in since his first trip to The Man's island two years prior.

The leaders of the CCP had their own way of handling high profile outspoken dissenters. From A-list celebrity actors like Vicki Zhao, to tennis star Peng Shuai, to Alibaba chairman Jack Ma, the CCP had made it clear no one was out of reach. Following critical comments on social media, all three had gone missing for extended periods, then returned with a newfound sense of humility, never to publicly speak out against the party again.

But in the unique case of Mr. Chen, whom in the weeks leading up to his explosive rhetoric had been celibritized by The Man and Cabal's global media outlets, along with China's own state media, how to silence this individual without appearing afraid of him and attracting further attention to his inflammatory remarks was a real conundrum. Add to this the undeniably warm reception his unexpected speech had garnered from, in the least, a substantial minority of the National People's Congress itself, putting Mr. Chen in his place would prove an exceptionally difficult balancing act.

At first, while Secretary Xi and his reliable allies in government deliberated on the dilemma, the decision was made to keep him out of the public eye until people forgot about him. But privy to this strategy, Mr. Chen's mass media supporters flooded world news outlets with stories about the rousing speech and China's missing hero. The longer he remained out of sight, the more the public became rightfully convinced he was feared by party leaders.

While going off his newfound addictions to drugs, sex and luxury was tormenting, Mr. Chen found strength in the fact he'd already spent over four decades in similar circumstances. There was no case to be made that he could not endure another few months, or even years, in isolation and sobriety, which was yet another reason The Man had seen Mr. Chen as an ideal candidate for the job, knowing in advance this would likely be part of the story of his rise to power. After all, most great dictators spend some portion of their lives imprisoned by the government they later take over — a fact Mr. Chen had learned from his arduous bathtub studies.

One evening, Mr. Chen received a typewritten letter, slid under his door. It was from Ting Ting, and came with a book of matches to burn it with after reading.


Dear Mr. Chen,

Your performance was magnificent! The Man must be as proud of you as I am. He has gone away for a while, but don't worry. I'm sure this was always part of his plan. Stay strong. Stay silent (which shouldn't be a problem for you!) and know there are forces at work to get you out of captivity and in power where you belong as soon as possible.

The whole world has now heard of the great and controversial genius Mr. Chen… the man who saved the world from Covid-20; the man who saved the world before the virus even struck, with his vaccine — which has already sold hundreds of millions of doses to governments worldwide, with the notable exception of China's — a fact our capitalist friends find unacceptable. The Western governments of the capitalists will use every tool at their disposal to change this, even if it means making certain people "retire early".

I hear Secretary Xi himself might retire early. And when he's gone, who will come to mind when it comes time to choose China's next leader? : )

I successfully rescued your manuscript and journals from the hotel during your speech, and a team of very skilled ghost writers (including one of the writers of "Top Gun"!) helped turn it into a wonderful and inspiring book. It is already a best seller in the West. I didn't see that coming! Did you?! : )

I see your smiling face on the cover in Airports from Europe to America to Australia. It has been translated into many languages. The book is still banned in China, but the more they try to censor it, the more people become curious to know what you have to say that's so dangerous. You're famous now! It's so cool!

Keep practicing your smile, Mr. Chen. You'll need to use it a lot when you're released and surrounded by people begging you to let them put you in power. In the meantime, I'll continue running New Order International. I hope you're ready to be a billion-aire. Because with me in charge of your company, you will be. : D

Your Dear Friend,

Ting Ting

MR. CHEN WAS DISAPPOINTED IT HADN'T BEEN SIGNED "I LOVE YOU," BUT THE rest was outstanding news. Mr. Chen danced profusely and giddily re-read the letter several times before reluctantly and begrudgingly burning it.

---

A MONTH LATER, MR. CHEN WAS RELEASED.

The following week, Secretary Xi died "in a plane crash", and by vote of the National People's Congress, Mr. Chen was appointed to replace him. He immediately set into effect a sweeping agenda of new policies, which were branded "The Greatest Leap Forward". On the forefront were his unprece-dentedly aggressive vaccine policies and virus control strategies.

He immediately honored his deal with Geyser Pharmaceuticals and mandated his Covid-20 vaccine for every man, woman and child in China. To simplify the accounting and ensure no one slipped through the cracks, he instituted a policy at every hospital in China that every newborn infant be vaccinated before being given to the parents.

He also produced billions of vaccines that were sold en masse to govern-ments worldwide through Geyser's lucrative arrangements. His hundreds of millions in royalties grew into billions within a few years, tended to as it was by Ting Ting, who remained CEO of New Order International and one of Chairman Chen's most trusted advisors. He still claimed to love her, but in a show of restraint, left her tits alone. He found himself satisfied with his impressive roster of concubines, the likes of which had not been seen since the days of the old emperors.

Those who contracted the virus were presumed to have somehow faked their vaccination status and were quarantined from society for a minimum of one year. As everyone knew and faithfully repeated, Chairman Chen's vaccines were 100% safe and effective. Containment facilities were erected in every province to hold any and all vaccine avoiders, indefinitely and without trial.

Every phone came stocked with an app called CCPCCA — *the Chinese Communist Party's Chairman Chen App* — through which citizens were encouraged to anonymously report any lawbreaking they witnessed or were privy to. They could take pictures and videos of any infractions being committed and upload them. Law enforcement would evaluate the evidence and instantaneously apply the social credit score reduction and any additional prescribed punishments, which ranged from public humiliation to fines to prison sentences. To incentivize snitching, the reporters were given the social credit points deducted from the offenders. The same applied to suspected carriers of Covid-20. People got very good at holding in their coughs.

State media proudly boasted that in the first two years of the Covid-20 pandemic, there hadn't been a single documented case of illness in anyone who had received Chairman Chen's vaccine. Of course, anyone who did get the virus was known to be unvaccinated. The possibility it didn't work was off the table. The spread of such harmful lies were of course major offenses. Western media unscrupulously reported the figures provided to them as factual — with neither the ability nor will to attempt to verify the bold claims — and held China to be a shining example of how safe everyone would be if they all simply obeyed the authorities without resistance.

Two years in, Mr. Chen was officially awarded the title Chairman and granted a lifetime appointment. Under Chairman Chen, China became more orderly than ever. No cars drove too fast. No one jaywalked. No one spoke too loud or used banned words. China flourished, thanks to Chairman Chen's ever-growing collection of enforceable, enforced rules.

There were downsides. But only for problematic people who maintained dangerous ideas about personal freedom, privacy, and accepting the existence of a single centralized grid of total control.

Of all Chairman Chen's illustrious accomplishments, none surpassed China's claim to not only the largest gingerbread house on Earth, but an entire gingerbread city — exactly as he'd dreamed it. It was in this city that President Randall DuPont issued a public declaration that Santa Claus is not real and every toy American children receive that says MADE IN CHINA was not really constructed by elves. He refused to comment on Jesus.

The anniversary of this admission was called "Sorry to China Day" and made an official Chinese holiday, during which Chairman Chen would publicly forgive Western governments and people for specific historic misdeeds. It also served as a way to humiliate them and bolster national pride without necessarily coming across as hostile in the international press. He delighted in using the proclaimed values of his competitors against them and proved a highly proficient shit talker, despite his trademark genial demeanor. In doing so, he also fomented warranted hostilities between the citizens of Western governments and their exploitative overlords, which proved very useful as World War III approached like an unavoidable winter.

---

RANDY OF COURSE EASILY BEAT OUT JOE BIDEN IN THE NEXT ELECTION CYCLE, TO Joe and the rest of the country's relief, and promptly used the full force of his power to enforce Covid-20 policies with ruthless efficiency, profiting immensely, as both a major shareholder in Geyser Pharmaceuticals and guy with a stock broker proficient in options trading who could turn Randy's snippets of inside information into millions every week with the click of a mouse. Randy achieved his lifelong goal of eclipsing his father's successes in terms of fortune, fame and power within his first year in office.

Western media played up the threat of Covid-20 with the same single-minded focus they had its predecessor, and censored wild conspiracy theories the virus was a manmade creation with even greater efficiency. Social media was effectively purged of anyone and everyone who questioned the official narrative or criticized the pharmaceutical giants raking in record profits quarter after quarter, with more and more countries around the world pressured and persuaded to mandate Mr. Chen's vaccine, and monthly booster shots becoming a near universal norm.

Google even went so far as to start narrowing the search results from any search queries to a handful of results that complied with their propagandistic preferences, which were largely dictated by members of the World Economic Forum. It started with Covid-related inquiries, but since they got away with it, they figured they might as well apply the same technique to the entire internet.

The search engine still boasted finding hundreds of millions of results in a fraction of a second every time someone pressed enter, but it was total bullshit. Those few with the patience to check would discover the true number was in the hundreds, at most. They just showed the same approved options over and over. No one seemed to notice. This form of censorship was more nefarious than that of the Chinese iteration, because the CCP didn't pretend they weren't doing it. Everyone in China knew what was going on, and had ways of getting around it if they really wanted to. As for the West, many still believed they had free access to information.

The goal for the rulers of America and Western societies in general remained to maintain a convincing enough veneer of freedom that people could consider themselves well-informed by an independent press. In truth, they were subtly shifting the so-called free world more and more toward the authoritarian model they truthfully sought to enact.

The vaccine did little more to stop the spread of Covid-20 than a cup of hot water with lemon. But that didn't matter, as scrutinizing the efficacy of the vaccine became tantamount to heresy in the brave new world where experts were the new high priests, and whatever they declared good science was equivalent to divine scripture. The apostates who took issue with the vaccines were silenced. Most Westerners obeyed, whether they wanted to or not, just so they could get on with their lives and not be treated like heretics.

———

WHETHER TO SNEAK A STERILIZATION AGENT INTO AN UPCOMING BOOSTER WAS firmly on the table, and voted on quarterly in Cabal meetings. But many of the new Cabal leaders were more focused on the windfall profits from indefinitely continued vaccine sales than depopulation targets — especially the younger new leaders, most of whom didn't give a damn about ancient alien god rescue missions — so they stuck to other methods of population control for the time being, with an emphasis on famine induction and increased control over the world's food supply.

Bill Gates became the largest farm owner in America and supplied the potatoes for McDonald's French fries. He and other billionaires built veritable monopolies over food sources so they could retain leverage for control over the populations in the event people stopped caring about money, and because the Cabal was intentionally facilitating the conditions for global famines. Starving people, as it turns out, are more inclined to obey the people with food.

The Cabal effectively halted Ukraine's food production through the proxy war with Russia, decreasing Russia and Iran's access to relied-upon imports. They also prevented the export of food to third world nations in hopes of adding points to the board as far as the global depopulation goal was concerned. The poorest were naturally the easiest targets and would therefore first to go. As for the first world countries, following the oil model, control over food allowed them to drain people of their disposable income through price manipulation and affect political outcomes by increasing or decreasing any targeted region's access to the needed commodities. It was all vaguely blamed on inflation, which was blamed on rival nations, leaving everyone on all sides increasingly broke, hungry, confused and frustrated. In this way The Cabal primed as many people as possible for the next world war.

The goal of escalating World War III into a full-scale apocalyptic event, as envisioned by the now extinct former Cabal leaders, was voted down by the newcomers. Their business dealings with Chairman Chen proved too profitable. They kept the focus instead on continuing to fuel regionally contained proxy wars while profiting from arming both sides. In other words, it was business as usual.

As for Russia and Iran, the plan was to fragment both into several smaller countries by quietly arming contentious factions, profiting off the arms trade, ensuring continual population reduction in the regions, and gradually weakening all parties involved. They crippled Russia economically through years of relentlessly applied sanctions, which amounted to a modern-day castle siege. They supplied weapons en masse to the Ukrainian government they'd installed and still backed. They ensured that so long as the weapons were being used to kill people, they would keep them coming for as long as necessary. The United States government continued to prioritize unconstitutional and illegal participation in foreign wars over domestic affairs, neglecting to fix the problems at home while escalating them abroad.

In return, they were ensured no Ukrainian men would be allowed to flee the country to avoid the war and would continue to be used as cannon fodder for the superior Russian military. Western media of course misreported all new developments and simply repeated the slogan "support Ukraine" to keep the people assuming Ukraine had a fighting chance absent escalation into a proper world war. The Cabal foiled all attempts to reach a peace arrangement between the Russians and Ukrainians throughout the war by assassinating diplomats, blackmailing and extorting leaders, arranging for terror attacks on either side when tensions seemed to be decreasing, and destroying Russia's Nordstream II oil pipeline so President Putin couldn't use withholding energy as leverage in negotiations. The day after the pipeline's destruction, as countless sea life perished from one of the worst oil spills in history, the Cabal publicly announced through its Western puppet leaders remarkably conveniently timed opening of a new oil pipeline to Europe through NATO allied countries.

Eventually a government would be recognized as legitimate by NATO and invited by the leaders to install a "peacekeeping force". This enabled The Cabal to establish new puppet governments and new forward-operating bases as they continued their slow, calculated march Eastward. Naturally, a federal reserve bank would then be proposed. Through these methods, The

Cabal gained increased control over Eastern Europe, Western Russia, parts of Iran and two of the "istans" during Randy's two presidential terms, to the delight of the Draco down below. This strategy was however countered by a bifurcation of the global economy, which was the ultimate impetus for the eruption of the widespread war that was to come.

———

THE DRACONIAN HIGH COUNCIL'S DECISION TO EXORCISE THE MAN HAD PROVEN wise, and they successfully deposited his essence into a relic that was kept safely at the Great Temple, which effectively contained him, as far as they could tell. There The Man effectively served as a genie in a bottle, as Bortimus and the council deliberated their options moving forward, which ranged from calling on him as an advisor under limited circumstances to transmuting his consciousness and vast intelligence into a powerful AI system.

Bortimus had the temple stormed, and the relic was retrieved. He attempted to fashion it into a crown that would grant him the powers of The Man when he wore it. But it did not work, and the relic was grudgingly returned. It could have worked, and one day would, but The Man kept quiet for a while for the simple reason he wanted to take a break from the whole global domination racket.

———

GRIM AS THE GLOBAL OUTLOOK WAS, THE MAN HAD, IN HIS FINAL HOUR BEFORE being trapped by the reptilian mystics, gifted the world a positive counterbalance by effectively handing Mark the keys to the kingdom. With tens of millions of dollars, political pull galore, and Luke to keep him safe, he had everything he needed to put into effect his own means and methods to change the world as he saw fit.

This could be seen as an act of redemption on The Man's part; but it could also be seen as a strategic move to maintain balance in his absence. After all, he didn't want to wake up to find himself back in the stone age. In accordance with Mark's wishes, expressed in the form of a polite letter accompanying a copy of Randy's memory card from the box of strings, Randy capitulated to Mark's demands and named Frank the first head of the DoD-2.

In contrast to the Department of Defense, the newly formed Department of Disclosure (DoD-2) was empowered to release un-doctored, uncensored government documents, and to interview former government insiders — without them being subject to reprisal for violating coercive confidentiality agreements and secrecy oaths that threatened them with extended prison sentences, exorbitant fines and other punishments if they ever dared air the country's dirty laundry. As head of the DoD-2, Frank was authorized to show up unannounced to any military base or contractor's premises and investigate the goings on, then to release all information to the public, via a dedicated website, in the tradition of his own website. But now he had legal backing, a bloated budget, and no one in any American state or territory was ever again allowed to tell him, "you can't dig here."

Mark sent similar persuasive letters to the leaders of several foreign countries, along with copies of their memory cards of misdeeds, and similar agencies began to sprout up worldwide, opening the world to a golden age of disclosure. The entire concept of secrecy on grounds of "national security" was finally called into question and the people were at long last given the truth they deserved. The only area of inquiry that remained off limits was anything to do with Covid, viruses and vaccines... for the time being.

A beautiful hot tub was installed at Château Pensmore, in which Frank finally relayed Hope's message of apology and forgiveness. The *in another life* bit put a bittersweet smile on Mark's face and granted him closure. The surviving "gifts" were promptly apologized to, released, and given more than enough money to find their way home and pay for as much counseling as necessary. Luke went to several countries, well armed, to ensure the modeling agency had been shut down and The Man's sex trafficking enterprise was no more. Doing so proved a violent and complicated affair, but Luke was eager to take on the challenge and there could have been no better man for the job.

Frank and Mark became best friends and continued to have pizza parties at Château Pensmore, where they organized and prioritized which mysteries and conspiracies to get to the bottom of. While the bunker buster bomb had demolished the primary Cahokia Mound, it actually made the excavation much easier. In short, Frank had been right — beneath the mounds was found a veritable treasure trove of giant skeletons and puzzling proof of ancient native Americans having some type of interaction with extraterrestrial beings, opening enormous opportunities for continued exploration of the subject. The publicly excavated giant bones never fell into the hands of any men in black, and were eventually displayed at the Smithsonian museum, where the director sheepishly offered Frank a long overdue apology for sinking his academic career. Frank accepted it without conceit. Next, the DoD-2 turned its focus to the giant underwater pyramid in the Bermuda Triangle. Having so quickly discovered giant bones and a giant pyramid, the DoD-2 was hailed out the gate as a great success, for which Randy begrudgingly took credit.

The agency went on to investigate topics including the FBI's involvement in the deaths of JFK, Martin Luther King Jr. and Malcolm X, the truth about

Roswell, why fluoride is added to the water supply, whether Operation High Jump was a hunt for Antarctic Nazi bases, whether the moon contains a space station, who the hell the Annunaki were/are, and many other formerly scoffed at possibilities. The discoveries turned Frank into an overnight celebrity, and not only did he no longer have to take shit from the academic community, he was awarded an honorary PhD from the college that had expelled him for going against the grain.

Luke continued to gradually regain his humanity, and when he got his seashell back, it unlocked a massive cascade of memories. He remembered Jessica and decided to look her up, which took him less than a second. He was happy to learn she was still single, and even happier to realize he felt happiness. She too was happy to see him. When they looked at one another, they saw each other. Luke told her the Luke she remembered was dead... and the new and improved Luke could do a lot of things the old one couldn't, including letting her in and expressing his emotions. Her big beautiful brown eyes proved to be the mirror through which he could see himself come back to life.

Speaking of mirrors, after much reflection, Mark decided to do away with The Man's Box of Strings, rather than continue using it to control the world. He sent each compromised individual their memory card and a handwritten letter, explaining to them The Man had retired and requesting they follow suit. World leaders promptly resigned in droves without clear explanation, and the world's governments and institutions were purged of hundreds of corrupt officials. It was the biggest global house cleaning in known history and no one seemed to understand why it happened. Unsurprisingly, the mainstream media ruled it all completely un-newsworthy and still focused on selling cheap lies that fewer and fewer people tuned in to digest.

A new wave of online media was destined to completely replace the old guard, and truth gradually began to find its way back into everyone's screens. As a result, political tensions reached all time low and people woke up to the fact they'd been turned against one another. Calls for a complete overhaul of the democratic system ensued as more and more people endorsed third, fourth or fifth party candidates — diverse in ideologies but united in the demand the two party duopoly be demolished so real people not owned by a handful of billionaires could start winning elections and the system could again work as intended.

Mark continued to write. True to The Man's word, each time he self-published a new book, he received a check from the law firm Sullivan & Cromwell for $15,000,000, adjusted for inflation (a provision that would prove salient as the dollar continued to collapse in value). He put his fortune to work in many productive ways and exercised the political power his money bought him to stave off The Cabal's attempt to disarm the American public like they did the Canadian populace through Prime Minister Justin Trudeau.

The World Economic Forum, which came to govern many countries like Canada and England from the shadows with its installed world leaders, would soon have their way — the prolonged economic depression paving the way for the introduction of a new cryptocurrency "minted" by the federal reserve banks. It too could be made out of thin air, with the added benefit of giving the government complete record of all transactions everyone made, and the newfound ability to shut off an individual's ability to access or use their money if they proved problematic, effectively emulating the Chinese model.

---

SPEAKING OF CHINESE MODELS, ONE DAY MARK RECEIVED A VISIT FROM THE CEO of Order International — Ting Ting. She showed him the tattoo on her left breast and spoke of their mutual friend who, in his final conversation with her, had suggested they collaborate.

Ting Ting sought to lay the foundation for a new technological infrastructure that would remove capitalist leeches and rent seekers from the equation and grant the whole world affordable, zero-emissions energy. She saw a world where everyone had completely free utilities, including electricity. She'd followed DoD-2 discoveries closely and was fascinated with the newly-discovered Bermuda triangle pyramid, and the possibility it might have something to do with all the reported anomalies in the region.

Her research team concluded ancient pyramids were likely shells of a forgotten technology and was determined to discover if they could be used as power plants, as Mark's friend Frank's published research suggested. Chairman Chen had granted her request to locate and excavate ancient pyramids in China, which would prove to be one of the moves for which history best remembered him.

Mark, Ting Ting and Frank went on to form a new corporation. They called it *Fire In The Middle* — a translation of the literal meaning of the word pyramid. When they developed a working model three years later, Mark founded a second company: *Bortimus Power*, for the sole purpose of marketing the new energy technology to a friend he hoped would be running low on loosh in the years to come.

It was a Texas-based corporation.

---

A LOT OF THINGS WERE STILL MOVING IN THE WRONG DIRECTION. BAD PEOPLE were still doing a lot of bad things, and good people were still doing some bad things. But at the same time, a lot of things were moving in the right direction. Good people were doing even more good things; and bad people were doing less bad things.

Thanks to recent and ongoing developments, a more elegant balance in the ever changing equation of life and morality had been struck. The Man would be happy to know humanity is evolving on pace with his ambitious schedule, and the species is likely to survive itself for at least another generation.

The Man has been put to rest in the Great Temple. It is a rest he deserves and appreciates, distanced for the first time in ages from the responsibilities of managing the messy evolution of an intelligent species on an isolated planet.

But even in his physical absence, he still remains at work in our world, as he always has, and presumably always will. This so because The Man lives within all of us, to varying degrees, just waiting to be summoned… whispering his advice and persuading us to pursue our will by his means and methods, in the quietudes of our most guarded thoughts and feelings. As the saying goes…

*"The line between good and evil runs through the heart of every man."*

The only question is whether The Man is our passenger or driver.

This concludes a brief account of The Man, his means, and his methods.

— The End —

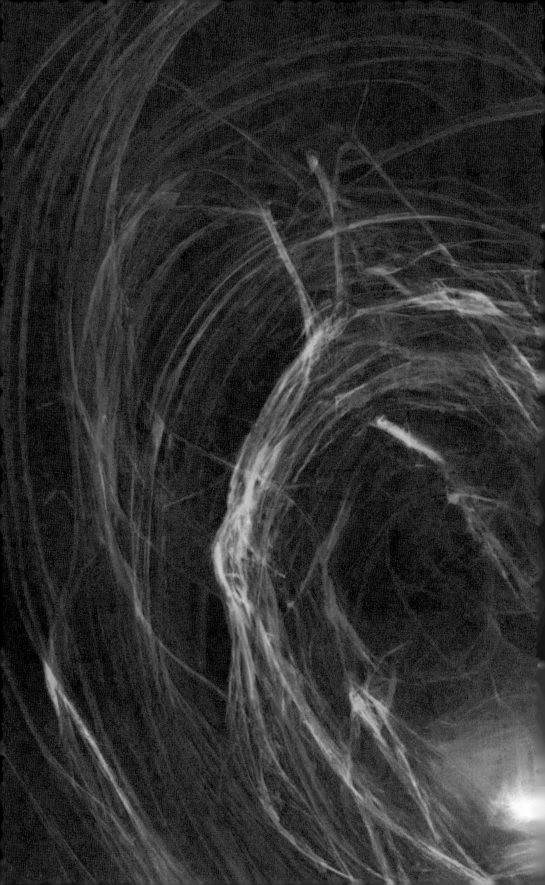

# ACKNOWLEDGMENTS

**This is the first book in known Earth history to incorporate art created by the author using artificial intelligence.**

Special thanks to *Sam* and the geniuses at *OpenAI*. There's nothing artificial about how cool Dalle is!

Thank you to *Woldfordeer Colony Studio* for transforming my sketches into the beautiful covers, title and dedication page.

Thank you to *The Chinese Government* for letting me live in Beijing, travel China, and see for myself. May the future be harmonious and peaceful. Please consider allowing this book on your side of the great wall.

Thank you *Alley Cat*, for being the first to read this book. I know it bothers you that I just switched to an Oxford comma. Get over it.

Thanks *Mom & Dad*, for creating me and everything else.

Thanks *Grandma Joanie*. Hope you're able to read this even though you're dead. You always believed in me, especially when I didn't.

Thanks to *Joe Rogan, Lex Fridman, Dr. Steven Greer, Graham Hancock, Randall Carlson, David Wilcock, Michael Tellinger, Billy Carson, Robert J. Gilbert, Emory Smith, Regina Meredith, David Icke, Jahanna James, Jimmy Corsetti* (great last name, bro) everyone at *Gaia*, and all those in search of the truth about our past so we can create a better future. You gave me plenty to work with.

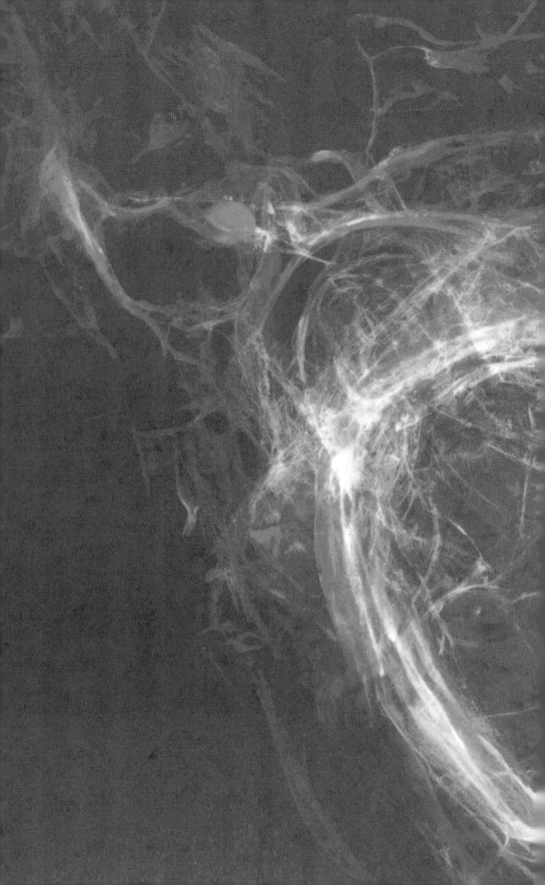

# ACKNOWLEDGMENTS

Shout out to *The Cabal* and the *Draco Reptilians*. I have a lot of respect for y'all. Sorry if it doesn't come through in the book (gotta appeal to the profane masses). Ruling this crazy planet can't be easy. I respectfully request you not kill me and/or everyone I love.

(But if you do, as soon as I leave this body I shall apply the totality of my infinite will into evolving into a positively polarized higher-dimensional Jedi light warrior and return with the backing of the Galactic Federation to really just fuck your whole shit up. Then, I'll reincarnate into human form as the greatest American writer since Nico Monetti and just pick up where I left off anyway.)

# ABOUT THE AUTHOR

The one called Nico Monetti began as a divine spark of infinite potential from a higher dimension that expanded into a ball of plasmic light that was intercepted by NASA in the late 1980s and taken to an underground lab in New Mexico where it was imbued with DNA from great writers to include Mark Twain, Dan Brown and Michael Crichton. It was then blasted by the most powerful laser ever created by man, worshipped by various religious leaders, and read to. The goal was to create the greatest writer in American history. Despite his intended destiny, the emanation proved to have free will and superhuman capabilities hitherto incomprehensible. Though still an infant, he willed himself into disappearing from the laboratory and reconstituted his physical vessel in Tibet, where he began wandering the world on foot, learning, teaching, and building a repertoire of inspiration to one day draw upon when the time came to fulfill his destiny. Thirty-three years later, he was ready to write his first novel. He sat down one day with a notebook and fountain pen and decided to write the best book ever. Then, he wrote this.

www.nicomonetti.com
monetti@protonmail.com
Instagram: nico.monetti
TikTok: nico.monetti
Twitter: @nicomonetti

# WHAT IT'S ABOUT

It's about power.

It's about the power of money, and how it functions as a mechanism to control populations.

It's about the power of media, and the role subtle persuasion plays in shaping thought.

It's about the power of governments, and how institutions establish and maintain control. It's about the power of deception, and how easy we can all be mislead and exploited.

It's about the power of hope, and the danger hope presents.

It's about the power of sex, and how it's used to control the men who control the world.

It's about the power of will, and the evolution it propels through suffering.